# Mystic INVISIBLE

## RYDER HUNTE CLANCY

Winter Goose
PUBLISHING
where words take flight
wintergoosepublishing.com

Winter Goose Publishing
45 Lafayette Road #114
North Hampton, NH 03862

www.wintergoosepublishing.com
Contact Information: info@wintergoosepublishing.com

Mystic Invisible

COPYRIGHT © 2021 by Ryder Hunte Clancy

First Edition, February 2021

Cover Design & Formatting by Winter Goose Publishing

ISBN: 978-1-952909-05-4

Published in the United States of America

To my children, may you always find joy in consuming literature,
to my nana and my grandmother, some of my first teachers,
and to Angie, the game changer

# CHAPTER 1
## Growing Pains

*[handwritten: A wetsuit & a Wand]*

*[handwritten: narrator judgement →]*

Monte's pulse thumped an encouraging beat, drumming from his chest to his fingertips as he hesitated at the threshold. The sun beat down on his mop of golden ringlets, its intense power a fiery blaze against his neck. *What are you waiting for? Just go in.* Norms of different ages and sizes bustled past him into the cool comfort of the supermarket, quite oblivious to the fact that he resembled a gimpy pelican hovering pointlessly in the doorframe. *I'll be grounded for a year if the International Mystic Bureau finds out what I'm about to do.* The sliding glass doors stalled on either side of him, groaning with his indecision as he stepped away from the entrance. *But you're moving in a few days. This might be your last chance.* *[handwritten: → Backed off & slouched by the window / into the store]*

A group of teenagers scampered past him, the effects of the heat apparent in their rosy cheeks. Monte recognized a couple of them from the Norm high school up the street. And from the park. And the beach. He shrunk against the store window, his breath catching in his throat as a girl with bright blonde hair and thick eyeliner brought up the rear. His pulse quickened, his resolve thickening. A little peek inside a Norm store never hurt anyone. He craned his neck after the eyeliner girl. It was now or never. *[handwritten: would he think like that?]*

He took a deep breath and slipped into the supermarket. A current of conditioned air greeted his face, carrying with it hints of cinnamon, sweet pastries, and other baked goods. He squinted, the store dim after the glare of outside. A Norm woman marched toward him, her arms packed with bulging paper grocery bags. *Oh great, now you've done it.* *[handwritten: we know]*

"Excuse me, young man," the Norm woman panted. A bunch of celery poked from one of her bags. Its bushy top bobbed up and down with her stiff stride.

Monte scurried out of her way, forcing a smile as she passed. His heart pounded along with the beeps and drone of the cash registers, his back sticky with sweat. He spotted Eyeliner's blonde hair near the produce section—a beacon amongst the general chaos. She joined the rest of the teens as they filtered toward an empty checkout stand, bound together like a cluster of grapes.

Monte inched toward them, careful to keep a casual distance. He was a Mystic, after all, and they mustn't suspect anything extraordinary. His kind rarely mixed with the non-magical Norms when it came to grocery stores. Turnip Sap, Toadflax, and Nettle Dust were hardly part of the Norm vernacular, and the International Mystic Bureau worked hard to keep it that way.

The group stopped near a shelf lined with candy. They joked amongst each other, their excitement almost tangible as they surveyed the sweets. "Hey, you!" someone shouted toward Monte. It was Eyeliner.

Monte froze. *Is she talking to me?*

Eyeliner waved.

Monte cleared his throat. "Hey." His voice cracked.

"Get over here, you dork." Eyeliner bounded toward him.

Monte gasped. He leaned back, bracing himself, prepared to run if needed. But Eyeliner brushed past him, leaping at a tall, hunky kid with a letterman jacket knotted at his waist.

"Hey, you spaz," the letterman kid said. He gave Eyeliner a playful shove.

Monte shrunk toward the produce section, his ears as hot as jalapeño peppers. *She wasn't talking to you, moron.*

"You sure the stuff's in?" Letterman asked Eyeliner. "It's barely even September."

"Yup," Eyeliner said as the pair returned to the group. "I saw them stocking it all last night." She grabbed a pack of bubble gum from the candy shelves. "This way." She strutted toward the back of the store, motioning for the others to follow.

*I might as well be invisible.* Monte moseyed after them, his pulse finally slowing. Norms really do have weak magic radars.

Eyeliner led them around a corner, stopping abruptly. She spun around, a smug grin pasted on her face. "See?"

"Awesome!" A scrawny girl, who looked more like someone's kid sister than a member of the high school pack, traipsed down the aisle. She grinned, her smile wired-up in braces.

"Oh, please." Another girl flipped her shiny blue braids around her as she sauntered away from the group. She folded her arms across her chest, batting her ridiculously long, mascaraed eyelashes in disapproval.

"You guys seriously still like this stuff? It's so babyish!"

"Well . . ." Eyeliner looked down at her feet, her shoulders slumping.

"Some of it's kinda fun." She fiddled with her pack of gum.

"Ah, lighten up, you killjoy." Letterman flashed a crooked grin at Blue Braids as the pack spread through the aisle.

Monte pretended to fumble with a packet of toothpicks at the endcap, peering at the group as they sniffed out their treasures. He smirked, suddenly realizing what all the hype was about. The aisle, adorned in an abundance of orange, black, and purple décor, was a Halloween paradise. Plastic wands, tin cauldrons, and pointed, cylindrical hats with round brims lined the wall in a variety of makes. *What's this supposed to be?* Monte snatched one of the hats and shoved it over his head. He flicked the flimsy cauldrons with his fingernails. *Not even a mild potion would last inside these pieces of garbage. And this . . .* He rolled a plastic wand across his palms. *This one takes the cake,* he laughed to himself. *Such blasphemy.*

The Norms never got it completely right—the whole magic thing. Yet he wasn't surprised. Mystics had lived alongside the non-magical Norms for centuries, their powers safely concealed within a well-maintained motherboard of magic. Every Mystic was educated from birth; Monte knew full well that the Norms were quite ignorant to their enchanted counterparts. He tossed the toy wand aside. The entire aisle was stockpiled with pretend magic items—all things that fueled the Norms' already strange obsession with what they called "witches" and "wizards." Unlike his parents, and most Mystics for that matter, Monte found the Norms' idea of magic quite amusing.

"I'm getting this one." Letterman grabbed a wand from a large bin at the other end of the aisle. "I gave my old one to my little brother for trick-or-treating last year."

"Fine. But don't think that'll make you more powerful," Eyeliner teased, rolling her eyes.

"There's only one way to find out!" Letterman lunged at her, playfully.

Eyeliner squealed as he spun her around, the plastic wand clenched between his teeth.

"Would you two knock it off?" Blue Braids chastised. "You're gonna get us kicked out."

Letterman joined Eyeliner in more eye rolling. "C'mon then." He twitched his wand at Blue Braids. "Let's go."

The pack trotted toward the front of the store, their arms full of new trinkets. Monte stuttered backward, nearly upsetting a display of Styrofoam pumpkins as the scrawny girl with braces bumped into him.

"Hey man, lose the hat," she said with a laugh. "You ain't no witch!"

"Uh . . ." Monte yanked the hat from his head.

"Psh." Blue Braids cocked an eyebrow at him as she passed. "Seriously, so immature."

*Touchy*, Monte thought, ambling after them. He plucked a tangerine from a nearby fruit barrel and tossed it between his hands.

Eyeliner and Letterman clacked their wands together, already engaged in a fake duel. *If they only knew*, Monte mused, training his eyes on the ignorant group as they paid for their loot. A tall girl with long black hair skirted around them, her brows pinched together like she was deep in thought.

"Tag the Hag at the park, then?" Letterman asked, nearly stumbling over the dark-haired girl as she weaved past them. He threw her a quizzical look before turning to face the rest of the group.

Something burned inside Monte's chest. A fleeting and unfamiliar heat.

"Really, guys?" Blue Braids whined. "I don't like that game. You know what people say about it."

Monte gulped, his fingers tingling.

"What?" Eyeliner asked. "That it's a mockery of the witches of old?" she snorted.

It was Blue Braids's turn to look at her feet.

Monte leaned forward. *Tag the Hag?* Another warm wave rushed through him.

"Don't come then, if you're too chicken," the scrawny girl teased as the group headed for the exit.

"Fine," Blue Braids huffed, marching after them.

Monte scooted in several paces behind the pack. Tag the Hag. At the park. With the Norms. The thoughts circuited through his head. He swallowed again, the residual warmth in his chest diminishing to a gentle thrum. It wasn't until they reached the park that he realized he still had the tangerine, clutched tightly in his hand. *Oh no. Monte, you dimwit!* His eyes darted from the tangerine to the Norm teens and back again. Spying on Norms . . . and now shoplifting. *Way to go*, he thought, half expecting to see the Norm police appear. Now he really could get in trouble. Double in trouble. He hunched behind a patchy hedge of shrubs. *I'll sneak the tangerine back in a minute*, he resolved. *But first, Tag the Hag.*

He watched through a hole in the bramble as Eyeliner and the others chose a large grassy spot for their game. The beachside park hosted a handful of picnic tables, plenty of mature trees, and several quaint paths that trailed to the shore below. *Not much has changed*, he told himself, remembering how his parents used to bring him here as a child. It had been one of their favorite haunts, a little oasis tucked away from the hustle and bustle of downtown Salem, Massachusetts. The park was often swarming with Norm vacationers. But not today. *Everyone's probably at the city center for Salem Heritage Days*, Monte thought, remembering what time of year it was. The past week's heat wave was tripping him up. It felt more like July than September.

He rubbed his thumbs over the bumpy pores of the tangerine, hardly eager to return to the monotony of the hotel room, his temporary home. His parents were probably signing closing papers for the sale of their house right about now. Sadness filled him at the thought of his childhood home, no longer his.

He crouched lower as the group turned his way. Blue Braids sat perched on a nearby bench, her hands knitted together. She scowled and wrinkled her mouth, her lipstick as pink as everyone else's faces. "You guys!" she whined. "It's like a million degrees out here. Can we at least move this nonsense indoors?"

The scrawny girl clucked like a chicken. Blue Braids stuck her tongue out at her.

"Well, we can't go to my place." Letterman tossed his pretend wand into the air and caught it again. "My parents are home."

Blue Braids frowned.

"What?" Letterman wiped at his sweaty hairline. "You know how my old man is about Tag the Hag."

Curiosity got the best of Monte. He was familiar with a few Norm games, but Tag the Hag wasn't one of them. His older brother, Garrick, thought they were downright shameful, especially since the sting of the Witch Hunts still resonated even hundreds of years later for the Mystics of Salem. But Monte disagreed. It was more fun to award the non-mysticals points for their recreational creativity than to scoff.

"All right, everyone!" Eyeliner barked through a large wad of gum, her wand clutched in her hand. "No need to go over the rules. Unless you're a softy and you need special rules." She raised her eyebrows at Blue Braids and then scowled. She swooshed her wand through the air. "Now get lost before I get ya!" she said, shoving Letterman. He laughed, stumbling across the grass with his own plastic wand as the rest of the pack dispersed around him.

"Double toil! Double trouble . . ." Eyeliner raised her wand above her head, whimsical and completely silly.

The teenagers erupted into organized madness. Strings of incantations, spells, and jumbled curses shot across the grassy lot as everyone tried to capture as many opponents as possible. Letterman tottered by the hedge, gripping his wand, pursued by Eyeliner.

"Abra-doo-da!" She laughed, thrusting her wand in his direction.

Letterman stuttered to a stop, poised in a comical attack stance. "Sha-zam!" he countered, a goofy grin spread across his face.

Eyeliner retaliated, brandishing her wand in a flutter of swirls around her head.

*Nice one*, Monte chuckled to himself. He wished he was old enough to carry a wand of his own—a genuine Mystic wand—so that he could give these Norms a taste of real magic. But he still had a few months before he turned fifteen-and-a-half, which was the official wand carrying age.

"I caught you! I caught you!" The scrawny girl appeared from behind a picnic table. She rushed at Letterman and shrieked with laughter, making Monte think she really was someone's little sister.

"Whatever," Letterman answered. "That was a stunning spell, not a capturing one, anyway. Dork."

Monte lowered himself to his stomach as the group backed closer to the hedge. The coarse grass was hardly soothing against his sweaty skin. Not even the briny breeze from the ocean below was a comfort against the throttling humidity.

"I'm not a dork!"

stomache?
hunger?

?

Monte flinched. Something stirred inside his chest—a deep, warm grumble. Sweat salted his forehead as a peculiar energy buoyed around his heart. He held his breath, trying not to gasp.

"Whoa!" he heard one of the pack yell. "Hey man, cut it out!"

Monte's insides buzzed as the foreign power moved through his body, the warmth escalating. *What's happening to me?* He peered through the shrubs where the Norms, several yards away, had halted their game.

"I didn't do anything!" Letterman demanded. "It just flew out of my hands."

"Just because you're a whiner and you're losing the game doesn't mean you have to start chucking things at us!" Blue Braids jumped to her feet, her eyes big and round.

"Oh, come off it. You're not even playing!" Letterman said through deep breaths.

Blue Braids flicked her glossy hair behind her. "I told you this was a bad idea. We should get out of here before—" She screamed as a stick hurtled past her head. "Who did that?"

Monte pressed his stomach further into the grass, his insides quivering. The strange warmth branched from his chest to his temples. He swallowed hard as the power begged to release.

"Maybe we should stop playing—hey?" Eyeliner's gum tumbled from her mouth as her wand was yanked into the air by an unseen force.

The power in Monte's chest pulsated. He dug his fingernails into the tangerine's skin.

"Watch out!" the scrawny girl squealed as her stick flew out of her hand.

Monte sunk his teeth into the tangerine, muffling a scream. He sucked in the citrus juices, his breath hot and steamy as the energy inside his chest threatened to give birth to something not unlike a hornet's nest. The Norms scattered across the grass, down the road, and away from the park, their exclamations of terror dense in the muggy air.

Finally, after several deep breaths, the strange vibrations ceased. An oppressive silence blanketed the now-empty park as the power diffused from Monte's body. He rose to his feet and stared at the mutilated tangerine. Chills skirted up his spine despite the heat of the day. He launched the decimated piece of fruit as far as he could and then dashed away, back to the hotel.

"You all right, young sir?" The front desk host cocked his head as Monte thudded into the lobby.

*Can't . . . talk . . . now.* The thought perspired from Monte as he padded past the desk, barely making eye contact with the bewildered clerk. He thudded up the stairs, silently grumbling at his dad for not booking a room on the main floor. He sludged down the hallway and teetered to a stop in front of their door, hoping that his family was still out as he jammed the plastic keycard into the handle.

To his great relief, the room was deserted.

The freshly laundered bed welcomed Monte as he collapsed face first onto the pillows. An odd sensation seeped through his sweaty skin as his mind battled the muddled events of the afternoon. He was trounced with confusion, shock, and an emptiness that shook his bones. But strangest of all, he felt a longing for more.

# CHAPTER 2
## The Birth of Bodmin

An icy darkness cloaked the man as he shivered on the frozen floor of the cave. He rubbed his purple hands across his ankle, pain etching the sturdy contours of his face.

"Take it," a woman's voice whispered from the darkness.

The man cringed. He shook his head in earnest, his light, feathery hair clinging to the woolen edges of his hat, his blue eyes almost wild.

"Take it now, or you'll surely die," the woman's voice continued, velvety yet threatening.

"I won't." The man's shaky voice matched his trembling hands as he pushed a small glass vial from his side. It clinked into the shadows, the noise echoing eerily through the hollows of the cave. The man rocked onto his hands and his knees, his gray lips set in a hard grimace, his slender torso convulsing with the cold.

"Don't move." The woman's voice, now lined with authority, grew closer. "The frostbite . . . you'll die if you don't hurry."

Agony contorted the man's brow as he sank back to the ground. He glared into the darkness as the rejected vial bobbed through the air, back toward him. It drifted in front of his face, its silvery contents an unwelcome beacon of his plight. "There has to be another way," he said through chattering teeth. He curled his legs into his chest, the shivers rolling through him.

"This is the only way," the woman's voice urged.

A single tear ran down the man's cheek as he stared at the floating vial. Slowly, he reached for the menacing bottle and, with quivering hands, uncorked the lid.

"Yes," the woman hissed from somewhere in the gloom.

"This is the end," the man whispered. He brought the vial to his lips, the last fragments of hope fading from his glassy eyes. With one firm shake, he dumped the misty liquid down his throat.

The vial clattered to the ground. The man's screams ripped through the cavern. He writhed on the floor, his fingers slashing the air in front of him as a cloud of darkness pressed in. The inky vapor stifled his cries until they were no more than a whimper, his torment finally giving way to a malicious and unnatural quiet. And then the dark cloud began to lift, exposing something much more treacherous.

Claws tore ice and a piercing shriek echoed through the cave. A sleek black panther blinked through the shadows, its pale eyes wide and vibrant. The large cat's tail flicked powerfully from side to side as it struggled to gain its footing on the icy ground. Claws scratched ice again and the cat stood, his mighty chest rising and falling in short, rapid puffs.

"Magnificent," the woman cooed from the darkness. "Absolutely astounding. You, my dark beauty, shall be called Bodmin, and you will be my crowning glory."

Her voice swam euphorically through the cave as she emerged from the shadows, tall and stately, wrapped in a cowled cape the color of midnight. She plucked the vial from the frosty ground, her eyes glinting beneath her hood.

The great cat squalled, his ears flattening against his head.

"Now, now," the woman said. "There's no need for that. You're saved now."

A low hiss caught in the cat's throat. Slowly, he lowered himself to the ground, his muscles twitching in submission.

"What a masterpiece . . . my masterpiece," the woman gloated. She kicked aside a heap of torn clothing, the articles no longer of use to the transformed man. A boot tumbled from the pile and skidded across the ground as the woman glided forward, her golden tresses flowing down the side of her neck in a loose braid. She whistled through her teeth and an enormous wolf appeared at her side. "Connery, call the others," she demanded of her canine charge. "There's work to be done."

Connery slinked to the mouth of the cave, her breath freezing in the mountainous night air. She pointed her snout toward the stars and yowled. Several beasts materialized from the darkness, the light from the moon splashing over their sharp features. She led the group back into the cave as the woman dropped the last of the ruined clothes into a newly conjured bonfire. The great cat crouched by her side, a thin, shimmery rope around his neck. His eyes darted around the cave, the brightness of the flames dancing through his whiskers.

"Come," the woman commanded as the wolves took their places around the fire. "My experiment has worked. My endless labor has finally paid off and now our plan can come to fruition. The time to strike draws near. I will prove my greatness to my people and eventually to the world." She clutched at the delicate rope around the cat's neck. "The master will worship me. I will be the most favored, once and for all." A devilish grin shadowed her face. "And when that happens, no one will ever dare to doubt me again—"

"Ah, man," Monte groaned as the television screen flickered. He tried to leap from the bed but instead found himself asphyxiated within a cocoon of bed covers. "Get . . . off of me," he grunted, yanking his arms from the scratchy clutches of the hotel blanket. He kicked his legs free and sprung from the bed. The aged mattress groaned, even under his light frame. He pounced in front of the TV and slapped his palm against the side of the box. Feeble strands of static streaked across the screen. "Stupid piece of junk." He pulled at the curls on the top of his head, a nervous habit his mother had given up trying to break him of.

The TV had been acting up all week. Of course it would die now, when he most needed the distraction. Goosebumps flecked his arms as he recalled his far-from-normal experience at the park the day before. He shook his head. *Probably just more growing pains*, he thought, wondering when his bones would finally stop stretching.

He tapped the side of the box again in one last attempt to restore the program. Nothing. He sighed. The movie had been interesting, unusually convincing for a Norm film. He had to give the non-mysticals credit for their imagination, at least.

He shuffled toward the window and pushed aside the heavy drapes. The late morning light leaked into the peaceful dimness of the room. He pressed his forehead against the glass and surveyed the scene a couple stories below him. It was another mellow day. Even the mist from the harbor seemed in no hurry to depart from the shore. It clung to the tree line that bordered the coast, the Pickering Lighthouse poking above the center, a lone bishop on a cloudy chessboard.

A taxi rolled leisurely through the parking lot below. Of the many things that kept society moving, automobiles were common instruments of transport for both the Norms and Mystic communities alike. This instrument, a dull, weather-worn yellow, spotted with rusty red patches, looked as though it had lived a long life of servitude. *It's probably shuttled thousands of Norm tourists all over Salem for years now*, Monte thought. He spun around as the room door creaked open behind him.

"Easy there, Jack-in-the-box," his older brother, Garrick, said as he stepped into the room. Sturdy and muscular, at seventeen years old, Garrick was their father's clone. Even down to the way his auburn hair waved over his forehead, he was every bit as identical to Mr. Esca Darrow as Monte was not.

"The man-child has returned," Monte joked. "Are we still going to the beach?"

Garrick wiped the sweat from his forehead with his arm. "Give me a sec, you skinny malinky," he said. He removed his damp t-shirt, pulling the sides of his hair up in the process so it looked like his head was growing wings. "Honestly, little bro. You look like a straw in search of a soda." Garrick eyed Monte up and down.

"Psh . . ." Monte puffed his chest out. "Just because I'm not a tall drink of water."

Garrick smirked. "Well played, Monte."

Monte pretended to take a bow and then shoved his shoes onto his oversized feet. "But seriously, this hotel room is depressing. I'm pretty sure the walls are sucking my brains out."

Garrick flexed his biceps, admiring his muscles as they rippled up and down. "What? You're bored? What about all of your summer reading?" He plucked a book from a small stack of novels at the foot of the bed and fluttered through the pages.

"I'm not like you, Garrick. I'd rather pour lemon juice over a freshly picked scab than read," Monte said. "Besides, even if I did fancy some literary education, it wouldn't matter since we're moving to the Highlands of Scotland tomorrow," he added in perfect imitation of Mr. Darrow and his Scottish brogue. He lifted his shirt to reveal his slender physique. "Wanna see my pec dance?"

"You're such a twerp." Garrick pushed Monte aside.

"Well at least I don't have stretch marks from pumping too much iron."

While Monte lacked the impressive physicality of his older brother, his crooked grin and playful eyes did prove that he was, indeed, a Darrow. For every pound of muscle Garrick carried, Monte had the same amount of wit. Monte had Mr. Darrow's Scottish blood to thank for that, although his long gangly limbs hardly passed him off as a rugged Highlander.

"Let's go, then," Monte said. "I don't think Mom and Dad realize the soul-eating potential of this room."

"Yeah okay, point taken. But it's not like you have to stay in here. You've been quite the couch potato since yesterday." Garrick raised his eyebrows.

"Hardly. I've been waiting on you all morning," Monte said, his stomach tightening at the thought of the Norm kids at the park. He didn't want anyone to know. Not even Garrick. "The TV stopped working and I'm going to die of boredom." *we know — enough already*

"Okay, okay. Quit squawking." Garrick secured his wand and a holster to his chest.

"You're bringing your wand?" Monte asked, grabbing a wetsuit from the floor.

"You're bringing that thing?" Garrick frowned at the suit and then pulled a fresh t-shirt over his head.

"Yeah, so?"

"Whatever." Garrick scooped up a backpack from the floor and heaved it onto his shoulders.

Monte grinned. A wet suit and a wand; sounded like a harmless afternoon to him.

*he sitting?* *how he it sees it?* *dropped*

Monte sloshed through the water and up toward the rock alcove. Saltwater and sand from his ocean gear splattered every which way as he plunked himself onto a large piece of driftwood.

"Ooft, watch it," Garrick complained, ~~wiping~~ *wiped* the sandy paste from his sunglasses. "Go collect your rocks somewhere else. The tide pools, perhaps?" he mocked, waving his hand at the shallow pools.

"These aren't rocks," Monte said as he dumped a handful of sand dollar*s* ~~pieces~~ at his feet. "And I had to have that rock collection for my report on Norm ecosystems, like, three years ago."

"Sure you did," Garrick teased. "You look like an octopus, by the way. Or a sea demon." *threw something at him*

Monte looked down at the wetsuit hugging his body. "Well in case you haven't noticed, the water's not exactly *freezing* warm." He ~~slapped~~ *pressed* his hands against his chest. Sea juices squelched out the sides. "And since we don't share any bloodlines with the Merpeople . . ." *from under then*

"Har-har." Garrick forced a grin. *? are we in Garrick's mind now?*

"If you don't like it, I can go starkers." Monte pretended to unzip the suit.

"Whatever you want," Garrick replied, clearly not fooled.

Monte placed the *sand* dollar fragments on a small boulder in front of him, *and* hunching down so that his eyes were level with ~~the pieces~~ *them*. *terrify*

"What're you doing?" Garrick questioned.

"Practicing levitation. I'm going to move these sand dollars . . . with my mind." Monte tapped his temples, secretly hoping to conjure the magic, that surge of energy he had felt in the park the day before, even though it had been nothing less than terrifying. *Who am I kidding?* *This heart pounded at the memory*

"Psh. Wouldn't that be amazing. Go ahead, then," Garrick urged.

Monte attempted to clear his mind, channeling every ounce of energy he could muster. "C'mon, move," he ~~implored through~~ *said* gritted teeth. "Move. Mooove!"

"You're doing it wrong." Garrick nudged Monte out of the way. "Watch and learn from the master." He pulled his wand from the holster and looked over his shoulder to ensure the beach was clear. With a subtle flick of his arm he sent the sand dollars dancing through the air. "A wand is always the way to go," he said, smugly.

"Wow. You're such a nerd. And that's real nice, seeing as I don't have a wand."

"Yet. Your half-birthday's coming. A little while longer and you'll get your wand." Garrick conducted the sand dollars back down to the top of the boulder and then opened his backpack, stowing the wand and holster safely inside.

*Show off.* Monte pursed his lips, annoyed. Recently, he had celebrated his fifteenth birthday which meant he had entered the year of his first wand. At Fifteen-and-a-half years old, a Mystic could officially advance in the magical community, and Monte was nearly at the threshold. Garrick liked to remind him about it frequently.

"My little baby is growing up so fast." Garrick patted Monte on the head.

Monte swatted at Garrick and a brief but vigorous skirmish ensued. Monte put his brother in a headlock, his maturing height finally proving useful. "Now who's the skinny malinky?" he laughed, accidentally giving Garrick the opportunity to slither from his grasp.

The pair tumbled into the sand. Monte quickly scrambled to his feet. Light, wiry, and all limbs, he was able to scurry away with considerable ease, wetsuit and all. Garrick stumbled after him, his flawless muscles quivering beneath smooth, sun-soaked skin. The pair collapsed near the tide pools in a mutual truce.

"I'll miss coming here." Monte unzipped his wetsuit and let his clammy skin breathe in the salty sea air. He turned his face upward, daring the sun to thicken the light dusting of freckles across his nose.

"We'll be back." Garrick sounded unsure.

"You think? How do you know that Dad won't get all caught up in the splendor of his heritage and keep us in Scotland forever?"

"He won't." Garrick shook sand from his shorts and staggered toward the nearest tidepool.

Monte followed. He peeled the wetsuit from his legs, revealing his clean but wrinkled swim shorts.

"I knew you weren't naked under there," Garrick said.

"Won't you miss it here?" Monte quipped. "I mean, Salem's our home."

"Of course I'm going to miss it, Mr. Sentimental, but there's not much we can do about it."

"I wish Mom and Dad would tell us more. The International Mystic Bureau is already getting on my nerves and we haven't even moved yet."

"They have to be secretive, Monte," Garrick said. "We don't want to risk exposing ourselves to the Norms, especially with everything going on in Scotland right now."

Monte sighed. Although their parents worked for the most influential governing body in the Mystic realm—the International Mystic Bureau, or IMB—never had they been summoned to a foreign country before. But then again, Scotland was hardly foreign, at least in the technical sense.

"When was the last time we visited the old country anyway?" Monte asked, sounding once again like their father.

Garrick brushed sand from his hands. "Been a little while now."

Monte tried to recall his most recent memories of the Scottish relatives. He smiled at the thought of Grandmother Meriweather Darrow. She would probably be the same as ever: perpetually old but definitely not ancient—spritely, in fact, with an unbreakable spirit. His only cousin, Maren, was older than he was and would likely be the most changed. "I wonder what Maren looks like now," he thought out loud.

"She's too old for you, if that's what you mean," Garrick teased. "Also, she's your cousin."

"Gross. I didn't mean it like that, you moron."

"Whatever." Garrick tilted his sunglasses up. His steely gray eyes danced with humor.

"I don't remember much about her, to be honest," Monte replied. "She's like seven years older than me." Memories of his father's family often evaded him, seeing as they hardly ever visited each other. The person who really threw him off was Uncle Jarus, his father's identical twin. On more than one occasion Monte had either confused the two or felt like he was seeing double. He liked to blame the family's lack of recurrent reunions for his confusion.

But the infrequent visits were about to end, thanks to the IMB's official orders. Mr. and Mrs. Darrow specialized in the study of enchanted forests and the evolutionary patterns of magical creatures. Their prestige had earned them a summons to the Highlands of Scotland where a menacing Mystic force was brewing. Since Mr. Darrow also had some experience in the area of Suspicious and Uncharted Magical Activity—and not to mention that he was a native to Scotland—he had been the first in line for the job.

"So, I guess Mom and Dad are bigwigs now? Since they'll be heading up their own Mystic team," Monte thought out loud.

"I suppose so," Garrick said with a shrug.

"They'll be tramping around that big mountain. What's it called again?"

"Ben Nevis."

"Right," Monte said. "Wish I could help. I'd quite enjoy a little mystical hunting."

"They won't be hunting, Monte."

"Tracking, then," Monte clarified. "What do you think they'll find? Some sort of scary creature? Hobgoblins? A witch's lair?" He snickered at his last suggestion. He was beginning to sound like a Norm.

"I dunno." Garrick turned to face the ocean, growing quiet. "Could be anything, really."

"Well whatever's going on—whatever's out there scaring the Scots out of their minds—Mom and Dad will solve it." Monte plunged his feet into the shallow water and watched as the loose sand melted from his toes to the bottom of the tide pool. He glanced at Garrick who wore a forced look of nonchalance. He could tell that his brother wasn't as tough as he looked. Garrick was as nervous as he was about the move. Yet it was the Darrow nature to buck up and be brave.

"I'm sure we'll be back before long," Monte resolved.

Garrick shook his hair from his eyes, causing sand to rain down on everything, including Monte. "Sure," he finally said.

Monte stared blankly into the tidepool. Something glinted in the water, like a flare against a magnifying glass. He leaned forward for a better look. Another twinkle revealed a small seashell resting on the bed of the pool.

"Cool." Monte plunged his hand into the water and retrieved the shell. Milky white with sparkly flecks, it was no bigger than a golf ball, and much flatter. A metallic spot dotted its middle from which bronzy, vein-like streaks emanated, dancing across the shell's surface as though alive.

"It's a seashell, Monte." Garrick mimed a yawn.

"Thanks, Captain Obvious. I was referring to the strange markings." Monte stroked his thumb over the shell's intricate ridges. "Look." He shoved the shell in his brother's face.

"Um, nope. Just a plain old seashell." Garrick stood. "You have fun with that; the makings of your very own shell collection," he said, dryly. "I'm gonna lay out more before Mom and Dad get back. This sunshine is too good to pass up and who knows what we'll get in Scotland. Stick around and stay out of trouble, will ya?"

"Yes, Mother," Monte said, full of sarcasm, as he rolled the shell through his fingers. He secured the curious object in the pocket of his swim shorts and then gazed at the undulating shoreline. A cluster of sea rocks jutted from the mainland a short distance ahead; a jetty shrouded in leftover morning mist—it was what the locals liked to call Witch's Pointe. Many claimed the great strip of rock had been bewitched centuries previously during the Salem Witch Hunts. The particularly superstitious folk avoided it altogether, and even Monte's parents, the accomplished Mystics that they were, steered clear of it.

Monte traipsed around the sea caves toward Witch's Pointe, leaving Garrick secluded in the rock alcove behind him. He trained his eyes on the Pointe, noting how majestic it was despite its bad name. Mist sprayed his ankles as he reached the base. He craned his neck toward the ocean's foam-topped waves. The tide wouldn't be in for several hours. Garrick was undoubtedly asleep by now. There was time for a quick climb.

Monte squinted at the top of Witch's Pointe. It was three stories high at the most—nothing he couldn't handle. He sprung onto the first boulder, ever mindful of the jagged edges infested with overgrown sea barnacles. He licked his salt-crusted lips, concentrating on the careful placement of his hands and feet as he climbed. The trouble wasn't the incline, but rather the small puddles of seawater that hosted thriving communities of slippery algae.

It didn't take Monte long to develop a steady climbing pattern and before he knew it, he was nearly at the top. He looked over his shoulder at the landscape below, his grip firm against the gritty rock structure. Warm shafts of light splashed down onto the rock alcove some fifty yards away, a natural vortex that formed a sunbather's paradise. The angle of the alcove, coupled with the position of the sea caves, shielded Garrick from Monte's line of sight.

Suddenly, something pricked Monte's leg. "Ouch!" he gasped. He tightened his grasp on the rock face and pulled up his swim shorts with his free hand. A raised red mark swelled on the front of his thigh, no larger than a fingerprint. "What in the world . . . ?" He shook out his shorts, wondering if a small sea crab had snuck in there. Nothing. He rubbed at the welt and then continued the last few stretches to the top.

The ocean breeze whipped through his hair as he pulled himself over the pinnacle. He spread his arms above his head in victory, panting only slightly. He picked his way to the tip of the Pointe, the mainland at his back, the rock rough under his bare feet, and peered over the ledge. The tide, still a good distance away, poured over itself in a soothing chorus of peaceful waves.

"Psh," Monte huffed. "This isn't dangerous at all." No sooner had the words left his mouth than another pain stabbed at his thigh. "Okay, seriously?" He sank onto the puddled rocks, his back to the ocean, and thumbed the seashell through the mesh lining of his pocket. "Little nuisance."

Just as he was considering chucking the unfortunate object over the ledge, a rumbling sound stampeded around the boulders below. Alarmed, Monte sprang to his feet, his teeth clattering as an intense watery roar rattled the entire peninsula. A monstrous wave crashed against the Pointe's crest, its spray hissing as he turned to face the awful noise. An entire cascade of frothy sea followed, each wave grander than the next, each breaker rolling toward the very spot where he stood. The tide wasn't due for several hours, yet here it was, unexpected and highly potent.

Monte ran the length of Witch's Pointe, stumbling toward the mainland. Water sprayed up in every direction as the sea continued its relentless pursuit. Something sharp sliced into the sole of his foot. He skittered across the rocky juts, his skin screaming as he keeled to a stop only inches from the rugged edge. Water crashed on the rocks. Mist as thick as a hurricane encircled him. Before he could regain his footing, an enormous wave swooped over the boulders and dragged him off the edge.

Monte fought against the churning sea with desperation. Another wave crashed over the top of him, thrusting him far beneath the water where he was thrown around like a puppet. He pedaled his legs against the turbulent undercurrent, gasping for air as his face finally broke the surface. He choked and water leaked down his throat and into his lungs. Another wave buried him as his final puffs of oxygen were pushed from his chest. Darkness invaded his peripheries, a blackness so intense that he was forced to succumb to the reality of death. He felt his body grow still. Time no longer existed. He was the ocean's victim, his body now swaying in perfect synchrony with the pattern of the sea.

*No!* his brain screamed. *Don't yield!* Monte flinched as his synapses fired the commands. He tried to reach his arms out in front of him as his body grew increasingly disconnected from his mind.

Then he felt it: an unmistakable burning sensation on his thigh, an energy that shook the very nucleus of his being. He seized the seashell in his pocket, his movements not his own. His body lurched forward. He squeezed the shell again and was propelled upward. He shot out of the water, bouncing over the swells, guided by a strange impetus. Seawater swirled from his lungs in a series of gritty gasps and coughs as he skidded onto dry land. Monte swallowed deeply, his throat stinging.

"Are you okay?" A voice pelted his head.

He didn't understand what it was saying.

"Are you okay?" the same voice repeated, this time closer and with far more clarity.

Monte slowly turned his head and rested his cheek against the warm sand. A peculiar smell permeated the air. Odd, but not unpleasant. Like damp soil fused with vanilla essence.

"Do you need any help?" The voice was female.

Monte raised his water-logged head and blinked, his eyelids out of sync as they stuttered over his throbbing eyeballs. He struggled to focus his vision as the figure in front of him went from single, to double, to single again. She planted a slender stick into the sand and then lowered herself to his level.

"Are you . . . all right?" The girl emphasized each word as she tucked a long strand of black hair behind her ear.

"I'm okay," Monte croaked. He rubbed at his eyes. The girl seemed familiar. "Do I know you from somewhere?"

"I don't think so." The girl sounded startled.

Monte blinked, trying to focus. He thought of the Norms from the day before. The park. The supermarket. "Were you at the Norm—er, I mean . . . the store yesterday?"

"Store?" the girl asked, her eyes widening.

Monte massaged his forehead, his thoughts foggy. There had been a dark-haired girl. The one Letterman had almost tripped over near the checkout stands. "Maybe I just imagined it," he mumbled.

The girl scooted closer. "I saw you fall from that sea stack thing." She motioned to Witch's Pointe. "You were nearly a goner."

Monte attempted to pull himself to his hands and knees but collapsed under rubbery limbs. He stifled a groan.

"You should stay put for a minute." The girl uprooted her stick and pointed it at Monte.

"Hey, watch it," he complained as she toggled the stick at his head, trying to remove a strand of seaweed that was dangling from his ear. Her face was a composition of curiosity and concern. She pinched her eyebrows together, her russet eyes boring into Monte.

Monte pulled himself to a sitting position. "So," he grunted. "You saw me go under?"

She turned to face the shoreline, twisting a slender rose-gold bracelet around her wrist. "I saw the ocean swoop up and grab you from the edge," she said. "I was about to run for help when you came hurtling to the top. It was . . . miraculous."

"Yeah," Monte said.

"I'm Cameron, by the way. Cameron Basu." The girl thrust her hand in Monte's face.

"M-Monte. I'm Monte." He shook her hand stiffly, unable to tear his gaze from Witch's Pointe. The tide had ebbed as quickly as it had appeared, the only sign of its recent presence the water-saturated sand. The whole thing was extremely confusing, and slightly eerie to say the least. "Bizarre," he whispered. "Maybe it really is haunted."

Cameron rested her elbows on her knees, propping her dainty chin in her hands. "Where'd the tide come from anyway?"

"You didn't see?"

"No." Cameron hugged her knees to her chest. "No, I guess I didn't," she said, kneading her forehead like she was the one who had hit the rocks. "I was kind of distracted—I tend to daydream. I didn't realize anything was wrong until the water was trying to eat you."

"Bih . . . zarre," Monte repeated, cupping his head in his palms.

"Monte. Monte!" Garrick's voice sang from the recesses of the rock alcove. Cameron jumped up as his large frame came into view, her face full of alarm.

"Oh, that's just my brother," Monte explained.

But Cameron was already skittering away, much like a frightened waterfowl.

"Wait!" Monte shouted after her.

She splashed through the puddles toward the apex of Witch's Pointe, pausing to look back at Monte, the slender contours of her body silhouetted against the distant ocean as she disappeared around the other side.

"Who was that? You find yourself a girlfriend?" Garrick yelled as he jogged the rest of the way over.

"Shut it, Garrick." Monte tottered to his feet.

"Sheesh. I was just making a joke. You ready? Mom and Dad'll be back soon. Wait, what happened to your back?" Garrick eyed the spot where Monte's shoulder blades had scraped across the boulders.

"Uh. I fell, that's all."

"Lies," Garrick said, surveying the wounds. "Some of these are quite gnarly, Monte. What happened?"

Monte pressed his lips together, his throat like fire, the burn of shame tracing his ears. "I . . . climbed Witch's Pointe," he said. "And then the tide . . . it came out of nowhere, and before I knew it the water had me."

"What? But the tide isn't due in for several hours."

"I know." Monte raised his shoulders, a reasonable explanation eluding him. "Look, if Mom and Dad ask, we were wrestling, and I fell against the boulders."

"No way. Then I'll get the blame for your stupidity."

"C'mon, Garrick. Dad'll skin me alive if he finds out."

"As he should. Witch's Pointe is no place to goof off. You could've . . . you almost . . . how did you even . . ." Garrick ran his fingers through his hair as he paced back and forth. "I'm glad you're okay," he finally said. "And I'm glad that I won't have to explain to Mom and Dad that I almost let you die. But this is the last secret I'm keeping. I mean it."

"Thanks Garrick," Monte said.

Garrick shook his head. "I can't believe you actually climbed that thing," he said, shoving a finger at the ominous rock structure. "You're such a moron."

Monte winced as a gush of ocean air swept across his back.

"C'mon. I think I know a few spells to patch you up."

Monte stole one last glance at Witch's Pointe and shuddered. He reached into his pocket and closed his fingers around the seashell. Instantly, he felt warmer.

CHAPTER 4

The Land of True Enchantment

The next morning found the Darrow family in front of a large block of a building. Composed of robust crimson brick, the structure sat regally on the corner of Washington Square in Downtown Salem, only a pebble's throw from the infamous Salem Witch Museum. Creamy rectangular chunks of stone trimmed its corners, climbing up the façade of the building, dividing the structure into equal segments. The windows spanned the impressive surface area with satisfying precision, adding more order to the already geometrical soundness of the building.

"The Hawthorne Hotel?" Monte stood on the corner of the block where a rustic wooden sign protruded from the building. In the distance a clock rang the top of the hour, its strokes drifting up from the Salem Common. Monte felt a surge of anticipation engulf him as the eighth and final chime dissipated into the muggy late-summer air. Eight o'clock. Their portal to Scotland would launch in thirty minutes.

"The Hawthorne Hotel houses one of the largest Mystic transportation portals on the east coast," Mr. Darrow explained as the family passed under the wooden sign.

"But it's a Norm facility." Monte paused outside the hotel's front doors.

"And it's haunted," Garrick added with a smirk. "Just like almost everything else in Salem."

"What's that supposed to mean?"

"Haven't you heard about the sixth floor?"

"Hush, boys." Mrs. Darrow's tone hinted at impending discipline as the family trod into the front lobby.

Mr. Darrow nodded politely to a pair of gentlemen at the front desk and then moseyed toward the back of the grand lobby. "This way." He motioned to the elevator in the far corner.

Monte shuffled across the deep green carpet after his father, almost forgetting about the tenderness of his wounds from the previous day. Thanks to Garrick's expert charm-work, his back was mostly healed, though still sensitive. His thigh, however, had proven more mysterious, the injury exceeding even Garrick's talent with a wand. Most confusing were the strange swirly-marks the seashell had left—much like burns but with far less pain. Guilt twinged in his gut as he brushed past his mother into the elevator. He had nearly died yesterday, and his parents were none the wiser.

Mr. Darrow waited for the elevator doors to slide shut before punching 2-5-2-2 into the worn copper buttons on the inside. Almost instantly the doors squealed open again, exposing a narrow, dingy room lit by a single incandescent light bulb that hung from a wire suspended from the ceiling. The needle at the top of the elevator indicated they were on the sixth floor, yet the décor shared no resemblance with the lobby downstairs.

"Garrick, this is the sixth floor," Monte said in an exaggerated whisper. He slid his thumbs through the shoulder straps of his backpack and then threaded his fingers together across his chest. He could feel the seashell tucked snugly inside his shirt pocket.

"Definitely haunted," Garrick remarked as the family filed out of the elevator.

The room certainly appeared as though it could house ghosts. The floor, no more than polished concrete, was cold and harsh. The room, surrounded by bare walls clothed in a yellowing nautical wallpaper, was devoid of furnishings save for a worn desk planted in its center. A young man sat behind the desk, trimming his fingernails with his teeth. He yawned and stretched as the family approached, showcasing the impressive span of his lanky arms.

"What can I do for you?" he asked in a Bostonian drawl. He brushed at the pile of dead finger skin littering the desk and then twiddled a wand through his fingers, his chair screeching as he leaned back.

"Ah, yes." Mr. Darrow reached the desk in three massive strides. "Hello, good sir. The name's Darrow."

The young man blinked back at him with sloth-like speed.

"Esca Darrow . . ." Mr. Darrow paused, met only by a blank stare. "Right," he continued, squaring his shoulders in a business-like manner. "The IMB—that is, the International Mystic Bureau—should've informed you we were coming this morning."

Monte glanced at a dilapidated clock hanging crooked on the wall: 8:12. They had less than twenty minutes to get to their portal.

"Hmm . . ." The young man pulled a crinkled paper from the corner of his desk and scanned a long, knobby finger down its middle.

Mr. Darrow cleared his throat and extricated a silver coin the size of a sand dollar from his pocket. "Our validation. From the Bureau—from the IMB." He rested the coin in his thick palm for the young man to see. Delicate vines intertwined around the coin's diameter where in the center was imprinted a rearing unicorn, the IMB's official crest.

"Oh . . . Darrow, yes," the young man exclaimed, his eyes suddenly knowing. "They did tell me you'd be coming this morning, but I completely spaced it."

"Interesting," Monte said, his voice laced with sarcasm.

Mrs. Darrow pinched his shoulder. Monte yelped, his skin still tender.

"Any luggage for scanning?" The young man stood, the tedium vanishing from his countenance as he peered around Mr. Darrow.

"No," Mr. Darrow replied. "It was sent on ahead."

"Right, I see." The young man plunked back into his chair. "I'll need to review your wands next, then."

Mr. and Mrs. Darrow produced their wands, followed by Garrick.

"And this is for my youngest." Mr. Darrow pulled a small purple booklet from his pocket. "He's not wand eligible just yet."

Monte felt his cheeks flush at Mr. Darrow's not-so-subtle reminder of his age. The young man inserted one of the wands into a narrow black tube at the head of his desk. A picture of Garrick materialized in the air. Strong but with a transparent quality, Garrick's face flickered back at them, his gray eyes almost as piercing as they were in real life. Several sentences, in bold typewriter font, hovered near the picture:

Darrow, Garrick Ian
DOB: 28 April
Height: 5' 10"
Hair: Auburn
Eyes: Gray
Origin: Massachusetts, USA
Status: Cleared

"Good." The young man extracted the wand from the tube and returned it to Garrick. The image and list receded as quickly as they had appeared. "Next."

He plugged in the second wand and this time Mr. Darrow's picture emerged in the same fashion.

Darrow, Esca Lawrence
DOB: 13 May
Height: 6' 3"
Hair: Auburn
Eyes: Gray
Origin: Scotland, UK
Status: Cleared

The image flickered away as the young man disengaged the wand. "And the third." He slid the final wand—a black, slender device with an eagle etched in the handle—into the tube:

Darrow, Vanessa Cly
DOB: 7 October
Height: 5' 5"
Hair: Brown
Eyes: Brown
Origin: New Mexico, USA
Status: Cleared

"Seems you three are in order." The young man handed back the wand. "Now for the minor." He opened the purple booklet and peered at Monte over the pages.

Monte waited, almost expecting his face and accompanying data to somehow project into the air. Instead, the young man read the information out loud: "Darrow, Montgomery McKay. Date of Birth: June thirtieth. Hair: Blonde. Check. Eyes: Hazel." The young man ogled Monte. "Hmm . . ." he said.

Monte held his breath and tried not to wrinkle his nose as the fellow leaned in, unintentionally blowing his breakfast into his face.

"Green . . ." the young man said. "No, gray."

Monte's eye color was always a topic of debate. Gray-green with a brown tracing around the outer edge of his irises, an interesting palette of colors.

"Eyes, hazel," the young man repeated. "Check. Origin: Massachusetts, United States. Status: Cleared. You're good to go." He handed the booklet back to Mr. Darrow and pointed his own wand toward the only door at the back of the room. Fluorescent light flooded across the cold concrete as the door swung open. "Safe travels."

Monte followed his family into the brightness of the adjoining room.

They were standing inside a giant warehouse—a warehouse on the sixth floor of the Hawthorne Hotel, apparently—where magic appeared alive and vibrant. Male and female Mystics dressed in business attire bustled past them. A handful of individuals wore traveling cloaks, but most of them carried folders and briefcases. Each eventually settled behind desks stationed throughout the expansive room. The walls, composed of bronzy brick, hosted sections dedicated to announcements and advertisements that materialized in bold, rigid lettering every few seconds. The words "International Mystic Bureau, Section 7" flashed across the wall parallel to them as though an invisible giant was writing in chalk.

Archways of varied craftsmanship lined nearly the entire perimeter of the enormous room. Some were twice the span of an average doorway, mostly constructed out of smooth stone. Others stood only four feet high and were devised of more curious materials such as clay, glass, and jewels. A ribbon of burgundy carpet ran snugly around the warehouse, serving as a divider between the archways and the activity of the room. Frosty orbs illuminated by soft golden light dangled from the ceiling—a friendly contrast to the buzzing fluorescents that hovered directly above them.

"Ah. Mr. Esca Darrow. Good to see you." A man in a pinstripe suit came forward to shake Mr. Darrow's hand.

"Hello, Kiernan." A smile spread across Mr. Darrow's face. "Vanessa, you remember Kiernan Calder? From my Uncharted Magical Investigation days?"

The man dabbed at his shiny forehead with a handkerchief before offering his hand to Mrs. Darrow. "Vanessa, it's been so long. And look at your boys." His thick, greasy eyebrows arched into his hairline.

"Nice to see you again," Mrs. Darrow said with a dewy smile.

"I hear you're heading up the Munro project in Scotland?" Kiernan asked.

"You heard correctly," Mr. Darrow answered.

"News is, it's kind of a mess over there," Kiernan said. "Rumor has it there's a large cat on the prowl, and that it's wreaking havoc."

"A large cat?" Monte piped in. "Like a lion?"

"Worse." Kiernan's caterpillars crawled even higher.

Monte raised his own eyebrows back. "Betcha Mom and Dad catch it on the first day."

Kiernan snorted and then smoothed over his black mustache with his spindly fingers. "Well . . ." He clutched his hands behind his back. "I'd love to catch up with you and your family, Esca, but it'll have to wait. I'm afraid I must take you straight to your portal. You launch in eleven minutes."

"Oh, of course. Off we go then." Mr. Darrow gestured for his family to follow.

Monte waited until Kiernan was a few paces ahead of them before making a face behind his back.

"Stop it." Garrick elbowed him as they scurried through the crowd.

"Ouch," Monte complained.

"Boys." Mrs. Darrow whipped around. "Stop messing around. And keep up, please."

"Sorry, Mom," Garrick and Monte mumbled in unison, trotting after her.

"I don't like him, that Kiernan guy," Monte whispered. "He's so . . . rickety. Like an old spider."

A Mystic woman in a red blazer and high-waisted skirt pranced past them as they weaved through the organized chaos. Monte watched as she marched over the burgundy carpet and disappeared beneath an archway lit in green. "Whoa, did you see that?" he exclaimed as they came to a stop near a small section of archways illuminated in purple.

"Here we are—your gateway." Kiernan flourished his twiggy wrists at a misty hole nuzzled in the wall at the end. "Poppy, here, will get you situated.

Safe travels now. And best of luck," he muttered, giving Mr. Darrow one final eyebrow raise before disappearing back into the crowd.

An official-looking lady with a pleasant face and a charming front-tooth gap greeted them. "Hello, Darrow family." She shoved a pin into the back of her tightly woven hair. "I'm Poppy. Please, follow me." She guided them to the entrance. "Excuse the haze," Poppy's voice echoed into the archway as she peered over her shoulder at them. "It's a foggy day in Scotland and some of it was brought back with our last traveler."

Monte took a deep breath. The air leaking from the portal was sweet and fresh. If this was any reflection of Scotland, he liked it already.

"This portal was used recently?" Mrs. Darrow asked.

"Very." Poppy turned to face them. "In fact, here comes our previous traveler now. Perhaps she forgot something."

A lofty woman approached. Her heeled boots clicked firmly against the stone floor. She radiated confidence, her light brown eyes sharp and alert as she peered down her straight, slender nose. She had a strong jawline and prominent cheekbones which were offset by thin, refined lips. A thick braid of blonde hair shone like twisted strands of honey beneath her sophisticated travel hat, which matched the rest of her pristine appearance.

"Moira? Moira Bryce?" Mr. Darrow asked in disbelief.

"Esca." A faint smile traced the corner of her mouth. She didn't seem as surprised as Mr. Darrow, yet she still exuded a subtle air of repressed pleasure.

"Wowza, she's pretty," Monte whispered.

A faint whistle left Garrick's lips.

"Shush," Mrs. Darrow warned through clenched teeth.

"You're the last person I expected to see here today," Mr. Darrow exclaimed. "But then again, you've always been a go-getter so I guess I shouldn't be so surprised. Oh . . ." Mr. Darrow interrupted himself. "Pardon my rudeness. This is my family." He swept his hand across the impressed bunch. "You remember Vanessa? And these are my sons."

"A pleasure," Moira said in a buttery voice. She extended her arms toward Mrs. Darrow and pulled her into a forceful hug. The pair embraced like a poorly matched figure-skating couple. Mrs. Darrow's hair snagged on the brass buttons dotting Moira's sleeve in a grand finale of forced affection.

"Whoops," Moira said, laughing. "Caught you there, Vanessa."

Mrs. Darrow cranked her neck to the side, her lips a solid line of vexation as she picked her hair from the clasps.

"And aren't you a strapping young lad?" Moira's face melted at the sight of Garrick. "My, he looks just like Jarus did at this age." She reached forward and cupped her fingers beneath his chin, several tendrils of Mrs. Darrow's hair still attached to her sleeve.

"Uh, thank you," Garrick said, choking on his tongue.

Monte snickered.

"Let me see . . . You're about nineteen, I'd say?" Moira took a step back to get a better look.

"Seventeen, actually." Garrick cleared his throat.

"A big lad!" Moira beamed. "Well done, Esca."

Mr. Darrow nodded proudly and slung his arm over his son's shoulder. Mrs. Darrow pursed her mouth into a sappy, muddled smile.

"And I'm Monte. The younger, often overlooked son," Monte joked.

Moira turned to face him. "Nonsense. I see a strong streak of Darrow in you, too," she said with a wink. "And I'm an expert, I'll have you know."

"Aha, well, I suppose you are," Mr. Darrow said, eyeing Mrs. Darrow with cautious regard. "So, what brings you to Salem?"

"Oh, you know . . . this and that. All business mostly."

"All work and far too little play. You haven't changed at all, Moira." There was a hint of camaraderie in Mr. Darrow's voice.

"You mean she's always been this pretty?" Monte asked. "Ouch! Mom!" he gasped as Mrs. Darrow grabbed his ear, twisting it just enough to make his eyes water.

"Sorry, Mr. Darrow," Poppy interrupted, "but I need to get you and your family situated. We are down to the final minutes. Can I assist you with anything, Ms. Bryce?"

"Oh, no. I thought I had forgotten something." Moira picked casually at a thistle pinned to her cloak. "But I was mistaken." She looked up, enthusiasm saturating her demeanor. "A wonderful family you have, Esca. Let's talk again soon." Her eyes glinted as she dismissed herself with a subtle nod. The sweet, earthy fragrance of her perfume lingered pleasantly in the air as she swept into the general bustle of Mystics.

"She's interesting." Garrick goggled after her. A twinkle of unrepressed admiration wavered on his face.

"Oh, knock it off," Mrs. Darrow hissed. "Honestly, the three of you." She glared at Mr. Darrow as she smoothed down her hair.

"I think Moira liked your muscles, Garrick," Monte teased.

"Indeed," Garrick said with a wink.

"Enough, boys," Mr. Darrow said. "Moira is a very old family friend, but I lost touch with her years ago. I had no idea that she was back in Britain." He seemed eager to change the subject. "She'll be working for the IMB on the other side of the pond, no doubt."

"Fabulous." Mrs. Darrow's voice was sour.

"Everybody ready?" Poppy said, already beneath the portal entrance.

The family shuffled after her through a short and stout archway fringed with mossy stone, and into a dark, drafty tunnel. Aside from the occasional road trip and a couple of flights to Scotland when he was very young, Monte was not accustomed to long-distance travel. The portal system was the swiftest and most secure means of Mystic transportation, usually reserved for prominent Bureau officials. They had Mr. and Mrs. Darrow's high standing with the IMB to thank for the privilege.

Monte rubbed his arms as the chilliness of the tunnel nipped his skin.

"First time travelers?" Poppy stopped as they reached a dead end.

"It is for my boys," Mrs. Darrow replied.

"Not a problem. It's really easy, actually," Poppy explained. "In a moment I will leave this corridor and activate the portal. Once opened, you will be magically conveyed to your destination."

"Won't that hurt?" Monte couldn't help himself. He had to know.

Poppy chuckled. "Not a bit. This is one of the most leisurely forms of Mystic transport. Not to mention the quickest—almost instantaneous. Now if you would all please have a seat we can get started." She pointed to a narrow brick bench, barely enough room for four, jutting from the wall.

"How come this portal is so deep?" Monte asked.

"They're all built differently, you see. Now please, if you would." Poppy motioned to the brick bench.

The family obeyed, squishing together like parakeets on a perch. It was a tight fit. Wedged between Garrick's and Mr. Darrow's massive frames, Monte had to stretch his neck awkwardly to avoid an armpit to his face.

"'Sake, Monte. Settle down," Mr. Darrow protested.

"My backpack," Monte grunted. "It's digging into my shoulder blades."

"Just leave it, son. We'll be there soon enough."

"Fine. But I hope everyone remembered to put on deodorant this morning," Monte teased. He rested the back of his head against the wall. Even from behind he could sense the moisture seeping from the mortar and stones.

"Ho, you sure are a funny bunch," Poppy said with a giggle. "Everyone ready?"

"Aye," Mr. Darrow replied.

"I understand it's a little jammed on that bench, but you must stay put. It'll only be for a moment," Poppy promised.

"Yeah . . . just a smidge . . . too tight." Garrick stretched his tree-trunk legs in front of him.

"Ha!" Monte clamped his teeth together, trapping his laughter inside.

"Remember, all you have to do is remain seated," Poppy continued. "You'll be on your way shortly." She smiled as she retreated into the corridor.

"Preparing for transportation," a female voice emanated from the walls.

Fireworks erupted in Monte's stomach. This was it. Even though it was rather immature to think it, Monte wished he had sat by his mom. Garrick whacked him in the face with his elbow as he hastily wiped a bead of sweat from his forehead.

"Ooft, Garrick. Your elbow—watch it." Monte's voice was sucked from his throat.

An odd pressure percolated in his chest, targeting his sternum as he was pressed against the wall. He tried to kick his legs in protest but they, too, had fallen victim to the invisible exertion. Light deserted the damp room, engulfing them in darkness. Perspiration tickled Monte's hairline as his blood thrummed in his ears. His stomach lurched as a torrent of wind spurted at him. *I'm going to suffocate before I even reach Scotland*, he thought as a colossal gush of air slapped his body. Then, all became still.

Monte heaved in and out, his head spinning from the miniature tornado that had just ripped through the portal. The air around him returned to a bearable temperature. Its warmth seeped into his wind-chilled skin as the mysterious weight was lifted from his body.

"Welcome to Scotland," the same feminine voice from before rang through the portal.

"That's it?" Monte asked as bright green-and-yellow specks paraded up the tunnel from which they had entered.

"Please stand and follow the lights to the end of your portal," the voice commanded.

"All right, Monte? Garrick?" Mr. Darrow pried himself from the bench. He pretended to yawn before offering his hand to Mrs. Darrow.

"Show off," Mrs. Darrow said, standing.

Monte stood and stretched, his fists nearly touching the ceiling.

"Your dad likes to pretend that portal travel doesn't faze him," Mrs. Darrow said. "But you boys should've seen him on his first trip."

"Too right. That was bad," Mr. Darrow said as the family plodded up the dim corridor. "I'm no novice now, though." He smiled at Mrs. Darrow.

Monte blinked heavily as they approached the portal opening, his eyes still favoring the gloom of the tunnel. It was a strange brightness; the light was natural yet dampened as though the sun wore a filter.

"Ah, brilliant." Mr. Darrow clapped his hands together. "Looks like they've sent us directly to the Banavie portal. It's one of the only outdoor channels left."

"Banavie?" Monte asked.

"Banavie is a sub-town of Fort William, not far from where your Uncle Jarus lives," Mr. Darrow replied.

"Fort William is your father's hometown," Mrs. Darrow added. "You probably won't remember much; you were quite young the last time we visited."

"Aye," Mr. Darrow answered as they stepped through the archway onto a path overgrown with moss. The earthy lane extended a short way ahead of them before joining with a crumbly sidewalk that lined an even more decrepit road. Fields, full of sleepy pre-autumn grass, stretched in an abundance of acreage on the other side of the road. The sky, burdened with a collection of wooly gray clouds, smelled of the luscious nectar of the land.

"Ah . . ." Mr. Darrow closed his eyes, a grin teasing his mouth. "It's good to be home."

"Welcome te Scotland, yeh bonnie bunch!" a cheery voice trailed from the sidewalk ahead. A small pixie of a woman with hair the color of strawberry cream danced around excitedly, several paces in front of them. Although wrinkles corrugated her face, she emitted a sense of matronly style. Her baby-fine hair fluffed over her head in short, playful tufts, perfectly poised yet with the potential for craziness.

"Mum!" Mr. Darrow exploded into a squeal.

"Oh wow, Grandmother Meriweather hasn't changed a bit." Monte turned to Garrick.

"And Dad . . ." Garrick cocked an eyebrow. "He's reverted back to a six-year-old. Look at him, doing the potty-dance and everything."

Monte chuckled.

Grandmother Meriweather bounded toward them with open arms. "Ah, yer here at long last!" She reached Mr. Darrow first. "Esca, how'd you manage at the portals? Yer looking overworked, I see. Vanessa, dear!"

The words spilled from her mouth, her Scottish accent thick and rich. "Garrick, son! I hardly recognized yeh," she said, using the highest form of endearment as she cupped his cheeks in the palms of her hands. "Ah, and Monte. My, how you've stretched!" She placed her hands on his shoulders. "Welcome, son." Her radiant blue eyes looked up at his. "Welcome te Scotland, the Land of True Enchantment."

# CHAPTER 5
## Troublemaker

Monte gazed around the office at Strathmartine Academy, his focus drawn to an inviting bay window which overlooked the rolling emerald hills and heavy clouds of the Scottish Highlands. *Just play it cool*, he told himself. *You didn't do anything wrong . . . at least not this time.* He swallowed and stared out the window. The weepy sky spoke of a tantrum, a habit which promised no end. Across the loosely populated landscape was Ben Nevis—or the Ben, as the locals called it—the mighty mountain Mr. and Mrs. Darrow had been assigned to survey. They were up there now, toiling through the mist in search of large cats and mysterious enchantments. Monte shook his head. The days were melting into weeks, already. It felt like they had just arrived yesterday.

"And what is this all about?"

He cringed at the sudden presence of the assistant headmistress's warbly voice.

"Ma'am?" he asked as Babs Campbell entered the office. She pattered past him, her puffy brown hair bobbing with every stride, her eyes as frantic and as bulbous as ever.

"Oh, come now, Master Darrow," she said, planting herself behind a glossy mahogany desk at the back of the room. "I know it was you." She twitched her nail-lacquered fingers in the air, signaling him forward.

Reluctantly, Monte obeyed. "It wasn't me. Honestly, Babs." He slumped into the chair opposite her.

"It's Mrs. Campbell," her voice vibrated like a taut rubber band. "And I don't believe you. Not for one minute."

Monte's steady composure flickered. Uncle Jarus had made the mistake of addressing his assistant as Babs at their first meeting, and the informal title had stuck, hard, in Monte's mind. Using her first name was a delightful way to fluster her.

"Chalk flying through the room," Babs continued, "a toupee hovering in the air as if possessed, and now this." A pungent smell attacked Monte as Babs pulled a blue-and-white-striped paper sack from her desk.

"I see your lunch has gone bad," he gasped as the odor drifted through the room.

"This is not my lunch!" Babs shot up. Her watery eyes darted around the room. "I know you are behind this, Master Monte Darrow," she said, enunciating every word. "You've been nothing but a troublemaker since your arrival to Strathmartine Academy. I've had it up to my neck with your mischievous . . . naughty . . . ways." Her lips trembled as the words fought their way from her mouth. "You've been here all of three weeks and look at the trouble you've already caused. Is that what we're going to get? An incident a week with you?"

"No, I—"

"Your uncle may run this school but that does not excuse you from your actions. This is the very type of paper sack you transport your school lunch in, is it not?"

*Affirmative.* It was the sort of bag Monte used for his pack lunches— Cousin Maren got them from the bakery up the road—but that was hardly reason for Babs to accuse him of mischief.

"It wasn't me," he persisted.

"Oh?" Babs bleated. Her confrontational courage, so gallantly mustered, was quickly diminishing.

"That . . . whatever is in there," Monte stammered, pointing to the paper sack. "Was not me."

A brown stain framed the bag as the decaying, syrupy fluid inside threatened to burst out.

Babs sank into her chair. Monte stared fixedly at a shiny golden name plate on the edge of the desk. The words "Assistant Headmistress" were stamped boldly across it.

"That's new, isn't it?" He gestured to the nameplate in an attempt to break the uncomfortable silence.

"Yes . . ." Babs's eyelids fluttered over her enormous eyes.

She was cracking. He gazed past her overly hair-sprayed head, pausing at the tall bookshelf just behind the desk. An impressive collection of nail polish vials stood at attention on the top shelf, tiny soldiers that overlooked the grand realm of Babs Campbell. Books, bound in an array of leathers, were posed on the shelves, many with worn spines. Another office, modest but dignified, was tucked adjacent to the back wall. Its large oaken door hung slightly ajar, labeled with a plaque that read "Headmaster Darrow." Uncle

Jarus's grandfather clock ticked through the narrow opening in the door. The tones sliced through the smelly air, a countdown to how long it would take until Babs finally broke.

Strathmartine Academy was a Norm institution, overseen by Uncle Jarus who, as usual, kept his magical capabilities under wraps. It sat atop a knoll in the center of Fort William, and was a landmark that the locals took much pride in. Monte had been less than disheartened to learn that the small town hosted no schools for Mystics and wondered how, exactly, his father had managed to grow up in a place so dismally devoid of magical influence.

A sharp wave of rotten egg blasted the thoughts out of Monte's head. Babs brushed her fingers across an open folder at her desk. A Polaroid of a kid with golden ringlets, a crooked grin, and playful eyes stared up at Monte. It was a photograph of him, stapled to the inside of a folder where Babs undoubtedly kept his naughty file.

Monte squirmed, Uncle Jarus's clock ticking louder. Babs looked up, expectantly. Monte clamped his jaw together. *You didn't do anything. Don't give in.* But eventually, Babs's goat-like ogling got the better of him. "How long do I—I mean—how long would you like for me to stay here?" he yielded.

Babs just blinked back at him.

"Look, I'm sorry about the chalk. And I did detention for the toupee. But I did not plant this disgusting bag on Mr. McCormack's chair."

"I have reason to believe otherwise," Babs said with a sniff. "Sofia Snee said she saw you with an identical paper sack this morning."

"Psh . . ." Monte snorted. "Surely I'm not the only one who uses the baker's paper bags to carry my lunch? Seriously. I mess up a couple times and suddenly I'm the school poltergeist."

"Your tone, Master Darrow, is far from appropriate," Babs warbled as the lunch bell clanged overhead.

"This is hardly fair, Babs—er, Mrs. Campbell. Look, why would I risk carrying something around that smells of death? What if it spilled?"

"You're blethering, Darrow."

"I didn't do it." Monte rose to his feet.

"We're not done." Babs looked panicked.

"Bring me back when you have evidence." Monte marched for the door.

Uncle Jarus's voice boomed from the hallway outside the office. "Off te lunch with yeh! Go on now."

"Now you're in for it," Babs crowed, pompously. "Headmaster Darrow doesn't put up with any nonsense. Don't expect any special treatment just because you're his nephew."

Uncle Jarus barged into the room. "Hey-ho, Monte!" He blew right past them, ushering a pale, petite boy into the office. "Finn, right this way, pal."

The boy's bright blonde hair was parted at the side, slicked severely against his head. He clutched a metal lunchbox decorated with a cartoon character Monte didn't recognize tightly in his hands.

"Yeh can eat in here, pal," Uncle Jarus said, pausing at Babs's desk. "Whoa! What in the name of Prince Charles is that ghastly smell?"

Babs thrust a quivering finger at the paper sack.

"Blech. It's stinkin' of rotten eggs." Uncle Jarus plucked the sack from the corner of the desk. Decomposing egg juice oozed from its bottom. He glared at the atrocity, finally daring a peek inside. "Gah, it *is* rotten eggs! Babs, why is this in here? It's pure minging. Get it out at once."

"Yes, Headmaster Darrow," Babs chirped. "It's just that your nephew placed this on Mr. McCormack's chair, and—"

"Monte . . ." Uncle Jarus turned on his nephew, his eyes sharp.

"Hey, it wasn't me." Monte held his hands up defensively.

Uncle Jarus raised his eyebrows in an I'll-tell-your-mother-on-you look.

"Honest, Uncle Jarus," Monte pleaded, still not used to how identical his uncle was to his father.

Finn, the pale boy, tiptoed around the desk and plopped into the chair Monte had just vacated. He gawked at the gooey residue leaking from the bag.

"A word please, Babs. Monte, yeh stay put, yeh hear?" Uncle Jarus shoved a finger toward his nephew, returning the repulsive bag to the desk with great care.

"Monte was seen with a paper sack just like that one this morning," Babs continued, her protests buckling through the air.

"Yeah, because that was my lunch!" Monte exclaimed as the door to Uncle Jarus's office closed. He huffed and marched to the bay window, throwing himself onto the cushioned seat with a heavy sigh.

"Are you a sorcerer?" Finn chimed from behind Babs's bulky armchair. His voice, though childlike, had an ageless quality.

"Are you talking to me?" Monte asked.

Finn's head peeped over the back of the chair. "Don't be a numpty. Who else would I be talkin' to?"

"Did you ask if I was . . . a sorcerer?"

Finn nodded, his dazzling jade eyes full of question.

"No . . . I'm not," Monte said slowly. "What kind of a question is that anyway?"

A smile stole across Finn's face. He shrugged.

"Why're you eating your lunch in here?"

"Nanny does'nae like me eating with the other kids," Finn said matter-of-factly as he slid back down the chair.

Does'nae . . . Monte still didn't understand how the word *doesn't* translated into does'nae. But that was Scottish slang. So many variations, so many blended words. In a few weeks' time it felt like he had learned a completely foreign language.

Uncle Jarus's office door swung open. "Ooft!" Uncle Jarus flared his nose. "Babs, please, for the love of goodness, get that bag out of here. And Monte, I'm not going te pretend that yer behavior hasn't been far from exemplary since yer arrival here at Strathmartine." He scratched his head aggressively. "But I'll tell yeh what . . . Take Babs te yer locker. If yeh can procure yer proclaimed lunch sack, I'll let yeh off, but not before yeh apologize for yer insolence."

"But—"

"Nah." Uncle Jarus knit his arms over his chest. "Not another word, yeh hear? Not in my school. Not anywhere, for that matter. Yeh ken?"

"Ken?" Monte scrunched his eyebrows together, stumped once again by the slang.

"You know? You understand?" Uncle Jarus said in an exaggerated American accent.

Finn chomped into a chicken salad sandwich, smacking his lips together with delight.

Monte's stomach growled. "Sorry," he sighed, glancing at Babs before turning to leave. He could feel Finn staring at the back of his neck.

"Wait for me, Master Darrow," Babs whinnied.

Monte heard a sickening squelch as Babs snatched the paper sack from the desk. "The old goat," he said through gritted teeth as she trotted behind him. *Always has it in for me.*

He reached his locker, cranked in the code, pulled out his sack lunch, and handed it to Babs.

"Oh." She eyed her own paper sack sheepishly. The bottom burst open, finally succumbing to its rotten contents. A slew of brown yolks and rancid slime splashed onto the wood floors of the hallway. Droplets of slop splattered across Babs's stubby, flat shoes.

"Have a lovely afternoon, then." Monte barely managed to choke out the words past his irritation, and the smell, as he turned on his heel.

"You've forgotten your lunch, Master Darrow!"

Scotland was turning out to be a bust after all. More than ever, Monte wanted to go home.

CHAPTER 6

The Rainbow Lights

The seashell sparkled under the perky light of the reading lamp at Monte's desk. He ran his finger over the ridges before tucking it safely inside his trouser pocket. The marks on his thigh had healed and were no longer bothersome, yet the memory of nearly being swallowed up by the ocean still made him shudder. He was convinced the shell had saved his life and he liked to keep it close—especially with all the rumors flying around.

It had not taken long to discover that Scotland was on the verge of magical upheaval. Mystic surveillance had been strict since the Darrow family arrived, beginning only moments after Grandmother Meriweather had greeted them outside their portal. Given the nature of their duties with the International Mystic Bureau, Mr. and Mrs. Darrow had been granted elite status, which meant they could use their wands freely and with little fuss. Unfortunately for Garrick—and even Monte, though still not wand eligible—the use of magic was, by order of British Mystic law, temporarily forbidden unless cleared by the IMB.

To make matters worse, Fort William, Scotland was home to some of the most superstitious Norms Monte had ever encountered, and that was saying a lot, coming from someone who had grown up in Salem. Then again, it didn't take a genius to realize that the large cat sightings, along with the unsettling aura that brewed over Ben Nevis, were far from normal. Regardless, the current IMB restrictions, paired with a heightened Norm intolerance for the extraordinary, were a recipe for extreme boredom. Monte hoped his parents would catch the source of all the trouble before his brain melted out of his ears. Or before the tedium of his studies crushed him.

Of course, it didn't help that Strathmartine Academy was a non-mystical school, meant only to host Norm kids. In all his years in Salem, Monte had never attended a Norm school. Such a thing was hardly heard of, especially for Mystics living in a town with a dark, sordid history of hunting witches. Up until now, the IMB had taken a much stauncher position outside of Scotland—and particularly in Salem—all nonsense, in Monte's newly formed opinion. Weirdly enough, Uncle Jarus, once a highly gifted Mystic, was now a simple headmaster. You would never see that in Salem, Monte mused; a

Mystic, mingling with and working for the Norms. The whole setup was peculiar, to say the least. Then again, there were many things about his uncle that he was yet to figure out.

Monte pulled his tie from his neck. *Wretched thing. Who invented school uniforms anyway?* He tossed the offending article on his bed and crept into the hallway.

Light spilled from the space beneath Garrick's closed bedroom door across the hall. Monte raised his hand to knock, then stopped. Garrick, once his closest friend and confidant, had been in a disagreeable mood the past little while. Adjusting to life in Scotland had been hard enough, and the absence of Garrick's usual camaraderie only made the days drearier. Monte jokingly blamed the drinking water but suspected there was a much deeper cause. Aside from all the magical restrictions, Mr. and Mrs. Darrow's fight to eradicate the inexplicable darkness surrounding Ben Nevis had proven incredibly demanding thus far. So much so, that they had opted to move into Downfield Place, the estate where Uncle Jarus and Cousin Maren resided. Here Monte and Garrick could be properly looked after while their parents were away. *Not that we need it*, Monte mused.

Uncle Jarus's car rumbled down the cobblestone driveway outside, as if on cue. Monte whizzed back into his room. His uncle would be expecting an explanation for the day's rotten egg incident. *Maybe if I hide up here long enough, he'll just forget about it*, Monte told himself as he thumbed through a stack of schoolwork on his desk. *If he catches me doing my homework, he might be less harsh.* He slid a packet from the mound of past-due assignments.

The cover page read "Unit 2. Scottish and Gaelic Mythology: Questions from the reading." Monte groaned, thinking it was hardly fair that he had to learn about Norm topics. Maybe he would take the conversation with Uncle Jarus after all. He scanned through the first question. He had no clue what it was talking about. The second question wasn't much better. He shook his head and skipped down to question number five.

*Scottish mythology tells of three ancient stones with exquisite powers. They are kept by the earth but are strongly desired by man, and date back to Pagan times. Collaboratively known as the "Deo Stones," which of the following is NOT mythed to be part of the trio?*

A) *The Moondrop*
B) *The Firepearl*
C) *The Woodland Ruby*
D) *The Mica Star*

Monte dug his chin into his knuckles. He knew a thing or two about rocks and gems, thanks to his mother, but was quite the amateur when it came to Celtic mythology. *These are dumb questions. Who even cares about the Deo Stones?* He huffed as Uncle Jarus's baritone voice meshed with Cousin Maren's staccato chuckle downstairs. The house was extensive, but not much could prevent the musical mirth of Uncle Jarus and Maren from singing through the walls. Already bored with homework, and distracted by the fun happening downstairs, Monte went to the window and stared aimlessly up at the night's first stars.

Downfield Place was constructed in an odd *L* formation and Monte's room sat within the vortex—the crook of the estate's elbow. His bedroom overlooked the driveway which trailed toward the road in a sturdy procession of cobblestones. Across the street was expansive greenery, stretching for miles into wild and hilly countryside, all sleepy in the looming darkness. Empty pastures lay to either side of the Downfield property. The majority of Uncle Jarus's land stretched behind the house where a forest-y patch of trees shadowed a blathering stream. Though dusk faded rapidly, there was still enough light to make out the Ben's smooth, rounded peak poking up from the mist which so constantly masked the great mountain. Guardian of the Highlands, Ben Nevis commanded attention, the great gem of the Mystic and Norm realms alike.

Monte pressed his hand against the cool windowpane. He wondered who was responsible for today's rotten egg prank. He understood why he had been a possible suspect. After all, he had already fostered a mischievous reputation at Strathmartine. But then again, he surely wasn't the only prankster in the school.

The chalk had been a mistake. But how was he to help it? One second it had been in his hands and the next it had rocketed across the classroom, barely missing his math teacher's ear. Then there was Mr. McCormack's toupee. A meticulous man who constantly preened his ever-so-obvious hairpiece, Mr. McCormack had been the unfortunate recipient of Monte's unintended magic trick. He smirked at the memory of his teacher's toupee peeling from his head. It had dangled several inches in the air—so subtly, so beautifully—for a full second before plopping to the ground. Even now, Monte wasn't sure how he had done it. News of "The Great Toupee Escape" spread quickly throughout the school, much to the chagrin of Uncle Jarus, who had to scramble to find an excuse for the baffling floating-hair incident. Monte wasn't helpful in his explanations of the experience either. It had just happened, and without warning. The IMB had acted with impressive speed on the matter. Luckily, Mr. and Mrs. Darrow's elite status had gotten Monte off the hook, but only just.

Monte watched as the window fogged up around his outstretched fingers. Something outside caught his attention. A figure, shrouded in a colorful display of lights, picked its way through the dim landscape across the lane. It moved toward Downfield Place, finally halting beneath the lamppost on the other side of the street.

"What the blaze?" Monte rubbed the condensation from the window.

A young lady stood beneath the gentle sheen of the lamppost. She wore a strand of what appeared to be Christmas lights loosely around her neck. Her long black hair was styled in a low ponytail. In her hand, she held a walking stick. There was a familiar look about her, yet Monte couldn't quite place where he'd seen her before.

His throat tingled. The scent of citrus stung his nose. He backed away from the window, his chest suddenly full of warm, buzzing energy—a feeling he hadn't experienced since . . . Salem. The park. The beach. Without questioning how or why, he snatched up his jacket and bolted out of the room.

"Whoa, there!" Uncle Jarus said from the kitchen as Monte pounded down the stairs. "Here comes a hungry ogre."

Monte burst into the kitchen, suddenly realizing the need to act inconspicuous.

"Hi, Monte," Cousin Maren sang out from the kitchen table.

"Oh, hi. Um, I'll be right back." Monte dashed through the kitchen toward the back service door.

"Just yeh hang on a minute, pal. It's getting dark out," Uncle Jarus called after him.

Monte waved his hand in hasty acknowledgement before slamming the door behind him. He wrangled into his jacket and then cut through the back garden, tumbling through the side gate and onto the driveway. Downfield Place towered above him, its rocky face almost spooky in the waning daylight. Monte's heart thumped vigorously as he padded up the driveway, compelled by the odd energy brewing inside of him. The mushroom-shaped ground lights cast strange shadows against the bumpy cobblestones, like lurking goblins. The lamppost's light radiated from across the lane, its circumference nearly reaching the edge of the Downfield driveway.

And there was the girl, just visible behind the metal stem of the lamppost. The Christmas-light contraption pulsated in a rainbow of colors around her slender neck. "Hey!" Monte panted as he reached the edge of the driveway. "You're from Salem, aren't you?" he yelled to her, hardly caring if he sounded crazy.

She startled at the sound of his voice.

"What's your name again?" Monte stepped onto the road.

The girl inched from behind the lamppost. "It's Cameron," she said, massaging her forehead. "Do you live here?"

"Yeah . . . I just moved here," Monte said, increasingly puzzled. "What're you doing here? You didn't follow me halfway across the world, did ya?"

Cameron's eyes crawled up Monte's sports jacket—a hand-me-down from Garrick—stopping once they reached his face. He gasped as a chill gushed through him.

"Monte," she said, her voice barely audible from across the street.

His spine tingled under her gaze. Suddenly, he was reliving his brush with death at Witch's Pointe all over again.

"Monte," she repeated, her voice louder. "I don't know how I . . ." She paused to rub her forehead again. She seemed to swoon a bit, and then finally blurted out, "Monte, you're in danger."

What little warmth remained in Monte's chest extinguished with Cameron's words. "I'm in danger? What do you mean?"

"Monte?" Uncle Jarus's voice echoed up the driveway. Monte heard a faint creak then a dull snap as the garden gate slammed shut below.

"In a minute!" Monte yelled down to his uncle, spinning back around to face Cameron. But she was already retreating into the field behind the lamppost, scarcely visible save for the twinkling lights around her neck.

"Cameron, come back!"

Cameron sprung further into the field, the looming darkness all but swallowing her.

"Wait," Monte whispered loudly. Cameron disappeared behind a hilly clump of bramble, her rainbow lights smothered by the darkness.

"Bizarre . . . honestly." Monte began to march across the lane, his eyes fixated on the spot where she had vanished.

"Monte . . . stop!" Uncle Jarus's voice thundered from behind.

Adrenaline pumped against Monte's temples. He paused. He knew that tone. It was the same as his dad's and it was not to be disregarded, no matter what the circumstance.

"What the devil are yeh doing?" Uncle Jarus placed a firm hand on Monte's shoulder and herded him back to the driveway. "How many times must I remind yeh that yer not allowed out here alone after dark? There are . . . things . . . happening."

Monte squinted hard at the trees, searching for Cameron. He turned to face his uncle. "Things happening? That really narrows it down." It wasn't like he was five years old. He hardly needed a babysitter to escort him up the driveway.

Uncle Jarus held his breath, as though trying to repress an explosive remark. "Fancy a walk then?" he asked. He pulled a glass orb the size of an orange from his jacket. He tapped it twice with his index finger, giving birth to a powerful white light. "Ooft. Too bright," he muttered, tapping the orb again. The light dimmed. "That's better." He propped the orb in his uplifted palm. It rose from his hand and hovered in the air near his shoulder, pitching light onto the tarmac ahead of them.

"You just used magic," Monte said, staring at the orb. "I thought—"

"When yer name is Jarus Darrow, yeh are afforded certain privileges in this town," Uncle Jarus said as he forged down the dark lane.

The Widow Smith's cottage—a dark lump with a glowing spec of light— sat several pastures away from Downfield Place, a feeble beacon in the deepening twilight. The Widow was their only neighbor for a couple miles, save for Grandmother Meriweather, and Monte had yet to see her. She favored seclusion, he was told.

A crisp darkness engulfed the surrounding landscape as the lit orb escorted them down the country road. Twigs snapped and leaves scratched across the ground, the night welcoming a chilly breeze. Monte dragged his head around, half expecting to see Cameron's creepy, twinkling rainbow lights.

Uncle Jarus cleared his throat. "I know yeh didn't do it." His voice was low and calm, unlike his tense and rigid posture. Even in the nightfall Monte could tell Uncle Jarus was on alert. The large cat rumors had even the bravest of Mystics in a hyper-vigilant mindset.

"Do what?" Monte pushed his hands deeper into his pockets.

"The rotten eggs. That was obviously the joke of a much less experienced prankster," Uncle Jarus said, only half joking.

Monte shivered, trying to forget about what Cameron had said about being in danger. "Oh, yeah. The eggs. Like I said before, it wasn't me."

"I ken. But let me remind yeh of the trouble yeh've already caused. The chalk, the . . . hairpiece," Uncle Jarus wavered as if not wanting to betray Mr. McCormack's far from discreet hair secret. "Too close for comfort, pal. We're lucky the Bureau was lenient."

"I already said I was sorry. I don't know how either of those things happened."

"Aye. But Monte, I don't think yeh understand the level of magical surveillance the country is under right now." Uncle Jarus's breath froze in large puffs as he spoke.

"Maybe I don't."

"Listen here, my boy. I cannot have yeh slipping up anymore. Not at school, not at Downfield, not anywhere. I won't emphasize this enough."

"Kind of a big deal over some lame cat sightings," Monte mumbled. He scanned the dark fields on either side of them. Where had Cameron come from, anyway?

"Yeh think this is all a big farce, do yeh?" Uncle Jarus spat. "Do yeh know why yer parents were ordered here in the first place?"

"To figure out what's going on in Ben Nevis?"

"Aye, partly. But do yeh know what kicked this all off?"

"Some overgrown cat that everyone's scared of for some reason?"

"It's killing people, Monte. This thing . . . this cat sith," Uncle Jarus said in a hushed tone. "And it's not just killing people at random. It's killing boys—laddies yer age." He looked over his shoulder. Monte whipped his head around too. The trees swayed in the windy blackness.

"The first incident was a couple months ago," Uncle Jarus continued. "A young lad was found dead near the foot of the Ben. He was a Mystic, here on summer holiday with his family. The only clue to the source of his death? Giant claw marks in a single swipe, across his face."

Monte's skin prickled with goosebumps. "Seems a strange way to die—only a flesh wound across his face?"

"Aye," Uncle Jarus agreed. "The IMB thought it te be a freak accident. But not two weeks later, it happened again. This time te a lad about Garrick's age, from right here in Fort William. Same area, same claw marks across his face. Further exploration led te the discovery of large cat tracks near both the death scenes, and a full investigation was launched."

Something crunched from the thickening tree line to Monte's side. He jumped, his skeleton nearly parting ways with his skin.

"Only a dead branch, pal," Uncle Jarus said, the glow of the orb continuing to guide them. "Not long after the second cat attack, the Ben began te show signs of dark, magical infection, and things rapidly spiraled out of control. Two more laddies—brothers—were attacked, this time on the outskirts of this very town."

"Which is when the IMB summoned my parents?"

"Aye." Uncle Jarus nodded. "And it's a good thing, too, because just days before your family's arrival, a Mystic man went missing on Ben Nevis."

"Was he from here, too?"

"Not originally, no." Uncle Jarus pulled at the stubble on his chin. "Brian Shaw was his name, and he was from clan McKnight in the Hebrides."

"The Heh-bri-dees?"

"Aye. A gathering of small islands northwest of here. Populated with all sorts of magic, those isles. Brian Shaw moved down this way for work, I was told." Uncle Jarus's voice swept into the wind.

"Did the cat sith catch him as well?"

"Nobody kens," Uncle Jarus sighed. "But no remains have been found. He's been missing for a while now. Poor bloke."

Monte pulled his coat tighter. His uncle had given him more information in the last two minutes than his parents had in the entire three weeks they had been here.

"No new attacks have occurred since yer parents' arrival, thank goodness," Uncle Jarus continued. "Regardless, this cat sith is a beast, Monte. It isn't some large, over-bred house feline. It is a magical mongrel that harbors much superstition and fear. And for all we know, there could be more than one. The unknown origin poses huge threats to the Mystic and Norm realms alike. Mystics are being hit at every angle at the moment. With each attack, the Norms have grown increasingly more aware that something is out of whack, which puts the IMB under that much more pressure. Hence the underage curfews and restrictions on magic." Uncle Jarus blew warm air into his hands. "We, under no condition, can expose our realm here in Britain, yet all the recent uproar is threatening te do just that. And mind who yer talking te . . . me . . . someone who tries te be as uninvolved in the IMB's doings as possible."

Monte burrowed his chin deeper into his chest as the wind whistled through the trees. He wished he was back in Salem. At least he had friends there, as well the opportunity to use a wand. And he would be far away from random people claiming he was in danger.

They came to a stop in front of the Widow Smith's cottage. Light from a single bulb spilled from her porch onto the front garden.

"I imagine it's been a lot te take in at once," Uncle Jarus said. He pointed his finger at the glowing orb. The light within tapered to a faint glow as it floated obediently beside them. "First, yeh moved from yer childhood home te a foreign country, for goodness sake. Now, all these extra stipulations and IMB regulations put in front of yeh, not te mention the frightening potential of a cat sith roaming about." He squeezed Monte's shoulder. "Believe it or not, I was young and wild once. Yer dad and I were quite the devious pair."

Monte allowed himself to smile, amused by the thought of his father ever being anything but orderly.

"Just remember that this hold on magic is only temporary," Uncle Jarus continued. "And, that I really need yeh te keep a lid on things until all of this clears up. Think of magic as invisible for the time being. Yer parents will get te the bottom of this and then yeh can have a little more fun."

"Okay, but what am I supposed to do until then? Just sit around, bored? Without magic?"

"Shh," Uncle Jarus interrupted. He slid his hand inside his jacket and cautiously extracted his wand, his eyes fixated on something on the road ahead of them. He cocked his wand-arm in a defensive stance above his head, guiding the glowing orb toward him with the other. It fought against the ripping wind, its brightness diminishing under Uncle Jarus's command.

A yell lodged in Monte's throat as a flowerpot tipped over, cracked, and rolled from the Widow Smith's cottage. Uncle Jarus remained still and unflinching. The light from the orb accentuated the hollows of his face as it contacted his palm. Monte strained against the gloom. Dead leaves scraped across his feet. He hardly dared to breathe. The shallow hoosh of his breath ached in his throat.

And then, he saw it. Large and hefty with a set of eerie amber eyes, a black beast lurked in the shadows ahead of them.

"Din'nae hex ma dog!" a woman's voice pierced the darkness. The thick Scottish brogue was unmistakable.

"Grandmother Meriweather!" Monte exclaimed as an enormous black Great Dane galumphed toward them. It pawed at him, an overzealous puppy the size of a pony. "Oi, Brotus! Down boy!" Monte laughed nervously, his hands shaking as the dog tried to smear a slobbery kiss across his face. He had thought the worst for a second there.

"Mum! What the blaze are yeh doing out after dark? Alone at that!" Uncle Jarus struggled to return his wand to his jacket as the orb bobbed from his clutches. "Do yeh pay any heed te the warnings?"

"Nonsense. Em not alone, son. I have the dogs." She whistled and a second Great Dane, a harlequin, coated in white with splotchy black patches, trotted forward.

"Saladin, you big beast." Monte patted the dog's firm head, causing his tail to whip back and forth. Eager for the same affection, Brotus nudged Monte from behind, barking loudly. His bellows cut through the blustery air.

"Monte, pal! How are yeh?" Grandmother Meriweather's navy eyes sparkled despite the oppressive darkness. She pulled him into a tight embrace.

"Hi, Gran," Monte said, taking in her pinewood scent. He pulled away and batted at the large pom-pom that was stitched atop her hat. He had seen his grandmother just yesterday, yet she treated their meeting like the most significant of reunions.

"Mum, really. What are yeh doing out right now? Are yeh a daftie? Took the notion for an evening stroll, I gather?" Uncle Jarus's voice dripped with sarcasm.

"Too right. I fancied a walk and the dogs had energy, so I thought we'd enjoy a wee saunter. We were headed te see yeh lot at Downfield Place, actually."

Brotus barked again.

"Easy, boys," Uncle Jarus warned, glancing at the Widow Smith's front door. The porch light seemed much brighter now. It spilled over them, elongating their shadows, emphasizing Uncle Jarus's already robust frame.

"Ah, come off it, Jarus. Yeh'd think we were past curfew or something." Grandmother Meriweather placed her hands on her hips. She trained her eyes up at her son like a sprite confronting a bridge troll. "It's no' like I bide all the way across toon," she continued, her voice climbing to uncomfortable decibels.

"Bide?" Monte interrupted. "Toon? As in cartoon?" He tried to make sense of the word. "It's not like I bide all the way across cartoon?"

"Reside, pal. Yeh know, like live, sojourn. In town," Grandmother Meriweather stretched the word town long and flat like an American. "Yer too much of a Yankee." She swiveled back to Uncle Jarus. "And I'm no' even a mile out from Downfield Place. I'm allowed te go for a walk when I please."

"Now isn't the time for dilly-dallying, Mother. Besides, it's cold out and I sense a gale brewing." Uncle Jarus held up his hand against the building breeze. "No more evening constitutionals, Mum. I mean it."

"I see yer really taking yer own words te heart." Grandmother Meriweather jabbed her thumb in Monte's direction. "Yeh don't see me pestering yeh about yer business with Master Monte, especially with all that's going on." She said the last with great indignation.

Monte refrained from chuckling. Grandmother Meriweather was so dramatic when she got worked up.

"Besides," she continued, "what's an old woman meant te do with herself, all cooped up inside?"

"Gah!" Uncle Jarus threw his hands up in exasperation.

Saladin barked, his howls echoing through the trees.

"Ack, Saladin!" Uncle Jarus hissed. "Let's move this circus away from here, before—"

"Excuse me," a woman's voice interrupted him. "I'd like te know what all the noise is about."

An oddly shaped person stood in the front walkway of the Widow Smith's cottage. Her stout figure cast a bumbling shadow over the pebble-crusted lawn. She suspended her arms above her head, a raincoat tenting her stubby physique as her fuzzy dressing gown swayed in the wind. A pair of oversized galoshes completed her ensemble, the tops curling over her ankles like flaps of seaweed. Although only a touch of precipitation scuttled through the air, the old woman cowered like a headless gargoyle in a torrential downpour.

Uncle Jarus snatched the hovering orb from the air and stuffed it into his jacket.

"Jivens Crivens," Grandmother Meriweather said, her tone far from enthusiastic. "It's the Widow Smith herself."

"Aw, Doris—Mrs. Doris Smith," Uncle Jarus stuttered. "My sincere apologies for all of the ruckus. We were just heading out."

"Humph," the Widow snorted. "I was tucked in all cozy-like in meh bed, about te drift into a peaceful slumber—perhaps meh last, heaven rest meh weary soul—and what yanks me from the brink of such pleasantries? A loud, silly dog wi' a foghorn for a snout!"

"Ack, calm yerself, Doris," Grandmother Meriweather spat. "Yeh were'nae in yer bed and yeh know it."

"Mum, hush," Uncle Jarus barked. "I do apologize, Mrs. Smith. We'll be leaving now." He put his arm around Grandmother Meriweather, gently prodding her forward. "Let's go, Monte." Uncle Jarus rolled his eyes. "Trust me on this, we don't want te encourage her," he said out of the corner of his mouth.

"Do yeh have any idea what time it is?" the Widow pressed on. Her raincoat lashed around her. "Yeh lot need te get off meh property before I call the polis!"

"Polis?" Monte stopped in his tracks.

"The police, pal." Uncle Jarus scooped his hand after Monte.

"The polis?" Monte frowned at the Widow Smith. "What they gonna do? *Pull* us out of here?"

Uncle Jarus glared down at Monte. "Enough," he rumbled.

"Yeh insolent numpty of a lad!" the Widow shrieked.

Grandmother Meriweather balled her hands into fists as she extricated herself from Uncle Jarus's arm. "Now that's too far, Doris Smith, yeh nutcase!" She stamped her foot into the ground. "And te answer yer question, it can't be a minute over seven o'clock."

The Widow Smith trembled in her galoshes.

"Nanny? What's going on?" A boy clad in exquisite powdery-blue pajamas stepped through the front door. His bright blonde hair, parted to the side and slicked against his head, glinted in the light.

"Finn?" Monte stared at the kid, puzzled.

Finn shuffled his hands over his silky pajamas, his white cheeks suddenly red and patchy.

"Finn Cornelius! Where is yer dressing gown? Yeh get back in that house before yeh catch a pneumonia," the Widow Smith snapped.

"Yes, Nanny." Finn sounded regretful as he retreated into the house. The front door remained slightly ajar.

"Meri, yeh get those dogs out of here or I swear te yeh, I'll call the officials." The Widow continued to launch threats at Grandmother Meriweather.

"Aye, yeh will," Grandmother Meriweather replied, with indignation. "I ken walk meh dogs wherever I please."

"Mother . . ." Uncle Jarus warned.

A pair of vivid jade eyes peered through the crack in the door.

"Finn Cornelius, shut that door and go te yer bed," the Widow Smith ordered without even turning around. The door snapped shut.

Monte started to question the possibility of the Widow possessing a third eye, perhaps at the base of her skull. *Like a true demon-witch*, he mused.

A set of snowy, slender fingers crept through the brass mail flap in the door. They slid to the side, propping the feed open as Finn's bright eyes peered through.

"Oi, meh head. Now yeh've done it," the Widow Smith wailed and slapped her hand against her forehead. Frizzy gray curls poked out from under her frilly nightcap. Monte suddenly felt a little bad. Maybe she really had been in bed.

Grandmother Meriweather huffed under her breath. "We'll be going then." She whistled to the dogs, dwarfed between their massive frames as they stationed themselves at her side.

Monte wondered if she ever rode them. He chuckled at the thought, resolving to ask her when they weren't at risk for having the polis called on them.

"We are truly sorry te have disturbed yeh," Uncle Jarus said with sincerity. He bowed his head and slowly retreated.

The Widow Smith clucked her tongue and backed toward the cottage like a disgruntled hen. The mail flap clicked shut. "Finn Cornelius!" Her trills melted into the storm as Monte traipsed after Uncle Jarus and Grandmother Meriweather.

"Poor old dearie. She dwells in such discontent." Uncle Jarus walked swiftly, forcing Monte and Gran to a trot to keep up with his long stride.

"Aye, bless her unhappy, cantankerous soul," Grandmother Meriweather said, dryly. "Crazy creature . . . and as superstitious as they come."

"Finn seems all right." Monte shivered as a gust of Baltic air broke through the insulated defenses of his jacket. "I didn't know he was her grandson. I met him today while I was . . ." He paused, not wishing to remind Uncle Jarus about his run-in with Babs. "I met him today when I was in Uncle Jarus's office."

"Aye." Uncle Jarus rubbed his hands together. "Finn is a nice wee lad. He came te live with his grandmother Smith about a year ago, although she's not his only legal guardian. They keep te themselves mostly. The Widow shelters him greatly."

"I sensed that," Monte said as the air churned around them. The gale Uncle Jarus predicted was fast approaching.

"Whew, that's a biting wind," Uncle Jarus said. "Let's hurry." He threw a sheltering arm around Grandmother Meriweather. "Still glad yeh went out for one of yer saunters?" he joked.

"Aye!" Grandmother Meriweather shouted as the sky began to squall. "'Tis nothing but a wee storm." She and Uncle Jarus scuttled ahead of Monte toward Downfield Place.

The lamppost leered at Monte as he approached the estate. The wind lashed at his clothing as icy rain bombarded his face. He blinked vigorously, searching the black night for Cameron. He wondered where she had gone to and if she was caught in the storm. He wondered about her warning and what it might mean. He wondered if he really was in some kind of danger.

Lightning buzzed through the sky, the smack of thunder close on its tail. All at once, a bolt of electricity struck the lamppost. Brightness, fleeting but spectacular, overtook the sky before darkness regained its authority. The bulb in the lamppost flickered as it surrendered its power.

"Monte, come along before the storm consumes yeh!" Grandmother Meriweather shouted from the top of the driveway.

"Coming!" Monte pushed through the forceful gusts. A trail of smoke spun from the top of the lamppost as he reached the driveway, the seashell heavy in his pocket. He plodded down the cobblestones as the air lamented around him. Golden lights winked through the windows of Downfield Place, a comforting invitation. For the first time since his arrival, Scotland was starting to feel like home.

# CHAPTER 7
## Conundrums

Monte basked by the fire in the living room of Downfield Place, munching on his third Mars bar of the afternoon as the rain spittered against the grand window. A mass of thick gray clouds congested the sky outside. It was a bleak day, the earth dreary and raw from the gale storm the night before.

Grandmother Meriweather occupied Uncle Jarus's oversized plaid armchair. Her legs dangled over one of the arms, her head nestled in the crook of the other. Brotus and Saladin sprawled on the floor below her, each gnawing on a hunk of bone from the butcher.

Earthy scents wafted from the glossy mantelpiece where a display of burnt orange leaves and bronzy ribbons intertwined through a freshly assembled garland of pine branches and dried citrus. A marble bust of a lion's head peeked from behind the pine needles, its mouth frozen in a majestic roar. It was only slightly larger than Monte's fist yet commanded authority as the king of the hearth. Suddenly, its sapphire eyes came to life.

"A message is coming!" Monte sprung up as a thin strand of paper curled from a narrow slit inside the lion's mouth.

"From yer parents, no doubt." Grandmother Meriweather bolted off the chair.

Garrick burst into the room as Monte plucked the paper from the bust. "What's it say?" He breathed down his brother's neck.

Monte stretched the strip of parchment between his fingers. It wasn't even a foot long. A transmission of Mr. Darrow's messy penmanship was scrawled across the note in tiny lettering. Monte read it out loud:

*New developments on the Ben today. We will be here longer than intended. More updates later. Hope all is well there.*

*Best,*
*E.D.*

"New developments?" Garrick asked. "Again?"

"Maybe this it. Maybe they're on to the cat sith," Monte said.

"Yeah." Garrick sounded unconvinced.

"Best te send them a quick response." Grandmother Meriweather scooted toward the lion bust. She held her wand to her mouth, much like a microphone. Monte was about to call her out for using magic but then remembered that mystical communication, especially when it involved IMB business, was allowed.

"Got yer message, son," Grandmother Meriweather spoke into her wand. "Sending all of our best. Hope yeh catch 'em skivers soon." She pressed the wand against her lips and then placed it in the jaws of the lion. Slowly, the teeth clamped around the wand. The regal sculpture's eyes flared. Somewhere on Ben Nevis the message would reach Mr. and Mrs. Darrow, likely through a similar bust.

Monte rambled into the kitchen. A peculiar smell dressed the air, as though someone's sneakers were baking in a bed of savory spices. The butcher-block countertops stretched before him, spotless and tidy. An old toaster oven roosted in the corner by the stove, companion to a radio every bit as ancient. The transmitter device, probably once Grandmother Meriweather's, droned the Lochabar Nightly News—a local Norm program—as he searched the refrigerator for something to wash the sticky Mars bar residue down his throat.

The radio crackled loudly as a new voice interrupted the weather forecaster.

"Hiya. Dean-o the Reporter here with some breaking news," the Norm man's voice buzzed through the speakers. "Another large cat sighting was reported here in Fort William this afternoon. Several accounts claim the black cat was on the prowl near the Dun Deardail trail, the very location where those teenage boys were found dead not too long ago. The beast is suspected to rival even the most massive of predatory cats, although we still await expert confirmation. No injuries or disruptions have been reported despite the sighting."

Monte chewed his lip. This had to be the new development Mr. Darrow's message had referred to. Hopefully, his parents would get to the cat in time.

"Hungry?" Maren's voice interrupted Monte's thoughts.

Monte jumped, nearly dropping the large glass of milk he had just poured.

"I didn't mean to startle you," Maren said with a chuckle. She wore a damp towel twisted around her head. A few strands of her short hair poked from the terry folds, her nursing uniform crisp from a recent ironing.

"No worries." Monte gulped down the milk before patting up the droplets he had splattered on the floor. "I was distracted by the radio."

"What's going on now?" Maren asked.

Dean-o the Reporter's voice continued to carry through the speakers. "Let's take some calls regarding this newest cat appearance."

Maren flashed Monte a knowing look. "Oh dear." She snapped the lid back on the milk bottle. "Not a good sign."

"Yeah," Monte said, trying not to think about the beast's past victims. Teenage boys. His age.

Maren peered into the oven, revealing a smooth lump of something the color of a dead fish. The savory sneaker odor intensified.

"What is that?" Monte asked as his cousin pulled the dish from the oven. "Looks like a lopsided volleyball."

Maren snorted as she turned to face him. "This, Monte, is haggis. Surely your dad has talked about it before?" She grabbed a knife from the drawer.

"Haggis?" Monte asked. The term wasn't familiar. Neither was the unusual smell. "Is it something you eat?"

"Of course it's something you eat." Maren plunged the knife into the center of the haggis, releasing a cascade of stinky steam and dark, crumbly innards.

"Ugh!" Monte held his nose. "What're you doing?"

"Letting the reek out," Maren said with an amused smile.

"The reek?" Monte coughed as the smell swirled around him.

"That's right," Maren said, far too casually. "It stinks a wee bit at first, but it tastes brilliant. Most particularly when paired with neeps and tatties."

"Neeps and what?" Monte asked, daring to let go of his nose. The stink was still there, but not as strong.

"You know, parsnips? Potatoes?" Maren dug through the haggis with the tip of her knife. "I would've thought you'd be well versed in Scottish cuisine by now," she teased. "I hear you and your dad do most of the cooking back home."

"Well, yeah," Monte agreed, reluctantly. He really wasn't interested in becoming Maren's sous chef, especially if this was the sort of thing she liked to make. "Mom's the best cook but she's always super busy with work. And Garrick doesn't know a spatula from his rear end, so . . ." Monte dared a closer look at the haggis, somehow mesmerized. "What's in it?"

"Sheep's pluck—liver, heart, and lungs—as well as oatmeal and onions, to name a few things."

"Heart and lungs? Of a sheep?"

"Aye."

Dean-o the Reporter's voice crackled loudly over the radio, as if in agreeance.

"Really now." Maren's dusky eyes locked with Monte's. "Haggis is quite lovely."

Monte took a step back, unsure if his cousin was being serious.

Maren chuckled. "Relax. I'll whip together a stew for my Yankee cousins, since you still haven't acquired your authentic taste buds." She pulled a pot from the cupboard and flourished her wand in front of her. The tap sprang to life, followed by a sack of dried lentils on the counter.

Monte ducked as a clump of potatoes joined the main procession. "Okay, really?" he huffed as the ingredients splashed into the pot. "You're allowed to use magic too?" He had been meaning to ask.

"This hardly qualifies as magic, Monte." Maren's smile widened. "But yes, to answer your question. I benefit from the privileges your parents hold with the IMB. And thank goodness. Without their immunities to the current restrictions, life would be pretty bleak." She clunked the pot onto the stove. "I mean, imagine if I had to make this soup the Norm way? Psh! I'd really be in a pinch tonight if that were the case, seeing as you won't eat my haggis," she said with a wink.

Monte suddenly felt like a wee lad. "Sorry," he mumbled.

"It's no bother." Maren's smile went from playful to endearing. "I have my shift at the Mystic Royal Infirmary soon, but I don't mind throwing together dinner for you lot, especially since I don't get to cook often. I'm too much like your mother, I suppose." She ignited the burner with her wand.

"Always busy with work." A cupboard to her side creaked open, displaying several tidy rows of jarred spices.

Monte had perused that cupboard several times. Some items were like what they had back home—elven turmeric, reindeer spice—but others were completely new to him. His nose burned as he noticed a tall, slender receptacle tucked in the corner. Ground dragon pepper. He had accidentally inhaled the fiery powder on his first day in Scotland while assisting Uncle Jarus in making a casserole for the family. A sneezing fit ensued, accompanied by fireballs the size of plums. Fortunately, Maren had known how to halt the sizzling spasms, but it had still taken a good week to fully clear the pepper from his system.

"Well, there you have it, everyone," Dean-o the Reporter sputtered through the radio. "A first-hand witness account of our most recent cat sighting. As always, we encourage everyone to use extreme caution until the professionals get to the bottom of this. In the meantime, please report any further suspicious activity to your local police department and remember to use the key words: cat sighting."

"Maren?" Monte asked, clicking off the radio.

"Hm?" Maren drew a figure-eight in the air with her wand. A puff of steam swirled from the pot.

"Do you think all this suspicious magical activity—the cat sith stuff and all that—is a sign of dark magic?" If there was anyone Monte could get answers from, it was Maren. Not only was she extremely smart, she was a trusted comrade.

Maren released the towel from her head and leaned in toward Monte, as though she had a secret to tell. "Here's the thing . . ." she said, slinging the towel over her shoulder. "It's believed that a long time ago—I mean, a really long time ago—enormous wildcats used to terrorize Britain. They were highly feared creatures, not only for the potential havoc they'd wreak as natural predators, but for their unexplained origins." Maren straightened and ruffled her damp hair with her fingers.

"What do you mean?"

"Magic." Maren grabbed a wooden mixing spoon from the counter. She swished the utensil through the air, as though conjuring a spell. "Even the

Norms developed theories around the unnatural appearances of these mysterious beasts."

Monte pulled at a ringlet on his head, winding it around his finger. "So, you're saying that large cats are naturally magical creatures, even in the Norm community? And that they just pop up? Out of nowhere?" He thought of the tigers he had seen at the zoo the summer before. There had been nothing magical about them.

"No to your first question, and yes to the second," Maren said. "Rather, the beastly cats of ancient Britain were believed to be the sign of evildoers. Especially the black ones."

"Okay . . ." Monte scratched his head, struggling to see her point.

Maren chuckled. "Most of it's just myth. It's what we do: fabricate tales to explain the unexplained. And stories evolve." She swirled the wooden spoon inside the pot. A comforting aroma filled the kitchen. "Where do you think all the delusion around black house cats comes from?"

"But what about those kids that were killed? The ones with the claw marks across their faces?" Monte asked. "That's gotta be more than just myth. I mean . . . they died." He struggled to say the last.

"Unfortunately, you're right," Maren said, her face suddenly solemn. "I saw the young lads who were attacked. You know, the ones the cat sith killed. Not the first two, but the pair of brothers who were found dead."

Monte gulped.

"Their corpses were brought to the Mystic Royal Infirmary for analysis. We got to take a look after the Norm investigators had seen their share," Maren explained, a hint of disgust in her voice. "It always turns into a real mess, whenever Mystic and Norm paths cross. It doesn't happen often, but when it does, we always end up with a big conundrum of a situation."

"Did someone say conundrum?" Uncle Jarus strolled into the kitchen. He tapped Monte on the head with a rolled-up newspaper, his eyes fixed on the stove. "Haggis! My favorite." He tossed the newspaper on the counter, completely ignoring the pot of soup. "Yeh two want te see a real conundrum? Yeh should check out this ingrown toenail I'm developing." He waggled his foot in front of him which was fortunately still sheathed by his sock. "Maren, might I trouble yeh te take a wee look?"

"Dad. Gross," Maren complained.

"What? Yeh care for strangers all the time but yeh won't help out yer old man?"

"Fine," Maren said, shaking her head. "My medical kit's in the living room."

Monte smoothed over the curled edges of Uncle Jarus's newspaper as the pair left the kitchen. He scanned through the haphazardly placed articles—the trademark layout for the British Mystic Gazette, the largest Mystic paper in Britain. A snapshot of a man's face almost covered the entire second page. He looked about Mr. Darrow's age, his light, feathery hair swooping over a sturdy forehead. Even with the brown undertones of the ink, a hint of whimsy was apparent in the minute lines of the man's clean-shaven face. A notice, printed in heavy typeface, completed the portrait: "HAVE YOU SEEN THIS MYSTIC?" Monte scrolled down to where a cluster of sentences fanned the bottom of the page.

*Missing Mystic, Brian Shaw, was last seen near Cow's Hill in Fort William. He is believed to have been carrying field gear at the time of his vanishing. If you have any tips on this Mystic's whereabouts please report them directly to the International Mystic Bureau, section 4-A, Missing Persons and Other Unexplainable Cases.*

Monte sighed. Brian Shaw, the missing Mystic from Clan McKnight. The one Uncle Jarus had mentioned the night before. This probably wasn't the first time he'd shown up in the paper. Monte wondered what had become of him, and if the cat sith had anything to do with his mysterious disappearance. He turned the page, his eyes drawn to a star scribbled in Uncle Jarus's characteristic navy ink. It glinted beside an article in the center of the page.

*MOIRA BRYCE EXERTS EXPERTISE ON LARGE CAT CASES*
*The International Mystic Bureau is pleased to announce the addition of Ms. Moira Bryce, recent member of the British Uncharted Magical Coalition, to the official Ben Nevis Investigative Team. Ms. Bryce has been appointed as one of the chief trackers and researchers on the project. Her specialties include predatory beasts—both Mystic and Norm—potions, and the investigation behind the use of illegal metamorphosis and transfiguration.*

"Are you reading?" Garrick moseyed into the kitchen. "You must be bored."

"Funny, Garrick." Monte rolled his eyes at his brother. "You're a total comedian."

"Whatcha got there?" Garrick snatched the newspaper from Monte. "Ah. It looks like that Moira lady will be working closely with Mom and Dad now."

"Yeah . . . Moira. Why do I feel like I've heard that name before?"

"Because you have," Garrick answered. "She's the blonde lady from the portal in Salem."

"Oh!" Monte said, quickly remembering. "The one who likes your muscles?" He leered.

"My muscles? Hold up, she does not!" Garrick demanded.

"Great blazes, you totally have a crush on her."

"No, I don't! She's like Dad's age." Pink splotches patched Garrick's face.

"You do too. Your face is turning red and everything."

"Whatever, Monte," Garrick huffed, showing sudden interest in an ad for Mr. Tolbert's Impenetrable Gardening Galoshes.

"She'll be working closely with Mom and Dad." Monte flicked the paper. "You may just get to see her again."

Garrick's eyes narrowed. He pivoted; his arms positioned to tackle.

"Psst." Grandmother Meriweather's fluffy head peeped through the door. "Come here, yeh two. I have something te show yeh."

Monte grinned as he followed Grandmother Meriweather out of the kitchen, past the grand entrance, and into Uncle Jarus's dimly lit den. Garrick stalked after him. *What is Gran up to now?* Monte mused. Last week, she had given him a miniscule Nutcracker painted with intricate and flawless detail. When he had asked where it came from, she said the Fae had given it to her.

"These are for yeh two." Grandmother Meriweather plucked something from Uncle Jarus's expansive desk. A leathery goggle contraption. "They were yer grandfather's from very long ago."

"Uh, thanks," Garrick said with furrowed brows.

"What are they?" Monte asked. "How do they work?" He stroked the soft leather band that secured the two black lenses in place.

"They're called madgers." Grandmother Meriweather beamed.

"Madgers?" Monte asked.

"Aye, madgers. See here." She attempted to wrap the strange eyepiece around Garrick's head. He bent down compliantly, his height cumbersome to her efforts.

Monte laughed as his brother pulled away from Grandmother Meriweather's fidgety hands. Garrick looked like a giant crazed insect, the goggles horribly askew on his perfectly chiseled face.

"Good look for you, Garrick," Monte crowed. "These oughta be popular with the ladies."

"Shut up, you." Garrick slapped at Monte.

Grandmother Meriweather switched off the lamp by the desk, dousing the room in darkness. A splotch of dreary daylight etched through a narrow gap in the drapes. "Turn the dial at the side there," she instructed, pointing to a knob at Garrick's temple.

Garrick obeyed. "Everything's a murky green color. Oooh."

"Night vision." Grandmother Meriweather clapped her hands together.

"Give me a shot, then," Monte demanded.

"Hold it, you eejit. I'm not finished yet," Garrick said, turning slowly on the spot.

"Eejit?" Monte teased Garrick. "Listen to you. You're getting more Scottish by the day."

"Who, me?" Garrick adjusted the madgers.

"Aye," Monte said. He clamped his hands over his mouth, suddenly realizing that he, too, had grown subject to the Scottish vocabulary.

"Oh, aye," Garrick snickered. He cupped his hands around the madger lenses. "These are pretty cool, Gran, but we're not really supposed to be out after dark."

Monte peeled the madgers from Garrick's face and strapped them over his own head. The shadows in the room lessened as his vision sharpened. "Brilliant."

"Ack, well. They're harmless, really." Grandmother Meriweather swatted her hand in the air. "I just thought yeh lads might like te have them."

Monte walked toward the bookshelves at the other end of the room. "These were Granddad's? What'd he use them for?" He twisted one of the dials at his temple back and forth. His eyesight faded in and out.

"Give me those." Garrick tripped through the dark after Monte. "You big buffoon. You're gonna break them, tinkering with them like that. I'll oversee these." He yanked the device from Monte's head.

"Ow, Garrick!"

"These are best kept with me." Garrick's voice was stern as he left the room, madgers in hand.

"Killjoy," Monte muttered. *I wonder what's gotten into him.*

"Ah, Garrick is a good lad," Grandmother Meriweather said with a smile. "But never mind the madgers just now, Monte." She flicked the lamp back on. "I have another wee treasure for yeh." Her smile broadened as she slid a slender box across the desk.

"Is that what I think it is?" Monte asked. He seized the box. The tiny hinges groaned as he opened it. "It is . . . It's a wand."

"Aye, so it is." Grandmother Meriweather winked. "It also belonged te yer Granddad. It was his first." Her voice was reflective. "And his only," she added quietly.

"Wow," Monte whispered. He pinched the wand from its velvet pillow. Slender, with a cherry stain, the wand gleamed as though it had recently undergone the finest of polishes. He hugged his fingers around the handle. It was a comfortable fit, a perfect weight. Not too tufty but with a satisfying amount of substance.

"Ah, yer granddad would've loved te see yeh with this."

"It's great," Monte said in awe, trying not to bubble over with boyish excitement. He had waited for this day—the day he received his first wand—for a long time. But just then, a disappointing realization hit him. "It's not my half-birthday yet. I can't . . . I'm not supposed to have this until I turn fifteen and a half."

"Aye, but yeh can, son," Grandmother Meriweather trilled.

"What d'you mean?"

"Here in Scotland, yeh can have a wand in yer possession before the halfway mark of yer fifteenth year, so long as it is three months past yer fifteenth birthday."

Monte tilted his head, unable to make sense of Grandmother Meriweather's unintentional math problem.

"Monte, what's today?" Grandmother Meriweather urged.

"It's Saturday."

"No, I mean what's the date?"

"Oh." Monte felt his entire face blush. *Monte, you dork.* "Let's see . . . The thirtieth of September."

"And when did yeh turn fifteen?"

"On June thirtieth. Wait a second . . . July, August, September," Monte counted the months out loud. "It's been exactly three months since I turned fifteen, so I can have a wand." He tried to hide his enthusiasm, almost dropping the prized possession in the process. "I can handle a wand!"

"Monte . . ."

"Sorry. Slipped."

"No, it's not that. The rules are very clear on one thing . . . yeh can have the wand in yer possession, but yeh can'nae actually use it until yer half-birthday."

Monte's elation quickly drained. "Seriously?" he grumbled. What was the point in having a wand if he couldn't use it?

"Aye," Grandmother Meriweather said, sounding almost as glum as Monte felt. "The IMB has grown very strict on the matter, as of late." She cast him a look of understanding. "But I thought yeh'd like te hold on te it in the meantime."

"Yeah. I suppose," Monte said. "At least, if you say so." He didn't dare disobey Grandmother Meriweather, though it was tempting. He already had a handful of spells that he was eager to experiment with. He ran his fingers along the bedding of the wand box. A silvery paper imprinted with rearing unicorn heads lined the inside of the lid. Each shared the same ferocious expression, their manes wild, their mouths open in a mighty bray.

"Aren't unicorns supposed to be tame?"

"What's that, pal?" Grandmother Meriweather turned from where she was peering out the window. The world outside looked weepy and gray.

"These unicorns look kinda vicious." Monte pointed to the designs inside the box. "I thought they were supposed to be gentle."

Monte knew that Scotland was home to a diverse array of ancient Mystic beasts, the unicorn being one. He had never encountered such a creature in Salem, where they were only briefly studied in school. In the United States, the majestic equines were seen only as fairytale creatures, by both Mystics and Norms alike.

Grandmother Meriweather chuckled. "No, unicorns are definitely not tame. They are amongst the purest and most primitive of magical creatures. A magnificent beast that should'nae be crossed, at least not by the untrained Mystic."

"Do they just roam around? Do you have any here, in Fort William?"

"Not nearby, no. Not many exist in the wild anymore. But there are unicorn proprietors—breeders and caretakers, if yeh will. Clan McKnight of the Hebrides keeps unicorns. It's a trade that requires much wisdom and respect. Tending unicorns is a touchy business and only the most skilled of Mystics can accomplish it."

Monte was intrigued. "Clan McKnight. Isn't that where Brian Shaw is from? The Mystic that disappeared?"

"Aye," Grandmother Meriweather sighed. "Good fellow, that Brian. I wish the IMB would hurry up and find him."

"You know Mr. Shaw? Personally?"

Grandmother Meriweather nodded. "I visit Clan McKnight at least once a year. Brian was always very welcoming. He has a real knack with the wilder unicorns."

"Awesome. You'll have to bring me along the next time you go."

"You visiting Clan McKnight, all the way out there in the rugged isles, is past my control, Master Monte." Grandmother Meriweather clapped him on the back. "A good proposition for yer father though, the next time the IMB gives him a spare minute," she said with a trickle of irritation. "Anyhow, mind yeh don't use that wand until yer proper age hits."

"Or until all of the restrictions are lifted," Monte said, wrinkling his nose. He was fed up with all the IMB rules.

Grandmother Meriweather gently shook his shoulder. "I ken, it's absurd." She took the wand from Monte and clutched it in her worn but sturdy hands. "But rules are rules, especially right now. Performing even the simplest of spells will activate it, and the Bureau will know." She held the wand like a scepter, her eyes searching. "Yer grandfather always kept this in such good repair. Never a scratch or a nick. I trust yeh'll treat it the same." She rested the wand inside the box and carefully folded the lid down. "And remember, when it comes te magic, yeh must use subtlety and discretion, even when yer free of restrictions. In fact, largely when." She tucked the box in Monte's hands. "Look at yeh. Growin' up so fast."

Monte fidgeted under Grandmother Meriweather's sentimental gaze. "Thank you very much for the wand. I'll make sure to take good care of it."

"No bother, son. Yer granddad would've loved te see yeh have it." Her eyes sparkled. "Now, I'd better go check on those dogs of mine."

Monte listened as Grandmother Meriweather's footsteps faded down the great hallway. He waited until he knew he was alone and then pumped his fist in the air, his shadow dancing victoriously around the columns of books lining the walls. Even though he couldn't use it yet, he finally had his own wand.

CHAPTER 8

The Shell Speaks

The long, wet grass pulled at Monte's trousers as he raced through the field. It was a tedious fall afternoon. The sky, clogged with dark clouds, leaked a steady mist upon the sodden countryside, making for an extra mopey Halloween.

"Monte!" Garrick yelled from the road. "Come back, you lunatic!"

But Monte plowed toward the spot where he had seen them, the rainbow lights.

"We're on an errand for Maren. This isn't an excuse to go exploring!" Garrick's voice grew distant as Monte plodded through the wet landscape.

Water leaked into Monte's sneakers. But he didn't care. He needed to get to those lights. He was sure it was Cameron, wandering around with that glowing necklace again. The drizzle coated his skin as he skidded to a stop. The shell, which he always kept close, felt heavy in his dampened pocket. He adjusted the wand holster inside his jacket. It was a bit of a nuisance, but his granddad's wand was fun to tote around, even if he wasn't allowed to use it.

"Seriously, man," Garrick trotted over, panting at Monte's side. "What're you doing?"

"I saw something." Monte wiped the dew from his eyes and pointed to the small bunch of trees where he had last seen the lights.

"Congratulations. You're a regular scientist now." Garrick grabbed Monte's elbow.

"No, wait!" Monte tried to yank his arm away. "I think this might have to do with what happened at Witch's Pointe."

Garrick halted, his grip tightening. "I thought we weren't going to talk about that again." His eyes sparked warning.

"Let go of me." Monte twisted his arm. Garrick squeezed tighter. "Ouch. Why are you treating me like your kid brother all of a sudden?"

"Um, because you *are* my kid brother," Garrick said, releasing Monte with a tiny shove.

Monte stared at the patch of trees and then turned to face Garrick. "Look, do you remember that girl on the beach in Salem? The one that ran away when you found me at Witch's Pointe?"

Garrick's eyes narrowed. "What about her?"

"Well, I think she's here."

"Here? In Scotland?" Garrick asked, puzzled.

"No, in Zimbabwe, you moron," Monte huffed. "Of course I meant here." He scanned the trees again.

"You're nuts, Monte," Garrick said. "C'mon. We're not supposed to be out here."

Monte glared at his brother and then sprinted for the trees. The rainbow lights appeared again, twinkling through the foliage as he closed in on the thicket.

"Cameron!" Monte yelled as the rainbow lights vanished.

"Have you gone berserk?" Garrick exclaimed, clumping after his brother.

"She's here." Monte scanned the mossy trunks.

"Who? Who's here?" Garrick asked. "Look, if anything it's probably just an early trick-or-treater."

Monte trampled through the cushy forest bed, spilling out into an abandoned soccer field. A thatch of clover spread around a timeworn goalpost at one end of the overgrown pitch. Rust scarred the frame's once-white paint. Across the field a thick row of firs served as a barrier between the field and a narrow, crumbling lane. "But . . ." Monte squinted across the gloomy field. "I saw the lights."

"I hate to break it to you, little bro . . ." Garrick paused, smirking. His large figure bulged beneath his slippery raincoat. "But I think you're in love with a phantom."

Monte grunted. "If I've gone bonkers, then you can't be much farther behind." He stabbed a finger at Garrick. "All you ever do anymore is stay locked in your room."

Garrick snorted. "I do not."

Monte stamped his feet into the mushy grass. His ears twitched against the squelch of his sneakers, alert for any irregular noises.

"Besides," Garrick continued. "What else am I supposed to do? There's not a lot of potential to make hard and fast friends here, seeing as we're the only Mystics around."

"You could play with those madger thingies," Monte suggested, as though he were the big brother, not Garrick. He squinted at the line of firs across the field.

"And when would I ever need night-vision goggles?" Garrick asked. "That's all they are. They're rudimentary."

"Rudimentary?" Monte could never keep up with Garrick's fancy words.

"Primal . . . basic . . . old," Garrick rattled off.

His rant was interrupted by a loud *whoop*. The shout crossed through the field—a teenage battle call—as a pale, springy kid scurried out from the firs.

"Finn?" Monte asked. "It's Finn Cornelius!"

Finn sprung through the jungle of grass like a nymph, fear plastered across his face, pursued by a posse of very large high school-aged boys.

"Hey!" Garrick tore toward the group. "Get away from him!"

Monte raced after his brother. A dark blur flashed in his peripheries, knocking him to the ground. Dull lights, like distant stars, mottled his vision as he tumbled to a stop in the muddy grass. A girl with scraggly black hair and bronzy skin stood above him. "Cameron?" He scrambled to his feet.

Cameron's stare met his, her caramel eyes familiar and intense. The rainbow lights hung around her neck, much dimmer than Monte remembered.

"I knew it! What're you doing here?"

Cameron waggled her head, her chin tight as she pointed to where the pack of boys converged on Finn.

"Get him!" a kid with no neck and long sideburns barked as Finn's tiny body disappeared underneath a heap of goons.

"You'll kill him!" Garrick shouted as he reached the pack. "Get off!" He yanked one of the smaller goons from the pile.

"Wait here," Monte shouted to Cameron as he sprinted toward the group, his brother already shoulder-deep in the dogpile.

A goon with a thick mohawk swung his fist at Garrick, clipping him in the face. Garrick retaliated with a haymaker, sending his assailant splattering into the mud.

"Garrick!" Monte skidded to a stop, several strides from the brawl. He quickly surveyed their odds. His brother was big, but so were the goons. Even with Monte's help, Garrick wouldn't be able to take them all. They were outnumbered.

The no-neck goon lunged for Garrick but was met with a swift uppercut, his teeth clashing together as he careened backward. A third goon with shaggy hair sprung from behind. He wrapped his fingers around Garrick's neck, his grip slippery from the rain.

"Oi, get 'im!" the shaggy kid shouted for reinforcements.

Garrick thrashed as No-Neck and two more goons lunged for his massive arms.

Monte charged toward the fight. He kicked Shaggy from behind, striking him in the back of his knee. A dastardly move, but the situation was dire. The goon squawked in pain, his leg crumpling from under him. Garrick wheezed as Shaggy's hands fell from his neck.

"Yeh three mind the big one," Shaggy growled at the goons holding Garrick's arms. "I'll take care o' the beanpole." He snarled at Monte, his new limp hardly slowing him.

"Stay away!" Monte raised his fists in front of him. The goon snorted like an enraged bull, his teeth crooked and yellow, his fingers also curled into fists. Only his were much bigger. Enormous, like bricks.

*There's no way we're surviving this*, Monte thought. Shaggy was already upon him, his steamy breath hissing across Monte's face.

"Wee maggot." The goon cranked his arm back, grabbing Monte by the collar.

Monte bicycled his fists at Shaggy's chest, each punch hitting with a leathery thud.

The goon snickered, hardly flinching as he sent Monte hurtling backward with his head.

"That all yeh got?" Shaggy's voice was distant and warped.

Monte shook his head, stunned and hardly aware of his throbbing cheek as he lay in the soaking grass. A dull prodding between his shoulders snapped him back to reality. The holster. Granddad's wand! Monte leapt to his feet, disengaging the wand from the holster inside his jacket. Shaggy was half-marching, half-limping toward him. Finn howled from the grassy clutches of his captors, Garrick several yards away in what looked to be the scuffle of his life.

Monte thrust his grandfather's wand in front of him. "Stop right there!" Sparks shot from the tip, whizzing over Shaggy's head and into the firs.

Monte flinched. *I just used my wand.* But what choice did he have? He wasn't about to let the goons make mincemeat out of Garrick and Finn. And it would be nice not to get the snot kicked out of him, either. Time felt heavy. He watched as Cameron skirted the perimeter of the field. The rainbow lights bounced against her chest like a chain of multicolored fireflies. *We need a diversion.* Monte punched his wand arm into the sky, barely thinking twice.

"Monte, no!" Garrick tried to clobber free from the goons.

Monte's heart walloped against his chest, Shaggy almost upon him. Before he knew it, a spell flared from his wand in a crescendo of pops and snaps. All heads whipped in his direction. Monte's hand quaked as the sparks petered out from the wand.

"What do yeh think yer playing at, yeh pyro?" the mohawk goon snarled from where he now restrained Finn.

Monte shoved the wand back into its holster and hastily re-zipped his jacket.

"He was holdin' somethin'. I saw'r it!" No-Neck exclaimed.

"Aye, he pointed it right at me! An explosive by the looks o' it," Shaggy verified, his voice as rough as his hair.

"I've got this one sorted," No-Neck said as he muscled his arms around Garrick's neck. "Everyone else, after the pyro!"

"Run, Monte!" Garrick choked, crashing to his knees.

Anger welled inside Monte's chest. He refused to budge. His eyes locked with Cameron at the edge of the field. She scrunched her forehead, her stare lively yet distant.

Suddenly, a penetrating sting, like a lump of hot coal, bored into Monte's thigh. He gasped in pain and dug into his pocket, the seashell sizzling against his skin. He closed his fingers around the fiery shell, the heat hardly bearable, yet completely fortifying. A Christmas-y smell, like spiced orange rinds, fizzled up his nose. Slowly, he backed away from the group, the long grass tangling around his ankles. "Look, everyone. This isn't a big deal," he petitioned. "If you'd just let us all go, there won't be any more trouble." He raised his free hand in surrender.

"Shut it, Goldilocks!" Mohawk said with a growl. Shaggy, still closest to Monte, cracked his neck from side to side.

"Toads!" Monte shouted back as the goons advanced on him. Any second and they would charge, like the predators they were.

Cameron remained glued to her spot, motionless. The rainbow lights refracted off her face, brighter than what they had been a few minutes before.

"Leave him alone, yeh numpty!" Finn spat. Bits of grass flew from his mouth. He squirmed against Mohawk's hold, wiggling one arm free.

"Cut it out, yeh wee bird dropping." Mohawk leaned into Finn's slender frame.

Garrick cried out as No-Neck kneed him in the back.

"Tha's right. Cry, yeh toe-rag," No-Neck taunted.

Garrick returned with a backwards elbow to his stomach.

"Oi!" No-Neck wailed, somehow maintaining his hold on Garrick's neck.

"Stop! I'm warning you," Monte shouted. Adrenaline cascaded through his body. He felt the shell pulsate in his hand. His arm shot forward of its own accord, his muscles solid and tight. He raised his other arm in front of him and continued his gradual retreat, the goons inching after him.

"Put yer hands down, yeh freak," Shaggy said.

Monte scrunched his fingers around the burning shell. It pulsated again. This time, a shockwave surged up his arm. The power buzzed through his limbs to the tips of his fingers and toes. His breath caught in his throat. A warm, electrifying energy pooled in his chest—the same sprawling force he had felt at the park in Salem. He bent both arms across his sternum, captained by the magic within, as the seashell whirred against his palm. Then, with a mighty yell, he punched his fists forward.

*Boom!* A noise rivaling a giant's cry rent the air. The earth trembled and the entire group tumbled to the ground like dominoes. The seashell hissed from between Monte's balled fingers. Another explosion cracked through the air. Monte's ribcage shook as an unearthly silence fell upon the field. He sank to his knees as the power drained from his chest.

The goons rocked back and forth in the sodden grass, shaking their heads from side to side. No-Neck dug his meaty fingers into his ears. He swatted the air around his head and then stuttered to his feet, his face frozen in a pallid stupor. "Everyone get lost," he finally cried.

"Aye." Mohawk stumbled after No-Neck. "I'm outta here."

Shaggy was the last to get up. He looked around frantically as his mates stampeded into the thicket.

"How dare you pick on someone so much smaller than you!" Garrick lunged at the goon. "You're really tough, you know that?" He grasped the front of Shaggy's jacket, yanking him from the ground. "You want me to squash you like a bug, do ya? You toilet sucker!"

"Garrick," Monte warned. He had never seen his brother behave so aggressively.

A strange sound leaked from Shaggy's mouth. It sounded like a whimper.

Garrick retracted his fingers. "It doesn't matter," he said, his voice deep and dangerous as Shaggy crumpled to the mud. "Just go. Get out of here."

Shaggy scampered away—half running, half crawling—almost tripping over Cameron who had fallen into a wilted heap on the ground. The rainbow lights wreathed her face, flickering a dazzling display of colors.

"Cameron?" Monte staggered toward her as Garrick saw to the mud-plastered Finn. "Cameron? You all right?"

"Monte," Cameron said in a hollow voice. "What happened?"

The seashell smoldered in Monte's hand. The scent of dirt and sugary cream floated around Cameron, a strangely pleasing perfume.

"My head feels weird." Cameron rubbed her temples.

"Probably the explosion," Monte muttered, the aromas fading into the wet air. He rubbed at his throbbing cheek.

Garrick helped Finn to his feet. "Why were they after you?"

"Nanny doesn't let me have sweets, save for those hideous, foosty licorice bites she keeps in her desk drawer," Finn said. "I didn't think those goons would miss just one chocolate bar. They had a whole heap of them."

"You stole a candy bar from them?" Monte pushed a droopy ringlet from his face. "They were gonna pummel you over a bit of chocolate?"

"It looked right tasty, okay?" Finn pulled the offending sweetie from his pocket. He peeled back the wrapper and bit into the chocolate-covered biscuit. "Oh, aye. It's dynamite."

"Those guys gang up on you often?" Garrick asked.

Finn shrugged and continued to gnaw away on the candy bar.

"I should get going," Cameron said quietly. She swayed unsteadily as she rose to her feet.

"No, wait." Monte grabbed her shoulder. "You said something before." He bowed closer. "You said I was in danger? Why?" The shell prickled against his palm.

Just then, a police siren wailed through the air. Cameron's mouth twitched. "Oh no." Her knees buckled. "I can't be here."

"The polis," Finn almost squeaked.

"Time to go," Garrick said as blue and yellow lights rippled through the fir trees. A second siren squealed in the distance.

Monte sunk to the ground beside Cameron. Her eyes were glassy and distant again. He couldn't leave her.

"Monte," Garrick implored. "Let's go."

"What about Cameron?" Monte said. "I don't think she can walk." He waved his hand in front of her expressionless face. "Cameron?" The pain from the seashell broiled up his arm.

Garrick's eyebrows convulsed in dismay. "Monte, those are Norm police," he hissed. "And you're carrying a wand."

"You have a wand?" Finn popped to Monte's side. "Like a real magic wand?"

A swell of heat crested over Monte.

"Son of a motherless goat, look at your hand!" Garrick grabbed Monte's wrist.

"Ugh," Monte complained, Garrick's touch firm and painful.

"Oi. That's impressive," Finn said.

The shell sat in Monte's palm, embedded around his discolored skin like a festering boil. He pushed on the spot with his thumb. A burning sensation trailed up his arm. The seashell didn't budge.

"Can you get it off?" Garrick whispered as a pair of police officers emerged from the firs.

Monte gently pried at the shell again. He trapped a yell behind his lips and shook his head at Garrick.

"Here." Garrick wrenched a pair of mittens from his jacket. "Hide your hand with one of these. Leave the talking to me," he ordered, using his broad frame to shield Monte. He took a deep breath and slowly turned to face the approaching Norm officers—a giant of a woman and a stumpy, bandy-legged man.

"Everyone hold yer hands in front of yeh," the female officer said in a heavy Highland brogue. A tassel of bushy red bangs exploded from beneath her police cap.

Monte bit his tongue as he shimmied the mitten over his scorching hand. Beads of perspiration slid down his back. Cameron snapped back to attention and slipped her necklace inside her jacket. She rose to her feet and obediently held her hands out in front of her.

"Hands in front of yeh, please," the male officer repeated in a wheezy voice. "Heard a loud noise over this way. Ken anything about that?"

Finn shook his head solemnly. Monte attempted to conceal the surges of pain now spreading over him.

"We heard it too, officer," Cameron said, her voice surprisingly steady. "We were all out for a walk. There was a loud bang, but we didn't see anything."

"That's right," Garrick continued the lie. "And then my brother, here . . ." He gestured to Monte. ". . . started to feel ill so we—"

"Save yer words," the female officer interrupted. She squinted at the group, stopping at Finn who wore a smear of chocolate on his bottom lip like it was the new fashion. Her male counterpart rattled a set of handcuffs on his belt. "Yeh four are going te need te come with us."

Monte, Garrick, and Finn sat wedged in the backseat of the parked police car. Cameron was perched in the passenger seat, yielding no words. She nestled her chin in her knees, her legs hugged to her chest. Monte peeled Garrick's mitten from his throbbing hand. The Norm officers hadn't noticed much, thankfully. Only Garrick had been subjected to a pat-down, another fortunate thing because he wasn't bearing his wand. He hardly ever carried it anymore, thanks to the IMB restrictions. Between Monte's own wand, the seashell stuck to his hand, and Cameron's psychedelic necklace, they would've had more than a little explaining to do if the Norm officers had looked close enough. And who knew what sort of surprises Finn was toting around.

"What is that thing?" Finn peered at Monte's hand.

The shell sparkled against Monte's skin, its bronzy veins pulsating like they had the day on the beach. "Nothing." Sweat pellets sponged his forehead. He cradled his hand against his chest as numbness began to take over.

"Oh, aye. And the third ear on top of my head is nothing, too." Finn rolled his eyes.

"You're quite feisty for a little peanut, aren't you?" Monte said.

"Hold the phone, I bet I'm barely younger than you." Finn leaned over Garrick, practically sliding onto his lap.

"Shut up, you two." Garrick pushed Finn back. He dabbed at his injured eye, which was growing puffier by the minute.

Silence fell over the interior of the car, the muffled voices of the Norm officers outside mixing with the hum of the engine.

"I'll be fourteen at the turn of the year," Finn said in quiet defiance.

"Nice," Garrick mumbled through a swollen lip.

Monte stared at Cameron through the reflection of the rearview mirror. She looked as perplexed as he felt. Why was she here? And what did her creepy message about danger mean? He was starting to think that she knew things, especially when it came to the seashell. His neck hairs stood on end at the thought. "What's taking those knuckleheads so long?" he blurted. He snooped at the officers through the waterdrop stained window.

"Gee, Monte, I don't know, seeing as I've never been detained in a cop car before," Garrick said.

"Why did they bring us straight to the car? I didn't have to explain hardly anything," Monte continued.

"Too right," Finn agreed.

"Probably trying to attract as little attention as possible. You know, with everything going on." Garrick gave Monte a meaningful look.

Cameron shifted in her seat.

Finn looked at Monte, then Garrick, scrutiny in his eyes. "They don't want anything else turning up on the news, even something as little as this," Finn said. "They're probably worried it would only fire suspicion."

"Yes . . ." Garrick replied in a wary tone.

"It's okay. I know what type you two are," Finn whispered. "I'm the same."

Cameron's back straightened.

"Ahem." It was Garrick's turn to shift uncomfortably in his seat.

"Type? The same?" Monte asked. Garrick nipped his arm. "Ouch," he complained.

Cameron whipped around in her seat, her face glowing, and not from her necklace. "You're all magical, aren't you?"

Monte blinked stupidly, caught off-guard.

"Mystics?" She craned her neck forward, lines arching her forehead.

Monte was stunned. "Yeah, um . . ."

"I don't know what you're talking about." Garrick crossed his arms over his chest, his shoulders nearly squashing Monte and Finn on either side of him.

"Ack, come off it." Finn pushed at Garrick's arm. "You guys reek of magic. Especially Monte."

"Me?" Monte asked.

Garrick huffed. "There's no such thing as magic. But if there was, it wouldn't have a smell."

"No such thing as magic?" Finn chortled. "Then how come her necklace is shining like that?" He pointed at Cameron's rainbow necklace. "That's no Norm piece of jewelry," he said, only further verifying his identity as a Mystic.

Cameron turned away and slanted against the back of her seat. "I'm not a Mystic." Her voice was soft. "But I've known a few."

"My whole family are Mystics," Finn rattled. "Even Nanny. Although she has nothing to do with magic anymore."

"You all need to shut it." Garrick's ears flushed scarlet.

"You've known a few?" Monte craned his neck at Cameron. "A few Mystics? What are you doing here, anyway? And what's with the necklace?"

Cameron remained still.

"Be quiet, Monte," Garrick warned.

"And you . . ." Monte spun on Finn. "Does our Uncle Jarus know you're a Mystic?"

"'Course he does." Finn scratched at the dried mud on his jacket. "It's the only reason Nanny lets me attend Strathmartine, on account of Headmaster Darrow being a Mystic. She likes that he keeps his identity so concealed."

Monte slumped back, dumbfounded. What else was being kept from him?

"They're coming," Garrick said, peeking out the window. "Everyone, zip it."

Monte peered through the glass. The female officer nodded to her stubby companion, who was already waddling toward his own vehicle. She brushed the rain from her jacket and clicked the driver door open. "Looks like I'm taking yeh all te Downfield Place," she said as she slid behind the wheel. The car bobbed with her weight. "Yeh belong te Jarus Darrow, aye?" Her seatbelt clicked over her broad chest.

"Yes, ma'am." Garrick sounded like he had a frog in his throat.

"Call me McTavish," the officer said as she steered the car down the lane. "None of yer silly Yankee formalities."

"Nanny's gonna skelp me," Finn whispered.

Silently, Monte agreed. There were some things not even magic could handle.

# CHAPTER 9
## The IMB Calls

Monte pressed his forehead against the cool, foggy window as the cop car rumbled down the Downfield Place driveway. His stomach churned, the shell's heat rushing through his arm. He watched with pity as Cameron wiped at her cheeks. *She didn't do anything out of line,* he told himself. *She was just in the wrong place at the wrong time.* The darkening sky remained congested, save for a blood-orange smear across the horizon where the sun prepared to retire for the evening.

"Everyone out," McTavish ordered as the car heaved to a stop in front of the mossy side-garden wall. "Come along now." She guided the group up the thistle-lined walkway to the grand entrance, a door rarely used save for the occasional Norm visitation. Thankfully, Uncle Jarus did a superb job of maintaining the protective spells that surrounded the Downfield property. It was one of the key reasons he refused to hire any outside help. He liked to handle the upkeep and affairs of the estate himself; another safeguard to ensure that any Mystical aspects would be invisible to the non-magical eye.

Monte pulled his feverish hand further into the arm of his jacket. His heart palpitated. The shell practically had a pulse of its own now.

McTavish tapped the knocker—a heavy metal ring wrapped in the talons of an iron falcon. The grand door creaked open. Uncle Jarus and an extremely disgruntled Widow Smith crowded in the doorframe.

"Finn Cornelius! I've been looking all over for yeh." The Widow snatched her grandson from McTavish's clutches with hardly so much as a glance. "Look at the state of yeh, covered head to toe in mud! What's this all about?"

"Officer McTavish, please come in," Uncle Jarus said. "The police station rang just minutes ago." He looked alarmed at the sight of Garrick's swollen eye.

Monte followed the procession down the grand hallway to the living room. Brotus and Saladin scrambled to their paws as the group entered. A freshly lit fire crackled in the hearth.

"Ah, yer all here, finally." Grandmother Meriweather sprung from the plaid armchair. She scanned the group, resting her eyes on McTavish. The look on her face suggested she was in a pestering mood. "Really now?" She planted her hands on her hips. "Is there need for all of this? These bairns—these kids—are not skivers . . ." Her eyes softened at the sight of Cameron. "And who might you be, meh dear?"

Cameron seemed to shrink at Grandmother Meriweather's question. She clamped her mouth shut, her normally soft lips a solid line across her face.

"Oi there, Cameron." Finn snapped his fingers in her face.

"Is that yer name, dearie?" Grandmother Meriweather pressed, her voice calm although her face suggested otherwise.

Cameron's chin quivered.

"Yes," Monte finally answered, growing increasingly puzzled. "This is Cameron."

"Aye, she's lovely," Grandmother Meriweather said with a smile before shooting a stony glance at the Norm officer.

McTavish cleared her throat. "As yeh know, these kids got in te a load of bother this afternoon. They created quite a commotion out at the old Hibernian Field. I suspect firecrackers were involved, although I can'nae find any proof." She pushed at her soggy bangs. "However, from what I'm led te believe, the rumpus was in defense of Master Smith here, who happened te provoke one of the roughest teenage crowds in Fort William."

"Finn Cornelius!" the Widow Smith exclaimed, her frizzy hair projecting from her head. "What are yeh doin', associating with such hooliganism? I absolutely forbid yeh te . . . ugh!" She snorted.

"Might I offer yeh a chair, Mrs. Smith?" Uncle Jarus asked. Distress etched the net of lines around his eyes.

McTavish stepped forward, commanding attention with her giant hound-like presence. "I'll be generous this time and let yeh all off with a warning. But let me make this a very harsh warning." She squeezed her hands together. "There's mention of rumors—strange things—in the area. Many claim there are unexplainable forces on the loose." She paused to look at

Uncle Jarus, who stroked the red stubble on his chin. "Altercations of today's nature—disturbing noises, gang-like fighting, and the likes—are only kindling te the spreading fires of apprehension. It is my job te protect this town and much of that boils down te maintaining the peace. Am I being clear enough?"

"Yes, ma'am—I mean, yes," Garrick said.

Monte's insides lurched as another pain clenched his arm. He forced a nod.

"Right then." McTavish turned to Cameron. "I'll see yeh home, lassie."

"Oh-no." Cameron sounded panicked. "It's all right. I'll find my own way," she stuttered. "It's not far."

"Not at all, yeh won't." McTavish thumped toward Cameron. "Nothing but mischief-makers out there tonight, what with it being All Hallows' Eve and all. I will be taking yeh home."

Cameron backed away. "No." Her voice was firm.

Monte's knees began to shake as the shell sizzled in his palm. A wave of Christmas spices, this time overbearing, smoldered in his nose.

"Excuse me?" McTavish clamped her hand over Cameron's shoulder, her eyes hinting at authority.

"Now just wait a minute, McTavish." Concern traced Uncle Jarus's voice.

"I really don't need any help," Cameron continued, her forehead wrinkling.

McTavish dropped her hand from Cameron's shoulder. She angled her head to the side like a wolfhound awaiting her master's mandates. "Very well then," she mumbled, her eyes suddenly blank. "Yeh all have a pleasant night." She turned for the hallway, her stride stiff.

"Too right, we will," Grandmother Meriweather called after McTavish. "Silly Norm eejit," she muttered, winking at Cameron.

"That was weird, Cameron," Monte said, sluggishly.

"Monte?" Garrick's voice sounded like it was traveling through water.

"I don't . . . feel . . . so . . . great . . ." Monte slurred, staggering backward into the plaid armchair.

"What's going on? Monte, what is it? What've yeh done?" Uncle Jarus's words echoed through Monte's head. "Garrick, what's yer brother doing?"

"It's his hand . . . something happened," Garrick stuttered. "It's that seashell."

Monte was barely conscious of the conversation around him. He felt his head fall into the back of the armchair.

"What the devil are yeh talking about?" Uncle Jarus asked, rushing for Monte. His lips tightened at the sight of the shell which remained pillowed in Monte's palm. "What in the name of Prince William? Garrick, take the others in te my office," he ordered, kneeling down. "Now."

"Dear me, lad. Yer hand is not of the right constitution!" the Widow Smith said from across the room.

"Everyone out," Uncle Jarus repeated. "And someone call for Maren."

Garrick ushered the Widow Smith out of the room. Finn and Cameron shuffled after them, clearly hesitant to leave.

"This way, dearies." Grandmother Meriweather shepherded the group from behind, Brotus and Saladin at her heels.

Monte bit away the agony as Uncle Jarus pushed back his jacket sleeve. The shell had scorched a pattern of inflamed, swirly marks into his skin. He groaned as the room started to spin.

"Monte, listen. I need yer full attention," Uncle Jarus urged. "Come on, pal!"

"Yeah . . . okay." Monte struggled to keep his neck vertical.

"Yer arm . . ." Uncle Jarus drew three silvery circles in the air with his wand. "Here. Place yer arm here, quickly."

With great deliberation Monte lifted his arm to the hovering rings. A cooling sensation rushed through him.

"Better?" Uncle Jarus asked.

Monte sighed and nodded as the floating rings vanished.

"Right, then." Uncle Jarus gingerly clasped Monte's hand. He shook his wrist and then directed his wand at the shell. Nothing happened. He repeated the motion, this time mouthing a silent incantation.

Monte writhed about, his skin prickling with pain.

Grandmother Meriweather rushed back into the room, her blue eyes deep and dark as she sank to her knees beside Monte. "Try again, son," she urged Uncle Jarus.

The creases in Uncle Jarus's forehead deepened as he tried to dislodge the shell for a third time.

Something buzzed up Monte's arm. "Argh!" He yanked his hand away.

"Sorry, pal." Uncle Jarus rocked back onto his heels in defeat. He pursed his lips together, his hairline fringed with sweat.

"Why won't it just magic off?" Finn drifted back into the living room, followed by Garrick. Cameron crept in behind them.

"I thought I told yeh lot te get out!" Uncle Jarus wiped his forehead with the back of his hand. "And I don't know why the devil it's stuck." He stared at the shell with contempt.

Monte swallowed his choking panic and closed his eyes. *Off! Off!* He sent the words flying through the dark chasms of his mind. He opened his eyes and looked down at his hand. The shell remained cemented to his palm.

"Where the Dickens is Maren when we need her?" Uncle Jarus said.

"Here, let me try." Grandmother Meriweather produced her wand.

"No! Wait—" Monte inhaled sharply. He reached even deeper, recalling the surge of energy he had felt in his chest at Hibernian Field, remembering the power he had experienced at the park in Salem. An image of the mangled tangerine raced through his head. He could almost taste its tangy juices again. *I need you to come off*, he thought to the shell. *I need you to release your hold.* The shell shifted slightly.

"It moved! I saw it!" Finn exclaimed.

Maren darted into the living room, still in her nursing uniform, her medical kit in hand. "How much pain are you in, Monte?" she asked, not wasting any time.

Monte didn't answer. *Release your hold*, he focused on the shell. *You will come off.* A warm sensation ballooned in his chest. *I need you to come off!* he urged. The power spread from his chest to his fingertips.

"That's it, Monte!" Uncle Jarus thumbed the wiggling shell. "Keep going."

*Release!* Monte thought, the energy flowing through him like waves. *Release!*

The shell detached from his hand in one vigorous surge of power. It sailed across the room, denting the wall with a loud clunk.

Uncle Jarus yanked a handkerchief from his pocket and pounced on the shell. "Where did yeh get this thing?" He wound the fine cloth around the sparkling seashell.

"Just at—whoa." The ground slanted as Monte tried to stand. "At the beach." He blinked, waiting for his vision to steady.

"Which beach?" Uncle Jarus demanded. "Was it one here in Scotland?"

"No. One in Salem," Garrick answered. "He found it the day before we moved here."

Monte chanced a look at his hand. He winced. Inflamed symbols, strange and mysterious, feathered from his palm up to his elbow—the work of the fiery seashell.

"Wow." Finn crept closer to Uncle Jarus, his eyes inquisitive.

"Stay back." Uncle Jarus raised the shell above his head. "Nobody will have anything te do with this thing until we figure out what's going on."

"Nobody?" Monte leaned his good arm against the back of the chair. "But that seashell saved my life."

"Sit down, Monte," Grandmother Meriweather coaxed.

"I don't know what you call it," Maren said, digging through her medical bag. "But I don't see anything lifesaving about the condition of Monte's arm." She swept her fingers over the marks.

"I'm not talking about my arm. I'm talking about what happened back at the beach in Salem."

"What do yeh mean, son?" Grandmother Meriweather asked.

The story rushed from Monte as he recounted what had transpired on Witch's Pointe. He didn't care what the adults thought; he just knew that he needed to defend the seashell.

"Cameron," he said. "You were there. Tell them what you saw."

"Hold the phone," Uncle Jarus said. "Cameron was there?"

"I didn't see much," Cameron said, her voice dense. "But from what I remember, everything Monte said is true."

"So, this really is the girl from the beach?" Garrick turned to Monte.

"Can someone please explain what's going on?" Uncle Jarus looked from Monte, to Garrick, to Cameron. "Who are you again, lass?"

"She's not a Mystic but has had associations with them," Finn piped in.

"But what's she doing here?" Uncle Jarus pressed, turning to face Cameron.

"That's exactly what I've been trying to figure out," Monte said.

"I'm allowed to go w-where I please!" Cameron lifted a shaking chin in the air. "Baap is gone," she said, her voice heavy with emotion. "So, I live here now, in this dangerous place."

"Baap?" Uncle Jarus asked, his voice soft.

"What do you mean by dangerous?" Monte thought back to that night by the lamppost. "You keep using that word."

Tears welled in Cameron's eyes.

"There, there now. Don't fret." Grandmother Meriweather swooped to Cameron's side. She brushed at the rainbow lights, her fingers hesitating over the glowing gems, her face curious. "Don't yeh pay any heed te them, dearie." She smiled, cupping Cameron's shoulder. "They laddies can be mongrels." She shot the group a warning look.

Uncle Jarus raked his fingers through his hair. "Mum, might yeh get this poor lassie something hot te drink?" he said, cautiously. "Then we can figure all of this out," he added under his breath as Grandmother Meriweather led Cameron to the kitchen.

Maren touched her wand to the deepest mark on Monte's palm. He flinched.

"These are presenting like burns," she said. A foamy cream spewed from the end of her wand. "This will provide some relief . . . but I'm sorry to say that these symbols are quite strange to me. They'll definitely take some time to heal and will likely leave you scarred, even with the most expert mending spells."

Uncle Jarus's shadowy eyes darted from Monte to Garrick, to Finn. "Now lads, I need te know what really happened this afternoon at Hibernian Field." He tucked the swaddled seashell in his pocket. "Any of yeh care te elaborate?"

Monte stared at Garrick, who looked like he had been caught shoplifting.

"We can wait here all night." Uncle Jarus folded his arms.

Monte grumbled inside. He was getting all too familiar with that look. "So . . ." he finally yielded as Maren sprinkled a glittery substance onto his arm. It sank into his skin, cool and soothing. "These goons were after Finn.

We went to help him. We were outnumbered. They had Garrick and Finn pinned down . . ." He exchanged a significant look with Garrick. He didn't want to admit he had used a wand, even if it had been in defense.

"And?" Uncle Jarus pressed.

Garrick paced the floor.

"I can't describe what happened next." Monte chose his words carefully. "The seashell—it's like it was alive. It had a power of some sort."

Uncle Jarus placed his hand over his pocket where the shell lay. "What do yeh mean by . . . power? As in it burned yeh?"

"Not just that. A feeling of warmth. Of energy. Something I've never felt before." *It's only a partial lie*, Monte justified, burying the guilt of having used the wand.

"Hmm." Uncle Jarus scratched his chin. "Officer McTavish mentioned firecrackers . . ."

Garrick opened and closed his mouth, soundless, like a fish out of water.

"The shell got really hot," Monte explained. "I held it in front me. There was a loud noise."

"And everyone fell to the ground." Garrick's voice returned.

"And what produced this loud noise?" Uncle Jarus asked, almost whispering.

Silence blanketed the room. Monte looked at Finn, who was suddenly very interested in his fingers.

"The seashell did it. Or maybe it was me . . . or possibly all of us?" Monte stuttered. "I don't really know what happened."

Uncle Jarus buried his face in his hands, shaking his head.

"Does this mean something bad?" Finn asked.

"I don't ken," Uncle Jarus said. "It is strange, indeed. I'd be lying if I said I wasn't a little concerned. Especially in light of everything that's happening right now. Then again, yeh said yeh found the seashell in the States?"

"Yeah," Monte said. "In Salem."

"Which means what, exactly?" Garrick asked.

"The chances of the Mystical disturbances here in Scotland correlating with whatever is going on with this seashell should'nae be that high, in all actuality."

"That's good then, right?" Monte asked, eager for some positive news.

"Dad . . ." Maren held Monte's arm up, his skin pink behind the glistening spiraled wounds. "These symbols kind of look like . . ." The color drained from her face.

"Finn Cornelius? Finn Cornelius!" The Widow Smith's shrill calls vibrated from the grand hallway. "Finn Cornelius, there yeh are." The Widow scuffed into the room, her face creased from sleep. "I dozed off and yeh were gone. Yeh can't just go wandering away like that. Yeh can't—ugh!" she gasped at the sight of Monte's arm. "It's . . . It's . . . It can't be! No. Those markings." She patted a stubby hand against her chest. "I've seen too much. We must go. We must *go*," she demanded as she clawed the air for her grandson. "Finn Cornelius, we're leaving. Now!" She scuttled back toward the hallway, dragging a confused Finn behind her.

"Nanny?" Finn grabbed at the Widow's hands. "What's wrong?"

"Yeh mustn't speak of this te anyone. Not ever. Do yeh understand?"

"Mrs. Smith, please. Calm yerself," Uncle Jarus implored.

"How am I supposed te be calm when that boy clearly bears the mark of the . . ." she started to wheeze.

Garrick rushed to her side. "What're you talking about, Mrs. Smith?"

The Widow clutched her throat, heaving in and out.

Maren dashed into the kitchen and returned with a small vial full of inky liquid. "You're having an anxiety attack, Mrs. Smith. Take some of this," she instructed, uncorking the lid.

"What's that? What're you giving her?" Finn asked, his voice filled with panic. "Nanny? Nanny?" He shook the Widow's shoulders, his face whiter than Monte had ever seen it before.

"It killed them! It killed them!" she wailed.

Garrick guided the Widow to the couch. She slumped into the cushions, her chin quivering, as Maren tilted the vial into her mouth. Instantly, the old woman's shoulders relaxed.

"What's she talking about?" Monte asked.

"Garrick, go get yer grandmother." Uncle Jarus nestled a pillow behind the Widow's head. Soft, silent tears stained her cheeks.

Just then, a strange knocking echoed into the living room. Saladin and Brotus bellowed and scampered into the kitchen.

"Is that someone knocking?" Monte asked, suddenly remembering that it was Halloween. Do you get trick-or-treaters at the—"

"The service door," Uncle Jarus said, dread etched across his forehead. "They're here."

"Who's here?" Monte leapt to his feet.

The knocking grew into a pattern of taps and drums, like a bodhran sounding through the great estate.

"Yer telling me the truth?" Uncle Jarus planted a forceful stare on Monte. "What happened this afternoon—the goons, the seashell, its power, everything—it's all true?"

"Yeah . . . yes," Monte stammered. After all, it was the truth. Even if it wasn't the entire truth.

"Garrick?" Uncle Jarus rounded on his other nephew.

"Yes. All true," Garrick said, although it looked like it pained him to say so.

The rhythmic knocking increased in tempo, sending Brotus and Saladin into a yapping frenzy.

"It's them pesky Bureau eejits, Jarus." Grandmother Meriweather appeared from the kitchen. "A leprechaun, by the sounds of it."

"Comerford, I'd wager," Uncle Jarus said.

"Should I ignore it?" Grandmother Meriweather asked. "Yeh know what happens when I do." Her lips twitched.

"No," Uncle Jarus said. "Not this time. I'm afraid this is something we must address. Especially with Esca out of the picture." He swapped apprehensive looks with Grandmother Meriweather. "Go ahead and answer it, Mum. I'll be right there."

"Who's Comerford?" Garrick asked.

"An IMB messenger," Uncle Jarus said. "I'm being summoned."

"Summoned? As in they want you at the IMB headquarters?" Monte asked. "Why?"

"They'll want te know about all the commotion this afternoon. I'm sure they expect an explanation for yer use of magic." Uncle Jarus pulled the wrapped seashell from his pocket. "Don't lose this." He handed the small bundle to Maren. "And whatever yeh do, don't open it."

Maren nodded then threw her arms around her father.

Some of the tension released from Uncle Jarus's face. "Don't yeh worry. I'll get this sorted and be back straight away."

The drumming stopped. "Aye, Comerford. Come in," Grandmother Meriweather said from the kitchen.

Uncle Jarus reached for his cloak, a dark, billowy mantle so long that it nearly brushed the floor, even when adorned.

"Hang on. I'll go with you," Monte said. You might need me to explain what happened."

"No," Uncle Jarus and Maren said in unison as Grandmother Meriweather entered the room.

"It *is* Comerford. He's waiting at the threshold, gave yeh thirty seconds before he comes in himself. Arrogant bloke," Grandmother Meriweather said with a sniff.

Uncle Jarus nodded. "Monte, yeh'll stay here with everyone else."

"But—"

"No, Monte. I'm the head of this estate and therefore I'm responsible for the actions of its inhabitants," Uncle Jarus said, eyeing the dressings on Monte's arm. "Besides . . ." His voice was barely audible. "There are some things yeh should know." He turned to Grandmother Meriweather. "Mum?" She nodded in understanding.

"Wait. This is just some freak accident, right?" Garrick asked as Uncle Jarus turned to leave. "The seashell, and what it did?"

Uncle Jarus paused, hesitating. "Aye," he said, slowly. "I'll be back soon." He bounded from the room, his cloak curling around his ankles.

The glow of the flames in the hearth skipped across Monte's face, flickering through the emptiness that Uncle Jarus had left behind. He looked at Grandmother Meriweather. "If this whole thing with the seashell was just an accident, then how come the Widow Smith was so upset when she saw my arm?"

Grandmother Meriweather sighed. "Everybody gather around. I think it's time for a wee story."

CHAPTER 10
The Nuckelavee's Kiss

Monte balanced a plate of beans, sausages, and toast on his knee. He shoveled a forkful of food into his mouth. Meat juice dribbled down his chin as he tried to grasp the utensil with his freshly bandaged hand. He had worked up quite an appetite despite the frightening events of the day. Plus, eating was a good distraction. The night waxed on and Uncle Jarus's absence grew ever concerning.

"You're an animal," Garrick said with an air of annoyance. He propped a similar plate across his lap. It remained untouched.

"What? I'm hungry," Monte said as the others took their places in front of the hearth.

"I can't believe you've even got an appetite right now," Garrick said.

"Here." Maren handed Garrick a slab of raw beef. "For your eye."

"Delicious," Monte teased as Garrick fumbled with the dripping piece of meat, finally managing to slap it over his swollen eye.

"Quiet, you," Garrick snapped. "You and your cheek are next."

Finn popped beans into his mouth at a rapid pace. The Widow lay draped across the couch behind him, deep in slumber. Cameron came in from the kitchen, already on her second plate. Monte smiled, he appreciated her hearty appetite.

"Okay, everyone. Are yeh all listening?" Grandmother Meriweather stood with her back to the crackling hearth. "Time for a little discussion. Cameron, dearie, yeh sit here, beside me." Her voice matched the warming comfort of the flames behind her. "Yer practically a Mystic yerself, after what yeh witnessed today. Yeh deserve te hear this too."

Cameron's hair fell in loose strands around her face, her skin soft against the brilliance of the rainbow lights around her neck. Her eyes met Monte's. A half-smile flickered across her face. Monte felt his cheeks grow red. It was the first time he had seen her smile, and he wished for more.

"Right, everyone," Grandmother Meriweather continued. "How familiar are yeh with Scottish folklore?"

"You mean like Bigfoot?" Monte chomped into a bit of sausage.

"Scottish folklore, Monte. Not American," Garrick said.

"Oh, right."

"We covered some Scottish mythology last week at Strathmartine Academy," Garrick said. "Ancient gems, the blue men, fairy civilizations, the Witches of Delnabo—all fairytales." He placed a mocking emphasis on the last.

Grandmother Meriweather smiled. "Yeh, that's right. Such stories are merely legends te the Norms. However, we know the truth. Sure, some tales are a wee bit dressed up, but most Norm myths actually happened. They are part of our Mystic past, pieces of history passed down through the years." Her blue eyes twinkled. "We Mystics are living folklore, yet the Norms don't realize it because they din'nae see us for who we really are. We're good at keeping ourselves secret."

"So, you're saying that fairytales are real-life Mystic stories that have carried over to the Norm culture?" Monte asked with newfound interest.

"Aye. In a way. Except even we Mystics enjoy a good fable," Grandmother Meriweather said.

"How's that?"

"Take the werewolf, for example," Maren butted in. "Unfortunately, such creatures still walk this earth. The Norms see them as beasts of myth, but we Mystics know they are very real. What we don't know, however, is whether their kindly and helpful cousins, the Wulvers, are a creature of reality or of folklore. Even in the Mystic community some things remain unclear."

"Wulvers are real," Finn said. "Cousin B's seen one."

"Who's Cousin B?" Monte asked.

"My cousin, obviously."

Monte shrugged. *Touché.*

"Perhaps your Cousin B *has* seen one." Maren looked at Finn. "But either way, Wulvers are an example of a myth that hasn't actually been verified into Mystic existence—a story that has likely morphed over time, likewise becoming more legend than fact."

"Fairies are real too." Cameron's eyes shone as the light from the flames lit her face. "That's how I got this necklace." She fingered the glowing gems at her neck.

"Aye, the Fae are definitely not myth," Grandmother Meriweather said with great fondness.

"But you're saying that some magical creatures are just myths, even in Mystic belief?" Garrick pressed.

"Well, the line is becoming increasingly unclear," Maren said. "Just look at the scare these large cats are causing. Not just in the Norm realm, but for Mystics, too. The presence of dangerous, magical—even enchanted—cats in Britain has been merely speculation until now." She sighed. "Cat siths originate from Fae folklore, ancient creatures that pop up from time to time. Sort of like the Loch Ness monster. Now any previous assumptions are being put to the test as what was once thought to be myth is becoming reality."

"Which brings me te my story," Grandmother Meriweather said. "As yeh may have noticed, the marks on Monte's arm caused quite the commotion with Doris over there." She glanced at the Widow Smith, who was snoring loudly on the couch. "Have any of yeh—with the exception of Maren—ever heard of the Nuckelavee?" She spat the name from her mouth as though it was poison.

"Nuck-eh-what?" Monte asked, his gut suddenly heavy.

"The Nuh-cah-la-vee," Grandmother Meriweather said. "The most feared of all Scottish creatures. A sinister fiend." She paused, her eyes unblinking. "A true demon."

The fire snapped and popped in the hearth. Even the Widow Smith seemed to be listening from her sleep. The name of the malevolent beast hung in the air, unrelenting, like the stench of rotting fish.

Grandmother Meriweather wove her fingers together. "The Nuckelavee was merely part of Mystic mythology until twenty-odd years ago, when . . ." Her voice fizzled into nothing.

"When new evidence surfaced suggesting its actual existence," Maren interjected.

"We call it the Great Nuckelavee Scare. It was a time when the dreadful monster attempted te rise te power," Grandmother Meriweather continued. "And he had followers, the Nuckelavee. Just as he existed te cause misery, his servants existed te bring doom upon the Mystic and the Norm realms. There were bletherings. Many claimed the Nuckelavee and his followers were in search of something—an object of power." Grandmother Meriweather's stare hooked on Monte. She took a deep breath. "Others believed that the

Nuckelavee wished te spread his darkness to the Norms. On any account, they were a loathsome bunch."

Monte swallowed hard, the beans and sausages now a greasy lump in his belly.

"Before the Great Scare, legend stated that the Nuckelavee of old haunted the shores of Scotland. It was said te bring severe misfortune, wretchedness, and even death wherever it roamed. Crops would die and disease would persist. There was'nae any escape if yeh encountered the horrible creature face te face."

"No escape, save for freshwater," Maren added, using her wand to guide the dirty dinner plates from the room.

"Freshwater?" Garrick asked.

"The Nuckelavee can'nae tread freshwater without catastrophic results," Grandmother Meriweather explained. "There's only one account of a Mystic who actually managed te escape the Nuckelavee's grasp . . . But that is a story for another time."

Monte placed his hand over his bandaged arm, suddenly feeling very protective of the symbols beneath.

"Our understanding of the Nuckelavee's curse is not great," Grandmother Meriweather continued. "But every mythical fandanglement I know of agrees on one thing: te undergo the wrath of the Nuckelavee is like experiencing death itself. If yeh are touched by the demon in any way, truly, yeh are touched by the darkest of magic."

A shudder jolted up Monte's back. He felt Finn inch closer to him. "What does this thing look like?" Monte asked. "The Nuckelavee?" A log, charred by the flames, collapsed inside the hearth. Grandmother Meriweather pulled Cameron out of the way as orange ash spewed from the crispy piece of wood.

"There aren't many illustrations but what we do have would certainly give yeh a right good fleg," Grandmother Meriweather said with a shiver. "Said te be birthed from the ocean, the Nuckelavee is partially human, partially beast. It appears as a man's torso attached te a horse's body, its teeth pointy and jagged. It has long, sinewy arms that drape nearly all the way down te its sharp, cloven hooves." She pinched her fingers between her eyes, as though she didn't wish to go on. "The Nuckelavee's face is skeletal, its eyes slanted and yellow with thin lips that stretch across a wide frog-like mouth. The rot of the sea lives on its breath. It lacks skin, its muscles red and raw with bits of bone jutting out."

"And there's just one? One Nuckelavee?" Finn asked, his eyes like saucers.

"The Nuckelavee wanders alone, raining torment and demise down upon anyone who crosses its path. It is a dark and relentless being," Grandmother Meriweather answered in a whisper. "No reports—recent or ancient—offer information as te whether the terrible beast has a mate or a herd."

The Widow Smith jumped in her sleep as if confirming Grandmother Meriweather's words.

"During the height of the scares twenty years ago, the Nuckelavee's followers were a highly secretive group, only recognized by strange markings on their skin," Grandmother Meriweather explained, her face the straightest Monte had ever seen it. "The symbols were a token of their allegiance te their master." Her eyes drifted down Monte's bandaged arm. "These symbols came te be known as the Nuckelavee's kiss. And te cross a follower bearing this mark meant sure doom."

Monte's arm stung beneath Maren's dressings. He could feel all eyes staring at him. "So that's what you think I have? The Nuckelavee's kiss?"

Grandmother Meriweather twisted her lips together like she was repressing an answer she didn't want to give.

"We don't know," Maren finally said.

"But," Garrick said, dropping the hunk of meat from his eye. "The Nuckelavee didn't make those marks. The seashell did."

"And Monte found the shell in the States," Cameron added.

"That's right," Monte demanded. "It saved my life."

"Not to mention Monte just used it to pound those goons," Finn said.

Monte nodded in agreement. "It's cool. It's brought lots of . . . goodness."

"None of us are denying that, son," Grandmother Meriweather said.

"It just doesn't quite all add up," Maren said. She swiped her wand over the bandages on Monte's arm. The prickling ceased.

"But the Great Nuckelavee Scare happened here in Scotland, not America," Garrick pushed. "How can Monte's shell even be related to any of that?"

"Because it's a seashell," Maren said.

"Yeah, so?"

"Where's the Nuckelavee supposed te bide?" Grandmother Meriweather asked. "Where did it originate?"

"It's from . . . the ocean." Garrick's voice faded into a look of understanding.

"So?" Monte asked.

Cameron stepped back onto the hearth, her face creased with worry. "You think the seashell is from the Nuckelavee." Her voice was resolute as she turned to face Grandmother Meriweather. "You think that someone placed Monte's shell in Salem deliberately?"

Grandmother Meriweather's shoulders slumped. "Hopefully not," she murmured. "But it's an idea we should'nae part ways with."

"Wait a second," Monte said, standing. "You said the Great Nuckelavee Scare was over twenty years ago. What happened? Where's this demon been since then?"

"Farwen," Grandmother Meriweather said.

"Farwen?" Garrick and Monte asked in unison.

"The queen of the unicorns," Finn said, his voice almost reverent. "Cousin B told me about her. Everyone calls her the Unicorn Witch."

"Witch? A unicorn?" Monte asked.

"Aye, a good one though," Finn explained.

Grandmother Meriweather nodded. "Farwen is the governing witch of all equines, both Mystic and Norm. She receives everlasting life in exchange for guardianship of the magical and non-magical realms of Britain. If there is one thing the Nuckelavee can'nae withstand, it's her."

"So Farwen killed the Nuckelavee?" Monte asked.

"No, but she did banish it."

"Then why are we so worried right now?" Garrick asked. "If Farwen banished the Nuckelavee, then surely the marks on Monte's arm aren't connected to it."

"Because Farwen—the purest Mystic creature of all—can'nae commit murder, even toward the most baleful of creatures," Grandmother Meriweather said. "She only banished the Nuckelavee te its realm, which is somewhere deep in the sea."

"Farwen maimed the Nuckelavee terribly," Maren explained further. "She didn't kill it, but she came close. It was forced back into the ocean. These lands haven't seen it since."

"Aye, 'twas a very promising banishment," Grandmother Meriweather said. "Many believe the Nuckelavee was so badly skelped that it died at sea. There haven't been any sightings or stirrings since . . ." She surveyed Monte's arm once again. "But we still ultimately face the unknown."

"All right." Monte nervously yanked at his hair. "But I still don't see how my seashell could save my life, then turn out to be bad." He refused to accept the idea that he'd been carrying around a dark Mystic artifact.

"Ah." Grandmother Meriweather nodded. "A stalwart notion if there ever was one, pal. But din'nae forget that looks—even actions—can be deceiving."

"So, the marks on Monte's arm," Garrick began. "They resemble the Nuckelavee's kiss exactly?"

"I've never seen a Nuckelavee's kiss in person—thank goodness," Grandmother Meriweather said.

"I have." Maren folded her arms tightly in front of her.

The hairs at the back of Monte's neck stood at attention, his ears ringing. All eyes slowly and reluctantly landed on Maren.

"Yes," Maren whispered. She cleared her throat. "I saw a Nuckelavee's kiss some time ago, right before the large cat problems began. A Mystic woman was admitted to the Royal Infirmary. I was assigned to her triage team. You can probably guess where they found her."

"Ben Nevis?" Cameron asked.

"That's right. Dun Deardail trail, to be exact."

"Where the cat attacks were?" Monte asked, the words of Dean-o the Reporter replaying in his mind.

"Aye." Maren nodded. "The woman was emaciated and barely alive. Frostbite and starvation had eaten away at her, and in the end . . . she died. No family or relations came forward and we never pinpointed where she was from. But she had the mark—the kiss—all up her neck." Maren bowed her head and shuddered. "Monte," she said, looking up, "I wouldn't be truthful if I said the symbols on your arm don't look similar to what I saw on that woman."

"So tragic," Grandmother Meriweather said. "The IMB hunted down and successfully located most of the Nuckelavee's followers a couple decades ago. The wee fearties tried te go underground once their master was banished. Some escaped the IMB's hold and disappeared. The woman from the Dun Deardail was the first we'd seen in twenty years."

"Then it is possible that Monte's seashell is a weapon left behind by the Nuckelavee?" Garrick asked.

Monte glared at his brother and plopped back into the armchair.

"I hope te goodness not," Grandmother Meriweather said.

The Widow Smith spoke in her sleep—something about "oatmeal stuffing" and "eat it all." Everyone jumped.

"Okay, so even if Monte's seashell is a sign of the Nuckelavee, why can't we just call on Farwen again for help?" Garrick asked, eyeing the Widow Smith.

"Unicorns, including Farwen, are extremely wild," Grandmother Meriweather explained. "Nobody—creature or Mystic—can control the Unicorn Witch. Not even Clan McKnight."

"Clan McKnight? The ones who keep unicorns?" Monte asked.

"Aye."

"So Farwen just comes and goes as she pleases?" Garrick asked.

"As guardian of the British Mystic and Norm realms, Farwen must remain completely unbridled te successfully perform her magic," Grandmother Meriweather replied. "She presents herself in times of extreme Mystic turmoil, when either realm faces doom. She decides when te help and when te stay hidden."

"Ooft, sounds a bit harsh to me," Finn said.

"It is possible te summon Farwen," Grandmother Meriweather continued. "So long as the cause is worthy. Trouble is, nobody can agree on how te do it. We don't really understand the particulars. The process is based mightily on the worthiness of the beckoner."

Cameron sank down in front of the hearth, her finger hooked around the rainbow lights.

"Was Farwen summoned twenty years ago, then?" Monte asked.

"We din'nae know the details but many say a child called for her."

"Which makes sense," Maren said. "A perfect and untainted creature such as Farwen would be more likely to respond to the pure intents of an innocent youth than to an unreliable adult."

"So, what happens now?" Garrick began to pace again.

"We keep quiet and search for answers," Cameron said, glassy-eyed.

"Mom and Dad will know what to do," Monte said as the clock chimed an hour till midnight. He fought back a yawn.

"Aye." Grandmother Meriweather stretched her arms. "For now, I suggest we all get some rest. What a carry-on yeh lot have been through today."

"Here, Monte, take this." Maren pulled a small square bottle full of silvery liquid from her medical bag. "It'll help relax you and speed the healing process."

Monte took the bottle and swirled the liquid. *But I don't want to sleep*, he thought.

"Take it, Monte." Maren's voice was stern.

Monte looked around the room. Cameron had lowered herself to the floor where Brotus and Saladin snoozed, clearly too tired to pay heed to formality. There was still so much to ask her. So much to figure out.

"I'll force it down if I have to, Monte," Maren threatened.

"Fine," Monte muttered. He removed his jacket, bunching it around his wand and holster, and then gulped the liquid down, reluctantly. The sweet, shimmery tonic rushed through his body, balmy and tranquilizing. He yawned. *Danger*, he thought as his mind surrendered to the comforting warmth of impending sleep. *Cameron said I was in danger.* He blinked, finally letting his heavy eyelids fall as he drifted into a dreamless slumber.

CHAPTER 11
Missing Mystics and Vanishing Beasts

"Calm down? I get word that some strange, possessed seashell nearly burned my son's arm off and you expect me to be calm about it?"

Monte's eyes shot open at the sound of his father's voice. He squinted, his cheek sore and tender, as the morning light poured through the living room window. His arm throbbed beneath the bandages. Someone had tucked a pillow behind his head and a fuzzy blanket engulfed his body. His shoes sat neatly in front of the hearth where the remaining cinders glowed from beneath cracked black skin.

"Shush, Esca. You'll wake the boys." Mrs. Darrow's voice drifted from the kitchen.

*Mom and Dad are back?* Monte heaved himself from the armchair and tiptoed past a heap of quilts on the couch. Garrick's hair poked out from the top of the blankets, his breathing deep and heavy. There was no sign of Cameron, Finn, or anyone else.

Slowly, Monte leaned toward the door separating the living room from the kitchen. He strained his ears, listening to the adults' hushed tones.

"I don't know what it all means . . ." Uncle Jarus's voice sifted through the narrow crack in the door. "But I'll be demmed if it doesn't resemble what we saw a couple decades ago."

"How is Monte?" Mrs. Darrow asked.

"He's fine," Grandmother Meriweather answered. "That boy has the Darrow constitution in his favor." Her voice was tired and dull.

"You say his arm is quite marked?"

"Aye," came Maren's voice.

"Permanently?"

"Hard to say, not knowing the true nature of this shell, but yes, it's likely."

"Either way, we must keep this quiet until we have some solid answers," Uncle Jarus said.

Someone coughed uncomfortably.

"You know what will happen if the symbols on Monte's arm are discovered," Mr. Darrow said.

"Calm yerself, Esca, and mind who yer family is," Grandmother Meriweather said. "We'll get it sorted without a bother, I'm sure."

"We heard there was another cat sighting," Maren said. "What's the latest?"

Mr. Darrow sighed.

"It's like the beast vanishes. Every time," Mrs. Darrow said, sounding discouraged. "And Ben Nevis—that mountain grows sicker by the day—yet the source of the problem remains hidden."

"We left Moira Bryce in charge so we could rush here," Mr. Darrow explained. "Perhaps she'll pick up the trail again."

Monte tilted his head closer to the crack in the door, his breath suspended.

"What about the missing Mystic case?" Uncle Jarus asked. "Brian Shaw, from clan McKnight. Any leads?"

"Nothing," Mr. Darrow replied. "It's been a balancing act, collaborating with both the IMB and the Norm officials on all of this."

"Speaking of the Bureau," Uncle Jarus said. "They're far from pleased about yesterday's events. I'm telling yeh, they're a bunch of bureaucratic numpties."

"Ack, they're not all that bad," Mr. Darrow defended. "You're speaking about my employers, after all."

Just then, a sharp pain shot through Monte's arm. A yelp escaped his lips. He cupped his hand over his mouth.

"Shh," Mrs. Darrow said. "I think we have an eavesdropper."

Kitchen chairs scraped the floor. Before Monte had time to scurry back to the plaid chair, Mrs. Darrow was at the door.

"Monte, son! How are you?" His mother pulled him into a hug.

"Fine, Mom. You're home early?"

"Heard what happened and came straight away." Mr. Darrow tousled Monte's hair.

"How is it?" Mrs. Darrow stroked the bandages on Monte's arm.

"It's all right." Monte winced as another pain zapped his skin.

"Probably time for another treatment." Maren bustled toward him with her medical kit.

"Where's everyone else?" Monte asked. "Cameron? Finn?"

"Finn and his nanny left shortly after you zonked out last night," Maren said.

"And Cameron?"

Maren exchanged an uneasy look with Grandmother Meriweather. "We actually don't know when she left."

"One minute she was there, petting the dogs . . ." Grandmother Meriweather pointed to the spot on the floor. "And the next, she was gone." She shook her head.

"What? Not again," Monte complained.

"Mom? Dad?" Garrick rolled from the couch, his voice groggy.

"Garrick. You've seen better mornings, son," Mr. Darrow said with a laugh.

"Why're you back so early?" Garrick asked.

"Came to check in on you after what happened yesterday." Mrs. Darrow greeted him with open arms.

"Er, yeah. Strange day, yesterday." Garrick pushed at his hair, which was like a sea of restless auburn waves atop his head. His mouth was far less swollen than the day before, the inflammation localized around a tiny slit in his lip from where his skin had broken. But his eye looked like a swollen plum. "How'd things go with the IMB?"

"The Bureau isn't happy," Uncle Jarus replied. He clasped his hands together and circled his thumbs around each other. "They had many questions regarding Monte's status and wand eligibility. I haggled with them late in te the night. Eventually, yer parents' prestigious standing with the IMB yielded some leniency."

"Leniency?" Garrick asked.

"Compassion . . . mercy . . ." Monte badgered.

"I know what it means, you moron."

"Settle, Garrick. And Monte, you'd best not be joking about all of this," Mr. Darrow said, his forehead wrinkling.

"The goons were after Finn." Monte raised his hands in protest. "We were only defending ourselves."

"Aye, defense." Uncle Jarus nodded. "Which is why the IMB is offering yeh some allowance. Under their current statutes, the use of magic is circumstantial, and I argued that very point te the brink of exhaustion. I convinced them that Monte produced magic out of defense in an obviously threatening situation. It was not intended te harm, but rather te guard. And they finally accepted my dispute."

"They did?" Garrick asked.

"Aye. However, two problems remain: the first being that magic was performed in the presence of Norms, and secondly, they have no explainable source of the magic. In other words, they want an answer as te exactly how Monte produced such a powerful enchantment." Uncle Jarus raised his eyebrows at Monte. "And I wasn't about te tell them about the seashell."

Mr. Darrow stepped forward, Monte's wand and holster in hand. Monte groaned, glancing at the floor where his jacket lay, strewn open.

"This was my father's wand." Mr. Darrow massaged the instrument between his fingers. "Your grandmother said she gifted it to you under very specific conditions?"

"Yes, but—"

"But you used it all the same."

"Yeah, only because—"

"Monte, when are you going to get it through your head that magic is not allowed right now?" Mr. Darrow's voice began to climb.

"I didn't know what else to do. Plus, the goons didn't see the wand. They thought it was a firecracker, right Garrick?"

Garrick nodded.

Mr. Darrow looked like he might blow his lid.

"Let's just pause and think this through," Uncle Jarus intervened. "I think we can count on the goons not saying much, especially since this all transpired on All Hallows' Eve. It's one of the rowdiest nights of the year—full of jest and mischievous play. They probably got in te far more trouble last night than what took place at Hibernian Field."

Mr. Darrow huffed. "You can't just assume."

"I'll check in with McTavish and do some damage control," Uncle Jarus continued. "As for Monte's wand . . . I think we can use it in our favor."

"Not another one of your anti-Bureau schemes, Jarus," Mr. Darrow accused.

Uncle Jarus shot his twin an exasperated look. "We'll present the wand te the IMB and explain that it's yet te be registered under the new regime. I will have te plead ignorant of its presence up until this point—which won't be hard, seeing as I didn't know Monte had it until returning home a few hours ago." He rolled his eyes at his nephew. "We'll probably face a heavy fine and a slap on our wee paws, but it'll distract from the real problem: the seashell."

"Jarus, I don't think it's wise—"

"The last thing we need right now is te have Monte's injury discovered," Uncle Jarus pressed. "Yeh know just as well as I do, Esca, that the IMB can't catch wind of anything pertaining te the seashell, at least not until we have some answers of our own. We need te discover what it all means before taking it te the Bureau. There's too much room for misinterpretation."

All eyes darted to Monte as Maren peeled the bandages from his arm. Mrs. Darrow put her hands to her mouth, stifling a gasp as the strange symbols were unveiled.

"It's fine. It'll be fine." Monte searched his parents' shocked faces. Panic percolated in his chest. "It's fine," he repeated, recalling the marks on his thigh. They had healed fine from what he could tell, and that was without any magical attention. Then again, that had been merely a sting, not a burn.

A brisk knock at the grand entrance cut through the tension.

"Now who could that be?" Grandmother Meriweather asked as Brotus and Saladin bayed loudly. "Oi, meh head is done in."

"Probably McTavish making her rounds. Only Norms use the grand door," Uncle Jarus said. "Get those symbols covered up." He pointed to Monte's arm before heading down the hall.

"Sorry," Maren said as she hastily re-wrapped Monte's arm.

"Here, son." Mrs. Darrow draped a blanket over Monte's shoulders, cloaking his torso entirely.

"Moira!" Uncle Jarus's voice echoed through the hallway, nearly an octave higher than it normally was. "Good te see yeh . . . come in."

"Moira Bryce?" Garrick attempted to smooth down his messy crop of hair.

"Ah, look who it is!" Mr. Darrow exclaimed as the tall and stately woman entered the room. She wore a thick green traveling cloak pinned neatly at her right shoulder. Her hair was pulled into a tidy bun, her cheeks rosy from her travels. An earthy aroma accompanied her like fresh rain upon grass. Uncle

Jarus lingered behind her, his ears scarlet. He fidgeted with a snag in his sweater like it was the most important task in the world.

Moira glanced from Mr. Darrow to Mrs. Darrow. "You will forgive me for not calling beforehand, Esca, but I had to make haste." Her boots clicked against the hardwood floor as she greeted her colleagues.

"Is that so?" Mrs. Darrow asked, her eyes sharp.

"What's going on?" Mr. Darrow said. "Why aren't you up at the Ben?"

"It's all right, Esca." Moira's eyes glowed. "Things are brilliant, actually. I wanted to give you the news in person. I came as quickly as I could."

"News? What happened?"

"We caught it," Moira said, her face radiant. "We caught the cat sith."

# CHAPTER 12
Improvements

"Ho, Monte!" Mr. Darrow stepped through the service door into the Downfield kitchen. "How goes it, Garrick?" Water splattered everywhere as he closed his umbrella.

"Ugh, Esca, you'll mark up the floors!" Mrs. Darrow scolded from the stove.

"Sorry. Forgot to shake it before I came in." Mr. Darrow bounded across the floor. He scooped her up into a twirl and planted a kiss on her cheek.

Garrick rose from the table, smirking at his parents. "What'd the IMB say?"

"Good things, I hope?" Mrs. Darrow added, pulling herself away from her husband to take a meat pie from the oven.

"The IMB accepted our case. Jarus was very convincing." Mr. Darrow shook the rain from his boots. "Moira's capture of the cat sith helped too. It turned the Bureau's attention. They've been too preoccupied to pay much attention to Monte's little mishap with the seashell."

"So, I'm off the hook?" Monte asked, eager for the official verdict.

"Aye."

"Excellent." Monte jabbed his fist in the air.

"Now just hold on a minute." Mr. Darrow's face was stern. "I hope you boys know exactly how serious this all could've been. I'd hardly be celebrating if I were you."

"But I thought the IMB was lifting all the magical restrictions since the cat sith was caught?" Monte asked.

"They are, gradually. But let's not forget the underlying principle here. You exposed yourself to the Norms, Monte. You broke the rules."

"I already told you, I couldn't help it with the shell. And I used Granddad's wand in defense of myself and my friends."

"That's another thing," Mr. Darrow said. "Finn should've never picked a quarrel with that pack of hooligans. It's fortunate that they didn't have more than five brain cells between them."

Garrick snorted. "Thick as mince, that lot."

"Speaking of mince, is that mince pie?" Monte asked as his mother set a steaming dish of pastry and meat on the table. He tore a piece of the golden crust from the edge of the pan.

"Stop that." Mrs. Darrow swatted at Monte's hand. "Nobody's getting anything to eat until this kitchen is tidied. Honestly, poor Jarus. Looking after you messy boys while we're away all the time."

"Hold on now," Monte protested. "I've made dinner the past two nights. And Garrick . . ." He paused to look at his brother, unable to pass up an opportunity to taunt. "Well, nobody can scrub a toilet like Garrick can."

"Shut it, you!" Garrick lunged for Monte.

"All right, all right," Mr. Darrow continued. "Hear me out, boys. While what took place at Hibernian Field may have been pardoned by the IMB, your mother and I will not soon forget it." He raised his eyebrows at Monte. "And for that reason, Monte, I'll be holding on to your grandfather's wand until we determine you are responsible enough to carry it."

"Ah, c'mon, Dad," Monte complained. "It's almost my half-birthday. What if another cat sith turns up? How am I supposed to defend myself?"

"Watch your tone, son," Mr. Darrow warned. "The captured cat sith has been eliminated. The days of large cats terrorizing Scotland are long past now. They're wrapping up the case as we speak. Even Ben Nevis is starting to look healthier. I don't anticipate you needing that wand any time soon."

"Okay." Monte scooped up a messy bundle of schoolwork and shoved it into his backpack. Disappointment and frustration wrapped around him like a glove. "You're probably right."

"Don't forget your laundry piles," Mrs. Darrow ordered as she sent plates and cutlery flying to the table with her wand.

Monte slung his backpack over his shoulder, struggling with a tall pile of towels and t-shirts.

"Easy there, pipsqueak," Garrick joked. He handed Monte his own backpack. "I'll get it."

"I'm not a wuss, you know." Monte surrendered the folded laundry and heaved Garrick's backpack over his other shoulder. "This thing weighs a ton. Did you get carried away at the library again?" The pair staggered up the stairs.

"Har-har. They're called textbooks, Monte. And yes, they're heavy."

"You're such a dork." Monte pushed Garrick's bedroom door open and plunked the backpack onto the bed. The zipper burst open. Books and papers tumbled every which way.

"Watch it, you moron!"

"Don't blame me. I'm not the one who packed it full with boring books," Monte said as he bent down to pick up the mess. Something small bounced off his shoe, tinkering across the hardwood floor. Garrick dove after it but Monte was quicker, snatching it just before it rolled under the radiator. A tiny glass vial.

"What's this?" Monte examined the bottle. The inside was empty save for a chalky residue that coated the sides.

"It's nothing. Give it back," Garrick said.

Monte took a step back. "It's nothing, eh?" He waved the vial above his head, continuing to taunt. "Is it candy? Medicine?"

Garrick grabbed at Monte's wrist, prying the vial from his fingers. "I said it's nothing. Just a little something I took the other day to boost my energy before rugby practice."

"Ooh, like a special potion? Did Maren give it to you?"

"No. I mean yeah, sort of." Garrick pocketed the tiny bottle. "Look, I wasn't feeling myself, so Maren gave it to me to try."

"Did it work? Can I try some?"

"No, you can't."

"Why not? It's one of those performance booster potions, isn't it? For your big rugby match on Friday?"

"Come off it, Monte. I told you, it's nothing. I'm actually quite offended right now that you think I'd cheat with a performance booster."

"Well, I dunno. You haven't really been yourself lately . . . and they say that's when people turn to this kind of thing," Monte said, half-teasing. He wouldn't have expected Garrick, of all people, to meddle in unauthorized potions.

"Yeah, all right. That's it. I'm taking magical pick-me-ups." Garrick rolled his eyes. "That's not me at all and you know it."

"Then why are you being so defensive about it?"

"Shut it, Monte."

Monte held his hands up in surrender. "Just sayin'."

"Look, it was only a calming tonic."

"Oh yeah, of course it was." Monte turned for the door.

"Wait." Garrick grabbed Monte's shoulder. "Don't mention this to Mom and Dad, okay? I don't want them worrying. I'm fine and they're busy enough as it is trying to wrap up the cat sith case."

"Well, I dunno . . ."

"C'mon, bro. You owe me for keeping your secret about Witch's Point."

"That doesn't count since I ended up having to spill the beans anyway."

"I just don't want Mom and Dad to worry when it's not even a big deal. They might jump to conclusions."

"Okay, but if it's not a big deal . . ."

"Just leave it, Monte."

"Boooys!" Mrs. Darrow's voice trailed up from the bottom of the stairs. "Come, before dinner gets cold."

Monte tweaked Garrick's ear and then bounded down the stairs before his brother could retaliate. "Dinner smells brilliant, Mom," he said, tucking himself in behind the table.

"Your mother's mince pie is dynamite. Almost as good as mine," Mr. Darrow teased.

"Oh, stop it." Mrs. Darrow nudged him playfully.

"Well, I don't care whose mince pie this is," Monte said as he heaped enormous portions of the entree onto his plate. "I just know that I'm starving."

"And growing, I'd say." Mrs. Darrow pointed her fork at Monte. "I've let down all of your school trousers since being home and they're still too short."

"Ah, it's the Darrow gene kicking in." Mr. Darrow's eyes glinted.

"Maybe the seashell gave me superpowers when it burned me."

Garrick kicked Monte under the table.

"I don't think you should joke about that, son." Mrs. Darrow's voice was harsh.

"Why? Nothing else has happened," Monte objected through a forkful of potatoes. "Dad, you even said the other day that you hadn't detected any further signs of the Nuckelavee's return."

Mr. Darrow choked on his food. He hit his fist against his chest. "When did I say that?" he gasped.

"The other night, when you and Uncle Jarus were talking."

"Esca," Mrs. Darrow declared. "I told you to keep it down."

"That wasn't a discussion meant for your ears, Monte." Mr. Darrow slanted his brows. "What were you doing up in the middle of the night?"

Monte looked down at his plate. He'd been having trouble sleeping ever since the seashell burned him, though he didn't wish to admit it. After all, he was supposed to be well past the age of scary dreams.

"The late hour aside, you know you're not supposed to listen in when I talk about work," Mr. Darrow continued. "What else did you hear?"

"Nothing, really."

Mr. Darrow tilted his head in disbelief.

"I was on my way to the kitchen," Monte explained. "And I heard you mention that the seashell probably has no connection with the Nuckelavee. That it's probably a chameleon fossil, whatever that means," he added quietly.

"Chameleon fossils are exactly what they sound like," Garrick interjected. "Basically, things like rocks, tree bark, or shells—all enchanted—that have calcified over thousands of years, their magic preserved over time."

"And that's what you think my seashell is?"

"Aye," Mr. Darrow replied. "They're typically not harmful, although it's possible this particular shell has been gleaning magic from the Earth's core for some time now."

"Dynamite," Monte said, borrowing from his father's vocabulary.

"Sometimes these fossils, if left without disturbance for a long span of time, can gain more power than they already possess. Their initial magic—the enchantment that is calcified within them—is attracted to the natural powers of the Earth, much like a magnet. The longer they sit untouched, the more magic they collect. When finally used, they produce a single magically explosive incident like the one you experienced at Hibernian Field. It's likely that the rebound from that magic caused the seashell to fuse to Monte's hand, creating a sort of bond between them."

"Which would be a valid explanation for why only Monte could remove it in the end," Mrs. Darrow added.

"So that's it?" Monte asked. "The shell won't produce magic anymore?"

"It's not likely," Mr. Darrow said. "Once exploited, the chameleon fossil essentially turns into a dud, no matter how powerful it was to begin with."

"Bummer," Monte said. He had secretly hoped for something more out of the seashell. He wasn't sure exactly what, but something. He had felt a keen, unexplainable connection to it ever since that day on the beach. "I guess that means I can have it back now, right? Since it's no longer a threat?"

"None of you are going near that thing until we have an expert take a final assessment of it." Mrs. Darrow wrapped her knuckles on the table. "Its power seems to have fizzled out, but I'd like to be absolutely sure."

"Aye," Mr. Darrow agreed. "I'm almost positive it's a chameleon fossil now devoid of its power but perhaps we can seek Moira Bryce's opinion before drawing a final conclusion?"

Mrs. Darrow huffed. "I suppose we could ask her."

"Did you know that Uncle Jarus used to date Moira?" Monte asked, attempting to change the subject. All eyes turned to him, his mother's the most curious of all.

"Now, did he?" Mrs. Darrow cocked an eyebrow.

"Yeah, Maren told me."

An amused smile stole across Mrs. Darrow's face. "So that's why Jarus seemed a little out of sorts the other day when Moira was here."

"Aye." Mr. Darrow nodded. "They dated before I moved to the States, when we were all young whipper-snappers . . . at the pinnacle of our youth. We all became close colleagues and comrades—Jarus, Moira, and myself. Jarus and Moira hit it off particularly well."

"Aaand?" Garrick pried.

"They dated seriously, but only for a short time. They began to butt heads and, you see . . . it didn't end well. Quite bitterly, in fact." Mr. Darrow leaned back in his chair, his hands propped behind his head. "Moira and Jarus were both too brilliant for their own good. Their ingenuity and individuality were always the source of their disagreements. They had such different views of the Mystic realm—still do, for that matter. But there now, look at me, rambling on about failed romances and the like."

As if on cue, a dog bellowed from outside, followed by a rapping at the service door.

"Aye, come in!" Mr. Darrow shouted.

Brotus and Saladin belted into the kitchen, their sleek coats dripping with rain. Grandmother Meriweather followed, equally as wet.

"Oh, hello Mum. Did you walk all the way here?" Mr. Darrow chastised.

"Yeah, so I did. What's it to yeh? It's nice te see yeh too, by the way," Grandmother Meriweather replied, her lips tight.

"Mum . . ." Mr. Darrow nudged. "You really shouldn't be out alone after dark, regardless of the lifted restrictions."

"Yeh, all right, son. I hear yeh." Grandmother Meriweather scanned the kitchen like a raccoon on the prowl. "I'm missing meh teeth, have yeh seen them?" She put her hand over her mouth to cover the absence of her misplaced chompers. Monte snorted back a laugh.

"Your teeth, Meri?" Mrs. Darrow asked. The corner of her mouth twitched.

"Yeh, meh dentures. Can't find 'em anywhere. Must've left 'em 'ere last night." Grandmother Meriweather rummaged through the cupboards, her speech muffled and slurred.

"And you're just realizing this now?" Mr. Darrow asked.

"Well, I live by mysel' in case yeh forgot. Not exactly in the company of anyone that could remind me about 'em." Her voice was heavy with sarcasm. "No, Esca. I noticed they were missing this morning when I tried te eat meh cheese toasty."

"Then why didn't you come over first thing?" Mr. Darrow asked. "While the sun was still up," he added, under his breath.

"Been busy with the planning of meh annual fairy ball. Yeh bairns are coming, aye?"

"Of course, Gran," Garrick said.

"Good!" Grandmother Meriweather smiled, showing off her gums.

Monte suppressed a giggle.

"And Monte, make sure yeh invite those pals of yers. Finn, and that sweet lass, Cameron," Grandmother Meriweather said. She peeked inside the toaster oven.

*Sure thing,* Monte thought. *If I can even find her.*

"You're pretty sure your teeth are somewhere here in the kitchen, then?" Garrick asked as Grandmother Meriweather ran her foot underneath the gap between the floor and the cupboard.

"Almost certain of it," Grandmother Meriweather replied. She strutted to the planted pot by the sink. "This thing needs watering again," she said, delicately tapping the leaves. "Aha!" Her face broke into a triumphant smile, revealing her toothless grin once again as she plucked something from the base of the pot.

"Jivens Crivens, Mother, your teeth!" Mr. Darrow exclaimed. "Why were they in there?"

Monte chortled out loud, the laugh finally escaping. He looked at Garrick, who joined him in a chuckling duet.

"Well, obviously I'm the only person that keeps this plant alive," Grandmother Meriweather said. "Yeh lot are all useless—haven't got a green thumb between yeh. I took meh teeth out when I was over for supper last night and must've used the glass they were soaking in te water the plant. Dear me, I do forget about these sorts of things."

Laughter erupted through the kitchen. Monte clutched his cramping sides.

"Honestly, Mother. What're we going to do with you?" Mr. Darrow asked, his face red with laughter.

Monte wiped tears from his eyes. Everyone seemed genuinely happy for once, including Garrick. He looked down at his arm. The wounds, still healing, tingled slightly as he ran his fingers across his sleeve. He wondered if the seashell really was just a chameleon fossil. Deep down, he knew it was harmless. It had to be. It had saved his life, after all.

CHAPTER 13
Cat's Out of the Bag

The air was unusually warm for a November evening, at least by Scottish standards. Clouds, heavy and dark, hung in the evening sky like great ships in a black sea.

"We'll definitely be getting some rain," Mr. Darrow said as the family walked through the parking lot toward the Fort William Sports Arena.

"I wonder if Garrick's any good at rugby," Monte said as hordes of people flocked into the arena. "This kinda looks like a big deal."

"He'll do fine, I'm sure," Mrs. Darrow said. "Remember all of the football madness back in the States? He excelled above and beyond all expectations—most especially when he was under high pressure." Her face beamed with the memories.

"Rugby's loads of fun," Finn said. "Much better than Yankee football."

"Are you talking smack on my country?" Monte asked.

"Maybe," Finn said with a crooked grin. "But smack or no smack, Garrick's team is gonna win tonight."

"Really?" Monte asked, amused. "How's that?"

"I found a four-leaf clover in the back garden this morning." Finn patted his pocket. "We have luck on our side."

"Not if you used it all in getting yourself here," Monte said. "I can't believe your nanny actually let you come tonight."

Finn shrugged.

*Especially with my cursed arm*, Monte thought.

"Ho, yeh guys! Over here!" Uncle Jarus waved to them from a set of bleachers.

"Aye, Jarus!" Mr. Darrow said. He cleared a path through the crowd with his large frame as they filtered further into the stadium.

"Reserved us some spots." Uncle Jarus motioned to a row of sideline seats.

"Cheers, mate," Mr. Darrow said as they climbed several steps to their designated row. "This is excellent. Middle of the pitch and everything."

"Too right, it is." Finn sidled down the row with the skill of a bird on a clothesline.

Monte followed, feeling far less graceful as he carefully stepped along the narrow bleacher.

"Oh . . ." a familiar voice warbled.

Monte froze in his tracks, dread soaking through him. He knew that voice.

"Are you all joining us?" the voice asked.

Monte slowly looked up to see Babs Campbell, the assistant headmistress of Strathmartine Academy, tottering across the row toward them. "What's she doing here?" he whispered to Finn.

"Hush, Monte." Uncle Jarus shot a warning glance over his shoulder. "Babs always supports the annual rugby match."

Monte sighed loudly as Babs plunked herself into the best spot in the row. She shifted on her bottom like a cow bedding down for the night, her hair as big and as bushy as wild heather.

"Good evening, Master Darrow." Babs's voice was stiff. She seemed just as pleased to see Monte as he was to see her.

Monte grunted, forcing Finn to sit between himself and Babs.

"The teams haven't come out yet, I take it?" Mrs. Darrow asked as she and Mr. Darrow squeezed past Babs.

"No, they haven't. Exciting, isn't it?" Uncle Jarus rubbed his hands together. "It's going te be brilliant. This is the most anticipated event of the school year."

"Ha-looo!" a female voice boomed through the speakers.

A thrill of energy spread through the crowd.

"Are we ready for some *rugby*?" the voice bellowed.

The crowd erupted into a chorus of cheers.

Babs jumped to her feet and let out a boisterous whoop. Mrs. Darrow startled at the sound. She fished around her pocket and pulled out a set of ear plugs. Monte was sorry that his mother was stuck next to Babs, but not sorry enough to move. Mrs. Darrow twisted the plugs into her ears and then gave her son a wink.

"Tonight, we bring you a lovely match," the commentator continued, her voice doused with enthusiasm. "A great line-up between the Broughty Toads and the Strathmartine Panthers!"

More cheers and whistles filled the air.

"And here they come, folks. The Broughty Toads! Let's give them a warm welcome, shall we?"

The Toads' section lit up with golden banners and flags as the team—wearing yellow and khaki-colored uniforms—thundered onto the pitch.

One of the players faced the crowd and pumped his fists in the air. Even from across the field it was clear that he was the star of the team, his biceps bulging from underneath his jersey, his calves rippling as he jumped up and down. He kissed his fingers and stretched his arm to the stands. A small section of teenage girls flew into a frenzy of screams.

"Who's that?" Monte shouted through the noise.

"That . . . is Scotty Boyles," Uncle Jarus replied. "But everybody calls him the Tractor."

"Is he a big deal or something?" Monte asked.

"Aye," Uncle Jarus replied. "He plays in the private league. First in the division, and only sixteen years old."

"And I thought Garrick was the mammoth," Monte exclaimed.

"What a peacock." Finn's white eyelashes fluttered into a scowl as Scotty Boyles continued to pump his fists in the air.

"Agreed," Monte said. "I hope Garrick runs him into the ground."

The commentator's voice boomed, "Now, let's bring out the champions of last year's match: the Strathmartine Paaanthers!"

The crowd exploded into a roar as the Panthers, in their slick black uniforms with purple trim, charged onto the pitch.

"There's Garrick! Number three!" Monte cheered as Garrick sped onto the field.

"Go Garrick!" Babs shrieked. Her hair bobbed in one large bundle as she jumped up and down.

The Panthers formed a huddle. They stomped their feet, swaying side to side. The marching grew faster. The cluster tightened. With one final cheer, the team broke apart and pounded onto the field.

"That's right, laddies!" Babs yelled. She batted her mittens together. Her hood flopped against her back, the fake fur trim dancing like a deranged ferret.

Monte cringed, wondering if his mom had any more ear plugs. Scotty Boyles made a fist with one of his hands and punched it into the other as he strutted across the field. Monte massaged his own knuckles together, eager to see Garrick pummel the Tractor.

"And here we go!" the commentator belted. The crowd thundered with anticipation as the teams took their starting positions. "The Panthers kick off to the Toads . . . and that's the start of the game!"

"So, what happens when someone scores a touchdown?" Monte yelled as the Toads zigzagged the ball down the field.

"It's called a try, which means the team that scored gets five points," Uncle Jarus explained through the noise. "Once a try is scored, the team has a chance te gain two conversion points by kicking the ball through the opponent's goalpost."

As though dictated by Uncle Jarus's narration, the Toads passed the ball to Scotty Boyles who touched it down inside the goal.

"Tryyy!" the commentator exploded through the speakers. "That's a try for the Toads and our first points of the match!"

"Ah, really now!" Babs shouted as Scotty Boyles paraded around the pitch.

*Yeah, get it together,* Monte silently agreed.

"C'mon, yeh Panthers!" Uncle Jarus cheered. "Block the conversion!"

"And the Toads score the conversion points!" The commentator yelled as the kicker sent the ball sailing between the goalposts.

"Ugh," Monte glowered.

"Here we go," the commentator proceeded. "The Panthers are in possession of the ball. Passed to Darrow, number three. And look at him go. Astounding peripheral vision, folks."

The entire row jumped to their feet. "Go, Garrick!" Monte screeched.

"Ball thrown wide. Got loads of players over on the left-hand side," the commentator continued. "To Snee, to McLellan, the twenty-meter line, the ten . . ."

The Panthers weaved rapidly through their opponents' formation, black blurs against the green turf and gold Toads.

"Passed off to Darrow again . . . and a try! Darrow scores a try!"

The crowd cheered wildly, Mr. Darrow even louder than Babs.

"Yaaas!" Monte yelled as Garrick spotted the Darrow fan club from the field. He raised his hands in celebration.

Finn pulled a wilted four-leaf clover from his pocket. "Told ya!" He waggled it in front of Monte's face.

"And here we go again, everyone. Uh-oh, free ball. No one has possession of the ball! The referee calls for a pause. This will likely be a scrum."

"A scrum?" Monte asked.

But nobody answered. Everyone was too engaged in the game. He watched as each team fought to gain possession of the ball.

"And here it is, the scrum," the commentator continued as the players moved in one large mass, the ball tangled somewhere in their web of feet.

"The ball is still in there . . . no, it's loose! Toads with possession! Number twenty is away with it. He's away! A flick pass—oh *my*, Darrow with an interception!"

The Panthers' fans roared victoriously. Babs whooped again, her voice cracking.

*Maybe she'll go hoarse*, Monte thought, his excitement surging.

"What a handful young Darrow has turned into tonight," the commentator bellowed. "And there he goes. Boyles is after him. Boyles is after him!"

Monte held his breath and watched as the Tractor closed in on Garrick. A clap of thunder rumbled through the sky as the pair collided.

"And Darrow is down, but not before he sneaks the ball away to Montague, who's sliding to get back into line!"

Scotty Boyles lingered over Garrick. He pressed him into the turf with his gigantic knee, a snarl smeared across his face.

"Ah, ya scumbag!" Finn shouted. "Penalty! That's a penalty!"

Boyles shoved Garrick across the turf and then sped off down the pitch. Garrick sprung up and tore after him, a panther pursuing its prey.

"Shake it off, Garrick!" Mr. Darrow shouted from the sideline.

"The Panthers are heavily guarded. They're in a tight spot. The ball is sent back. Oh! Dropped by McLellan. The Toads regain it!"

Panthers fans groaned. Monte stared across the pitch at the Toads' fan section as another round of thunder sounded from above. Something colorful flickered in and out of view amongst the sea of gold spectators. Rainbow lights. "Cameron?" Monte whispered as the world grew quiet around him. The lights disappeared. He rubbed his eyes. "Where'd they go?" he thought out loud.

A tap on Monte's shoulder pulled him back into reality. He jumped, his mouth dropping as Moira Bryce smiled down at him. Her golden locks fell past her shoulders, her face framed beneath a woolen hood trimmed in fluffy white fur.

"What're you doing here?" The words escaped Monte's mouth before he could think.

"Nice to see you too, Master Monte," Moira said with a laugh. She looked like an Elven queen. "Is that your brother? Number three, for the Panthers?" Her voice spread smoothly through the rumble of the crowd as she motioned to the field.

"Uh, yeah. That's Garrick."

"My, he's good. What a beast of a lad."

"Who's the pretty lady?" Finn said, gawking at Moira.

"Not now." Monte elbowed Finn.

"Moira?" Uncle Jarus said, the enthusiasm draining from his face.

"Hello, Jarus." Moira stiffened, her voice suddenly hollow.

"Stewart gives it to Darrow who dives in to score!" the commentator's voice rebounded through the arena.

"Moira Bryce?" Finn shouted through the rumbling spectators, his eyes like emerald jewels. "The cat sith lady?"

"Er, pardon me," Uncle Jarus mumbled as he got to his feet. "I'm in need of a walk," he said, stumbling down the bleachers.

"Oh . . ." Babs quavered as Uncle Jarus hastily picked his way through the disgruntled fans. She surveyed Moira with her buggy eyes. "Is this your friend, Monte?"

"What's that?" Monte asked, forgetting his annoyance with Babs.

Babs continued to goggle at Moira.

"Oh, yeah. She's a family friend," Monte said, suddenly extra proud to be associated with the likes of Moira Bryce.

Lightning streaked across the clouds. A round of thunder clapped through the sky, clamoring over the noise of the crowd. Moira peered down at the pitch, her attention fixated on Garrick.

"Did you really catch the cat sith?" Finn inched closer to the stately woman.

Moira cocked her head, her attention shifting back to the bleachers. "Aye, I did." Her face softened. "And who might you be?"

"I'm Finn Cornelius Smith," he said, offering Moira his hand.

"And so you are." Moira smiled. She extended her own hand, which was clothed in a green leather glove. A line of amber pearls that matched the color of her eyes studded the smooth material. "It's a pleasure, Master Finn."

"Moira?" Mr. Darrow shouted across the row, suddenly aware of his colleague's presence. A whistle rang across the pitch, signaling the end of the first half. "Nothing's happened, surely?" He scooted across the bleacher, nearly tripping over Babs. "Excuse me, lads," he said as he shouldered past Monte and Finn. Mrs. Darrow followed, her face pinched with concern.

"No, no," Moira reassured them. "All is well. I only stopped by to deliver this week's reports." She handed over what appeared to be a deck of cards.

"Official IMB notes," Monte whispered to Finn, shocked that Moira displayed the forms so openly.

"Crikey, Moira." Mr. Darrow snatched the notes. "A wee bit more discretion, will you?"

"Oh Esca, stop." Moira tugged at her gloves, pulling the leather tighter around her fingers. "These aren't confidential notes. Simply some reports I thought you might want to look over before returning to the Ben. You know . . ." She leaned in closer. "Since we're about to wrap up the cat sith case."

"Indeed, yes. But you really didn't have to come all this way," Mr. Darrow said as he secured the notes inside his jacket.

"It was no bother, really," Moira said, staring down at Garrick. "Quite a sturdy lad, isn't he? Your Garrick."

"Ah, yes," Mrs. Darrow said, flashing a suspicious look. "He's getting lots of playing time tonight, too."

"So I noticed," Moira said over the buzz of the crowd, her gaze unfaltering.

"I think Garrick's got himself an admirer," Finn whispered in Monte's ear, voicing what everyone else was thinking.

"The referee turns over the ball, and the second half begins!" the commentator bellowed over the crowd as the players sprang into action.

"We've appreciated you taking over, Moira, while we've stayed closer to our boys this past little while," Mrs. Darrow said over the noise.

"It's been my pleasure, Vanessa," Moira said, sounding almost bored. "Nothing to it, really, when all's said and done."

Mrs. Darrow's lips formed a tight smile as Babs, still seated and out of ear shot, peeked around her.

"Things have run like clockwork," Moira continued. "Everything is lining up superbly." Suddenly, her face froze. In unison, Moira, Vanessa, and Esca rummaged through their pockets, all of them pulling out their telestones, official property of the IMB, magical communication devices used by Mystic investigators during times of urgency. Moira examined hers first: a flat, sleek slab of rock. Monte had only seen his parents consult theirs on one other occasion.

"We're needed on the site," Moira said.

"Aye, immediately," Mr. Darrow agreed. He stared down at his telestone as though he didn't believe the information he was receiving. "Trouble," he said.

"Another cat sith . . ." Mrs. Darrow read.

"At the foot of the Ben," Moira completed the sentence.

Mrs. Darrow hugged Monte. "I'm so sorry, but it's an emergency. Your uncle and Maren will look after you, as always. We'll be back as soon as we can."

"Right." Monte squirmed out of his mother's tight embrace. "We'll be fine."

Mr. Darrow clapped his hand over Monte's shoulder. His face was all business as he brushed past with a nod.

"Be good." Mrs. Darrow ruffled Monte's hair.

Monte watched as the adults shuffled away, his father's large figure eventually disappearing amongst the spectators below.

"You don't think there's really another cat sith, do you?" Finn leaned toward Monte, making certain Babs was out of earshot.

"I dunno," Monte said, distracted. "Say Finn, do you see anything odd over there, in the Toads' fan section?" He squinted across the field again.

"Like what?" Finn asked.

"I thought I saw something earlier." Monte scanned the crowd. "I think it was Cameron's rainbow lights."

"Ack, come off it, mate," Finn said as the players dashed around the field. "There's no way she's here. Honestly, I think that girl has put a spell on you."

Monte huffed. "She has not."

"Whatever you say." Finn wore a steady expression. "Anyway, what're you up to tomorrow night?"

"Nothing," Monte said. *Now that my parents are gone again,* he thought to himself, careful not to let his disappointment show. *This cat sith hype is really getting out of control.*

"Meet me in my nanny's back garden around half-nine tomorrow night," Finn said.

"Why?"

"I wanna show you something." A smile crept across Finn's face. "Something that'll make you forget all about cat siths."

CHAPTER 14
Brooms and Goons

Monte traipsed toward the rear of the Widow Smith's property, careful to keep a safe distance between himself and the cottage. He blew warm air into his hands, grateful that he had worn thick boots and his heaviest coat, yet sorry that he had left his gloves behind. Hazy clouds stretched through the sky. They sheltered the light of the moon and stars, casting shadows upon the fields. A row of meticulously trimmed shrubs served as a divider between the Widow's back garden and the wild field from which Monte trudged. *I wonder what Finn could be up to now*, he thought as he closed in on the garden. He jumped, caught off-guard, as Finn himself popped up on the other side of the hedge.

"Argh!" Monte fumbled for the flashlight in his coat.

"'Sake, keep it down," Finn buzzed as he adjusted a woolen cap with large ear flaps over his head. "And don't turn that thing on." He pointed at the flashlight.

"Sorry." Monte stowed the flashlight away. "But what do you expect me to do when a little garden maggot pops up out of nowhere?"

Finn smirked and beckoned Monte closer with a mittened hand. "Nanny took a heavy dose of cold medicine about an hour ago. That'll be her knackered until morning. You bring the stuff?"

"Yeah." Monte squeezed through a break in the bushes. He pulled Grandmother Meriweather's madgers from around his neck for Finn to see.

"Brilliant." Finn led them toward a ramshackle shed in the back corner of the garden. "And what about the other thing?"

"Oh, right." Monte fished through his pockets until he found the candy bar he had promised.

"Thanks, mate. My favorite kind as well." Finn snatched the chocolate from Monte.

"Your nanny feeds you, right?"

"Aye, but nothing like this." Finn held the candy bar up to his nose. "Aaah," he sighed. He slipped the treat into the chest pocket of his form-fitting coat. Complete with matching hat and mittens, the ensemble gave him the appearance of a woodland pixie doll. "Well, let's hurry then. We don't have all night." He flicked on the old shed's outside light. A musty yellow brightness spread across the muddy earth as he pranced around to the back. Monte followed, curious. "Look what I found." Finn pawed through a patch of odd-looking plants with spiny leaves and prickly bulbs the size of apples.

"Scotch thistle?" Monte asked, confused as to why the shrub—one of Scotland's most common flowers—was so special.

"Not the flowers, you eejit." Finn pulled something that resembled a smooth, shiny tree branch from the shrubs. "This."

"What is it?" Monte's breath froze in front of him.

Finn handed the branch to Monte, his eyes shining against the shed's dingy lamp. Monte wrapped his fingers around the branch, surprised at how light the wood felt. Warmth swelled in his palms. Something poked against his leg—twiggy bristles at the end of the long stem. It wasn't a tree branch at all.

"A broomstick?" Monte rolled the stem in his hands. It remained warm despite the frigid night air.

Finn nodded, his face eager and expectant.

"Who's is it? Where'd it come from?" Monte asked.

"It's Cousin B's."

"Who's Cousin B again?"

"You know, my legal guardian?" Finn said, as though that would jog Monte's memory. "His work keeps him away most of the time so that's why I stay here with Nanny."

A wave of realization rolled over Monte. "Oh, right. You've mentioned him before. I didn't know he was your legal guardian though."

"Didn't feel the need to say anything." Finn kicked against the mushy grass. "I saw Cousin B hide the broomstick out here the last time he visited. I was just gonna leave it alone but then I met you and . . ."

"And what?"

"I think you can make it fly."

"What do you mean? Doesn't it float on its own?" Monte stretched the broomstick out in front of him.

Finn shook his head. "It's the Mystic that makes a broom fly, not the broomstick itself. And it takes talent. Like what you have."

"Like what I have?" Monte snorted in amusement. He had never ridden a real broomstick before, nor did he know anyone who could. Broom travel wasn't very common in the States.

"Aye, I think there's a good chance that you can." Finn took the broomstick from Monte. He propped it upwards. The stem extended a good two feet above his head. "You're different from other Mystics. The same kind of different as Cousin B."

Monte grabbed the broomstick from Finn and squeezed his fingers around the handle. Warmth surged through his hands again, tingling in his fingertips. It was an energy not unlike what he had felt in Salem and again at Hibernian Field with the seashell. The broomstick began to buzz. A soft but lively hum emanated from its core. Monte tightened his grip as the sleek stem of wood tugged him forward. "Yikes!" he exclaimed as it shot from his hands. The broom tilted so that it was parallel to the ground, hovering steadily in front of him, no higher than his hip.

"Oh, aye! That's dynamite." Finn beat his hands together in an eruption of glee. "Let's ride it!" he said, darting into the shed.

"What? Are you crazy?" Monte followed him, leaving the broomstick to float mysteriously on its own. The smell of paint and mildew permeated the air as Finn rummaged through a wooden crate.

"The broomstick is big enough for two people, and I don't even count as a whole person." Finn pulled a familiar-looking goggle device from the crate. Madgers.

"Whose are those?" Monte clasped at his own madgers.

"Cousin B's, of course." Finn pulled the device around his head. The lenses looked ridiculous against his narrow face. "What're you waiting for? Put yours on."

"Are you kidding me? My parents already have me on high-watch as it is," Monte exclaimed. But Finn was already back outside and hopping onto the broomstick. "I won't live until my next birthday if I break the rules again, and this is definitely not allowed. The broom zoomed toward Monte. "Whoa!" he shouted as it knocked him in the knees, scooping him from the ground before he knew what was happening.

"Finn, cut it out!" Monte's legs straddled the stem as the broom slowly inched upward. He hugged his arms awkwardly around the handle.

"It's not me," Finn said from behind. "It's the broom. It's connecting with you."

"We've gotta get off this thing." Monte tried to swing his leg over the handle, but the broom sailed upwards. A yell lodged in his throat as air gushed past them.

"Quick!" Finn shouted from behind. "Say something to it!"

"I can't! I don't know how." Monte gripped the handle. Warmth pulsed through his palms and into the broomstick. Slowly, they came to a halt.

"Whew," Finn exclaimed. "You're a natural. And look at that view, will ya?"

Monte widened his eyes, suddenly aware that he was squinting. "I can't see much of anything," he said, his voice shaky.

"Your madgers," Finn said.

Awkwardly, and with one hand, Monte strapped his madgers over his eyes. He clicked the dial at his temple. His eyesight sharpened as the night vision was activated. He raised his marked hand in front of him. The swirly symbols on his palm shimmered eerily in the greenish light. He took a deep breath and dared a peek at the world below.

Thickets, and expansive fields dotted with tiny lights, winked back at him. A car inched along the main road. It seemed to move much slower at this altitude. Monte guessed they were several stories up, maybe ten to twelve. In front of them, shrouded in a halo of thick mist, was Ben Nevis—majestic and foreboding, the master of the land. He shivered, remembering that his parents were somewhere in that mountain of darkness and mystery.

"Pretty cool, aye?" Finn whispered.

"Yeah," Monte admitted, his confidence building. "But I'm gonna be so busted if the parentals or the IMB find out about this."

"No, you won't." The broomstick tottered as Finn shifted his weight around.

"How's that?" Monte asked.

"Because they won't find out. This is Cousin B's broom, and he gets special clearance, thanks to his job."

"So?" Monte asked as the energy from the broomstick warmed his hands. The powerful connection grew stronger with each passing second.

"So, the IMB can't track it," Finn said.

"Well . . ." A gentle vibration traveled up Monte's arms. He willed his body to relax, enticing the power to flow into his chest. Heat swelled in his torso.

Suddenly, they whizzed upward, the damp air whistling around his ears. Finn clutched him from behind, his grip surprisingly strong. Monte twisted his hands around the broomstick, his legs curling backward as they zoomed to a halt.

"Oi!" Finn tightened his death-grip on Monte. "Get a handle on this thing, will ya?"

"Oh-aye," Monte said, sarcastically. "It's not like this is my first time flying a broom or anything."

"Fair point." Finn loosened his hold.

"All right," Monte resolved. The damp air nipped at his face, but his hands remained toasty. "Let's do this." He bent into the broom. They pelted forward, this time with more poise, as they skimmed through the clouds. The Caledonian Canal snaked below them, the moon's mottled reflection shining up from the water below.

Monte tilted further into the broomstick as they reached the main motorway, sending them into a downward trajectory. Finn yelled in delight. His voice fizzled into the torrents of wind on either side of them. The motorway, growing closer, was dark and desolate save for the stream of road markers gleaming up from the asphalt, the colors somehow vibrant despite the lack of light below. Monte guided the broomstick lower, wondering if their speed could rival a car. He smiled at the thought.

"Monte, ahead of you!" Finn screeched in his ear.

Monte looked up to see an automobile, its headlights still pinholes against the darkness, racing toward them. He yanked on the broomstick. They swerved out of control, sinking lower and lower. Monte's feet scraped against the pavement as they hurtled for the oncoming car.

"We're gonna crash!" Finn squealed, his body molding into Monte's back.

Monte fumbled with the handle, his hands slippery with sweat. He pulled upward, propelling them into an uncontrollable arc. "Nooo!" he shouted as they descended upon the car once again. The vehicle swerved in a rapid serpentine motion, its horn wailing a final warning. Monte felt heat surge through his palms and into his chest. He tugged on the handle for a third time. His boots jutted over the car's hood as it whooshed beneath them, the smell of burnt rubber smoldering in the air. The boys clutched the broom as they bolted into the clouds, the car's Horn of Death still resounding in Monte's ears.

"I'm pretty sure you're trying to kill me," Finn said as they slowed to a cruising speed above the foggy veil.

"Sorry." Monte quivered as he tried to regain a steady breathing pattern. "The broomstick . . . it just went berserk."

"Too right, it did."

"It's touchy, okay?" Monte said, feeling defensive as they brushed over the town below. He wished desperately for a cold drink to extinguish the fire burning in his chest.

They floated toward the local market. Its parking lot was vacant save for a couple of teenagers standing at the side of the building. A young man and a young woman. The girl rested her back against the wall. The boy faced her, his hands interlocked with hers. Monte squinted at them, his hands shaky as he tried to keep the broomstick from catapulting downward. The boy combed his fingers through his hair and then placed his hands on the wall above the girl.

"Garrick?" Monte whispered in disbelief.

"Are they about to snog?" Finn hissed as Garrick leaned toward the girl.

"Snog?" Monte asked. "You mean kiss?"

"Oh aye, they're gonna," Finn squeaked as Garrick pressed his lips against the girl's mouth.

"Ah, sick! Monte griped.

"It's a snog-fest!"

Monte groaned. "Let's get out of here." He wasn't about to watch his brother suck the lips off a girl, no matter how shook up and unable to fly he felt.

They zoomed away from the market as fast as Monte dared. The remaining adrenaline oozed from his body as bountiful shrubbery and rolling mounds zipped beneath them. The image of Garrick smooching that girl replayed in his head and a knot formed in his gut. It wasn't envy. Far from it. Rather, he was annoyed with his brother. He missed their camaraderie—the jokes, the fun, the play. Scotland had turned Garrick into some sort of moody, distant troll. One that cared more about girls than anything else. Though Monte would never admit it, he missed the old Garrick.

The low-lying clouds seeped through a cluster of trees below them. Suddenly, Monte recognized where they were, the border of Hibernian Field. The knot in his stomach tightened as they inched through the murky night toward the overgrown soccer pitch. They slowed to a stop. Something twinkled in the corner of Monte's eye. "Whoa!" He squeezed his eyelids open and shut.

"What?" Finn asked. "You've never seen two people snog before?"

"No, not that. Look!" Monte pointed to a rainbow of luminescent colors on the field. He homed in his vision with the dial on the madgers. *Cameron?*

"I see it," Finn whispered loudly. "Oh no." He pointed to the rusty goalpost where a handful of figures were congregated.

It was the group of goons from Halloween, dark boulders in the thick fog. They shifted about, their voices muffled and disgruntled. In the center of it all stood Cameron, the rainbow lights flashing around her neck.

"No." Monte's hands nearly slipped from the broomstick. "She can't be . . . with them."

"Where do yeh think yer going?" Mohawk shouted, his voice surprisingly clear as Cameron tumbled from the pack.

"Aye," No-Neck said. "There's still business te conduct."

Cameron slowly inched backward, her face like stone.

Monte's breath grew shallow. It was Halloween night all over again. Except this time, he didn't have a wand. Or the seashell. And this time, the goons were after Cameron. Without further thought he plunged the broomstick downward. They dashed toward the pack, clipping No-Neck in the head before shooting back into the clouds.

"Wha' was that?" Shaggy yelled as No-Neck crumpled into a discombobulated heap beside him.

"Here we go again," Monte warned Finn as he pelted for the goons. He swooped down, sending Mohawk and two others to the ground before disappearing once more into the fog.

"Oi!" Shaggy roared. "You!" His voice bled with aggression as he stomped toward Cameron. "Yeh stop with the magic tricks this minute, yeh hear?"

Cameron yelled as he grabbed her by the wrist. "Get your grubby hands off me!" She strained against his grasp, her thin limbs no match for his stocky build.

*Oh, no you don't!* Monte thought as he zoomed toward the struggling pair.

"I've got him!" Finn pinged Shaggy on the side of the head.

Monte swung the broom around, this time keeping it low as he flew for the cluster of trees.

"Maggots!" one of the goons swore as they whizzed past.

They came to a halt inside the thicket, safely concealed by fog and trees. The broom bobbed unsteadily as they dismounted.

"Stay here," Monte ordered, shoving the broom at Finn. "And hold this."

"Never. I'm coming with you," Finn demanded, his pointy chin defiant, his pale face as silvery as the moon.

Monte tore the madgers from his face, his eyesight suddenly dim without the help of the night vision. He could hear the goons arguing through the trees. He brought a finger to his lips, gesturing for Finn to stay behind with the broomstick. His boots crunched through the dead twigs and mulch as he stepped from the tree line and into the dense fog that coated the field.

"Whoever yeh are, stay back or I'll whoop yeh!" No-Neck pressed his meaty hand against his head, apparently still feeling the blow.

Monte plowed forward. He swallowed his pounding heart.

"I said stay back!" No-Neck warned.

"Let her go," Monte demanded, surprised by the power in his voice. The goons materialized in front of him, hobgoblins in a sea of fog.

"Monte?" Cameron continued to pull against the goon's grasp.

"Hold the phone," No-Neck said. "It's that freaky bloke from Halloween! The one wi' the firecrackers."

"Oi, you!" Mohawk staggered forward. "No big brother here te protect yeh this time, aye?"

Laughter rippled through the cluster of goons.

"Let my friend go," Monte said, his chest fiery.

"Oh . . . I'm sorry," Shaggy replied. "I did'nae realize that this fine young bird was yer girlfriend."

Cameron squealed with displeasure as Shaggy tightened his hold.

"You're making a big mistake." Monte continued to plod forward. His eyes were almost completely adjusted to the darkness now. "I'm warning you. Let her go or—"

"Or what? Eh?" No-Neck stomped his feet. "This lassie owes us. She's no' holding up her end o' the deal."

"If you don't release her, I'll hex you!" Finn's voice swam through the fog.

Monte paused, the sound of Finn's footsteps barely noticeable as he padded from behind. Mist curled around his pixie-like frame as he stopped at Monte's side, his face free of Cousin B's oversized madgers.

"Oh-ho! The freak show really has begun," Mohawk sneered. "Sorry, no candy bars te steal te night, fairy-boy!"

"Aye." No-Neck shuffled forward, cracking his knuckles. "I think it's time we stopped these freaks, once and for all."

Monte flexed his fingers, filled with anticipation as the goons inched closer.

"Ready, boys?" Mohawk snarled. "On my count; one . . . two . . ." All at once, confusion washed over his face. Even in the gloom, Monte could tell that something was wrong.

"I . . . need te go home." Mohawk staggered backward. "I should'nae be here."

"Aye, me too," Shaggy muttered. He released his hold on Cameron and brought his hand to his forehead.

"Have yeh both gone mad?" one of the smaller goons spat. "Don't let her go. We can take 'em."

Cameron stood very still, rigid and barely visible as the fog embraced her legs. *Why doesn't she run?* Monte wondered.

No-Neck cowered in the dense fog and then grabbed his head and groaned. "What are yeh freaks playin' at?"

"I'm outta 'ere!" Mohawk vanished into the mist.

"Aye!" Shaggy scampered after his accomplice.

The rest of the goons followed, dispersing into the fog like large, clumsy bats.

"What just happened?" Finn asked.

"No clue." Monte rubbed his hands together. His fingers were cold. No magic remained. Oddly, the smell of cake wafted through the mist, as if someone was baking nearby. *White cake. Or maybe vanilla? Weird.*

Cameron's shoulders heaved up and down as she pressed her fingers to her temples.

"It was you, wasn't it?" Finn thrust a slender finger at Cameron.

"Stay away from me." Her voice was shaky and full of warning.

"What are you talking about, Finn?" Monte demanded.

"She stopped those goons." Finn advanced toward Cameron. "She's a Mystic, I can tell."

Cameron's eyes shifted from Finn to Monte. "I didn't want to do it." She sounded like she was about to cry.

"What's wrong with her?" Finn asked.

"Hush, Finn." Monte raised his hands for silence, scared that Cameron might run away again. He wasn't going to lose her this time. "Is Finn right?" he tried to keep his voice quiet. "Are you . . . a Mystic?"

Cameron brushed a stray tear from her face. She nodded her head in confirmation, bathed in apprehension.

"Then why'd you say you weren't?" Monte tried to keep his voice gentle.

"Does it really matter what I said?" Cameron replied, a hint of guilt in her voice.

"Hey, I hate to break up the banter," Finn interjected, "but I think we have a visitor."

A car's engine rumbled through the firs at the other end of the field. The vehicle screeched to a stop, its blue and yellow lights painting stripes through the trees.

"It's the polis," Finn said.

"Run!" Monte seized Cameron's wrist. The madgers banged against his collarbone as the trio darted into the thicket.

"Hey, yeh skivers!" a familiar voice shouted after them. It was McTavish. "Get back here!"

The threesome tore into the trees. Monte skidded to a halt, heat swelling in his palms as he grabbed Cousin B's broom. He swung his leg over the stem. "Get on," he yelled. Finn sprung on behind him, but Cameron stood planted in place, her face a mixture of bewilderment and alarm. A beam of light broke through the trees as McTavish approached. "C'mon," Monte pleaded with Cameron. "You have to trust me."

"Hold it right there!" McTavish shouted after them.

Monte strapped the madgers over his eyes and reached for Cameron, who staggered onto the broom in front of him. Monte stretched his arms around her and pulled on the handle, McTavish's light shooting after them as they raced through the trees and into the cloudy night. Up and up they climbed, never slowing until Monte was sure they were past the limits of human visibility.

CHAPTER 15
Clover Crystals and Fairy Piksels

Monte, Finn, and Cameron laid out their buffet of hot chocolate, doughnuts, potato chips, and other petrol station savories across the dirty floorboards of the Widow Smith's shed—all well-deserved prizes after their close encounter with the goons and McTavish. Monte, the only one with pocket money, was happy to treat his friends to a feast. He rested his back against a heap of musty woolen blankets, his muscles finally loose. He wondered if McTavish was still looking for them.

The shed was as cozy on the inside as it was tattered on the outside. Save for a smattering of garden soil and some moss patches on the walls, it was a suitable refuge. They sat cross-legged on the floor, warmed by a trinket Finn called his firelog, a petrified chunk of wood that worked like a radiator. Apparently, it was one of the only Mystic items the Widow Smith allowed in the house.

Cameron chomped on a pre-packaged egg salad sandwich. The light from Finn's plastic lantern cast playful shadows across her slender features. A thin golden chain glinted around her wrist as she reached for her third bag of potato chips—crisps, as Finn called them.

"Gee whiz, when was the last time you had a proper meal?" Monte braved asking.

Cameron looked up at him mid-swallow. "Been a couple of days, I think."

"That long?"

"I get snacks when I can," she replied, as though it was the most common thing in the world.

Monte wrapped his fingers around his hot chocolate cup, unsure of what to say.

"So, what'd those goons want, anyway?" Finn asked.

Cameron responded with a blank stare.

"They were acting like you did something to them?" Finn pressed.

Cameron buttoned up. Monte held his breath, glad that he wasn't the one asking the questions. It hadn't taken long to learn that silent-Cameron was far more perplexing than was talkative-Cameron.

"Clover crystals," Cameron finally said. She fingered the rainbow lights around her neck.

"Clover crystals?" Monte asked.

"You mean like leprechaun money?" Finn's eyes brightened.

"Yes." Cameron nodded. "And sometimes fairy piksels if I can find them. But they're harder to locate, especially lately."

"Where do you look for them?" Finn asked excitedly.

"Wait, pause." Monte held his hands up. "What're you guys talking about?"

Finn leaned forward, his eyebrows arched high. "Clover crystals and fairy piksels, mate. They're part of the Fae culture."

"And?" Monte asked, still confused.

"They're pretty gemstones, full of all sorts of magic," Finn explained.

"Like this necklace, here." Cameron wound her finger through the rainbow lights.

"They bring you luck, too." Finn licked his lips in excitement. "Cousin B told me that the Fae—especially leprechauns—like to have loads of parties, and that the leftovers from their feasts turn into clover crystals."

"And the fairy piksels?" Monte asked.

"They come from the Fae royalty, specifically," Cameron said, emptying potato chip crumbs into her hand.

"And those goons like the clover crystals?" Finn asked.

"Yes. But they love the fairy piksels the most." Cameron dumped the crumbs into her mouth. "The goons call them mood gems. They don't know they're magical," she defended, her eyes wide. "Tonight, I was supposed to deliver more fairy piksels to the goons in exchange for food, but they're growing scarce and . . . I didn't have enough."

"So, they got mad and you used your . . . powers . . . on them?" Monte asked, unable to hold the question in any longer.

Cameron traced her fingers along the bracelet around her wrist. "Yes," she said in a whisper.

"How come you told us you weren't a Mystic?" Monte continued, trying to control a wave of questions.

"Baap," Cameron said, looking down.

"Sorry?" There was that name again.

"Baap," Cameron repeated. "He said I was special."

"Special?" Monte pulled at one of his ringlets. Whoever this Baap was, he had to agree with him. Cameron was definitely unique.

"I can feel what other creatures are thinking," Cameron explained. "I can sense their intentions. And sometimes, I can influence their thoughts."

"That is purely brilliant!" Finn's white teeth flashed against the lantern.

"And who is Baap, exactly?" Monte asked.

"My father," Cameron said with great reserve.

"Wow. Where is he now?" Monte asked. "Does he know you're here?"

Cameron stared at her lap. "Baap is gone," she said softly.

A gentle hush hugged the shed. "Sorry," Monte mumbled, his ears burning.

"Well, you can stay here if you need a place," Finn chimed in.

"Yeah," Monte agreed, still digesting the information about Baap. "Unless . . . you have somewhere else you like to sleep." He felt extremely awkward.

Cameron crinkled the empty bag of crisps in her hands. "I just go wherever, really."

"It's decided then, you're staying here," Finn said with a grin. "Nanny never ventures all the way back here, so she won't find you. You already have the lantern and I'll keep my firelog out here for you. I don't mind, I have plenty to keep me warm inside."

An uneasy expression crossed Cameron's face, as though she was grateful for the offer but didn't know how to accept it.

"Or you can come to Downfield Place," Monte offered, thinking about Maren and how she seemed to appreciate conveniences such as a powder room with running water. He assumed Cameron would likely want the same, although he personally didn't think she needed any extra primping. She was pretty, even without styled hair and a painted face. "Uncle Jarus won't care," he urged. "And the house is plenty big."

"No," Cameron's voice was firm. "I mean, no thanks. I'll sleep here," she said with a forced smile.

"Just don't go back to those goons, okay?" Monte said. "You don't need them anymore. You have us now."

Cameron nodded.

"Oh no." Finn sprung to his feet.

"Darn it, Finn. Did you wet your pants again?" Monte joked.

"Ha, not funny." Finn shuffled through all the food wrappers on the floor. "Cousin B's madgers. I left them in the forest."

"You're kidding." Monte patted his chest where his own madgers hung.

"Wish I was."

"Well, I'm not going back there tonight, that's for sure." Monte got to his feet, his legs stiff. "Not with McTavish on the prowl. We'll have to check for them later." He had experienced enough adventure for one night. Plus, the chance of McTavish even finding the madgers was very slight. She was a Norm, after all.

CHAPTER 16
The Fairy Ball

Monte's breath turned frosty in the winter air. The sun had long since set, yet Grandmother Meriweather's property was as enchanting as ever. Even under the inky stillness of the night, it was apparent that she had been hard at work transforming every bit of outdoor space into a Christmas masterpiece.

Toadstools suffused with light jetted down the side of the house, marking the way to the festivities below. Each rounded top wore a dusting of emerald glitter, welcome beacons of holiday cheer. Monte padded down the pathway, the toadstools on either side of him, the bark beneath his sneakers a soft contrast to the coarse crunch of Grandmother Meriweather's gravel driveway. He slowed as he reached a patch of trees. Adorned in an abundance of red and white twinkle lights, the trunks looked like giant candy canes in a forest of murky blackness. The branches, majestic and strong with a thin coating of moss, extended over the path in an intersecting canopy of woven greenery. Clear glass baubles, each filled with a cloudy white mist, dangled from the arbor overhead. They swayed peacefully in the air as Monte passed, a succession of mini fireworks spurting within each one.

"You haven't seen any mistletoe out here, have you?" Finn's voice trilled from somewhere in the trees.

"Finn," Monte said, flinching only slightly. He was finally growing accustomed to his pal's phantom-like tendencies.

"Where've you been? The party started an hour ago." Finn stepped from behind one of the candy-cane tree trunks. He wore a soft cap traced in snowy fur, his face radiant beneath the pale fluffiness.

"Well, don't you look like your nanny's little angel," Monte teased.

He followed Finn down the path. They stopped before a row of large, bushy pines. The trees bordered Grandmother Meriweather's entire back garden like tall, sturdy soldiers, their branches sweet and dense. Music and sounds of merriment filtered through the thick needles, the citrusy aroma of wassail fragrant in the air. "Your nanny really likes to dress you up for these occasions, doesn't she?" Monte stared Finn up and down.

"Cameron keeps asking about you." Finn ignored the joke. "I told her I'd come find some mistletoe for when you arrived."

"Ah, c'mon," Monte said. "You did not."

"Aye, I did." Finn smirked. "And she seemed keen on the idea."

"Yeah, right," Monte huffed, grateful that Finn couldn't see him blushing in the dark. "I wish you'd quit teasing her like that. She may not know how to take it." Cameron was finally starting to feel like a close friend and the last thing Monte wanted was for her to disappear again.

"Where's Garrick?" Finn asked. A dog's bark echoed through the night.

"Garrick's . . . not coming," Monte said with an air of annoyance as Brotus and Saladin scampered up the trail. He grabbed at Saladin's tail, which whipped around like a propeller.

"Ah, the snogging girl strikes again." Finn made a kissing sound. Brotus jumped up and pushed him into the pines with his gigantic paws.

"Ha." Monte rubbed his hand over Saladin's muscular shoulders. Garrick had been extremely distant of late. And it was no mystery as to why. The kissing girl. Love. It spoiled everything.

"Ack." Finn fiddled with a large tartan bow around Brotus's neck—the artistic touch of Grandmother Meriweather. "Garrick'll tire of all the snogging soon enough. It's overrated. And gross." He patted Brotus's head. "Down, you big brute," he commanded before turning to face the pines. "Just wait until you feast your eyes on what's in there, Monte." Finn planted his hands on his hips. "Come on. I want to eat as many sweets as possible before Nanny gets here."

Monte followed Finn through a narrow slot in the pines, brushing the tickly branches from his face. A spectacular sight greeted his eyes. A unique array of fairies—ranging from six inches to thumb-size—buzzed through the air. Their wings shimmered under an expansive net of intricately laced holiday lights above. Some round, others slender, they were unlike any other Mystic creature Monte had ever seen. More glass ornaments, in a variety of festive colors, hovered in the air, casting an enchanting energy over the party. Fairies congregated near the center of the garden where a small, oval ice rink of sorts glistened.

"That's Grandmother Meriweather's pond," Monte exclaimed. "It's frozen over."

Fairies glided around the homemade rink. Some fluttered above it, others sashayed across, as a miniscule band atop a moss-covered tree stump accompanied them. The musicians' miniature bells, fiddles, and wind instruments sang merrily, working in harmony to play a spritely jig.

Monte crept toward the stump, hardly believing his eyes. A tall, lanky fairy with large goggles tooted away on a piccolo, surrounded by a pixie on a trumpet and a quartet of gnomes playing stringed instruments. A rugged, bearded fairy blasted the main melody on a set of tiny bagpipes. He tapped his foot to the beat as the miniature kilt at his waist swayed back and forth. He looked up and winked, his chest hard at work as he blew into the pipes.

"Incredible," Monte whispered.

"Over here!" Finn galloped toward the refreshment table in the back corner of the garden. "I'm starving."

A column of small kegs and metallic bowls, each heaping with cakes, biscuits, Christmas sausages, and cheeses skewered on toothpicks, lined each side of the table. A runner comprised of dried oranges, cinnamon sticks, holly, and evergreen branches banded the center. Grandmother Meriweather stood at the far end of the table, engaged in a boisterous conversation with a small bundle of fairies. Dressed in her finest tartan—complete with cloak and a feathered Glengarry cap—she too could have passed as a Christmas fairy. An elegant brooch dotted with a purple gem the size of a gumdrop decorated her petite shoulder. A similar but even larger ornament was pinned at her waist.

"Monte!" Grandmother Meriweather exclaimed. "Nice of yeh te show up," she said with a wink as she wrapped her arms around Monte. The smell of evergreen and gingerbread lingered in the air around her. "My, but yeh're freezing." She patted his shoulders and then plunged a ladle into a large silver cauldron at the end of the table. "Here, drink this." She dumped a steaming brown liquid into a sturdy mug etched with intricate engravings.

Monte clasped his half-frozen hands around the mug and brought it to his lips. A sweet, chocolatey aroma greeted him. He sent the smooth liquid gushing down his throat, pleased to find it a very comforting temperature.

"Finn, young lad? Would yeh like some as well?" Grandmother Meriweather swirled the ladle around the belly of the cauldron. "Ho, there. But yeh've already helped yerself, I see." She laughed as Finn clasped his white fingers around his own mug, his lips already stained with the chocolate.

"And where is Garrick up and about te tonight?" Grandmother Meriweather squinted around her as though she expected him to pop out of the pines.

"He, uh, couldn't come after all, Gran." Monte wiped his mouth on his sleeve.

Grandmother Meriweather's eyes narrowed.

"He had a test to study for or something," Monte added to ease the disappointing news. *Just wait until I see Garrick next, the eejit,* he thought. He felt angered on his grandmother's behalf.

"Shame, really." Grandmother Meriweather clicked her tongue. "I've been planning this for months."

"Yeah, I know." Monte looked down at his feet.

As a Mystic ambassador to the Fae, Grandmother Meriweather's annual Fairy Ball was quite the prestigious gathering, even from the IMB's point of view. Uncle Jarus had taken care to place extra shield enchantments around the property to promote maximum protection.

"Ack, but never mind." Grandmother Meriweather swatted the air with her hand. Something twinkled behind her.

"Cameron?" Monte spluttered, nearly choking on his drink.

"Whoa. Watch yerself." Grandmother Meriweather chuckled. "Yeh don't want chocolate spewing out yer nose, now. Especially in the presence of such a bonnie young lass." She smiled as Cameron stepped forward.

Cameron's gown swirled around her as she approached, the champagne-colored folds adding to her elegance. She was barely recognizable with her dark hair, which was normally straight and scraggly, wound around her head in a tight, silky braid. Her skin, the color of caramel, shimmered against the rainbow lights that rested around her slender neck.

"Mistletoe." The word involuntarily left Monte's lips. He bit his tongue, his heart suddenly pounding.

Finn snorted, hot chocolate spraying over the lid of his mug.

"Hey, Monte." Cameron's voice was quiet and choppy. She fumbled with the small cloak at her shoulders, her delicate brown fingers threading around the clasp.

"Hi," Monte's voice cracked. *Get a grip. It's just Cameron, you dimwit!*

"What do yeh think, Monte?" Grandmother Meriweather's eyes twinkled. "I did a no' bad job, I'd say?"

"You did this?" Monte asked. "I mean, you did a good job, Gran. I mean, your dress is very nice, Cameron." He fumbled through the compliments.

"Thanks." Cameron smiled bashfully.

"Ah!" Grandmother Meriweather exclaimed as a small bunch of fairies glided through the air toward them. "I'd like yeh all te meet the Devon Pixie tribe. This is Cahal and some of his clan brothers, from the Isle of Skye."

Monte peeled his eyes from Cameron and stared hard at the pixies as they approached, feeling completely ridiculous. Each pixie lad boasted rigid, muscular bodies. Their bright-eyed, clean-shaven faces suggested youth. Several had blue paint dotted across their faces, and despite the frigid temperature, all were shirtless.

The largest of the bunch sped forward, his wings fanning the air like a large dragonfly. He held out his tiny hand and bobbed his bright blonde head up and down in greeting. He looked like a miniature version of Finn, except more mature and lacking any wispy qualities. Even his hair seemed fortified, unlike Finn's baby-fine locks.

"Hi." Monte awkwardly held out his own hand. The pixie shook Monte's index finger with a strength unparalleled to his tiny stature. Then he turned to face Grandmother Meriweather, his voice musical and staccato-like as he rattled a chorus of clicks and rolling chimes in a foreign tongue.

Grandmother Meriweather interpreted. "Cahal, here, welcomes yeh te Scotland, the Land of True Enchantment, and would like te invite yeh and yer friends te the Isle of Skye one of these nights for an evening of pixie games and fairy jest."

Monte nodded his head. "Sounds great."

"Too right," Finn added, his incandescent skin brightening by the second. "I've always wanted to spend more time with the pixies."

"More time?" Monte asked. "Have you visited them before?"

"Well, it's been a long time . . ." Finn twiddled his thumbs.

"Such an invite is a true honor, I'll have yeh know," Grandmother Meriweather said. "All of yeh should be proud. Thank you, Cahal." She smiled at the pixie, who saluted in return.

"Well." Grandmother Meriweather clapped her hands together. "I think this calls for some dancin'!"

Cameron, who had been quietly munching on a piece of shortbread, looked startled at such a thought.

"Come on, yeh silly lot." Grandmother Meriweather grabbed Monte's elbow, scooping her other arm around Cameron's shoulders. "Yeh two seem like a well-matched pair." They weaved through the fairies toward the ice rink.

"Oh, we're not together," Monte said. He could feel his cheeks growing rosy.

"No, no, pal. I mean yeh two are suitable dancing partners," she explained as they reached the edge of the pond.

Monte glanced at Cameron. She looked just as puzzled as he felt. "Gran, I don't really dance." The heat rushed from his face. "And the ice looks pretty slippery."

"Nonsense," Grandmother Meriweather crooned. "Now go."

She sent the pair staggering onto the rink with a little shove. A curious sensation rushed through Monte. He heard Cameron gasp beside him. A feeling of weightlessness began to flow through him, satisfying and warm.

"What's happening?" Monte exclaimed as he rose slowly above the ice. He bicycled his legs in the air. His body wobbled awkwardly as Cameron rocked back and forth at his side.

A choir of chimes and bells erupted nearby. Monte glanced over to see Cahal and the other Devon pixies laughing heartily from the edge of the rink. Finn joined in as though he were one of them.

"It's not funny, Finn," Monte warned.

"Here!" Grandmother Meriweather yelled. "Yeh'll need these." She tossed a set of thin, silvery cords at them.

Monte nearly nose-dived as he caught the string. Another wave of pixie laughter rolled at him. "What is this stuff?" He pulled the wispy coils through his fingers.

"I think it's fairy thread." Cameron clasped the magical rope.

"Fairy thread?"

"Put it behind yer necks," Grandmother Meriweather instructed from her post.

Monte tossed the gentle rope over his head. An abrupt steadiness washed over him as the thread draped across the back of his neck.

"Better?" Grandmother Meriweather suddenly appeared at his side. She, too, hovered above the ice but without the assistance of Mystic fairy thread.

"Gran, how're you doing that?" Monte asked as the band struck up an old Irish folk tune.

"I'm well practiced in Fae magic, I'll have yeh know." Grandmother Meriweather grinned. She glided through the air to the center of the rink. "Yeh two coming?"

Monte pulled his leg forward in a walking motion. His body followed, slowly drifting toward where Grandmother Meriweather floated. Cameron joined him, her cloak flowing behind her. She smiled and Monte's heart skipped a beat. He looked down, his feet still dangling in the air. Several fairies drew pirouettes with their feet in the ice below him.

"Here I come!" Finn hurtled through the air. He moved to the music in a series of poised twirls and spins, skillfully dodging the groups of fairies that buzzed around him.

"How're you doing that?" Monte asked as Finn whooshed past.

"I don't know. I'm a natural, I guess." Finn laughed.

Monte felt a gentle tug at the thread around his neck. A girlish fairy with copper hair and gold skin had hold of the rope. Monte gasped as she flew backward, pulling him along. She tugged the thread to one side, encouraging him to dance.

"Yikes!" Monte said.

The fairy laughed, her voice like a windchime, and then guided him toward Cameron.

Monte twisted his mouth into a half smile. "All right. I get it." He took a deep breath and reached his hands out to Cameron. She placed her palms inside his, her skin smooth. The golden fairy clapped her hands together with delight and then sped off. Monte felt his ears burn again.

He looked over the top of Cameron's head. The lights from the trees above shone down on her glossy braids. He could feel her eyes on him. "So," he mumbled, "this is fun."

"Too right, it is!" Finn flashed by them.

Cameron laughed, the sound like the gentle waves of the ocean. Monte felt his shoulders relax. He smiled and dared to sway to the music. Cameron followed his lead. The tune switched from a jig to a reel and before Monte knew what was happening, he and Cameron were twisting around the rink.

"You're not bad!" he said as they bobbed in synchrony to the music. He squeezed her hands.

Cameron grinned and tightened her fingers around Monte's.

*I could get used to this*, Monte admitted to himself as the reel ended. He waited for the music to start back up, enjoying the velvety feel of Cameron's hands in his. But much to his dismay, the band fluttered toward the refreshment table.

"Well, look at you two," Finn said with a smirk as he followed the Devon pixies from the rink.

Monte quickly dropped Cameron's hands.

"Good fun, right?" Grandmother Meriweather drifted toward the edge of the frozen pond, waving for the pair to follow. She touched her toes to the ground, nimbly and with great skill.

Cameron landed with similar grace, only floundering slightly when her feet hit the ground. Monte's transition was far less elegant. He came down with a hard thud, his knees almost buckling as the fairy thread slipped from his neck.

"Easy there, pal." Grandmother Meriweather took the fairy thread and led him to a nearby bench. "Yeh don't have yer ground legs back quite yet."

"I'm fine." Monte massaged the scars on his arm, more out of habit than physical discomfort.

"I'm going te have a wee banter with the band," Grandmother Meriweather said. She winked, her eyes shifting from Monte to Cameron. "Yeh two have fun now. And no skiving about!"

*What is it with everyone tonight?* Monte thought as Grandmother Meriweather bobbed away. Yes, Cameron was enchanting, but it was like she had everyone magically captivated with her fancy dress and her pretty hair. He pulled at a curl on top of his head, thinking back to the day when he first met her in Salem. "Say, Cameron?" he asked.

"Yes, Monte?" Cameron sounded as sophisticated as she looked.

"Where did you . . . I mean, how did you come to live here? In Scotland?" The words burned in Monte's throat, the question finally escaping after weeks of ambiguity.

Cameron looked down at her hands. "Baap . . ."

*Baap.* Monte sighed. He was beginning to wonder if he'd ever understand Cameron's elusive father. "Did Baap send you here?"

Cameron stroked her golden bracelet, pinching the small gem that connected the two ends. "Yeah . . . sort of."

Monte held his breath. He could tell he was about to reach a dead end, already. The pair sat in silence, the gaieties around them suddenly more prominent. He heard Finn's mirthful giggle nearby, joined by the bell-like tinkles of pixie laughter.

"Cameron?" Monte asked again. Cameron's eyes remained fixated on her hands, but he knew she was listening. "That night by the lamppost. When you said I was . . . in danger. What did you mean?" Another pressing question to which he wasn't sure he wanted the answer.

Cameron looked up, her face rigid. "I say a lot of silly things." Her voice was suddenly dull.

"Right . . ." Monte mustered the courage to keep pressing. "But you didn't sound silly that night. In fact, you sounded the opposite."

Cameron knitted her eyebrows together. "You know I daydream a lot, right?"

"Yeah. You've mentioned that before."

"Well, it's a common side effect of being an Influencer."

"An Influencer?"

"Yes," she said. "It's a Mystic slang term for people like me."

"You mean people who can read minds?"

"Sort of." Cameron nodded. "More like, for people who can sense the intentions of others."

"Okay . . ."

A loud clatter interrupted their conversation. Monte whipped around to see a very disgruntled Grandmother Meriweather standing before a heap of upturned refreshment baskets. "Oh, Jivens Crivens!" The feather in her cap quivered. "Yeh gnomes are at it again!"

"Gnomes?" Monte rushed over to where a tiny brawl had broken out on top of the refreshment table.

Grandmother Meriweather plucked a stubby, wingless fairy from the middle of the fight. "Just sit yerself here, laddie." Her voice was thick with irritation. "I'll deal wi' yeh in a minute." She placed the young gnome by a basket of chipolata sausages. Finn stood behind the table near a pile of disrupted fairy cakes, a bemused grin plastered across his face. Not far from him was the rugged, bagpipe-playing fairy, stuck in a platter of shortbread, his face as red as his hair.

"How dare he! How dare he!" the bagpipe fairy yelled in a strong Highland brogue. His band members rushed to his aid. He launched a chunk of the Scottish delicacy in the direction of the gnome. "Oi! See here, yeh hooligan!" The bagpipe fairy brushed the sugary residue from his kilt. "If I find any crumbs up meh tartan, yer gonna git a right doin' in!" He balled up his hands in front of him.

Monte repressed a laugh, trying not to make eye contact with Finn.

"Now, Angus," Grandmother warned the bagpipe fairy. "Manners, mind yeh."

"Sorry, Madam Meriweather. It's jus' that this ruffian . . ." Angus huffed. He stared daggers at the young gnome. "He hopped up 'ere outta nowhere, with a full cat sith mask on and everything. He scared the livin' daylights outta me. Sent me flyin' a way back into yer fine shortbread here."

"Pech! Is this true?" Grandmother Meriweather asked.

The young gnome, not yet of age, lumbered forward. He stood about six inches tall and wore a billowy, black satin shirt with matching slacks. His silvery-white hair was braided into cornrows, his smooth, round face playful. A foolish grin formed across his face as he held up a small black-cat mask for Grandmother Meriweather to see.

Monte bit his lip. It was a good prank, although he could tell that for some reason, this was no laughing matter.

"Wipe that silly smile off yer face, yeh daftie! What exactly were yeh thinking?" Grandmother Meriweather shook her finger at Pech. "I'm partial te a good joke myself, but yeh could've chose something a little less alarming. There are proper ways te behave at my Fairy Ball, and this certainly is'nae one of them."

Pech stared down at his feet.

"Where's yer father?" Grandmother Meriweather demanded.

"Here, Lady Meriweather." A gnome with a thick, snowy beard came forward. Behind all the facial hair, his face was a portrait of humiliation.

"Odaq. This is very disappointing," Grandmother Meriweather reprimanded. "I expected better of yeh and yer family."

"I know, my lady." Odaq's voice was gravelly. "My lad is too rowdy for his own good, but let me assure you, I had no previous knowledge of my son's prank." He glared at Pech. "And you have my word that nothing of this sort will ever happen again."

"I would trust not," Grandmother Meriweather said. "These cat siths are not te be taken lightly, especially on an evening of gaiety and fairy jest. Now for goodness sake, get rid of that mask before Old Nick, the devil himself, visits us."

"You heard the lady." Odaq turned to Pech. "Lose the mask . . . now!"

Pech cast a very glum but apologetic look at Grandmother Meriweather before jumping from the table. He disappeared into the brush that bordered the back of the garden, the cat sith mask in hand.

"Some joke, eh?" Monte whispered to Finn, who had skirted around the table. Cameron rolled her eyes at Monte.

"Aye," Finn said. "Right good laugh, although I don't like to think about the real large cats lurking out there." The grin faded from his face.

"Yeah, but my parents will take care of it," Monte said. "I mean, how many more cat siths can there be?"

"Hush, Monte." Grandmother Meriweather dashed over, her eyes pierced with warning. "That is not a welcome term amongst the Fae."

"What? Cat sith?" Monte lowered his voice.

"Aye. The Fae are particularly sensitive te it because . . . it is one of their own."

"One of their own?" Monte scratched his head. Finn stood as still as a statue, his face bright and attentive.

Grandmother Meriweather leaned in closer. "Remember how I told yeh the cat sith is an ancient fairy creation? It is feared above all other beasts in the Fae culture."

"Oh, like the Nuckelavee?" Monte asked.

"Shh! Don't yeh dare say that name out loud here." Grandmother Meriweather cupped her hand over Monte's mouth. "The Fae are a very agreeable culture, but they also have turbulent tempers. They are quick te offense—it's in their nature—so we must take heed when speaking of such matters."

Suddenly, a strange, spine-tingling cry cut through the air. A hush spread through the party—eerie, heavy, and deadly.

"What was that?" Monte shivered.

"Hush." Grandmother Meriweather cocked her head to the side.

Another piercing shriek, this time closer, echoed through the pines. Monte reached for Cameron's hand. Finn was already at his other side, his shoulders trembling. A third cry rent the air, so sharp that Monte had to cover his ears.

Just then, Pech tore through the brush, his tiny face devoid of color. "Sith! Cat sith!" he screamed. "Run!"

A feline yowl ripped through the air. Monte stood frozen in place, his insides like lead as he fixated on the pines at the edge of the garden. The branches shifted and shook. Something snarled. And then, it appeared. A giant black panther. A cat sith.

The great cat jumped onto the refreshment table, scattering pastries every which way. Its eyes, like glossy balls of steel, darted through the party. Monte struggled to breathe against his pounding heart. His feet refused to budge. The panther wrinkled its snout and screamed then punched an enormous paw through the air, its black claws gleaming beneath the festive lights. Fairies buzzed through the air in a flurry of panic, their cries like a symphony of ill-matched bells. Cahal and his tribe flew together and clasped hands, forming a net with their bodies.

"Get back!" Grandmother Meriweather placed herself between Monte and the refreshment table. She held her wand above her head, her body sharp and poised.

Monte locked hands tighter with Cameron. He reached for Finn whose body was as cold and as tense as an icicle. Finn pointed upwards, his jaw gaping open. Not far above them hovered Cahal and the others. Their live fairy net had already tripled in size.

The panther growled and crouched down, as though in preparation to spring. Grandmother Meriweather slashed her arm downward. A stream of red light shot from her wand. The great cat screeched as the spell pelted it between the eyes. It staggered from the table with a terrible crash. Without hesitation, the fairy-net zoomed upon the panther. The great cat yowled and slashed its paws through the web. Some of the fairies broke from formation in a sequence of sickening cracks and pops.

"Cahal!" Monte yelled as the pale pixie hurtled past him, his body limp and lifeless.

"Nooo!" Finn sparked to life, darting after Cahal.

"Monte!" Cameron yelled. She squeezed the rainbow lights around her neck, which had turned a murky purple color. "Fear!" she exclaimed, as Grandmother Meriweather shot a second stream of red light through a gap in the fairy net.

A large gash appeared in the panther's shoulder. It shrieked, enraged, lunging for Grandmother Meriweather. The fairy net snapped and popped as more fairies were expelled from the gossamer clutches.

Just then, Brotus bounded from the pines. He charged at the panther, teeth bared and scruff on end.

"No! Not meh dog!" Grandmother Meriweather yelled as cat sith and canine engaged in a fatal wrestling match.

"Monte, fear!" Cameron shrieked, as Saladin joined the black mass of tangled legs and snapping jaws. He latched onto the back of the panther's neck with his teeth, the remaining fairies scattering from the brawl. Some pixies flew for shelter while others, including the Devon pixies, returned with rocks and pointy sticks.

"Fear!" Cameron wailed as the panther's screams shredded through the night sky. She clamped her hands against the sides of her head.

"Fear?" Monte whispered. He forced himself to stare at the terrible scene. Time whistled around him as the panther flailed its legs against the attacking dogs, its gray eyes large and glossy. Something wasn't right.

Cognizance bombarded Monte like a blanket of bricks. "Stop!" he yelled. "It's not here to hurt us!" But his voice was consumed by the noise of the fight. "No. No. No!" He watched in horror as Saladin and Brotus pinned the panther to the ground. Just then, something burned against his thigh. He dug into his pocket. There it was. Out of nowhere. The seashell. Hot and fierce, its lifesaving-power throbbing in his palm. Monte held the shell in front of him. Its milky-white coat shone brightly, the metallic spot in its center orange and hot.

Another flash of scarlet light. Another yowl from the panther, this time more feeble.

A bizarre but familiar feeling enveloped Monte, extending from his chest to the very tips of his fingers. The smell of Grandmother Meriweather's wassail surged up his nose. He squeezed the sizzling shell in his hand, letting the energy run through his veins. He didn't care how or why. He only knew what he had to do.

He rubbed the shell between his palms, compelled by an impulsive, overpowering force. He raised his arms high above his head, his hands cupped tightly around the shell and then slammed his fists against the frozen ground, a terrible yell tearing from his lungs.

*Boom!* The ground rumbled. A shockwave throttled the entire garden. Bark whizzed through the air and fog rose from the earth. Then, a dense silence seeped into the landscape.

Monte rubbed his head. He heard Cameron groan nearby. Finn muttered something from behind, his voice faint against the heavy air.

"Monte? Monte!" Grandmother Meriweather yelled.

"Here, Gran," Monte said with a cough. His eyes stung from the force of the explosion. He struggled to his feet. His scarred arm thumped as he clutched the seashell tightly in his fist. It was already cooling off.

"You okay?" Monte asked Cameron. He tucked the seashell back inside his pocket.

She swabbed at her eyes and nodded.

"Where's Finn?"

"Is everyone all right?" Grandmother Meriweather's voice chopped through the murky gloom.

Fairies buzzed dazedly through the air, many rushing to the aid of the fallen. Monte staggered forward.

"Wait!" Grandmother Meriweather ordered. "Nobody move. The cat sith is still here somewhere." Fog grabbed at her tartan skirt as she navigated her way through the garden, her wand aimed to stun. A dog's whimper swam through the clearing mist. A dark mass limped toward her. It was Brotus. Several fairies hovered in the air behind him, their faces pictures of terror.

"Jivens Crivens!" Grandmother Meriweather stopped dead in her tracks.

Monte rushed to her side, unprepared for the sight that awaited him. Saladin lay on the ground, his tail thumping dully against the bark. Beside him, covered in earth and blood, his body unclothed, bruised, and swollen, lay Garrick.

The panther was nowhere to be seen.

# CHAPTER 17
## A Sinister Enchantment

"Clear this area, quickly!" Grandmother Meriweather shouted as she swiped her wand across the kitchen table. Fine napkins and doilies scattered to the floor and chairs bolted for the wall. Monte dived out of the way as a stool barreled toward him.

"Here! Set Garrick here!" Grandmother Meriweather exclaimed.

Garrick's limp body, draped in Grandmother Meriweather's tartan cloak, floated into the kitchen, supported by a small army of fairies. An angry welt the size of a cherry pulsated on his forehead, blending with the dark circles that masked his swollen eyes. Cuts and scratches streaked across his body, the lacerations on his shoulder and the back of his neck deep and gaping. Monte clutched a chair for support, his stomach suddenly queasy as the fairies lowered his brother to the table. The injuries looked far worse under Gran's kitchen chandelier.

Finn teetered through the door, his usual luster washed from his face. A wide-eyed Cameron followed.

Monte heard the front door swing open. "Gran? Monte?" Maren's voice echoed from the entryway.

"In the kitchen, Maren! Hurry!" Grandmother Meriweather shouted as she rummaged through a small apothecary of potions, her hands shaky.

"I got your message and came straight from the hospital." Maren rushed into the room, accompanied by Angus, the bagpipe-playing fairy. Her face was traced with concern, her knuckles white as she clutched the handle of her medical bag. "What's going on?" Her jaw dropped at the sight of Garrick.

"Quickly, Maren. We need yer help." Grandmother Meriweather piled a small heap of potions at Garrick's side. "Come!" She shook Maren's shoulder. "Has anybody reached Jarus?"

"Still tryin', madam," Angus replied. "It seems he is nowhere to be found."

Grandmother Meriweather nodded. "Keep at it, then."

Maren took a deep breath, her lips pursed. She inched toward Garrick, apprehensive. "Garrick?" she whispered. "Can you hear me?" She touched his cheek and then lowered her ear to his bare chest.

"Is he dead?" Monte croaked.

"No . . . he's breathing." Maren grabbed Garrick's wrist, snapping into action. "And there's a pulse . . . but it's weak. We need to re-energize his system." She pulled a narrow bottle from her medical kit and tilted Garrick's head back. "Somebody steady his head while I administer this tonic," Maren barked as she uncorked the bottle.

Monte pinned himself to the wall, his body wracked with worry, as Grandmother Meriweather assisted Maren. The liquid slithered out of the bottle and into Garrick's mouth in a thick brownish goo. Almost immediately, the color rushed back into Garrick's pallid cheeks. His chest rose in one large breath. His eyes shot open, bloodshot and crazed beneath the swelling. He screamed and clawed at the air.

"Help me pin him down!" Maren yelled as Garrick clobbered at the table. She pulled a syringe from her bag.

Grandmother Meriweather leaned her entire body on top of Garrick. His eyes rolled back as Maren injected the needle, closing in pitiful surrender as his body succumbed to unconsciousness.

Slowly, Maren released her grip. She swooshed her wand above Garrick and a wispy cloud materialized. The medicinal fog sparkled as tiny droplets misted his body. "What happened to him?" Maren finally asked. Her voice was deep and quiet as she surveyed Garrick's torn up body.

"There was . . . an accident." Grandmother Meriweather released her hold on Garrick, blotting at a patch of blood spotting her blouse. Garrick's blood.

"An accident?" Maren asked. She placed her hand over Garrick's chest which now rose and fell in a steady rhythm. "What's all this?" She brushed at something on his ribs. Several coarse black hairs fell from his skin. She pinched them between her fingers. "This isn't Garrick's hair." Maren held the hairs against the light. "This is an animal of some kind." She looked down at Brotus and Saladin, who were busy licking their wounds. "And it doesn't belong to Gran's dogs. What's going on?"

"A cat sith," Finn said, his voice barely above a whisper.

Maren gasped, her eyes locking on Finn. "What do you mean a cat sith?"

A loud pounding sounded at the front door before anyone had a chance to answer. "Finn Cornelius? Finn Cornelius!" the Widow Smith's voice rang into the kitchen.

"Nanny." Finn sat rigid in his chair.

"Finn Cornelius!" The Widow Smith waddled into the kitchen as fast as her stubby legs would allow. She swung her arms back and forth as if she were sprinting, her arms catching on her buxom chest.

Finn jumped to his feet. "Finn Cornelius, it is well past yer curfew!" the Widow Smith panted as she latched her fingers around Finn's ear. "I should never have let yeh out tonight. I thought the Fairy Ball might do yeh some good, but no. I knew I couldn't trust yeh te be home on time—Gah!" Her gaze landed upon Garrick. She stumbled backward and clasped her fist to her chest. "No," she whispered. Her untidy gray hair sprung out from beneath a flowery rain bonnet, her face a mask of shock.

"Doris, take a seat, will yeh?" Grandmother Meriweather ushered the Widow Smith to an empty chair.

"Blood. Why is there blood? And . . . and . . ."

"Yer all right, yer all right," Grandmother Meriweather coaxed.

"I feel funny." Finn plunked back into his chair. He sunk his head into his hands.

"Finn Cornelius!" the Widow Smith shrieked. "He's in shock. Are yeh bleeding too, son?"

Uncle Jarus appeared in the doorway, Angus fluttering at his shoulder. "Angus, here, said there was an attack." He rushed to the kitchen table where Maren worked over Garrick's beaten frame. The color drained from his face. "By George," he whispered.

"These wounds are deep," Maren said, barely looking up. "But I think I can treat them."

"Angus." Grandmother Meriweather turned to the bagpipe fairy. "Yeh've seen te Cahal? The others? How's the state of the garden?"

"Fine, madam. All fine, including Cahal," Angus answered. "There were many injuries, but no fatalities. Odaq has cast reinforcement charms around the entire property. It seems that whatever magic the . . ." He paused to look at Garrick. ". . . cat possessed was mighty powerful. It shattered right through all yer protective barriers."

"Cat? What in the name of Queen Victoria are yeh talkin' about?" the Widow Smith exclaimed, pressing her hands against her cheeks.

Finn slowly raised his head. Dark circles outlined his eyes, his skin an ashy gray.

"Fear," Cameron whispered. She stared at her feet. "There was so much fear."

"You could feel him, couldn't you?" Monte turned to face Cameron.

"Hold the phone," Uncle Jarus exclaimed. "What the blaze is going on here?"

"A cat sith," Finn said.

Monte's chest began to burn.

"Cat sith! Here?" the Widow Smith gasped. Finn swayed unsteadily at her side, his eyes wide and vacant.

"A cat sith attacked Garrick?" Uncle Jarus asked.

"No." Monte shot to his feet. Was nobody getting it? "Garrick was the cat sith!"

"Garrick was the cat sith?" Uncle Jarus's voice was hollow. "Are yeh sure?"

"Yes." Monte looked at Cameron for support. "He came tearing into the garden, as big and as black as can be."

"Huge claws," Finn added quietly.

"But how?" Maren asked. She sent a flask of calming tonic flying toward the Widow Smith, whose breathing had become shallow. "Sip on that, Mrs. Smith. It'll help your nerves."

Grandmother Meriweather stepped forward, her lips pinched, her eyes deep, ominous pools of dread. "Transfiguration." The word stung the air.

"No," Uncle Jarus said with a gasp. Alarm seeped through the kitchen. The Widow Smith choked on her calming tonic.

"Aye, I do fear so. The darkest and most vicious of any metamorphosis," Grandmother Meriweather continued, her voice heavy. "And somehow, our Garrick has fallen victim to it."

"He was scared." Monte recalled the look in the cat's—in Garrick's— eyes before the seashell had dismantled the enchantment. "Cameron sensed it and I saw it in his eyes."

"It can't be." Maren stepped away from the table, shaking her head in disbelief.

"Aye." Grandmother Meriweather nodded. The wrinkles on her forehead deepened, sorrow emanating from her bones. "Undoubtedly, a sinister magic has been at play."

CHAPTER 18

Ripples and Repercussions

"Garrick?" Monte leaned over his brother's bed. He thought he had seen movement—a twitch, maybe. But Garrick just lay there, his body tranquil save for the gentle rising and falling of his chest, his mind seemingly vacant and unaware.

Monte sighed. Garrick had only resurfaced to consciousness a handful of times since the night of the Fairy Ball, and each instance had been brief, not to mention confusing. He would stare around the room with glassy eyes, as though he didn't know where he was. Slurred, incomprehensible words sometimes dribbled from his lips before he would drift away again.

Monte slumped back into the chair. Grandmother Meriweather's far from dulcet tones coasted up the stairs from below, followed by Kiernan Calder's strong English accent. Monte sighed, annoyed. Kiernan Calder. They hadn't seen Mr. Darrow's colleague since the day of their big move, when he had escorted them to their portal at the Hawthorne Hotel in Salem. Now, Kiernan frequented Downfield Place on the regular, like a dark, spindly spider waiting for his catch. News of a cat sith at the Fairy Ball had leaked out and he seemed determined to leech whatever information he could from whomever he could.

Someone knocked on the bedroom door.

"Yeah," Monte replied. It was probably Mrs. Darrow. She hardly ever left Garrick's side these days.

Instead, Mr. Darrow's head popped in. "How goes it, son?"

"You're back." Monte jumped up from his chair. "Did you see Finn?"

"No." Mr. Darrow shook his head. His face was worn and tired as he shuffled toward the bed. "No, I didn't. But I talked with the Widow Smith and she reassured me that Finn is doing much better."

"Awesome." Monte didn't even try to withhold the sarcasm. Finn had fallen ill shortly after the Fairy Ball. So ill, that no one had seen him for weeks.

"The Widow is a very protective woman," Mr. Darrow said. "I'm sure she's just being extra cautious. Especially after . . ." His voice drifted away as he swiped his hand over Garrick's forehead.

Monte stared at his unconscious brother. Physically, Garrick appeared much better. The bruises had healed and the claw marks and gashes from his fight with Saladin and Brotus looked pink and healthy. Even the red welt at his forehead was hardly noticeable anymore. "When do you think he'll wake up?" Monte asked.

Mr. Darrow sighed and raked his hands through his thick mane of hair. "We're not sure," he finally said. "Whatever enchantment—whatever means of transfiguration—Garrick experienced, still has a hold on him. Your uncle and I have combed through countless books: Unusual Magical Anatomies, Mystical Oddities and Other Strange Enchantments, The Changing. We can't find answers. This is unlike anything we've ever seen."

"I see." Monte felt bad for his father, who had a multitude of issues pressing down on him. Superstition and fear within Fort William and the surrounding towns were at a record high. The pressure of solving the cat sith problem was anything but light. "What about Moira?" A rush of hope spread over Monte at the thought of Mr. Darrow's much more pleasant colleague. "What does she think's going on?"

"Moira is busy enough with the work on Ben Nevis. She's also preoccupied with the slack your mother and I leave when we're away from the site. She doesn't have time to help us solve this."

"She sure doesn't seem shy of time whenever she visits here," Monte said under his breath.

Unlike Kiernan Calder, whose presence was like a cramp in one's side, Moira Bryce was well-received at Downfield, her visits having increased since the night of the Fairy Ball. Apart from Uncle Jarus, who tended to disappear whenever his old acquaintance was around, Moira's drop-ins were always welcomed. Even Mrs. Darrow had warmed up to her presence. *If Garrick only knew what he was missing*, Monte thought with a smile.

"What about that Mystic hospital in Edinburgh?" Monte offered. "Maren said there are experts there who could maybe help Garrick."

Mr. Darrow scratched his chin. "It's a tough thing, Monte. This whole transfiguration business." He took a seat on the edge of the bed. "Especially since Garrick isn't awake to tell us what happened."

"I know transfiguration is . . . bad." Monte paused. "But it's all gotta be an accident. Garrick would never do anything so terrible."

"Not only is undocumented transfiguration illegal across the Mystic realm, it is a form of dark metamorphosis." Mr. Darrow continued to stroke his chin, his eyes the color of charcoal. "Ever since the Great Nuckelavee Scare a couple of decades ago, anything related to transfiguration is scrutinized to the greatest degree. It is one of the highest Mystic offenses and the IMB will not stand for it. It is very rare to have a legal reason to transform oneself these days."

"Wow," Monte said. "I didn't realize."

"Aye," Mr. Darrow agreed. "We don't know how all of this came upon Garrick. He could face harsh retributions with the IMB, regardless of his young age."

"Retributions?"

"Heavy court hearings in front of the most prestigious Bureau officials. Even imprisonment," Mr. Darrow answered. "The IMB gives no leeway in situations like this. It wouldn't be good."

"Do you think that's why Kiernan Calder keeps bugging us? Does he suspect what really happened?"

Mr. Darrow glanced at the bedroom door, which was ajar. "I doubt it," he whispered. "But it does leave us in a very tough position, especially considering the standing your mother and I hold with the IMB. When you reach the levels we have, integrity and trust are everything." He rubbed his eyes. "Somehow, a warped account of what happened to Garrick has leaked out. The public has lapped it up like the eager Norm bloodhounds that they are. Whether or not the IMB believes it, is another story. They've been a wee bit aloof on the matter, save for Kiernan."

"So, we keep lying?" Monte asked.

Mr. Darrow's gray eyes bored into Monte. "Listen here, son. There are times when we must hold silent until the truth presents itself. Do you understand?"

Monte nodded.

"We will solve this," Mr. Darrow continued. "If we focus on the greater good, we will discover the larger truth."

Monte looked away, his father's gaze too intense.

Mr. Darrow sighed. "It's imperative that we get to the bottom of this, especially with the unexplainable happening to your seashell."

Guilt surged over Monte.

"It disappeared after you used it at the Fairy Ball, you say?"

Monte looked at his hands. The seashell sat like a heavy lump inside his pocket. "Yes," he finally whispered.

Mr. Darrow sighed. "I don't know. I just . . . don't know," he muttered.

Monte choked on the shame building up in his chest. He didn't want his family to fall into trouble with the IMB, yet he felt the unwavering need to protect the seashell. It had saved his life—everyone's lives. It had somehow broken Garrick's enchantment. It had presented itself to him in a time of life or death. Surely, that was significant. Yet the adults wouldn't see it that way. He couldn't tell them that he still had it. No. It was better for the shell to disappear from everyone's memory, to stay hidden for now, for the greater good.

"Well, we'll keep hunting around for some answers," Mr. Darrow said.

Monte gulped, his throat like sandpaper.

Grandmother Meriweather's disgruntled voice leaked through the bedroom door from where she battled Kiernan Calder below. "That is'nae true and yeh know it!"

"Good gracious." Mr. Darrow shook his head. "Kiernan's still pestering her."

"Gran should just set Brotus and Saladin on him," Monte said. "He's such a poky old doofus."

"I'll see to them in a moment, son, but first, come sit." Mr. Darrow patted the foot of the bed. "Your mother and I have been meaning to return this to you." He reached into his jacket and pulled out an old, slender box.

"Granddad's wand?" Monte leapt from the chair and onto the bed.

"Watch yourself, Monte," Mr. Darrow warned as the mattress bounced beneath Garrick's comatose body.

"Sorry," Monte mumbled. The tiny hinges squeaked as he opened the box.

"See here," Mr. Darrow began. "I know that Garrick's accident has overshadowed many things, including your half-birthday."

"It's all right."

"The wand has been registered with the IMB and is officially yours now," Mr. Darrow continued.

"So that's it?" Monte stroked his fingers over the wand's velvet bed. "No final words or warnings?"

Mr. Darrow's mouth formed a tight smile. "What transpired with the seashell the night of the Fairy Ball was very miraculous. However, it was also extremely dangerous. It terrifies your mother and me to think about how that shell's powers could've backfired on you."

"Yeah," Monte said. "But it didn't."

"A wand, Monte, would've been a much safer form of defense," Mr. Darrow continued. "The use of a wand in times of life-threatening situations is not punishable by Mystic law, even with all the current restrictions. Although you weren't technically of age, there wouldn't have been anything the IMB could've done to punish you, had you used it."

"But I didn't have a wand that night. I only had—"

"I know," Mr. Darrow said. "As your parents, we made a mistake in keeping this wand from you. By allowing you to wander about without any form of defense, we put you at great risk. Your mother and I face unspeakable threats every day up on Ben Nevis, but we never once thought that our children would need their own defenses, especially within the protection of our own estate." He kneaded his forehead. "Unfortunately, it took Garrick's accident to realize all of this. We should've returned the wand to you after Jarus cleared it with the IMB, and for that, I am truly sorry."

Monte nodded. He felt ready to burst with all the mixed emotions swirling around.

"Whatever you do, don't lose it." Mr. Darrow mussed Monte's hair.

Monte flinched. "Dad . . ." he said, embarrassed.

"All right?" Mr. Darrow nearly chuckled. "Just remember, a wand is the most valuable tool a Mystic can possess, and I don't have the time to go about replacing this one." Playful consternation laced his voice. "And mind you, although you are of age, the restrictions are still firmly in place. You are not to use your wand unless presented with extreme danger."

"What? Am I in danger or something?"

"No . . ." Mr. Darrow's voice dropped nearly an octave. "But let's not leave any more room for risk, aye?"

A noise, like a small stampede, thundered up the stairs. "I will not talk te yeh any further!" Grandmother Meriweather belted from the hallway. "Go away and quit nagging me!" She burst into the bedroom, her face contorted with annoyance. Kiernan slid in behind her, his shiny black mustache twitching, his forehead red under a slick layer of sweat.

"What the blaze is going on here?" Mr. Darrow jumped to his feet. "Keep it down, will you?" He patted the air in front of him as though trying to push the noise from the room.

"This Kiernan fellow is interrogating me about meh Fairy Ball." Grandmother Meriweather scurried over to Mr. Darrow. "Blamin' me for inviting the Fae. Accusing me of not taking the proper precautions." She spun around to face Kiernan, her eyes as fierce as frostbite as she stamped her foot against the floor.

"I simply came with a few questions, Madam Meriweather," Kiernan said. He peered over his shoulder at Garrick and then quickly looked away. "I'm on official orders from the Bureau."

"Oh, hang the Bureau!" Grandmother Meriweather spat.

"Mum," Mr. Darrow warned under his breath.

"Humph," Kiernan snorted. He smoothed over his mustache with his abnormally skinny fingers.

"May I suggest we move this wee gathering back downstairs?" Mr. Darrow eyed Garrick. "My son needs to rest."

Kiernan peeked at Garrick again, his eyes widening as though he expected him to jolt to life. "I do have some questions for young Monte."

"Me?" Monte asked as they tiptoed out of the bedroom. He tucked his wand under his arm, his heart pounding.

"Aye." Kiernan pulled a small notebook and pen from his suit pocket.

"That's all very well, Kiernan." Mr. Darrow exchanged nervous looks with Grandmother Meriweather. "But for the love of goodness, let's continue all of this somewhere else, away from Garrick's room."

"Very well." Kiernan's upper lip stiffened as he turned and loped down the stairs.

Grandmother Meriweather grabbed Monte's elbow. "I gave Kiernan everything I could," she whispered in his ear. "All of the details. Every tidbit. Yeh'll be just fine," she said with a wink.

*I sure hope so*, Monte thought. As if he wasn't disgusted enough, now he had to follow the trail of dandruff snowing from Kiernan's shoulders as they made their way down the stairs.

"Oh . . ." an all-too-familiar voice warbled as they neared the bottom of the stairs. *Babs! What could she possibly want, today of all days?* Monte thought, quickly hiding his wand beneath his shirt. Another familiar voice, velvety and pleasant, flowed from the living room as a musky aroma, like sandalwood and violets, greeted his nose.

"So, Mrs. Campbell, you're assistant headmistress at Jarus's school, you say?" the velvety voice continued as the entire group rounded the corner. The adults paraded into the living room first, Monte bringing up the rear. He crossed the threshold, Babs and Moira coming into view.

"Oh, hey Moira," Monte said, paying no heed to Babs.

"Master Monte," Moira said with a smile as she lounged in Uncle Jarus's plaid armchair. She clutched a bouquet of flowers in her hands.

"What's going on here?" Mr. Darrow asked, confusion tracing his face.

"Hello, Esca." Moira pressed the flowers into her face and inhaled deeply. "Lovely," she sighed. "For Garrick. I stopped by the florist on the way here. I couldn't resist."

"Uh, Moira. Good to see you again . . . so soon." Mr. Darrow took the flowers and handed them to Monte.

"Mrs. Campbell," Mr. Darrow continued. "Are you here to see Jarus? He's not in, I'm afraid."

Brotus and Saladin bounded in from the kitchen. They jumped at Babs, pestering her with kisses. She looked ridiculous, her eyelids fluttering as she batted at the dogs.

"Down, boys," Grandmother Meriweather said, half-heartedly, her attention still focused on Kiernan.

"No, I'm not here to see Jarus," Babs answered, flicking dog hair from her sleeves. "I actually came to check on Master Darrow. Winter break is over, and Monte hasn't returned to school." She raised her nose in the air. "It is my duty to oversee all reasons of absence, you see."

"Indeed, yes," Mr. Darrow agreed, an air of professionalism masking his growing alarm.

Only Monte could see past his father's stealthy spy skills. Mystics and Norms in the same room, Kiernan's interrogations, an illegally transfigured Garrick just up the stairs . . . Mr. Darrow was in a state.

"Garrick's been ill," Monte piped in.

"As has Finn, I understand," Babs said. "I've been taking Master Smith his weekly lessons for a while now. His nanny is so concerned about him falling behind. Yet you, Monte, are facing allegations of academic negligence. And pardon me, Mr. Darrow . . . Garrick and Finn may be ill, but Monte hardly looks sick to me."

Monte felt short of breath, as though Babs had stolen all the oxygen from the room. *Prying dingbat.*

"Right," Mr. Darrow said.

Moira leaned back in the armchair, her fingers clasped together over her crossed legs as she listened, only slightly amused.

"I understand Jarus is the headmaster, but I really can't allow a student in my charge to fall behind," Babs said.

Moira swung herself from the chair. "While this is all very important, I'm sure, I'm afraid I have some urgent business matters to run by you, Esca."

"Too right, Moira. Give me just a moment." Mr. Darrow guided a reluctant Babs from the room. "I so appreciate your attentiveness to my boys, Mrs. Campbell . . ." His voice trailed off as he escorted her down the grand hallway.

"Well, in that case, I'll be going as well," Grandmother Meriweather said. She whistled for her dogs. "There's fairy business to be addressed and alliances to be preserved." She pitched an advisory glance at Moira. "Watch out, dearie," she warned. "That Kiernan. He's really on one of his shenanigans today." She thrust her thumb at Mr. Calder.

"Psh." Kiernan peeled through his notebook.

"Thank you, Meri. I'm sure I can handle him." Moira patted Grandmother Meriweather's arm.

Saladin bared his teeth and growled at Moira. "Oh, stop it, yeh silly brute," Grandmother Meriweather scolded, shooing the dogs into the kitchen.

The whole house seemed to heave a sigh of relief as the last of the commotion pattered out the service door with the Danes and Gran.

"Now." Mr. Darrow returned, looking somewhat relieved. "You were saying, Moira?"

"Oh, yes. If I could just borrow you for a few minutes . . ." she said.

"I'll be with you shortly. I believe Mr. Calder has some questions for Monte and I'd like to be here for that."

"I'm afraid this is high priority, Esca," Moira pushed.

Mr. Darrow's eyes darted from Kiernan to Monte.

"Some more people have gone missing," Moira explained with an undertone of severity. "Norm boys. From the area. It really can't wait."

"Missing Norm boys?" Kiernan's eyebrows shimmied up his forehead.

"Where?" Mr. Darrow's jaw tightened. "And when?"

"They were last seen at a certain Hibernian Field, which I understand isn't too far from here," she said.

Monte's heart froze, his hands clammy around the flower stems. *Cousin B's broomstick. McTavish. The goons. Surely it wasn't the goons?*

"Sounds pressing, indeed," Kiernan said. "Perhaps I should listen in." He turned to a fresh page in his notebook.

"This really isn't your concern, Kiernan," Moira said. "The reports hit the IMB circuit just this morning. We all fear the worst."

"A cat sith?" Mr. Darrow rubbed the back of his neck, tension apparently returning.

"Affirmative," Moira whispered as Kiernan creaked forward. "Apparently these lads were part of a rougher crowd. They were thought to be up to no good, so they weren't reported missing . . . until now."

Monte listened intently.

"Which means the Mystic realm will be jeopardized even further," Mr. Darrow said. "Especially if this is anything like the other disappearances . . . Brian Shaw, the Mystic boys."

Moira nodded. "The Norm officials have been extra diligent with this case. They've even managed to keep their news networks quiet, until recently. We'll need our teams to perform with an even higher standard of vigilance on this one. Who knows how far the Norms have already dug." Moira craned her neck around at Kiernan. Her irritation seemed to simmer as she peered down her nose at him. He lingered directly behind her, practically crawling up her back. "Let's continue this in the kitchen, shall we?" she said, a strain of annoyance tracing her voice. "Kiernan, I believe you had an interview to conduct with Master Monte?"

"That's right," Kiernan said.

Monte locked eyes with a concerned Mr. Darrow. "Go ahead, Dad." He handed the flowers back to his father. "I've got this, if you'll take these."

"That's a good lad, Monte. Too right, this can't wait. I'll be back in two shakes of a lamb's tail." Mr. Darrow squeezed Monte's shoulder meaningfully and then followed Moira from the room, flowers in hand.

Monte sank into the plaid armchair, trying to ignore the growing knot of nerves in his stomach. The goons. Hibernian Field. Cat siths. The jumbled pieces seemed to puzzle together too well. Yet still, maybe it was only a coincidence. Monte glared at Kiernan, who looked as hampered as he felt. *What could the spider possibly want to ask me?* he wondered as Kiernan shook the final dusting of dandruff from his spiny frame in one raspy cough. *Does he . . . know?* Monte squeezed the seashell, still tucked safely inside of his pocket.

"Where were you on the night of your Grandmother Meriweather's Fairy Ball?" Kiernan began. His eyebrows arched over the tiny notebook.

"I was there. At the party." Monte already didn't like where this was going.

Kiernan scribbled a few notes. "Tell me about it. This Fairy Ball. What were the guests like? Anything strange happen?"

"You've got to be kidding me," Monte mumbled.

Kiernan's brows rose further.

Monte was beginning to understand why Grandmother Meriweather had been so annoyed. "The Fairy Ball was enchanting," he began. "Lots of fun. Tons of nice pixies . . . I quite enjoyed the Fae," he added with a twitch of his lips. A subtle drive of the dagger. *That was for Gran,* he smiled to himself.

"I see." Kiernan feigned disinterest. "And now for the oddities. Did anything strange happen?"

Monte coughed up the rehearsed details, impatient to have things over with. He recounted the arrival of the cat sith, how it had come from the woods, and how Grandmother Meriweather had used her wand against it.

"And your brother, Garrick? He was there?"

Now came the tricky part. Garrick had been there, technically, only not in human form.

"Yeah. He was there," Monte said with great deliberation.

"And Garrick fought the cat sith?"

Monte gave a little nod, biting his lip. "Well, he didn't fight the cat sith exactly, but he was battling the spells." *That's not a lie, exactly*, he thought.

"Battling the spells? With what?" Kiernan asked.

"With Grandmother Meriweather and the dogs' help," Monte said, avoiding the answer.

"So I've heard."

"Are we done yet?" Monte rubbed his sweaty palms on his trousers.

"Well," Kiernan muttered as he twiddled through the notepad. "Things aren't quite adding up."

Monte's stomach twisted. "They're not?" he asked, trying to play it cool.

"Everyone's stories match, yet there is something off about it all."

Monte continued to chew on his lip. The tension was hardly tolerable.

"Aside from whatever fairy contraptions were used, your Grandmother Meriweather's wand was the only magical tool exploited against the cat sith. As far as I've been led to believe, that is." Kiernan stroked his mustache. "However, the IMB's analysis of the attack site suggests a greater force to have acted there."

"Okay . . ." Monte replied. "Are you some sort of detective now?" he added under his breath. The topic was veering dangerously close to the shell, to the reverse transfiguration of cat-sith-Garrick to human-Garrick. He wished his dad would hurry and come back.

"Loads of magical residue was found in your grandmother's back garden," Kiernan explained. "More than what a single wand could produce. Any idea how that is?"

Monte gulped and tucked his scarred hand safely inside his sleeve. His grandfather's wand slipped from underneath his shirt and rolled across the floor.

"Is that yours?" Kiernan snatched the wand before Monte could catch it.

"Yeah, so?" Monte replied, his panic mounting.

"Very nice." Kiernan curled a bony finger over the handle. "I haven't seen very many of this model before. Has the IMB examined this wand since the incident at the Fairy Ball?" His eyes gripped Monte's.

"No," Monte stammered. "I mean, I don't think so. Dad just gave it to me today."

Kiernan smiled, exposing a set of crooked, coffee-stained teeth. "Intriguing," he said. "I think it would be prudent to have this wand analyzed."

"Excuse me?" Monte shot to his feet, now almost eye-level with Kiernan. "You can't take my wand away."

"This is not a confiscation, Master Darrow, only an investigation." Kiernan swung his own wand in front of him. A burgundy briefcase bobbed through the air, its smooth skin oily from excessive conditioning. "Don't fret. I'll have your wand back to you shortly." The briefcase sprung open. An expansive collection of fancy pens and silk handkerchiefs jeered back at Monte.

Monte balled his hands into fists. "This is so lame. How do I defend myself? What if another cat sith appears?"

"Ah, that reminds me of something else I need to clarify," Kiernan said. "Do you have any idea what happened to the cat sith? We've yet to find a body or any further signs that the beast may still be roaming about."

Moira strutted into the room. "Oh, Kiernan! Stop interrogating the kid. That's quite enough, really." Kiernan snapped his briefcase shut, trapping Monte's wand inside. "The discovery of the wounded cat—or its body, as it has likely perished—is something my team is investigating as we speak," she said with an air of impatience. "Leave the cat sith investigations to the experts, will you?"

Kiernan scratched his head, his mustache drooping. Moira winked at Monte.

"It appears as though we have another visitor." She nodded toward the hallway.

Cameron drifted through the door frame.

Like Kiernan and Moira, Cameron had become a regular visitor at Downfield Place. Yet somehow, she always managed to miss all the excitement. Today was the first time that all three guests were in the house together.

"Hiya, Cameron," Monte said, giving Moira a reassuring nod.

"Hello . . ." Cameron's voice faltered at the sight of Moira and Kiernan. Her face froze, as though she was in a trance. She brought her fingers to her neck, which looked bare without her rainbow lights.

"Who is this? Why is she doing that with her face?" Kiernan asked.

"Oh, she's fine. She just daydreams," Monte said, shooting Cameron a warning glance. The last thing anybody needed was for her to display her powers in front of Kiernan Calder, even if she was a Mystic. *It's probably a good thing she's not wearing the rainbow lights today*, he thought.

Cameron sneezed. The blank stare melted from her face. "Yeah. Just had a twitch . . . I mean, I had an itch," she replied, sinking into the couch. She caressed her temples and then glanced up at Kiernan, wincing.

"This must be another one of your charming pals, Monte?" Moira asked.

"Pleasure, Cameron," Kiernan said, not even bothering to look up as he gathered his things.

"Fear," Cameron whispered.

"What's that, lass?" Kiernan yanked his head up. "What'd she say?"

Monte's ears tingled with despair. "It's nothing," he said. Sweat beaded the back of his neck. He shot Cameron another look of caution. *What's wrong with her?*

"Oh, right." Moira chuckled. "Nothing, I'm sure." She flapped her hand at Kiernan as though trying to shoo him out the door. "Headed off so soon?"

Kiernan huffed. "I think I've gotten sufficient evidence, erm, information, for one day." He drummed his fingers over the briefcase.

"Did you use the Banavie portal?" Moira asked.

"No," Kiernan said, looking embarrassed.

"Oh, that's right." Moira snapped her fingers together. "I forgot. You need special clearance for that portal."

Monte snickered despite his unease.

"Humph." Kiernan brushed past them. He disappeared down the hall toward the grand entrance, apparently too important to use the service door.

Monte's tension lessened as Kiernan's footsteps faded. Finally, he heard the grand entrance door creak shut. "Good riddance." He slumped down beside Cameron who looked as though she wished the couch would swallow her.

"Was Kiernan giving you a hard time, Master Monte?" Moira's voice was as buttery as Kiernan's had been sour. "He can be a real ogre with his questions."

Monte bit his lip, unsure of how to answer. He didn't like Kiernan Calder at all, but did he dare tell Moira that? They were both employees of the Bureau, after all.

Moira's mouth flickered with amusement. "See here," she said. "I've been there, in your position." She clasped her hands together.

"You've been here?" Monte asked.

"Certainly," she said.

"You've had your wand confiscated before?" The words fell out of his mouth before he had a chance to think.

"Was that your wand Kiernan had? In his briefcase?" Moira asked.

Anticipation swelled inside of Monte. "I didn't even have it back five minutes before he took it away." He tried to sound casual and collected. Inside, he was fuming.

"You don't say?" Moira draped her arm over the plaid chair.

Cameron brought her knees to her chest, gaping at her feet.

"My dad's gonna kill me when he finds out," Monte said. "There's no way I'm getting that wand back now."

Moira nodded, pensive. "Listen." She glided toward him. "I've known Esca for an awfully long time. I realize he's strict, but believe me, he has your best interest at heart." She bent down beside Monte, her eyes warm.

Cameron's back stiffened. She hugged her knees tighter.

"Yeah," Monte agreed. "He's no rule breaker, that's for sure."

Moira smiled. "He certainly isn't." She rapped her fingers over the arm of the couch. "Let me see what I can do. I just might be able to get that wand back for you before Kiernan gets his knobby fingers all over it." She wiggled her own fingers in front of her, her eyelids creasing.

"Really?" Hope gushed through Monte. "I suppose things would be looking up again if I had my wand."

"Naturally," Moira agreed. "I'll work on it for you. Sometimes, you need to bend the rules a smidge to regain that which has been lost," she said. And with that, she disappeared into the kitchen.

"She's not good," Cameron said.

"Who?" Monte demanded. "Moira?"

Cameron continued to stare at her shoes, her eyes distant. "Moira, yes. She's not good at all, Monte."

"Ha. You don't know what you're talking about," Monte said, surprised by the force in his own voice. "Speaking of . . . what's with all your fear business? You could've given us away."

Cameron pursed her lips. Her eyes spoke a thousand confusing words, as usual. "I'm telling you, there's something off about Moira."

"Hardly." Monte folded his arms across his chest.

"Monte," Cameron urged. "I don't know what it is, but she doesn't have a good feel."

"Oh no, do not bring your telepathic nonsense into this one." Frustration welled up in Monte's chest.

"It's not nonsense, and it's not telepathy." Cameron's voice raised to a new level.

"Look." Monte took a deep breath. "Moira has been there for my family, through all of this. Ever since Garrick's accident at the Fairy Ball. You heard her. She's only here to help."

"Does she know about your seashell?" Cameron asked.

"No." Monte grappled with his rising emotions.

"Good," Cameron said. "Keep it that way."

"Why? What do you know about it?" His insides burned as he pulled himself off the couch.

"Nothing." Cameron closed her eyes and squeezed the bridge of her nose.

*So much mystery*, Monte thought. He was tired of it. "You're uncomfortable around Moira because she's so big with the Bureau," he accused. "Moira's smart, and you're worried that she'll take you away from here. Back to wherever it is you came from."

Cameron looked indignant, shocked even.

"Where is your long-lost family, anyway?" Monte asked. He knew he was being downright rude, but he didn't know why, and he couldn't make himself stop. "Surely you have one, a family, that is?"

Cameron jerked her head up, her eyes like spears. "How . . . dare you." Her voice was injected with anger and hurt. "I'm only telling you what I felt just now, when Moira was here." A tear slid down her cheek. "Take it for what you will. I won't bother you about this anymore." She untangled her legs from the couch, her face pale and melancholy. "You won't see me from now on. I won't try to interfere again."

Monte's heart dropped to his stomach. Why couldn't he keep his mouth shut?

"Cameron, wait," Monte said as she retreated into the shadowy gloom of the hallway. "You're just being dramatic." He winced at himself. *There I go again. What's wrong with me?* His throat swelled as the sound of the grand door slamming shut echoed into the living room. He wanted to run after Cameron. To apologize. To warn her about the missing boys. To tell her to be careful. Instead, he punched the couch. He yelled into a pillow and then stumbled back up the stairs into Garrick's room. Dusk crept through the window as he sank to his knees beside the bed. "Garrick, everything's falling apart." Hot tears stung Monte's eyes. "I need you to come back. Please."

CHAPTER 19
Monte Spills the Beans

Monte hesitated before rapping his knuckles across the cottage door. The Widow Smith would not be happy to see him. But he didn't care. He needed to talk to Finn. The door swung open. A disgruntled Widow stared down at him. She brushed her hands against her woolen skirt, her frilly, button-up blouse poking from beneath a yellow napkin at her throat.

"What are yeh doin' here?" she asked as a clump of porridge dribbled down her chest.

"I was hoping to see Finn," Monte said, his courage already ebbing.

"He's not well," the Widow said with a sniff.

She tried to close the door, but Monte stuck his foot out just in time. "Please?" he insisted.

"Why would I ever let my grandson communicate with the likes of yeh again?" she said, practically spitting nails. "With what happened at the Fairy Ball?"

"I just wanted to check on Finn," Monte persisted. "To make sure he's all right."

"I don't care what yeh have te say, yeh impudent laddie," the Widow said. "Yer not getting te see Finn Cornelius. He hasn't been right since yer grandmother's fairy party. And it's no matter why, after witnessing the things he did. Why I had the mind te even let him go in the first place is beyond me."

Monte took a deep breath, determined to persevere.

"Finn Cornelius trusted yeh," she rattled on. "He spoke very highly of yer family and seemed te be thriving under yer supposed friendship. But then yer crazy brother had te go and pull a stunt like that and now look at the mess we're all in." Her saggy lips trembled.

Monte choked back a retort, the wasted insult scraping against his throat. He desperately needed to talk to Finn, to tell him about Cameron, the missing Norms, his wand, and everything else. "Maybe Finn would snap out of whatever it is he's got if he saw me?" Monte offered one last feeble attempt.

"Gah!" The Widow squished her knuckles into her ample sides. "Yeh'd likely trigger him in the process."

"Trigger him?"

The Widow clamped her mouth shut, mumbling something about blood and fairies.

*She's actually gone crazy,* Monte concluded. He peered past her pear-shaped body, anxious for any sign of his pixie-like friend. The Widow shuffled forward, knocking him backward off the porch with her spongy chest. "The audacity," she gawked as she returned to the house, slamming the door behind her.

Monte stood on the front pathway, defeated, the steady drizzle of the morning rain his only company. "Crazy old cow." He scowled at the cottage and then scurried toward the back garden. Wet moss and bark soiled his clothes as he slid through the thick hedging and into the yard. He darted for the old shed, annoyed at himself for wearing Garrick's rain boots. Though slick and stylish, they were rather clunky and far from stealthy.

"Cameron?" he whispered through the door. "Psst . . . Cameron? It's Monte." Nobody answered. "I need to talk to you." He pushed his way into the shed.

All was dark within. The musty blankets from the night of the broom flight lay folded neatly in the corner, Finn's firelog nestled on top. Cousin B's broom sat propped against the wall, the skeleton of an adventure long-since past. But there was no sign of Cameron.

Monte sighed, his mood turning soggy like the world around him. He kicked at the pile of blankets.

"She left," a faint voice trickled behind him.

"Holy blazes, Finn! That gets me every time," Monte exclaimed as his pale friend appeared at the door.

"Nanny's got me all locked up," Finn whispered as he stepped into the shed. The door creaked shut behind him. "She's worried that whatever Garrick's got will get on me." The muted light from the shed's single moss-crusted window leaked down on him. He was even wispier than usual, with rings beneath his eyes—charcoal smudges against his pasty, soft skin. His eyes lacked their usual luster, his face as pointy as ever.

"It's good to see you, mate," Monte said, genuinely relieved to find Finn up and about. "A lot has happened."

"Aye, including Cameron leaving." Finn looked around the shed.

"She left?"

Finn bobbed his head up and down.

Monte shivered. Finn's glassy eyes were giving him the creeps. Something was very different about him.

"She took off yesterday," Finn explained. "Seemed pretty upset. She kept saying that something wasn't right. Something about a bad feeling."

Monte pulled at a lock of his hair. "Yeah. I think I know what that was all about." His chest felt heavy as the uneasiness seeped in—further, deeper.

"Nice going," Finn teased.

Monte tried to chuckle, the attempt painful. "I'm sure she'll come back soon; don't you think?"

Finn shrugged.

"I'm worried about her," Monte admitted. "You know the goons from Hibernian Field? I think they're missing."

"Missing?"

"Yeah." Monte recounted the information Moira had delivered the previous day.

Finn shook his head. "But the goons aren't the only numpties that hang about Hibernian Field. It could be anybody."

Monte chewed his lip. "Possibly, but the odds don't look good."

Finn nodded, though denial saturated his afflicted eyes. "Well, one thing's for certain . . ." He hopped onto the pile of blankets. "Nanny definitely won't be letting me out any time soon. Too many mental things going on right now. She'd have a fit if she knew I was out here."

Monte smiled, defying his mounting anxiety. "It's a shame that you're bound to the house," he paused. "Especially since Moira visits Downfield Place all the time now." There was no harm in tossing some bait.

"The pretty cat-sith lady?" Life sparked across Finn's face.

*Bingo*, Monte smiled to himself. "Yeah. Cameron thinks Moira's bad, but she only just met her. I mean, Moira's an old family friend. She's even going to help me get my wand back." Monte stopped, suddenly aware of how quickly he was talking. "Sorry," he muttered. "Life hasn't exactly been a party lately; Downfield is mega dreary these days. I feel like I'm stuck in a mortuary. Haven't gotten out much myself."

A half-smile cut across Finn's slender face.

"Are you sure you're all right, mate?" Monte asked. "Usually I can't get you to shut up." He slugged Finn playfully. "Oft!" His knuckles cracked against Finn's shoulder. "What're you wearing under there? A breastplate?"

Finn's pupils expanded, his irises thin bands of green. He shook his head, his face solemn.

"Dude, what's going on with you? Are you still sick?"

"Not really." The words rang from Finn's mouth like a bell. "I've been . . . I'm just . . ." He dug his fingers over his head, upsetting his smooth, slicked hair.

"What's wrong?"

"I'd better go." Finn leapt from the blankets and burst out the door.

"Come back!" Monte ran after him. But Finn was already at the cottage. He slipped skillfully through the back window, swallowed by the Widow's pristine muslin curtains.

"Bizarre," Monte whispered as he pushed back through the hedge. What was going on with everyone?

He trudged through the back fields, stopping to take in the small stream that stretched along the rear of the Downfield Place property. He stood on the mushy bank, lost in thought, the water babbling around him, the cold rain misting his face. For the first time in a long while, he felt lonely. Finn was behaving so oddly. And Cameron. Monte hardly knew what to think about her anymore, especially after what she'd said about Moira. Besides, it looked like she was back to her old habits of running away. How much more unreliable could someone get? Yet still, he couldn't help but worry after her.

Monte thumbed the seashell in his pocket. He had no clue as to how Cameron's mind worked, but surely, she was mistaken. Moira wasn't a bad person.

As if on cue, a woman's voice drifted through the sodden landscape. "I thought you might be down here."

Moira traipsed gracefully along the bank. An enormous umbrella canopied her frame, protecting her flawless hair, which was woven into a loose braid.

"I never really come down here, actually," Monte said, careful not to let his sudden excitement show. Now, more than ever, did he appreciate Moira's new liking for Downfield and its inhabitants.

"Oh, of course not," Moira said with an airy laugh. "A lucky guess on my part, then."

Monte nodded, his neck a little too stiff. *Don't be such an eejit*, he thought.

"I have something for you." She retrieved a long and slender object from her cloak.

"My wand? You got it back?"

Moira smiled. "I managed to pull a few strings. Mind you, our dear friend Mr. Calder wasn't overly pleased." She almost smirked.

"Excellent." Monte trundled the wand in his hands, unsure of how to behave. All at once, a curious thought popped into his head. The seashell. *Moira always has answers. I bet she can help me solve this whole thing.*

"Something bothering you, Master Monte?" Moira asked, as though she was reading his thoughts. "You seem troubled."

Monte looked down, embarrassed by her attentiveness. Should he tell her? She was smart, after all. And she had gained back his wand so easily.

"Are your friends giving you grief?"

*How does she know these things?* Monte wondered. "Not really . . . maybe a little." The seashell felt like a brick inside his pocket.

"I remember being your age." Moira's words were etched with sympathy. "You're a very strong lad, I hope you know."

Monte's ears burned with the compliment as he stowed his wand inside his jacket. Normally he would not tolerate such attempts at flattery, but Moira was an exception. Somehow, he didn't mind her praise.

"Truly, you are." Moira trained her eyes on Monte. "Not many Mystics your age could go through everything you have with such finesse."

"Thanks," Monte mumbled. He stared past Moira, quite aware of her studious gaze.

"My, but you are like Esca after all. Just there," she tapped the bridge of Monte's nose. "A sturdy brow. Garrick has it too . . . poor lad." She straightened, her last remark like a fleeting afterthought. "Well, you'll have to excuse me for being so brief today. I'm off to the Ben. Lots of work to get done, specifically now that we have these new missing Norms to deal with." She shook the rain from her umbrella. "I hope you enjoy your wand while I'm away," she encouraged.

Monte's heart rattled against his ribcage. *Tell her. Tell her about the seashell. She can help.*

"Don't hesitate to call on me, you hear? And take care of those parents of yours."

She was halfway up the bank before Monte found his voice. "Moira?" he croaked.

She stopped, rain pattering gently against her umbrella. "Yes?"

"I, um, was wondering if you might be able to help me with something else?" He climbed up the bank after her, reaching inside his pocket. The shell's ridges soothed his tingling fingers. *It's fine*, he reassured himself. *Moira will know what to do. She'll understand.*

Moira arched an eyebrow. "Anything for Esca's lad."

Monte held open a shaking hand. The shell glimmered in his palm. "Can you identify this shell?"

"What a curious looking thing." Moira plucked the seashell from his hand. She traced her finger over the grooves, her eyes laced with intrigue. "Where'd you find this?"

Monte hesitated. The seashell was his most prized possession. Yet Moira's expertise extended beyond even that of Mr. Darrow's. Who knew what valuable information she could provide? He took in a deep breath and then the entire story spilled from his mouth. Witch's Pointe, Hibernian Field, the strange marks on his arm, the Nuckelavee's kiss, and finally, what had happened at the Fairy Ball. Everything. It all spewed out. Moira listened, unblinking, as she absorbed the information.

"So, I really don't know what to do now," Monte disclosed his deepest trouble. He wrung his fingers. The guilt would strike any second now, like an anvil to his already-knotted stomach. Instead, he felt relieved.

"Well," Moira said significantly. "That certainly is quite the chain of events. But you're correct, Master Monte. I believe I can help you figure this out. Mind you . . . don't go mentioning this to anyone, not even to your parents."

"Not even Mom and Dad can know?"

Moira shook her head. "They love and care about you, Monte. But we cannot risk having them or the IMB finding out about this. At least not yet. I need to examine the seashell more thoroughly," she explained. "To see what we're up against before we start involving the others." She placed her hand on his shoulder. "Not to worry. I've got this handled. You can trust me."

Monte twisted his wet hair. *Cameron must be wrong about Moira, surely.* It was a shame they had argued, for that he was deeply sorry. He missed his friend and was worried for her. But at the same time, how was he supposed to trust someone who kept running off? He bit his bottom lip and nodded at Moira as the final hints of doubt fizzled from his mind. *It's time to get all this solved,* he told himself as Moira pulled a small red canister from her pocket. It was the same type of bottle his parents used to collect specimens while in the field.

"Then that settles it." The umbrella dangled in the air above Moira's head of its own accord as she used both hands to secure the seashell inside the canister. "I'll begin my assessments straight away."

Monte dared to grin.

"That's a good lad," Moira said with a smile. "Now get inside. You're soaked to the bone." She slipped the precious package inside her cloak. "I'll see you soon . . . very soon."

A blanket of comfort covered Monte as she swept up the bank. Moira would solve this. She would bring Garrick back. She would help him fix everything.

CHAPTER 20
The Mind of a Predator

Stern voices drifted from the living room as Monte crept through the service door at Downfield Place. He tiptoed through the kitchen, his boots squeaky against the tile.

"Officer McTavish." Uncle Jarus's voice flowed from the living room. "I really don't understand what all of this is about. Yeh say yeh found them where?"

Monte froze. Why was McTavish here? He thumped toward the living room, careful not to breathe too loudly as he peeked through the adjoining door.

"The woods at Hibernian Field," Officer McTavish said. Something brown and leathery hung at her side. "Your laddie. I need te talk te him."

Dread filled Monte as he recognized the goggle contraption in McTavish's hands. Finn's madgers. He plastered himself against the wall near the stairwell, grateful for the dim lighting.

"I know you think our Monte has something to do with this, but I can assure you, we've kept a close watch on him," Mr. Darrow said.

Monte peeled his head from the wall and squinted through the cracked door.

"I saw yer son and two other bairns when I was called te Hibernian Field all those weeks ago. There were complaints about a gang gathering, yeh see. And seeing as those teen boys went missing that very same night—"

"Monte? Part of a gang?" Mr. Darrow asked. "You think that my son is connected to the disappearance of those teenagers?"

McTavish raised her shoulders. "All I'm saying is that Monte was there. He and another lad. And a girl."

Mr. Darrow raised his eyebrows at Uncle Jarus.

"They took off when I tried te question them. Ran in te the woods. And then . . ." McTavish paused.

"Aye?"

"Now, don't think me a fool or anything, but I swear on my life that I saw them fly away."

Monte's heart stopped dead in his chest.

"Fly?" Mr. Darrow asked.

"Like birds?" Uncle Jarus said.

"No . . ." McTavish hesitated. "On a broomstick, yeh see."

A long, forced laugh droned from Uncle Jarus's mouth. "Now that, McTavish, is pure ridiculous!"

"I'm tellin' yeh, I saw it," McTavish protested.

"Really, officer," Mr. Darrow said. "I think this is just the young hooligans pulling a prank." He cocked his head at Uncle Jarus.

"Aye. I wouldn't be surprised if some clever bloke put all of this together te generate more attention for the town," Uncle Jarus added. "Fort William has become quite the target for entertainment and misfortune lately."

"Well . . ." McTavish shifted from side to side. "What about this odd contraption?"

She dangled the madgers in front of her, which, up until now, Mr. Darrow and Uncle Jarus had skillfully given little attention to.

"Yeh say yeh found them in the Hibernian thicket?" Uncle Jarus stroked the stubble on his chin.

"Aye." McTavish turned to face Mr. Darrow. "Your son was wearing something like this the night I saw him."

Monte gripped his reclaimed wand. He wished he knew a good mind-altering spell right about now. But his skills were far too rudimentary. Plus, the IMB would likely turn him to mincemeat if he attempted anything.

Out of nowhere, something pounded against the service door. "Holy blazes," Monte hissed under his breath.

Uncle Jarus pummeled into the kitchen. "Monte," he exclaimed as a tapping, smooth and steady in tempo, started thrumming on the service door. "How long have yeh been standing there?" The creases in his forehead deepened as the tapping melded into a rhythmic knocking.

"It's Comerford. From the IMB." Mr. Darrow barreled in from the living room.

"Not a good sign at all." Uncle Jarus's lips turned white. "He's an obnoxious git, with all that knocking."

Mr. Darrow marched for the service door. "Get rid of McTavish," he said. "She's seen too much. This is all going to fall apart if we're not careful."

Uncle Jarus nodded. "Yeh stay put, yeh hear?" He jabbed a finger at Monte as he slid back into the living room.

"What's going on?" Monte asked.

"I'm afraid we have some unexpected visitors, Officer McTavish." Uncle Jarus's voice was choppy and exaggerated. "I don't mean te be rude, but we'll have te continue this business another time."

"But I'm with the law, mind yeh!" McTavish shook the madgers in Uncle Jarus's face, her frizzy ginger bangs bobbing against her forehead.

"Yes, the law. Aye," Uncle Jarus said as he ushered an irritated McTavish down the grand hallway.

Monte could hear her confused protests trailing from the front entrance until the grand door finally slammed shut. He turned his attention to his father, who held his hand over the service door handle, as though bracing himself for a mighty gust of wind. His gray eyes darkened as he reeled the door open.

Kiernan Calder, dressed in a rain-splattered black suit complete with a puce-colored bowtie, stepped over the threshold. To his side, wearing heeled boots and a fancy all-in-one dress suit, was the most eccentric little man Monte had ever seen. He stood no taller than four feet and sported a silky copper beard that flowed around his pink face. Though he had never met one before, Monte was willing to bet a whole bucket of candy bars that the wee character was a leprechaun.

"Welcome, gentlemen," Mr. Darrow said, a smile plastered across his face. "Please, do come in."

"Esca." Kiernan ambled through the kitchen as though he owned the place. "This way, Comerford." He gestured. "Monte," his voice was stiff as they passed into the living room.

Monte followed, anticipation overcoming him.

"Do fetch your wife, Esca." Kiernan took his usual place by the hearth. "This is quite urgent. I assume you didn't receive my message?" He eyed the marble lion bust on the mantle. A long, narrow parchment curled from its mouth. The gems in the beast's eyes lacked a sapphire glow, an indication that the note was at least several minutes old.

"No, so sorry, Kiernan." Mr. Darrow's face flushed as he snatched the message from the lionhead, not even reading it. "We were entertaining someone and must've missed it," he added as Mrs. Darrow and Uncle Jarus entered the room.

"Did someone say urgent?" Mrs. Darrow asked, her eyes pricked with alarm.

"Ah, Vanessa." Kiernan's lips curled into an unpleasant smile. He looked from Mrs. Darrow to Uncle Jarus to Mr. Darrow as though they were all subjects about to undergo an experiment. Monte waited, feeling much like a specimen himself under Kiernan's unrepressed scrutiny.

"There really isn't any need for formality." Kiernan took a small wooden chest from Comerford. "So, I'll skip right to the bare bones of it all." He clicked the chest open. An exquisite glass vial the size of Monte's baby finger floated from the tiny box, rotating through the air as though part of a fancy department-store display.

"This was uncovered just last night near the top of Ben Nevis." Kiernan tapped the bottle with his wand.

"By Moira's team?" Mrs. Darrow asked.

"No, a Mystic volunteer," Kiernan said. "As you know, the IMB has accelerated the search program since Garrick's . . . accident." A second vial, as immaculate as the first, drifted from the chest. "This other was discovered early this morning, on the outskirts of your mother's property, Esca."

"On Meriweather's land?" Mrs. Darrow asked.

"Both vials, though found empty, were analyzed by IMB experts." He guided the tiny ornaments back to their container. "And both vials . . ." He paused, his voice quiet and tense, ". . . Yielded almost identical results."

"What do you mean, Kiernan?" Mrs. Darrow asked.

"Both vials contained the residue from a complicated potion. A concoction that we rarely encounter these days." Kiernan snapped the chest closed. "A formula concentrated with transfiguration compounds."

"Now see here, Kiernan—" Mr. Darrow raised his voice.

"Secondly," Kiernan spoke right over Mr. Darrow, "we found the second vial—the one near Meriweather Darrow's property—littered with fingerprints."

Mrs. Darrow brought her hand to her mouth.

"The fingerprints of a single individual," Kiernan said.

"And the owner of these fingerprints?" Mrs. Darrow whispered through the pressing silence.

Kiernan cleared his throat, Comerford, like a garden statue, poised beside him. "Garrick," he rasped. "The fingerprints are an exact match to your eldest son."

"No," Mrs. Darrow proclaimed, disbelief shaking through her. "No."

*It can't be.* Monte's head began to swirl. Surely Garrick wouldn't have taken such a thing? But, then again . . . Sudden recognition gushed through Monte as he recalled the vial he had discovered in Garrick's room so many weeks ago. His brother had claimed it was an energy-booster and had committed him to secrecy. Monte had been too careless to investigate it further. He had trusted Garrick.

"Lies." Uncle Jarus raised his voice. "All of it, lies!"

"Kiernan, perhaps the IMB is mistaken," Mr. Darrow suggested, his voice a degree below frantic.

"Afraid not," Kiernan said. "Esca and Vanessa Darrow," he asserted, "having means to suspect your disclosure of untrue and unlawful information to the IMB, we hereby take you into custody for official interrogation. To deny these accusations will only hinder the process."

Comerford lifted a pair of thin chains dotted with gems from his vest pocket.

"Now see here, gentlemen." Mr. Darrow took a step backward.

"Any poor cooperation would be unwise." Kiernan clasped his hands together, vibrating head to toe with the excitement of it all as Comerford threaded the chains around Mr. and Mrs. Darrow's wrists.

"Oh, come now, yeh bunch of Bureau buffoons," Uncle Jarus protested. "What are yeh on about with the clover cuffs? They're hardly criminals!"

"Let them go!" Monte yelled, finally finding his voice.

"Kiernan, we've never done anything but work hard for the IMB." Mrs. Darrow's voice was dense as Comerford nudged her toward the hallway. "You can attest to that, surely."

"Perhaps." Kiernan slicked a spindly finger over his mustache. "But I suggest you all keep your thoughts to yourselves until we reach IMB headquarters."

"You can't take my parents away! Where are you going? Wait!" Monte shouted as Kiernan and Comerford led Mr. and Mrs. Darrow down the hall.

"Monte, leave it." Uncle Jarus restrained him. "Let them go," he hissed. The grand entryway door slammed shut.

"They can't take them!" Monte yelled. "They can't!"

"Dad?" Maren's voice sailed down the hallway from the kitchen. "Monte?" She rushed into the living room, the sterile smell of the Royal Infirmary still fresh on her uniform. "What's wrong?"

"They have Mom and Dad!" Monte fought against Uncle Jarus's grip.

"Who has them? What's happening?"

"A weird-o leprechaun and that slimy Kiernan Calder," Monte grunted.

Maren looked at Uncle Jarus, dread on her face.

"Monte, will yeh just settle for a minute so we can figure this out?" Uncle Jarus said.

Monte forced himself to relax, his pulse bulging through his neck. Finally, Uncle Jarus relinquished his hold.

"Monte." Maren knelt beside him. "Don't take this the wrong way, but we need you to be calm, okay?"

Monte snorted, trying to ignore the fact that Maren sounded like his mother. McTavish was on to him, the IMB had his parents, and Garrick lay upstairs like a useless lump, now a confirmed suspect in the cat sith mysteries. How was he supposed to be calm?

Just then, something battered down the stairs.

"What in the name of Prince George was that?" Uncle Jarus exclaimed.

The living room door creaked open and a very groggy-looking Garrick stumbled over the threshold.

"Garrick?" Monte staggered backward as his brother teetered toward them.

"You're awake . . . y-you're walking!" Maren rushed to Garrick's aid. "Can you talk?" She placed a hand on his forehead. "Say something."

Garrick blinked heavily, his expression flat as he homed in on Monte. His gaze was quizzical, doused with a hint of sorrow, as Maren guided him to the plaid armchair. "Where're Mom and Dad?" he finally asked, his voice hoarse.

"They'll be back shortly, pal." Uncle Jarus's face suggested otherwise.

Tears flooded Garrick's eyes.

"Garrick?" Monte asked, the most shocked he had been all day.

"I didn't mean to," Garrick choked, as though he had wanted to say it for a very long time.

Monte bent down next to his brother. "What, Garrick? What happened?"

Garrick shook his head, his nostrils flaring as several tears dripped down his cheeks. "I can't."

"Look, whatever happened, it's okay," Maren coaxed.

"Aye, there's a good lad." Uncle Jarus patted Garrick's head. "Go ahead. Tell us."

Garrick's breathing grew shallow. "Moira," he said.

Something jabbed within Monte's chest. "Moira Bryce?"

"Yes." Garrick's face turned the color of ash. "It was Moira," he growled. "She transformed me into a predator."

"No." Monte took a step backward, in disbelief.

Garrick's eyes slanted, his jaw tight as he wobbled to his feet. "Yes," he almost yelled. "Moira Bryce did this to me. Moira Bryce turned me into a cat sith."

Voices of exclamation swam around Monte. He lowered himself to the floor, his knees weak. Moira? The woman he had just given all his secrets to? He bit his knuckles, refusing to believe Garrick's claims.

"Whatever do yeh mean?" Uncle Jarus guided Garrick back into the plaid chair, his eyes the size of golf balls.

"Moira's experimenting," Garrick's voice crackled. "I don't know why. My memory's shadowy. I have fragments. Pieces from the night when . . . when I was transfigured." He planted his face in his palms. "I made a mistake. I didn't realize the repercussions. I just wanted everything to be normal again."

"Whoa, hold up," Uncle Jarus said. "What do yeh mean Moira is experimenting?"

Garrick pushed his fingers through his shaggy, unkempt hair. "I tasted something I shouldn't have. I was unhappy. She told me it would help."

"Who? Moira?" Maren asked.

Garrick bowed his head and nodded.

"But how? When?" Maren asked.

Uncle Jarus marched across the room, his face growing redder by the second. "That awful, leaky chimney of a woman." He sounded like he might explode. "I knew she was never te be trusted. Not now, not back then."

"Dad," Maren warned as Uncle Jarus paced the room. "Please. We must all keep our heads on straight, now more than ever."

Monte put his head to his knees, too numb to speak or move.

"How did yeh get involved with Moira?" Uncle Jarus demanded.

"I ran into her at the florist, not long after we moved here. She asked how I was doing. I confided in her a little—she has this way about her." Garrick paused, his face pleading. "I was so homesick, so desperate to feel better, that I took this potion she offered me. She told me it would help with the adjustment of being in a new land, and I stupidly believed her."

"Oh, Garrick." Pity crossed Maren's face.

"If I'd only known," Garrick said. "If I'd only had the sense to sniff out the trouble. But no, all I cared about was feeling better. And Moira's potion—the tincture, as she called it—certainly did just that."

Monte thought once again about the night he had discovered the empty potion vial in Garrick's room. Garrick had brushed it off as nothing. He had lied. It had been Moira all along.

"How many did yeh take? How many instances?" Uncle Jarus demanded.

"A few." Garrick looked down at his hands. "They all seemed harmless, her concoctions. Until the last one."

"The night of the Fairy Ball," Maren whispered.

Shame darkened Garrick's face. "I was particularly upset that night. I'd been seeing this girl . . ."

*The snogging girl from the gas station*, Monte remembered.

"Well, it doesn't matter," Garrick muttered, as though the memory still pained him. "We broke up, this girl and me. And in an attempt to cool my mind I headed for a walk in the hills."

"After dark?" Uncle Jarus threw his hands up in the air.

"Hush, Dad. Let him finish."

"I thought a brisk walk would help," Garrick said in misery.

"And that's when Moira crossed yeh, I take it?" Uncle Jarus dabbed sweat from his forehead.

"Yes," Garrick whispered.

"Didn't yeh think it was strange that Moira would show up in the woods, out of nowhere? When yeh were feeling yer worst, at that?" Uncle Jarus interrogated.

Garrick pressed his fingers against his temples. "I don't know! Maybe. I just assumed she was scoping the area for work."

"Aye." Uncle Jarus sighed. "She is very convincing that way."

"And so, you were . . . transfigured?" Maren struggled to say the last word.

"Within seconds of consuming Moira's tincture, I started to feel funny," Garrick explained. "I remember it was freezing that night, yet somehow I was sweating heavily, as though it was a hot summer day. Seconds more, and it felt like my insides were burning. Then, I collapsed."

"Moira just stood and watched, sneering at me," Garrick continued. "And her eyes . . ." He shuddered. "They haunt me. She was so cold, so changed. So unlike what I thought I knew. It was like living a nightmare. Confusion, misery, despair, anger—I felt it all at once." He lowered his head, the scars at the back of his neck shiny and pink.

Monte gnawed on his lip, the metallic taste of blood leaking into his mouth as the truth of everything Garrick was saying pressed down upon him. *This isn't happening! Not Garrick. Not . . . Moira.*

"Moira was ecstatic," Garrick spat. "She congratulated herself, right then and there. She said something about her 'hypothesis proving right.' And all I could do was thrash around on the ground. It was then that I became aware of what was happening. Of what I was becoming." He flexed his fingers in front of him.

"I could feel my body and my brain changing, which only increased my panic," he continued. "It was like I had two minds, and they were battling each other. Part of me—the animal part—desired loyalty to Moira. The other, demanded freedom. Escape. It was that part of my brain that won in the end, which allowed me to break free from whatever dark, magical clutches Moira had over me."

Garrick shuddered. "I tore from her through the night, willing myself away despite the impulse to turn back. I was fast on all fours. My senses were heightened. It was a challenge to not completely surrender to the beast growing inside of me. Grandmother Meriweather's property was closest. I knew it was my only chance for survival. I raced against my changing body, holding on to every sliver of human logic I could muster."

He began to pant, as though he was reliving the entire experience.

"The rest is a blur." Garrick took a deep breath. "I remember seeing Monte and Grandmother Meriweather. I remember there was a fight . . ." His focus shifted around the room. "Did anyone . . . die?"

"No, pal," Uncle Jarus said.

Garrick's chin quivered. "I didn't mean to. I'm so sorry. I should've known better. I did know better."

Monte pushed himself against the wall, his muscles tight and aching. He could hardly breathe. The seashell. It had broken Moira's enchantment on Garrick the night of the Fairy Ball, and now she had it. What had he done? A wave of paralyzing panic embraced him. He was afraid to move or speak lest his disloyalty be discovered.

Uncle Jarus sighed. "It'll be okay, pal." His face was unconvincing. "Do you remember anything else? Yeh were lost te unconsciousness for quite some time."

Garrick stared at the dwindling fire in the hearth.

*You need to get out of here*, Monte told himself. He forced himself to his feet, sliding his back up the wall as his heart climbed up his throat. He needed to run, yet his legs felt like lead.

"There was, this dream," Garrick said. "Actually, it was more like a nightmare. I kept having it, again and again."

"Tell us, Garrick.," Maren urged. "It's all right."

"It was terrible," Garrick said. "I dreamed I was in the woods, trying to find my way home. But every time I thought I was getting close, Moira would turn up. She'd capture me and make me follow her commands. She was searching for something. She wanted it desperately."

"I'd beg her to let me go. But instead, she'd turn me into a cat sith and then order me to hunt people for this thing she wanted. And I had to do it, no matter how much I willed myself not to. I was a slave to her powers, to her desires."

Monte slipped into the shadows of the grand hallway.

"In a particularly vivid dream she sent me after Monte. It felt so real, and Monte seemed so tangible, as though I was stuck between sleeping and waking, in some sort of subconscious reality," Garrick explained. "I know it was just a nightmare, yet something was very real about it all."

"And do you remember what she was after? In your dream?" Uncle Jarus asked.

"No." Garrick sounded crushed. "No. I can't remember."

*The shell. She wanted my seashell.* Monte inched down the hallway, desperate to get away before Garrick said anything more. He fought past the burning tightness in his chest. He knew what he had to do.

He would fix everything.

He would track Moira down, and he would stop her.

He would get the seashell back, even if it meant dying in the process.

CHAPTER 21

The Summoning

The sky wept as Monte sprinted through the patch of woods behind Downfield Place. The pain of his decision was much harder to bear than the pinching of his boots as he plodded along, his backpack bouncing against his body. He pressed his hand against his chest pocket where his mother's telestone was stored. He had been in search of a pair of thick socks, which had led him to Garrick's room where the telestone, shiny and black, had sat nestled within the folds of the bed covers. It had probably slipped from Mrs. Darrow's pocket during her last vigil, and now Monte had it. Although he hardly knew how to operate the strange stone, he hoped it would come in useful at some point. He quickened his pace. He knew where he had to go, and he'd need Cousin B's broomstick to do so.

With trembling hands, he entered the Widow Smith's shed. A warm energy flowed up his arms as he grabbed the broomstick.

"Stealing is a felony," a quiet voice said.

Monte whipped around. Finn stood in the doorframe. "Really, Finn? You gotta sneak up on me like that twice in one day?"

"I'm starting to believe that you want to live in here, given how much you stop by." Finn's mouth twisted into a grin. "Where do you think you're going with Cousin B's broom?"

Monte stared at his friend, the broom's heat pulsating through him. "I . . ."

"You're up to something huge, so don't bother lying to me." Finn planted himself in the doorway.

Monte sighed. Finn had the right to know. "I'm going after Moira."

Finn's eyes widened, a look of knowing striking his face. "Cameron was right."

Monte nodded, the grim truth sinking in once again. "Moira transfigured Garrick into a cat sith the night of the Fairy Ball. She's got my seashell and she's going to use it to . . . well, I don't know what she's gonna do with it. But it'll be lethal." The words tumbled from his mouth.

"What? How'd she get the seashell?"

"It's all my fault," Monte admitted, bravely. "But there's no time to explain. If you want to come with me, then fine. But the decision is on you." He pulled the madgers from his backpack.

"I'm coming," Finn said without hesitation.

Monte knew he should force his friend to stay, yet he was relieved to have a fellow comrade at his side. "Get your heaviest coat and your thickest shoes." Monte secured the madgers around his head. Instantly, his vision brightened in the dullness of the shed, as though the goggles knew his very needs. "And be sneaky," Monte said as Finn bounded for the cottage. "Let's not give your nanny a chance to skin me alive just yet."

Finn returned wrapped in a puffy jacket and tightly clasped boots that climbed halfway up his calves. "Well, let's go, then." He slung a satchel over his shoulder.

"Glad to see you're finally back to your old self," Monte said.

Finn grinned.

"Right." Monte swung his leg over the broom. He'd have to question Finn more later.

"You know," Finn said, straddling the broom behind Monte. "I've seen more action since meeting you than I have in my entire time here with Nanny."

"No doubt." Monte smiled to himself. The rain stung his face as they whizzed into the sky, the clouds like a stormy sea of foam below them. Not far ahead, crowned in a thick layer of mist, stood Ben Nevis.

"So, where're you taking us?" Finn shouted.

"There." Monte pointed to the ominous black mountain.

"The Ben?"

"If Moira is anywhere, it's gotta be that mountain," Monte shouted as the frigid air whooshed around them.

They dipped below the main cloud layer, engulfed by thick mist and mushy snowflakes. A rippling lake glowered up at them, a match to the dismal landscape. The Ben, shrouded in a cloak of heavy gray clouds, beckoned them forward. *The heart of the mountain*, Monte thought as they flew over the foothills. Something told him that's where Moira would be.

Fog hugged the great mass as they soared toward its center, passing dormant foliage and chunky boulders the color of steel. *We'll never see anything from up here*, Monte thought. He pushed the broom handle downward as they reached the Ben's midriff. They glided over the somber earth, their feet dangling above the soppy ground as Monte searched for a place to land. His boots dragged across the muddy, dead grass, finally squelching to a stop near a wet, murky hiking trail.

"Now what?" Finn leapt from the broom.

"We find Moira." Monte removed the madgers and squinted through the rain.

"Any bright ideas on where she might be?"

"I have an inkling." Monte pulled the telestone from his jacket. "Have you ever worked one of these, by chance?"

"No. But Cousin B used to have one."

"Is there anything your Cousin B doesn't have?" Monte asked as he massaged his fingers over the telestone. It felt cold and lifeless against his already freezing fingers.

"Sure, lots of things," Finn replied.

"But you never saw him work his telestone?" Monte asked, tucking the madgers and the curious stone away. He propped the broomstick across the back of his neck and trampled through a scrap of bramble toward the narrow hiking trail.

"Not really," Finn replied as they began to climb. "All I know is that you have to activate it somehow, to get the magic flowing. Once that's done, you should be able to send messages and stuff."

Monte trudged forward. He tried to stamp out the doubt that festered inside of him. His courage seemed to be dimming with the waning daylight, the threat of doom growing with every step he took.

The trail led them up a steep incline and along a shallow ravine before opening into a small meadow. It would've been a welcoming place were it not for the blotchy darkness brought on by the overcast sky above.

"My feet are killing me," Finn said after a while.

"Maybe if your nanny didn't dress you like a little prince . . ." Monte limped toward the nearest boulder. He set Cousin B's broom down and pressed his fingers against the toe of his own boot.

Finn looked around, barely aware of the joke. "This place is too open." He scanned the meadow. "I feel like I'm being watched."

"You're right." Monte rummaged inside his backpack. "We'll only take a quick rest," he reassured, pulling out a sausage roll. "Here, eat this. You're all skin and bones these days."

Finn's eyes lit up. "I'm much tougher than I look," he said as he tore the striped paper from the savory pastry.

"Speaking of tough," Monte said, jabbing Finn's chest. "Since when were you made of steel?"

Finn shrugged, already halfway through his pastry.

"Seriously, though," Monte continued. "You gave my knuckles quite the crunch when I punched you earlier."

Finn's face grew serious, his eyes enormous orbs above slender cheekbones. "Nanny told you I fell sick right after the Fairy Ball, aye?"

"Yeah, something I'm actually starting to believe." Monte plunked down on the boulder. "I mean, I've seen you better, mate."

Finn kicked his fancy boots through the mud.

"Look," Monte said. "What happened at the Fairy Ball . . . It's totally fine to be scared. In fact, I'm still not sleeping well."

Finn shook his head. "I'm not scared of what happened," he said, suddenly looking much older than he was. "It's like this . . . I was sick, but not in a way that you'd guess."

"Okay."

"Have you ever wondered how I came to stay with my nanny?"

"Well, yeah." Monte frowned. "But since you never brought it up . . . I assumed it was a touchy subject." Something flashed in his peripheries. He jumped up, his body rigid.

"What?" Finn dropped his final bite of sausage roll in the mud.

Monte scrambled to the top of the boulder. A figure stood at the other end of the tiny ravine, inching toward them, gliding through the mist. A glimmer of colors broke through the growing darkness.

"What is it?" Finn hissed.

"Shhh."

The thing stopped at the sound of their voices.

"I see it." Finn mounted the boulder in a single leap. The figure moved forward again. "It's coming for us," his voice rang out.

The mysterious figure continued to weave toward them. Slender in form, it wore a dark, oversized raincoat that flapped with each step. Around its neck, was a halo of colors. Rainbow lights.

"Cameron," Monte croaked.

The figure pushed back her hood, exposing damp, stringy hair pulled back into a low ponytail. The rainbow lights sparkled around her neck.

Monte jumped from the boulder.

Cameron stared at him, her eyes as deep as ever. Her face contorted. She rushed forward and threw her arms around Monte. "I'm so glad you're here," she whispered.

"What's going on?" Monte stammered, awkwardly returning the hug. Cameron's toasty, vanilla scent washed over him. "Why? When? How'd you get up here?" The questions shot like pellets from his mouth.

"I knew it was you, Cameron!" Finn shimmied down the boulder.

"Ha, yeah right." Monte finally relinquished the hug. "You were about wetting your pants thirty seconds ago."

"Was not," Finn demanded.

Cameron smiled and fingered the rainbow lights. The gems pulsated independently of each other, as though alive, each as bright as the summer sun at midday. "I had a feeling you'd come." She flipped the large hood back over her head. "I've been waiting all day."

"You have?" Monte cocked his head. "You know, I really don't get you, Cameron."

"What's there to get, mate?" Finn asked. "Her special powers are an automatic explanation for everything." He turned to face Cameron, hardly fazed by the fact that she had just shown up, out of nowhere. "So, you wanna help us find Moira?"

Cameron recoiled at the name. "Moira?"

"Aye. Turns out she's a real baddy," Finn said.

Monte fumbled with Cousin B's broom, melting with shame. "I know," he mumbled. "Just say it . . . I told you so."

Cameron's eyes softened, offering reprieve. "I'm just so glad you're here," she said for a second time.

"I'm glad too," Monte whispered, although he wondered if she held a secret grudge against him.

"I need your help with something." Cameron began to traipse back across the meadow, never one to waste time or words.

"With what?" Both Monte and Finn asked at the same time.

Cameron looked over her shoulder, never stopping. "You two are going to help me summon the Unicorn Witch."

"Farwen?" Monte returned Cousin B's broom to the back of his neck and sloshed after Cameron.

"You want to summon the Unicorn Witch?" Finn followed.

"Yes." Cameron plodded steadily through the wet grass.

"Do you even know how?" Monte asked.

Cameron hooked her thumb around the rainbow lights. "You see these?"

"Yeah, yeah, your fairy piksels," Monte said.

"These gems are more than just something pretty to wear," Cameron explained. "They glow whenever I'm in the presence of good Mystics or friendly magic—that's how I found the two of you."

"That's brilliant." Finn trotted alongside her.

"I've been using them to pinpoint the perfect summoning location here on the Ben," Cameron continued. "The Unicorn Witch is very particular, you see."

"Okay. So pretty colors mean good magic," Monte ruminated. "What about when there's bad magic around? Like at the Fairy Ball. When Garrick showed up as a cat sith? The lights went all dark then."

"The piksels become inky whenever dark magic is near," Cameron answered.

"So how do you summon Farwen?" Finn pressed.

"In order to summon the Unicorn Witch, we need four things," Cameron said as the last of the daylight surrendered to the oncoming night. She veered onto another hiking trail, this one even steeper than the last. "First, we need a proper site. Someplace that's free of human contact and that's untainted by flawed magic. Such locations are surprisingly hard to come by. Secondly, a circle of fairy piksels is required." She clasped at her necklace, the lights falling in a vibrant halo in front of her. "Third, we must have the blood of a Fae child." She paused to scan the trail and then pointed to a narrow, muddy path that cut up the side of the mountain. "This way."

"And the fourth thing?" Monte panted, wondering how Cameron planned to produce the child of a fairy.

"A summoner. Someone to call upon the Unicorn Witch," Cameron said. "But it can't just be anyone. This person must have a courageous heart and pure intent."

"Where'd you learn all of this?" Monte struggled up the slippery incline, Cousin B's broom like a crowbar against his neck.

"Baap," Cameron said.

*Of course,* Monte thought. *The mysterious Baap. No point in questioning any further.*

"So, what happened with Moira?" Cameron asked.

Monte snarled to himself. He wanted to believe that this was all a bad dream. That Moira wasn't the villain. But he knew Cameron had been right all along. Moira's charisma had shaded who she really was, and Monte had fallen for her ploy. On top of that, she had toyed with his whole family and his friends. It was time for her to pay.

"C'mon, Monte," Cameron urged. "Out with it."

Monte bit his lip, not wishing to elaborate on the dreadful situation. At long last, he let it all out. The confession of how he had given the seashell to Moira burned in his throat as he told his friends everything.

"So, the pretty lady is the bad guy," Finn said as they inched up the mountain. "I always knew she was a weirdy."

"Sure you did," Monte huffed as the muddy slope leveled out into an expansive ridge.

Cameron stopped, turning to face him. "It's okay, Monte. You're here now, doing the right thing."

"Cameron, there's something I need to say . . ." Monte hesitated.

Cameron held up her hand. "Wait, this is it," she interrupted. The rainbow lights twinkled all around them, bouncing off the jagged rock walls. "This is the spot."

The platform, a natural ledge that cut into the side of the mountain, was at least thirty feet wide and double that in length. Patches of snow flashed on the frozen ground, brought to life by the lively glow of Cameron's magic gems.

"This is the purest spot on the mountain." Cameron removed the rainbow lights from her neck. She held them in front of her, their glow bright against her face as she examined them.

Monte laid Cousin B's broomstick on the ground, grateful to have full use of his arms again. "So, what do we do now?" he asked.

"We summon Farwen," Cameron said. She formed the strand of rainbow lights into a circle on the ground.

"And then when she shows up, we beg her to help us?" Finn kneeled beside the lights.

"Essentially, yes." Cameron's face radiated confidence. "Monte, I think you have the strongest heart of us all. You'll do the summoning. Which leaves . . ."

"The blood of a Fae child," Finn said.

"Yes," Cameron whispered. "I just need a little. I promise it won't hurt for too long."

"Hold up," Monte interrupted. "What're you saying? I don't exactly see any tiny, fluttering people around."

Cameron exchanged sharp looks with Finn, who was already pulling off his mittens.

"You're going to use Finn's blood?" Monte asked. "But that would mean . . ."

"Yes," Finn affirmed, the rainbow lights shedding crystalline patterns of light across his face.

"You're a fairy?"

"Part fairy," Finn clarified. "I'm three-quarters human and a quarter Devon pixie."

Monte turned to Cameron. "And you knew about this?"

"Not until after the Fairy Ball." Cameron rounded the circle of rainbow lights with the toe of her shoe. "That's when Finn's change began."

"I barely knew of my roots myself," Finn said. "It was scary, the change, but Cameron was there for me."

"The change?" Monte stared at Finn, whose hair and face shone against the inky blackness of the night.

"It's what happens when a fairy comes of age," Finn explained.

Monte dug his fist into his forehead. After today, nothing would surprise him. "How come you didn't tell me?"

"Nanny kept a close watch on me," Finn explained. "She wasn't pleased that the change was occurring. It wasn't technically supposed to happen to someone like me, someone who is more human than fairy. But . . ." He lowered his voice. "The cat sith is the darkest and the most feared of all Fae demons. My close contact with one at the Fairy Ball ignited the Fae blood in my veins. That's why Nanny hasn't wanted me anywhere near Garrick, or you, or your family. She didn't want to set me off any further. But it was too late. The change awakened my heritage and now I basically have Fae powers." Finn thrummed his fingers across his chest.

Monte massaged his knuckles, pensive. "So, you like, have really strong muscles now?"

Finn smirked. "Amongst other things. Kinda dynamite, aye?"

Monte shook his head. "Bizarre."

"Too right, it is," Finn chimed.

"The night's taking over." Cameron craned her neck at the cloud-mottled sky. "We should summon Farwen before anything else weird—or bad—happens." She stepped inside the circle of rainbow lights.

Monte followed, Finn at his side, the weight of what they were about to do suddenly sinking in.

"We'll need something to draw Finn's blood with," Cameron said.

"I have a pocketknife." Monte winced at the very thought of hurting Finn. He reached inside his backpack, reluctant. "Don't worry," he hesitated. "It's clean."

"That'll work," Cameron said. "A small amount should do it, but not yet," she warned as Monte released the blade from the trigger. "Monte, you must say these exact words then immediately draw the blood from Finn."

Monte nodded and tightened his grip around the knife handle.

Cameron took a deep breath. "The words are: I, Monte Darrow, summon thee, Farwen, the Unicorn Witch and queen of all creatures Mystical, with the purest intent . . . got it?"

"Yes," Monte said, though denial beat through him.

"Once Finn's blood has contacted the earth, you must state the reason you are calling upon her. These can be your own words, just make them sincere."

"Right. And how do you know this'll work?" Monte asked. "Have you ever summoned the Unicorn Witch before?"

Cameron returned his question with a stony stare. "No. But Baap—"

"Say no more," Monte interrupted. "Baap taught you, I get it."

Cameron's forehead wrinkled, her eyes sharp beneath her slanted brows.

"Sorry, I shouldn't have said that," Monte said.

"Look!" Finn jabbed his finger at the ground.

The rainbow lights faded, their brightness rapidly diminishing until only a cinder of color remained in the center of each.

"That can't be good," Monte said as the embers flickered out like hearts succumbing to death. A wolf howled nearby, sending shivers crawling up his spine. Cameron grew stiff at his side, her gaze deep, her stance vigilant. The fairy crystals sparked to life again, but this time something was wrong. Dark and tainted with black streaks, the gems cast a sickly violet glow across their feet.

"Dark magic," Cameron whispered. "She's coming."

"Moira?" Monte gasped.

"Quick, say the words." Finn snatched Monte's knife and held the blade against his palm.

"I can't, I . . ." Monte's head felt fuzzy.

"Do it," Finn demanded.

"I, Monte Darrow, summon thee, Farwen, the Unicorn Witch and queen of all creatures Mystical, with the purest intent," Monte stammered.

Finn grazed the knife blade across the inside of his hand. Blood dripped from the gash and splattered into the wet soil.

Another canine howl, this time closer, rent the air.

"Now the reason. Hurry," Cameron exclaimed.

"There isn't time." Panic wracked through Monte.

"Monte, please," Cameron begged.

"Help, Farwen! We need your help!" Monte pleaded to the ground and then grabbed the knife from Finn. He fumbled for the telestone, their only line of communication. "C'mon, work. Work!" he begged. But the stone remained as dark as the night around them.

A third howl drifted up from the trail below.

"We've gotta hide," Finn said.

Monte shoved the telestone inside his boot and stared at Cameron, whose wealth of wisdom and words seemed to have died along with the rainbow lights. "The broom." He plucked Cousin's B's broomstick from the ground. It felt as dead as the rainbow lights looked.

"Hurry! Make it go," Finn wailed.

Monte squeezed the handle, which was as cold as ice. "It's not working!" He whipped around in search of another escape route. But there was nowhere for them to go. The mountain shot up vertically behind them, too steep to climb, and the muddy trail that had led them to the ledge was now overtaken by sure doom. A small cluster of boulders near the back of the platform would provide merely temporary concealment, but it was their only chance. "Behind the rocks." Monte scooped the sickly purple gems from the ground.

"Here, let me." Cameron took the piksels with shaking hands as the trio squeezed in behind the rocks. She stuffed the lights down her coat as another howl pierced the air.

"Look," Finn squealed, pointing through a crack in the boulders.

An enormous wolf hopped over the ledge. It scanned the ground with its snout, its back slender yet strong beneath a coat of thick, grizzly fur. The wolf paused, sniffing aggressively at the spot where the threesome had stood only seconds before.

"It smells my blood," Finn whispered in agony.

A tall figure emerged from the path below. Though a hooded traveling cloak masked most of her willowy frame, there was no mistaking it was Moira. Monte carefully slid his wand from his backpack as she drifted toward where the wolf stood, grand and stately. In one hand, she clasped her wand. In the other, she held a small orb, its bright green glow stunning against the darkness.

"Good girl, Connery," Moira praised the wolf. "The intruders are near." She tapped the glowing orb with her wand, and it floated from her hands, scanning the platform like a giant all-seeing eye.

Monte ducked as the green light passed over the boulders. To his side, Finn began to quake. A wisp of a whimper leaked from his lips. Monte clapped his hand over Finn's mouth, the silence heavier than the freezing air surrounding them.

"There." Moira's voice scored the steely night.

Monte squeezed his fingers around his wand with his free hand as Connery's claws clicked against the frozen ground. There was no time to make plans. This was fight or flight. Or rather, fight or be captured. Monte vaulted from the boulders, slashing his wand through the air. A frail strand of sparks leaked from the tip.

"Really, Master Monte," Moira said through the stillness. "You shouldn't handle a wand unless you know how to use it."

Monte backed against the boulders, Connery's hot, musky breath bathing his face, her eyes yellow beads embedded in splotchy sable fur. "I'm gonna need my shell back," he said, forcing himself to ignore the wolf's massive teeth.

Moira laughed, the sound harsh as it reverberated off the mountain. "I must admit, Master Monte, I am only half-shocked to see you here. You came sooner than I expected, but I always knew you'd show up. Tell me, how long did it take for the regret to set in?"

"Garrick woke up," Monte growled. The green orb circled his head, like it was surveying his thoughts. "And he told us everything." He flinched as Connery snapped her teeth at him. He tried to direct his wand at the wolf's chest.

Moira strutted toward him, her cloak billowing behind her. "I'll take that," she said, commanding Monte's wand into her possession. "Anything else?" she asked, barely moving as his backpack, the pocketknife, and Cousin B's broom shot into the air toward her. Monte felt the telestone fighting to escape from inside his boot as his other belongings clattered to the ground.

"Oh." Moira cocked her head. "You brought accomplices." She stared at the boulders behind Monte.

"No, I'm alone."

"Nonsense. Lying doesn't suit you." Moira dashed her wand through the air.

"Stop!" Finn leapt from behind the boulders. Instantly, his travel satchel was ripped from his shoulders.

"Ah, our little pixie friend," Moira mocked.

"You skiving hag!" Finn balled his hands into fists and sprung at Moira. Connery intercepted him, sending him tumbling to the ground.

"Stay there, little pixie," Moira ordered. "It'd be a shame to have to waste you." She gazed ahead of her, eyes glassed over, as though communicating with an invisible force. "There's another . . ." She fluttered her wand in front of her. Cameron's rainbow lights whipped from behind the boulders. "Fairy piksels. Clever. Now who could these possibly belong to?" Moira's voice hinted at amusement. "Surely, such fine gems have an equally as fine owner?"

Cameron emerged from behind the rocky barricade, her face shadowed.

"Leave my friends alone." Monte glared at Moira. "You'll never get away with this."

The green orb hovered near Moira's head, elongating her shadow. "Oh, but I already have, Master Monte." She grabbed his shoulder, her grip like iron talons as she led him to the border of the ledge. Cameron and Finn, herded by a snarling Connery, followed. Debris crumbled from the edge of the platform as Monte teetered against Moira's grasp. He looked down to see blackness, like a bottomless pit.

Moira swooped her arms around the trio. "This will only hurt a little bit." She laughed wickedly and then shoved them from the ledge.

# CHAPTER 22
## The Firepearl

Somehow, Monte was still alive. He plummeted down the mountain on his backside, dragged by an unseen force, the wind sucked from his lungs. He clenched his teeth together, half-expecting to collide with a tree or a boulder as Finn careened in front of him. But whatever power was pulling them down the mountain didn't seem interested in taking their lives. At least not yet.

All at once, a flash of green light swallowed Finn from sight. Another flash and Monte found himself skidding down a narrow channel. His bare hands burned against the frozen ground as the tunnel spit him across a smooth, icy surface. Cameron hurtled past him on her stomach, her body sprawled out in a star formation as she struggled to slow down. She bumped into Finn who spun across the ice with a loud yelp.

Monte slid to a stop, his groans echoing off the bluish ice that coated the walls. He looked around, mesmerized by the gargantuan icicles hanging from above—sharp, magnificent teeth ready to pierce.

"We're in a snow monster's den," Finn said as he struggled to his hands and knees.

"Or a giant's igloo." Monte stood and turned slowly in a circle, his legs unsteady. "The tunnel!" He slipped toward the small opening they had just come through. "Maybe we can climb back up and—oh, Crivens!" A thick sheet of ice fused over the hole, as if the walls were alive.

"I don't see another exit." Finn whipped his head around.

"This isn't good," Cameron said, rising from the ice.

"We've gotta get out of here," Monte said.

"But how?" Finn asked. "We need magic to do that and Moira took your wand."

"Indeed, you will need magic to escape this place, my young pixie." Moira's voice rang through the cave. "Or a miracle."

Monte whirled around, nearly losing his footing as the slick ground began to quiver. The icy floor cracked near the center of the cave, giving way to a deep, circular rift, the walls groaning with the weight of the ice coat. A large glass bowl emerged from the growing hole. Its frosty surface, plated in a golden rim, glowed with Celtic knots that shone a plethora of colors.

"Welcome to the heart of Ben Nevis," Moira's voice rang through the icicles. The bowl continued to slowly rise until it hovered in the air above the hole.

"You!" Monte snarled as Moira materialized from the darkness. She grasped Cousin B's broomstick at her side. His pack and Finn's satchel swung from her other arm. Cameron's rainbow lights studded her neck, two shades away from complete blackness.

"I'm so glad you've joined me tonight." Moira tossed the packs aside. The broom whizzed from her hand, hitting the icicles overhead with a loud smash, the icy teeth swallowing the pieces away.

"Something very important is about to take place, and I need your help." Moira's lips curled into a sneer, her cheekbones high and imposing beneath her deep-set eyes. A clicking of nails against the frozen ground announced Connery's arrival. "You've already met Connery," Moira continued. "But let me introduce you to the others."

Over a dozen pairs of amber eyes emerged from the darkness behind Connery. The wolves padded forward on all fours, their rigid ears and long snouts menacing against the dull luminosity of the cavern walls.

"Master Monte . . ." Moira swept her eyes across the trio. ". . . friends. Meet the Munro Majesties."

The great dogs yipped and howled, showing off sets of sharp yellow teeth as they bounded around each other. A single wolf with a thick muzzle and fur the color of copper broke from the pack with a snarl. He barked and threw himself at Connery. The pair growled and yelped as they crashed to the ground, barely missing the floating glass basin.

"Enough!" Moira whistled through her teeth. "Please, my darlings. We have visitors, after all." The coppery wolf whimpered as Connery released her jaws from the back of his neck. He tussled to his paws and shook his coat, his fur shifting over a thatch of scars on his withers.

Monte squinted at the great dog's back. Across his auburn shoulders, intertwined through irregular patches of fur, swirled an interesting pattern of symbols.

Shadows brushed over Moira's face. "My Munro Majesties are very special, each and every one." She stroked the coppery wolf's head. "I created them, you see."

"What're you talking about?" Monte demanded.

"They're humans," Cameron said, her voice low and deep. "The Munro Majesties. They're not wolves at all."

"Ah." Moira's head snapped in Cameron's direction. "Witty, young lady."

"You transfigured them," Monte said. "Just like Garrick."

"Calm, Master Monte. Assumption is often the predecessor to disfavor," Moira said. "The Majesties provide me with their unwavering servitude in exchange for disguise within the Mystic and Norm realms."

"But they were humans," Cameron protested. "I can sense it."

"Once humans, yes, the Munro Majesties were amongst the Nuckelavee's most devout followers," Moira said. "Each bears the mark of our master." Moira pushed back the fur between the coppery wolf's shoulders. "The Nuckelavee's kiss."

"No." Monte felt sickened by the thought.

"When the Unicorn Witch banished the Nuckelavee we suffered a great loss," Moira said. "However, I was determined not to sit idly and wait for our master's return. Instead, I focused my energy into locating what was left of his followers. I succeeded in rescuing a good few before the IMB discovered them." Moira turned to the pack. "For them, it was a life of being hunted, of always ducking and diving. A life filled with the impending doom of capture." The pack fell into formation, an imposing row of vicious beasts. "So, I offered them an alternative. A life free from such threats, concealed from the eye of the IMB, safely disguised by my transfiguration expertise."

Monte bared his teeth, wanting to lash out, just like one of the wolves. Finn quivered at his side. Whether from anger or from fear, Monte was unsure.

Moira drifted across the line of Munro Majesties, her gaze harsh. "Saving the Nuckelavee's followers from a life of Bureau torture was the perfect opportunity to test out my formula. If the tincture worked, they could live out their days in peace, serving me in exchange for their secrecy."

"In peace? They're rabid wolves now," Monte exclaimed.

"I admire your passion, Master Monte," Moira leered. "You remind me so much of Esca."

"How dare you mention my father," Monte said. "Here, of all places. Pretending to be his friend. You're nothing but an old hag. Wait until my parents find out about this place." He took a step forward but was met by a chorus of gnashing teeth.

The mirth drained from Moira's face. "Let me assure you, Monte, that the next time you leave this cave you'll either be dead or . . . unable to conduct yourself in a humanly nature."

"Never!" Finn trumpeted.

"Foolish kids," Moira leered. She tapped the levitating basin with her wand, sending an eruption of colors through the ancient symbols. "Not even Mr. and Mrs. Darrow, the highly trained experts that they are, have unearthed this cavern, the heart of Ben Nevis."

"Perhaps not," Cameron finally spoke. "But there's a sickness on this mountain. It's spreading. And soon, everyone will see it."

"Hush," Moira said.

Cameron began to whimper. She clutched her head and sank to her knees.

"Cameron?" Monte exclaimed.

"What's wrong?" Finn asked.

Cameron continued to cradle her head.

"Leave her alone!" Finn glared at Moira, braced like a bobcat ready to lunge.

"The young lady is correct." Moira's voice rose over their protests. "The longer I labor in this cavern, the more influenced the mountain becomes. The magic—superior and grand—seeps through the walls, manifesting itself on the outside." She looked around her, as though admiring the cavern for the first time. "Very few Mystics recognize the potential such higher magic possesses. Instead, they succumb to fear. They label what they see and feel as dark and evil. But it doesn't have to be that way at all."

"Yes, it does." Cameron trembled. "Dark magic is dark magic."

Moira cocked an eyebrow. "Pretentious girl. You're just as irrational as the rest," she said. "But you'll see. Once the master has risen again, your eyes will be opened. You'll view everything in a new light, just as I did so many years ago, when the great Nuckelavee promised to exchange my servitude for what I desired most."

"This . . ." Monte pointed to the Munro Majesties. ". . . goes against Mystic law, and you won't get away with it."

Cameron returned to her feet beside him, her body rigid, her eyes distant.

Moira's nostrils flared. She glided across the ice, scoffing, as she slid to a graceful stop in front of the trio. "Let's not do this again, Cameron." She dismissed Monte with a flick of her hand. "Stop trying to tap into my head. Remember what happened last time?"

Cameron stood stiff and quiet, deep in concentration. "I'm done with your mind games, Moira," she said in a low voice. "I'm done with all of this."

Moira smirked. The necklace hung like black lumps of coal against her chest. "Silly girl. You've yet to experience what evil is."

"What's she talking about?" Monte stared at Cameron. "Mind games?"

Cameron's eyebrows wrinkled together, her lips clamped with focus.

"You'll never be as powerful as me." Moira's voice climbed. "You may be an Influencer, but I've delved deep into the offences of telepathy. Even the most practiced of your kind cannot command me."

"Cameron, what's going on?" Monte's heart raced.

Cameron began to shake. "She made me do it. I didn't want to!"

"Do what?"

"She's been using my powers as an Influencer to spy on you." The words burst from Cameron's mouth.

"Monte," Moira said with great pleasure as she swept her hand in front of Cameron. "Meet the half-wit responsible for nearly drowning you at Witch's Pointe."

"No," Cameron pleaded. "I never wanted to!"

"Meet the ninny from whose eyes and from whose mind I have gained valuable information about you."

"She got into my head. I had no choice!" Cameron wailed. "I tried to fight back, but she forced me. Again and again—" She halted, as though someone had grabbed the words from her throat.

"Just you have a seat, young lady," Moira said as Cameron collapsed against the ice.

"You've been messing with her to get to me?" Monte asked, disgusted.

Moira reached into her pocket. "No, Master Monte. I exploited Cameron's rare talents to get to this." She plucked the seashell from the red canister and thrust it in his face, tauntingly.

"That's mine, hand it over!" Monte pounced at Moira, frantic to regain his prize, to make her suffer. But Moira dashed her arm across his face, sending him and the red container clattering to the ground.

"Monte!" Cameron screamed.

"Quiet." Moira tucked the seashell back inside her cloak.

Monte gasped, his vision fuzzy, his nose pulsating, as Moira grabbed a handful of his hair.

"Get your hands off of him!" Finn lunged after Moira.

With a snap of her wrist Moira sent a fiery green rope flying from her fingertips.

Finn hollered and crashed to the ice as the emerald cord snaked around him.

"Finn!" Cameron yelled. "No!"

"Leave him alone!" Monte swung his fists at Moira as she dragged him across the ice.

"Take him to the basin," Moira ordered. Connery sprung forward, clamping down on Monte's wrist.

Monte kicked and twisted, clenching his jaw in agony as the wolf's teeth threatened to puncture through his jacket. She hauled him to the glass bowl, which now glowed the color of molten lava.

Across the ice, the crackling green cable whipped from Finn's slender frame. It circled above Cameron as she scrambled toward him, sizzling through the air like a menacing lasso. It crashed to the ground with a great hiss, imprisoning the pair in a ring of fiery green flames.

"Don't either of you two move from that circle," Moira ordered. "Or you'll receive a most unpleasant shock."

Cameron cradled Finn's head in her arms, the green rope snapping and popping around them.

"My singe cords are one of a kind," Moira explained, waving at the offending rope. "They don't just burn. They bite."

Cameron screamed as the singe cord's flames licked the icy floor around her in an array of hostile zaps.

"Let . . . them . . . go!" Monte demanded, his fingers tingling against Connery's vice.

"And why would I do that, Master Monte?" Moira weaved toward him. "Especially when there are still introductions to be made?" She clicked her fingers together and a piercing shriek echoed through the cave.

Claws scratched ice, the wretched sound grinding up the walls, ricocheting through the tangle of stalactites above.

"Cat sith." Cameron's body went rigid.

Finn shot to a sitting position, the pallor of his face only intensifying against the green light of the singe cord.

Monte froze as the great cat materialized from the shadows. The beast's bulging muscles rippled beneath a sleek coat of ebony fur, its eyes glinting.

"Meet Bodmin, my greatest triumph yet." Moira cupped her hand under the beast's chin.

Monte's head swam as hints of recognition rang through him. Something was very familiar about this scene. The cave. The cat sith. The wolves.

Cave . . .

Cat Sith . . .

Monte gasped, sick with realization. The Norm film he had seen back in the hotel in Salem . . . with the lady who transformed the man into a black panther. He was living it.

"Something wrong, Master Monte?" Moira asked from where she caressed Bodmin's chin.

"You." Monte choked out the word. "How?"

"Whatever do you mean?" Moira straightened.

"This," Monte answered, waving his free hand in front of him. His voice felt disconnected, faraway. "I saw it all on television. Months ago."

"Isn't magic just marvelous?" Moira said, viciously smug.

"I don't understand," Monte growled through his teeth.

"Some time ago I came across a lone hiker here on Ben Nevis," Moira explained. "He was badly injured—unable to move. Hypothermia was overtaking him. He was dying."

Monte's pulse beat against his ears. He already knew where this was going, and he didn't want to hear it.

"I offered the hiker a remedy," Moira continued. "If he partook of my newest tincture—a highly refined formula—I'd not only save his life but provide for him until his death." She smiled, a barbarous admiration lining her face. "Being a Mystic himself, he agreed." Bodmin's tail flicked from side to side as he stared up at his master.

"You tricked him," Monte said, remembering the man's desperate face on the TV. "Just like you tricked Garrick."

Moira's smile morphed from amused to wicked. "Once again, my potion worked spectacularly. Not only did he transform into this striking beauty, but he has served me well in my preparations for the Nuckelavee's return."

"Yeah, against his will!" Monte protested.

"On the contrary, Master Monte," Moira said. "My potions are most effective when the candidate has a profound, ardent desire. To live, in this case. A life as a noble predator is far better than no life at all. I merely offered another choice to impending death."

"I would've died rather than be held captive to you," Monte spat.

Moira charged at Monte. She grabbed him by the collar of his jacket, yanking him to his feet. He bellowed as Connery's teeth tore down his arm, grating across his bare hand. Moira pivoted so that Monte was facing the glass bowl. Slowly, she extended her arm, her eyes crazed like the Munro Majesties behind her. "Your hand, Master Monte."

"Never!"

"Your hand. Give it to me now." Moira pulled him toward her. Monte narrowed his eyes in defiance.

"Stupid boy." Moira snatched his wrist. She twisted his hand upward and placed the seashell in his palm, the blood from Connery's bite staining its milky white grooves. Cameron's gems clinked around Moira's neck, inky and black. "To the basin." She scrunched Monte's fingers around the shell.

A familiar sensation swelled in Monte's chest as the shell's energy began to spread up his arm.

"You've yet to realize the power you hold, Master Monte." Moira yanked up his jacket sleeve, maintaining her grip on his tingling hand. She pulled her wand forward and pointed it at his fist.

Monte's arm twinged. The pain from Connery's bite paled next to the shell's fiery surface. Beads of sweat trickled down his temples as a strange incantation rolled from Moira's lips. Her mouth fluttered as she chanted the foreign words, growing louder with each syllable until finally, with a mighty shout, she looked to the icicles above. Her voice whirred through the cave, echoing through the icicles, a foreboding poem of doom. Then, all was quiet. She pried Monte's fist open, her fingers like marble against his flaming skin. Fine, powdery ashes spilled from his palm, the swirly scars on his hand red and inflamed beneath Connery's fresh teeth marks. Moira leaned closer, her hair brushing across Monte's arm, her warm breath scattering the ashes like dull pixie dust. "I knew it." She licked her lips. The Munro Majesties yipped from the shadows, their excitement bouncing through the cavern.

Monte stared at his palm in disbelief. A dense black ball with a metallic sheen glinted in his hand where the seashell had been.

"The Firepearl," Moira said with hushed awe as she scooped the dark stone from Monte's hand. "My suspicions did not fail me."

"Where's the seashell?" Finn staggered to his feet. The flames of the singe cord licked at his waist. "You demented hag," he howled at Moira. "You cursed it away!"

"There was never a seashell," Moira said, her face flecked with triumph. "Only this." She brought the gleaming pearl to her lips and kissed it.

Monte wiggled against her grasp, overcome with confusion and a sense of loss. "My seashell . . . you nixed it!"

"No, Master Monte. You destroyed the shell. Just now." Moira cradled the pearl in her palm. "I have you to thank for unveiling its true identity . . . for unveiling the Firepearl."

"Witchcraft," Monte seethed. "I trusted you with my seashell, and now look what you've done."

Moira's smile curled into a smirk. "The Firepearl . . ." She held the dark pearl to her cheek. ". . . is the brother to the Moondrop and the Mica Star. Together, the three make up the legendary Deo Stones. Really, Monte, surely you would've learned about this in school?" she mocked.

Monte panted, lost for words. Anger meshed with fear inside of him. He wished desperately that he had his wand. Or his pocketknife. Anything.

"The master has sought after you for many decades," Moira spoke to the Firepearl. "But to no avail . . . until now. We have our good friends here to thank for your discovery," she almost cooed. "Especially Cameron. She awakened my understanding of your disguise."

Cameron squealed from inside the singe cord, like an invisible hand was clamped over her mouth.

"Years of studying, of traveling around the globe," Moira prattled. "It all would've been nothing were it not for that young lady's distinctive abilities."

"Don't believe anything she says," Cameron wailed.

"I could tell the moment in which the Firepearl was discovered," Moira continued. "That day, months ago, when you, Monte, plucked it from oblivion on the beaches of Salem. I felt a great shift in the earth's energy that day, its magical patterns all leading to Witch's Pointe." She looked up at Monte, her eyes curious. "It's a wonder your father, the great Mystic that he is, didn't sense the surge himself. Yet I'm sure pleased he didn't." A small chuckle left her throat. "But what was I to do? Unfortunately, I was here, in Scotland, hundreds of miles away. I needed to get to the Firepearl, but how? It was physically impossible, even with my access to the portal system. I required a messenger. A host. Someone to conceal my identity while I watched from afar." Moira stared at Cameron. "And my, did I find one."

"No." Cameron clasped her forehead. "Stop."

Moira traced her finger across the rim of the glass basin. "I plunged into my clairvoyant capacities, and, to my pleasure, found Cameron. Right there. First in the Norm grocery store and then again on the very beach where Monte and the Firepearl were. Though I paid her little heed that day in the store. Her significance didn't awaken until the next day."

"I knew it," Monte said, thinking back to that hot summer day in Salem. "I knew I saw you in the grocery store." He looked at Cameron, who stared at her feet. He turned to Moira. "But it didn't work," Monte said. "You tried to use Cameron to set the tide on me, to get to the seashell, the pearl, but you failed." He swiped his hand at Moira, nearly knocking the Firepearl from her grasp.

"You moronic boy! I have half a mind to end you right here, without further word," Moira barked, thrusting Monte at the pack of Munro Majesties. "You've been nothing but a troublemaker, right from the start."

Monte kicked at the howling beasts, shielding his head from the frenzy of snapping teeth.

Finally, Moira dragged him back toward the basin. "I knew from the moment the ocean ejected you that there was a special connection between you and what I suspected to be the Firepearl. It was hard, seeing you and your family at the Hawthorne Hotel portals the next day, knowing what I knew. But I couldn't make a scene there, of all places. So, I retrieved Cameron from Salem and brought her here to Scotland. I used her skills to keep a close watch on you. However . . ." Moira's voice dropped. ". . . it wasn't until I came across Garrick that I knew I had a real chance of getting my hands on that shell."

"You tried to use my brother against me?" Monte spat. "You could've killed him!"

"It was the perfect plan. I could build my cat sith army all while hunting down the shell." Moira's lips creased together, her brow reflective. "All the other boys before Garrick couldn't withstand the potion. They were too weak. But your brother showed great promise. I knew that if my potion didn't kill Garrick, then I'd still be able to use him to get the shell."

The other boys. Monte's mind rolled back to the night he had seen Cameron at the lamppost, the night Uncle Jarus had told him all about the mysterious cat attacks. Boys his age. They hadn't been attacked by a cat sith at all. They *were* the cat siths. But none of them had survived the full transformation. None of them, except Garrick. "You are a disgusting, evil woman." Monte's throat swelled, furious.

Moira swept her hair behind her shoulders, almost as if she were proud to be titled as such. "I thought I finally had the shell the night of your grandmother's Fairy Ball. But Garrick was stronger than I ever expected. He fought my tincture, and, with the help of that seashell, broke from the enchantment—something I never thought was possible."

"I bet that infuriated you," Monte said, suppressing his rage.

Moira's face sharpened, her eyes like daggers. "No, not entirely," she almost whispered. "I'll admit it was another setback, but thanks to Cameron, I discovered an additional set of sturdy specimens."

"The goons?" Monte choked, thinking of the most recent missing Norm teens.

"That's right." Moira rolled the Firepearl through her fingers. "Not the brightest bunch, I'll admit. But still quite promising."

"Where are they? What'd you do with them?" Finn shouted from the fiery ring.

"Oh, I'm sure they'll be joining us shortly," Moira said, unconcerned.

Monte scanned the ice cavern, straining for any sign of movement. He had to fix this. Now.

"Just when things were looking rather ghastly, you, Monte, so openly divulged your sorry little story to me," Moira continued. "Like a clueless idiot you presented me with the object of my greatest desire. And that is all that matters."

Monte glared at Moira, tempted to lunge at her were it not for the army of wolves at her back.

"A brief inspection affirmed that it was no ordinary shell. It possessed a heart foreign to its sediment, yet I could not extract it. The shell needed coaxing in order to birth the Firepearl within."

"That's mental . . . *you* are mental," Finn shouted.

Moira snapped her fingers. The singe cord grew from a warm blaze to ferocious flames. "Hardly," Moira said, the hush of danger in her voice. "It's actually miraculous." Her eyes locked with Monte's. "You, Master Monte, were my accomplice in freeing the Firepearl, and you didn't even see it," she crowed. "You showed up here, on Ben Nevis, completely oblivious and practically on my doorstep. Cameron deserves a special thanks for leading you here."

"That wasn't my plan," Cameron cried.

"Settle down, lass. It is no secret that you Influencers are a conniving species. Stop trying to hide behind your tender-faced façade." Moira clutched the pearl in her palm, her other hand tightening around Monte's wrist.

The glass bowl began to spin, its primeval symbols blurring as it gathered speed. A heavy hum whirred from Moira's mouth, her knuckles white around the Firepearl. With a single incomprehensible word, she dropped the metallic ball into the bowl.

"No!" Monte sprung for the basin, the spinning bowl tearing at his fingers as he snatched the Firepearl. Connery charged. Her teeth snapped around his calf with a gruesome crunch. Monte screamed, his leg throbbing as a warm energy spilled from the Firepearl.

"You!" Moira slashed her wand at Monte. He catapulted through the air, his leg tearing from Connery's jaw. The wind whooshed from his lungs as he thudded to the icy ground. He was lost in a sea of dizziness. Light flickered in and out of his peripheries. And then, everything went black.

Sounds faded in and out. Monte's head buzzed, his body numb. Darkness surrounded him, the twinkling of a thousand stars swirling in and out of view. He blinked his eyes, the enormous stalactite tips staring down at him. Slowly, he turned his head. A single singe cord crackled around him. Finally, he recognized his name.

"Monte," Cameron said through the flames.

He raised his head. The cave spun around him.

"No, no. Get down," he heard Finn whisper.

Alarm stabbed through him as the cave came into focus. He didn't dare move. Across the ice, not ten feet from him, Cameron was kneeling, encompassed inside a separate singe ring. To her side, in an identical sizzling circle, squatted Finn.

Cameron's eyes met Monte's, her face full of warning as she thrust her finger to the center of the cave.

Monte craned his neck over the flames. Moira stood near the glass bowl, her back to them. Flasks full of steaming fluids orbited around her, the molten basin casting a demonic glow against her figure. Her sharp profile danced across the cavern walls, joined by the Munro Majesties as they faded in and out of the shadows. Bodmin was nowhere to be seen. Moira rolled something dark and shiny through her slender fingers. The Firepearl.

"Monte," Finn hissed. He pointed to something near Monte's feet, his eyes wide, his mouth forming a silent word.

Monte looked down at his feet but saw nothing. *What?* he mimed back.

*The telestone,* Cameron mouthed, jabbing her finger at the same spot.

*The telestone?*

"Yes, yes," Finn whispered, bouncing on his toes. "At your feet."

Monte flipped to his stomach, his pulse throbbing in his ears. A small, dark object clinked off his boot.

"Get it, quick," Finn buzzed.

Monte squirmed over the ice. He slapped his hand over the smooth, flat object, catching it just before it slid into the flaming green cord.

"It's on," Finn whispered. "Say something to it."

Violet streaks marbled the stone's sleek surface, each threading through the other, together forming a border around the edge. Monte flattened himself against the ice, ever mindful of Connery's bite marks beating in his calf, as Moira bustled from flask to flask in front of them. She worked quickly, her gaze intense and distant as she muttered something in a strange language.

"Hurry, Monte," Cameron urged, the singe circle drowning out her whisper.

Monte rolled to his side, his back to Moira as he cupped the glowing telestone to his mouth. "Mom? Dad . . ." The purple strands of light brightened and then faded, as though the telestone was absorbing his words. Perhaps his parents were out of custody by now. Just maybe, someone would be listening. "Uncle Jarus? Somebody, please, help us," Monte whispered into the stone. "We're in a secret cavern on Ben Nevis. Moira. It's Moira."

"She's coming," Cameron squealed.

Monte flipped to his back, the stone tumbling from his fingers. It bounced across the ice with a clang and a snap, skirting into Cameron's circle. She pounced on it, her eyes wide as she fumbled it into her pocket.

"What's going on here?" Moira demanded.

The hairs on Monte's neck prickled, his chest rising and falling in terrified waves as he glared up at his adversary.

"Impertinent fool." Moira stood over Monte. She tossed the Firepearl from hand to hand like it was some sort of plaything.

Monte clambered to his hands and knees, his insides blazing with anger and fear.

"Retribution is in order." Moira trickled her fingers around the pearl, her eyes narrowing. Slowly, she brought her fist to her mouth, the Firepearl trapped inside her fingers. She stared at Monte for a long second and then, without warning, punched her fist into the air.

Monte winced, expecting a catastrophic blow like what he'd experienced at Hibernian Field and again at Grandmother Meriweather's Fairy Ball. Instead, a hush cloaked the cavern.

Moira thrust her fist to the icicles again. The air remained still. "No," she whispered, repeating the action for a third time, unsuccessfully. Panic flickered across her face. She lowered the Firepearl, her wand clutched tightly in her other hand, the wolves erupting into an agitated madness behind her. Bodmin's yowls echoed through the shadows. "I will not fail again!" Moira shouted, swirling the wand around her head, her arm angled for attack. A spell shot from the end, clattering into the icicles above.

"Watch out!" Monte hunkered against the cave floor as Moira's dismay ignited into rage around them.

The ground trembled. The walls quivered. Shards of ice crashed from the ceiling. Moira descended upon the molten bowl, cave debris skittering around her as the frozen cavern walls creaked. "Master!" she wailed. "The prize!" A look of crazed satisfaction coated her face as she fed the Firepearl to the bubbling potion within the basin. An ear-splitting pop tore through the air and more sharp masses smashed to the ground. And then, like a dying thunderstorm, the cave's rumbling groans began to fade.

"Crikey!" Finn pointed to a massive hole in the wall behind them.

A silvery mist oozed from the earthy wound, creeping across the cavern floor in a thick sheet as something stirred from the depths within.

Monte struggled to his feet. He clenched his hands into fists, bracing himself as rubble tumbled from the great hole, the final crashes echoing off the ice-stripped slate. Something big and dark stirred within the breach of the cave wall.

CHAPTER 23

The Queen of the Unicorns

A masculine figure stepped into the cave. He wore a thick cloak, his face shadowed inside a deep, soft hood. His frame, tall and broad, matched the strength of his gait as his shoes tapped against the ice. He glanced at Monte, his steely eyes barely noticeable beneath the dark hood, his chin firm and prominent.

"Dad?" Monte whispered.

The figure raised his wand to his lips, signaling Monte to stay quiet. He picked his way across the ice like a nocturnal beast on the prowl, his focus on Moira. "I demand yeh release my son at once, Moira," he said in a booming voice. Bodmin hissed from the recesses of the cave.

"Esca," Moira said, her face cool as she smoothed her hands over her robes. "Out of custody so soon? Shocking." She tapped her wand across her palm, the glass bowl spinning beside her. "After all, your eldest son committed such a grievous crime."

"Yeh have some nerve." His voice matched the temperature of the cavern as he weaved through the wreckage. "I was a fool te ever trust yeh, especially with our shaky past."

"Ah, come now, Esca." Moira's face contorted. "It almost sounds like *you* were the one in love with me, not Jarus."

"Yer still pining over that?" He slowly raised his arm, his wand positioned to stun.

Moira lifted her chin, her fair locks the only bright quality about her. "That's all long passed now, Esca. But if you care to discuss—"

"I am not here te discuss the past," he said. "I'm here for Monte, and te detain yeh on behalf of the IMB."

"Ha! You're here to have me arrested?" Moira raised her wand.

"Release the children and I'll consider hearing what yeh have te say." His own wand shook in his hand.

Moira's eyes darkened. "I don't need to plead my case like I'm one of your useless, pitiful children."

"Moira . . ." he said.

With a snap of her wrist Moira dispelled a thin, shimmery string from the end of her wand.

"No! Dad!" Monte yelled.

"Stay back!" he choked as the string wound around his shoulders and neck.

"Fairy thread," Moira said as she yanked the wand from his hand. "One wrong move and it becomes a noose." She pushed him to his knees and stripped the hood from his head. His weary face stared back at her, his auburn hair swooping across his forehead. But it wasn't Esca Darrow.

"Jarus," Moira stammered, her voice caught between a whisper and a gasp.

"Yer surprised, Moira?" Uncle Jarus struggled against his bonds.

"That would please you, wouldn't it?" Moira said with a bitter laugh. "I assume you're here posing as your mightier brother as a ruse to ensnare me? You're a fool," she spat. "Have you forgotten how well I know you? Don't you remember all that we were? Now look at what you've become." She slapped his face. "Rusty and weak. Unimportant and disconnected from our kind. Desolate."

"Maybe I am all those things," Uncle Jarus grunted against the tightening snare. "Except for one. I am not desolate."

"I could finish you off right now." The fairy thread constricted as Moira pointed her wand at his neck.

"Let Monte and the others go," Uncle Jarus gasped.

Moira dug the tip of her wand into the side of his neck. "We could've had it all, Jarus," she hissed. "Just you remember that."

"Let them go . . . and yeh can have me," Uncle Jarus wheezed as the fairy thread sunk deeper into his skin. "I can help yeh be happy again."

"No, don't do it!" Monte shouted at Uncle Jarus.

His protests bounced off the walls and a painful hush fell over the cave. Conflicted, Moira's hesitation was tangible.

Suddenly, a jet of light whizzed from the giant hole in the wall, landing in a fiery coil in front of Uncle Jarus. He leaned into the tiny inferno and the fairy thread disintegrated from his cloak. He plucked his wand from the shocked Moira, his movements nimble despite his close call with the fairy thread. "Nice of yeh te join us, brother," he sputtered.

"Dad," Monte exclaimed as the real Mr. Darrow slid into the cave.

Mr. Darrow raised his wand, his face like granite as he shot a cluster of spells at Moira. They pinged off her, useless against whatever protective ward she had conjured. She retaliated with a ball of white light, which Mr. Darrow deflected with a swish of his wand. Bodmin shrieked and sprung forward, engulfing Uncle Jarus with his giant claws as the Munro Majesties charged for Mr. Darrow.

"Get away from them!" Mrs. Darrow's voice broiled through the cave. Her hair whipped around her face, her eyes searing as she bolted from the cavity. She lassoed her wand above her head, sending a wall of orange sparks soaring toward the converging pack of dogs.

"Seize her," Moira shouted. The wolves whimpered in pain as the blazing sparks showered down on them. "Seize her, now!"

"Let us out," Monte demanded of Mrs. Darrow. "We can help!" He kicked against the singe cord encircling him. Shocks zapped through him in bone-shattering waves.

"You're safer there," Mrs. Darrow yelled. She sliced her wand above her, emitting another cluster of sparks. The coppery wolf dodged the spell, diving at her with a great snarl.

"Mom," Monte shouted. "Watch out!"

Mrs. Darrow produced an enormous shimmering bubble from her wand. It folded around her like a great glass sphere, fluid yet impenetrable. The coppery wolf smashed into the bubble with a painful howl as the cave erupted in a rainbow of spells. "Away with you, beasts!" Mrs. Darrow added to the cacophony of noises and colors, her wand flaring as the Munro Majesties swarmed at her.

"Vanessa," Mr. Darrow bellowed from where he and Moira viciously dueled. A whirlwind of hexes and counter-hexes flew from their wands, so quickly that it was impossible to decipher who was casting what. "Vanessa! The cat sith . . . Jarus!"

Mrs. Darrow whipped around, a pair of wolves dashing against her protective bubble. Uncle Jarus lay pinned beneath Bodmin's clutches at the other end of the cave. A chain of defensive charms spurted from his wand, the only shield against the great beast's lethal claws and teeth. "I'm coming,

Jarus," Mrs. Darrow yelled. The bubble shivered, weakening, as she broke through the Majesties.

"We've gotta help them," Monte said.

"I'm trying," Finn protested. "I can't get out."

"The Firepearl!" Cameron kicked at her singe cord entrapment and was repelled backward with a terrible zap.

Monte watched in horror as Moira shot a succession of spells at Mr. Darrow. Many clanged off the rotating basin, where the Firepearl was still spinning.

"But it's all the way over there, in that bowl thingy, you numpties," Finn shouted.

A torrent of sparks collided with the bowl, breaking its rotation and sending it clattering to the ground. The coppery wolf, which was nearest to the disaster, dashed away with a whimper as Moira's potions sizzled into the ice. Cameron's eyes narrowed as she focused in on the cowering wolf. "Come on, boy," she said, her brow bunched. "Go fetch." She craned her neck forward, her profile like stone as the coppery wolf padded toward the overturned bowl, his stride uneven yet obedient. He nudged his pointy nose beneath the basin and retrieved the Firepearl.

"Cameron, hurry," Monte pleaded.

"Good dog," Cameron said, her voice steady despite the vicious battle echoing around her. "Now . . . come here." The coppery wolf slinked toward them, oblivious to the surrounding commotion. "Drop it," she commanded as the creature reached Monte's singe ring. The wolf bowed his head and spat the Firepearl from his mouth. It clinked through the sizzling barrier, bouncing from one end of the circle to the next. Monte dove on top of it, hugging it to his chest as the edge of the singe cord charred his hair.

"Can only control . . . one dog at a time," Cameron grunted as the coppery wolf retreated to the back of the cave. "And I can't influence him for much longer. End this, Monte. End it now."

Monte clutched the Firepearl in his hand. It was cold and glacial. Several yards away, the Munro Majesties paced around his mother, closing in on her fading protective bubble. Bodmin's scream rebounded through the cave, followed by Uncle Jarus's wails of agony, his chain of spells now only a feeble shield against the large cat's swipes.

"Monte. Do something!" Finn urged.

"I'm trying!" Monte squeezed his eyes shut, searching for a connection. But something was wrong. The Firepearl was icy. Void of power. Dead.

"I'm losing him." Cameron sank to her hands and knees as the coppery wolf pawed at his head from the shadows.

Monte massaged the Firepearl between his palms. It had worked before. It had freed Garrick. Why wouldn't it save them now? All at once a gust of air streamed up his back. Silence poured into the cave. He turned as a blinding white light splashed all around them.

A majestic creature surfaced from the radiance, her brightness shooting through the cave. A mane of wavy hair curled around her peaked ears, cascading down her smooth, robust neck. Her fur shone like crystalline specks of stardust, trailing into silky tufts of hair which clad her cloven hooves.

"Farwen," Finn said, hushed. "The Unicorn Witch."

The creature raised her horse-like head, her silvery spiral horn glistening. Her muscular chest and sturdy body suggested extreme power as her tail, like that of a lion, brushed the air behind her. A mixture of fear and wonderment rushed through Monte. The world grew still around him as he froze in terrified reverence.

*Monte Darrow*, a voice resembling the sound of a waterfall rushed through his head. *You summoned me. I have traveled a great distance. For what cause have you brought me here?*

A delicate breeze stroked Monte's face, bringing with it a smell like fresh rain. He clasped his quivering hands together, the Firepearl dense against his skin. *I . . . made a mistake.*

The Unicorn Witch bowed her majestic head.

*That is, I trusted someone I shouldn't have, and she betrayed me, my family, and my friends*, Monte continued. *And now I . . . we . . . need your help.*

*I know who you speak of*, the voice thundered through Monte. *Moira has betrayed many in her search for power. She has sickened this mountain with the darkest of magic in an attempt to bring forth the Nuckelavee once more. Yet deep down, a sliver of good still lives inside of her.*

*How do you know all this?* Monte asked.

*I am the mother guardian of this land. I am the perpetrator of all magic that is good and right.*

*Then why did you let this happen?*

Farwen pawed at the ground. *I am bound by the immortal laws of the Fae. Edicts that date back to our Mystic beginnings.*

Monte lowered his head, suddenly ashamed.

*But I sense your valiant heart and your pure intentions, Monte Darrow. And that is what has summoned me.*

Monte peered at Cameron out of the corner of his eye. She stared intently at Farwen. Could she hear her, too?

*What has transpired here tonight nearly resulted in the bidding of the Nuckelavee from his solitary existence,* Farwen continued. *Moira is very powerful and much of what she has accomplished will not be easily remedied.*

Dread rent through Monte.

*However, with darkness is coupled light. They pull against each other, battling for dominance. But in the end, light always wins.*

Monte looked around him. At his family and his friends. At Bodmin and the Munro Majesties. At Moira. All remained poised in battle, their movements labored as time morphed around them.

*I will help to eradicate some of what has been done tonight,* Farwen continued. *But remember, even my presence, though timeless, has its limits.* She stretched her head high. *Monte, I must bestow upon you a profound warning.* She stamped her hoof into the ground. *The demon hungers for the Firepearl. He will continue to enlist the help of others to obtain it. Many will come to desire its great potential in exchange for false satisfaction and artificial happiness. They will fall under the delusions of the Nuckelavee, just as Moira has, for his fuel is their confusion and his resolve is their sorrow.*

*So, the Nuckelavee still has power? To come back?*

Farwen bobbed her head, her mane tumbling in silky currents around her neck. *The Firepearl embodies the purity of the land, which is the very core of Mystic existence. The Nuckelavee strives to strip the Firepearl of that integrity, in turn using it to his own benefit. He wants that power, and he will keep coming after it, I fear.*

Monte's fingers tingled. He grasped the Firepearl tighter.

*Once robbed of its goodness, the Firepearl could become tainted, vulnerable to the dark forces that try to attack it. You must use extreme caution, Monte. Be wary of the Nuckelavee, of his evil grasp. For now you know the degree of his hunger.*

*Me? But what am I supposed to do with it?*

*In time you will learn how to best defend the Firepearl. Trust your instincts and learn to control the fire within, to exercise patience, to practice the art of discernment. And always remember that sometimes our most valuable possessions exist right before our eyes, even if we can't see them.* Farwen stared into Monte, her eyes like rays of noonday sun.

Monte rubbed the scars on his arm, at the marks the Firepearl—once hidden in the seashell—had created.

*Now free from its disguise—free from the shell which bound it—the Firepearl has no need to shout of its true identity. It is finally exposed. It will not burn you again. But remember, the use of its magic can come with great cost. May the marks you bear serve as a reminder of the power which you guard.* Farwen paused, her ears twitching. *The time has come, Monte. I will restore the Firepearl to its full form this once, but it will need time to heal. It has many capabilities, including to unbind that which is bound, but you will not be able to exploit its full powers now. No. You will have one chance, one surge of power, before the Firepearl recesses to a state of recovery. Choose wisely, Monte, and be swift.* She blew a gentle stream of air from her mouth.

Monte felt the Firepearl grow warm as Farwen's healing breath gushed between his fingers. His chest swelled with the familiar energy, time returning to its normal pace. The Unicorn Witch reared her head back and brayed, the sound like a thousand wind instruments. She thundered past him, her radiance piercing through the shadows, the ground shaking beneath her as she galloped toward the toppled basin in the center of the cave. She swooped her head down, her great horn like a fiery poker as it punctured the glass bowl. The basin hissed and screamed. A murky purple steam bled from its ancient designs, followed by the frothy remains of Moira's potion.

"No!" Moira threw sparks at Mr. Darrow with her wand, conjuring a green singe cord with her other hand.

The fiery cord writhed through the air toward Farwen, angry and sinister, turning to dust the moment it met her chest. The Unicorn Witch charged toward the Munro Majesties next, scattering the wolves from Mrs. Darrow with her horn-studded head. The great dogs yelped, darting for the hole in the cave with their tails between their legs. Connery brought up the rear, her whimpers uncharacteristically frantic, the mighty Unicorn Witch at her heels.

Monte gritted his teeth, the cave suddenly dim in Farwen's wake. He squeezed the Firepearl. Its warmth surged up his arm, but nothing more happened. "C'mon," he begged as Mrs. Darrow dashed to Uncle Jarus's aid. She shot a stream of darts at Bodmin, hitting the terrible cat in the side of the head.

"Vanessa," Moira snarled against the cat sith's shrieks, hatred in her eyes. She twisted her wand in front of her, catching Mr. Darrow in an invisible chokehold while Uncle Jarus, now free from Bodmin's clutches, heaved himself to his hands and knees, his cloak in tatters, his arms covered in bloody gashes.

"Moira, you witch!" A fresh, young, and very angry voice bounced through the cavern as Garrick's silhouette materialized from the great rift.

"Garrick," Mr. Darrow rasped, breaking free of Moira's magical vice only to be hit with a flurry of hexes.

"Master Darrow," Moira taunted Garrick. "I see you're back from cat sith hell." She dashed her wand at Esca, sending him flying across the cave.

"No!" Purple sparks pelted from Garrick's wand. "Leave . . . my family . . . alone!" The sparks fizzled unimpressively at Moira's feet.

The evil lady cackled. She punched her wand toward Mrs. Darrow, who shot across the cave, away from the staggering and winded Bodmin.

"Moira," Uncle Jarus said, weakly. "Please, stop." He crumpled to a pitiful heap, his shoulders sagging in defeat.

A feline yowl stabbed the air. Another cry, as dreadful as the first, rang through the remaining shards of icicles above.

"Ah, my beauties. What took you so long?" Moira flicked her golden hair from her face, pointing her wand at Mr. and Mrs. Darrow. Shadows lurked deep inside the cavern. "Come," Moira beckoned. The black figures crouched forward, one, two, and three sets of slanted eyes glowing from the darkness, their claws biting against the icy floor.

Bodmin, the mightiest of all, joined them, like a captain to his skulking charges. The three cats hissed, stooping further into submission, their coats just as sleek and just as black as their leader's.

"Cat siths . . ." Finn whispered. "The goons."

Mr. Darrow, now plastered to the wall, struggled against the spell Moira had him under. He looked at his wife, whose condition was no better. Garrick remained rooted in place, paralyzed by the newcomers.

Moira's lips curled over her teeth as she looked from the cat siths to Mr. and Mrs. Darrow. "They're all yours," she said to the cats, her voice hollow and cruel. "I'll take care of the rest."

The great cats padded toward Mr. and Mrs. Darrow, their muscular frames ready to kill.

"Monte," Cameron shrieked. "The Firepearl!"

Monte hobbled to the perimeter of his fiery prison, the Firepearl's warmth surging through his veins. He had only one chance. It must work this time. He squeezed the pearl and with a great shout, thrust his arm forward. Streaks of light shot from his fist in a rippling current of golden magic. Bodmin screamed, dodging the Firepearl's mystical energy in one massive leap. His three charges, not as capable as their leader, hissed in pain and tumbled to the ground as the magic cascaded over them. Bodmin bounded for Uncle Jarus, the Firepearl's light glinting across his fur.

Monte directed the golden current at the great beast.

The cat sith screeched as the Firepearl's power encompassed him. He collapsed in front of Uncle Jarus, the light shimmering into his body through a single, great vortex. He shrieked again, his jaw widening into a giant agonizing wail as the magic began to pour back out of his chest.

"My Magnificent!" Moira screamed as the Firepearl's power gushed around Bodmin.

Uncle Jarus scrambled away from the monstrous cat, Garrick dashing past him.

"Garrick, no!" Mrs. Darrow beat against Moira's invisible bonds.

Garrick stumbled against the river of magic spewing from Bodmin, his steely eyes blazing, his wand aimed at Moira.

"Stop, she'll kill you!" Mr. Darrow shouted. His large frame convulsed as Moira's hex squeezed the air from him.

Garrick swirled his wand above his head. Lavender flames exploded above him, burning through the frigid air as they propelled toward Moira.

"Idiot boy," Moira shrieked. She flicked the violet fire away, lunging at Garrick. "I should've ended you long ago." A strand of fairy thread shot from her wand, winding around Garrick's neck. A smoky cloud of mist followed, floating menacingly in the air beside her. "But I'll finish you now . . . while your entire family watches, helpless, as you perish."

"Not a chance!" Uncle Jarus sprang from where he crouched on the ice, his blood-splotted robe swelling around him. With a terrible crash he tackled Moira to the ground, ripping Cameron's rainbow lights from her neck. They scattered across the ice like tiny black imps as he clambered back to his feet, Moira at his back.

Monte tried to yell; tried to force his limbs to move. But his joints wouldn't budge, his arms locked straight in front of him as the golden magic continued to rage from the Firepearl.

Moira leapt in front of Uncle Jarus, sliding underneath his nose. He screamed in agony as she took out his eye with one fast, mighty jab of her wand. He tumbled to his knees, clutching the wound, blood oozing between his fingers.

Garrick wheezed against the choke of the fairy thread. He pointed his wand at Moira, conjuring another stream of purple fire.

The spell grazed Moira's cheek. She gasped, staggering backward, her face stricken with shock. The cloud, now a tornado of smoke, swirled around her. She yelled as her hair whipped around her face, her wand ripped from her grasp. Uncle Jarus dove at her, shoving her further into the cyclone. The fairy thread slithered away from Garrick's neck, coiling through the air as Moira disappeared into the cloud.

Mr. Darrow dashed for his brother, no longer spellbound. "Jarus, watch out!"

Suddenly, the fairy thread, already partially consumed by the dark twister, snapped around Uncle Jarus's wrist.

Mr. Darrow threw himself at his brother, clawing after him.

Uncle Jarus was yanked into the shrieking cloud, away from Esca's grasp. He opened his mouth in a pained but soundless cry as the darkness seeped into the cavity that was once his eye. The whirlwind wailed around him, eating away at his fading figure. Mr. Darrow grasped at his brother's shadowy fragments, now turning to particles of dust . . . but Jarus was gone, swallowed into oblivion along with Moira and the ominous mist.

"Jarus . . ." Mr. Darrow choked. "He's gone. They're gone."

Monte bolted forward, now free from the singe ring, the Firepearl smoldering into a cold lump against his palm.

"No. No! No!" Mr. Darrow hollered into the fading mist.

"He's gone, Esca," Mrs. Darrow said, her voice shaky. She grabbed Mr. Darrow's trembling arm. "They both are."

Denial pulsed through Monte. But not a single indication of Uncle Jarus's existence remained.

"The cat siths." Finn's voice broke through the terrible hush.

Bodmin. The goons. Monte whipped around.

"Everybody stay back," Mrs. Darrow warned, suddenly snapping to attention. She ran toward the steaming heap of flesh that was once Bodmin, leaving Mr. Darrow curled onto his knees.

Monte slid to his mother's side, Cameron, Finn, and Garrick on his heels. He waved away the steam, smothered by the smoky odor surrounding Bodmin's remains. He gasped. A man's bruised and emaciated body shivered inside a crater of melting ice. His chest rose and fell in rapid breaths, his skeleton poking from beneath taut skin.

"It can't be," Mrs. Darrow whispered. "It's Brian Shaw. The missing Mystic." She crouched down. "Garrick, help me lift him," she ordered. Together, they heaved Mr. Shaw's delicate body from the icy pool.

"Mr. Shaw? Can you hear me?" Mrs. Darrow wrapped her cloak around him. "Do you know where you are?"

Mr. Shaw's eyelids flickered in acknowledgement. "This is the end," he croaked, his voice hollow. He looked around the cave, his skin pimpled with cold, his gaunt face matted with whiskers.

Monte's stomach walloped as he recognized the line from the Norm movie back in Salem. Except it hadn't been a movie at all. It had been Moira from the very start. And the cat sith . . . Bodmin. Brian Shaw was Bodmin.

"The goons!" Finn darted to the opposite end of the cave. "Oi, it's them all right," he affirmed from where the Norm lads lay in a heap. One of the goons lifted his head and groaned, his eyelids droopy, his sideburns scruffy. It was No-Neck.

"The Firepearl," Cameron whispered. "It broke the enchantment. Just like it did with Garrick."

Farwen's words echoed through Monte's mind. *It has many capabilities, including to unbind that which is bound, but you will not be able to exploit its full powers now . . . You will have one chance, one surge of power.*

"You're okay. You're safe now," Mrs. Darrow reassured Mr. Shaw. She stood, wand in hand, her footsteps smooth as she headed toward the three goons. "We need to get everyone out of here," she said, perhaps the only one with her full wits about her. "But first, a dose of drowsiness for these poor Norm boys." She pointed her wand at the goons. A chalky cloud poofed from its end. No-Neck lowered his head, re-joining Mohawk and Shaggy on their bed of ice as the cloud sifted around them. Their breathing deepened and seconds later, they were fast asleep. "Now, we must move," Mrs. Darrow ordered. "Before these Norms wake back up and in case those wolves come back. Monte, your leg."

Monte looked down, his mind numb to the gaping teeth marks in his calf.

"I can help," Finn said. He cupped his slender hands over Monte's leg, his touch cool and appealing against the wound. He exhaled and slowly removed his hands, leaving behind tender pink skin.

Monte stroked his blood-crusted pant leg, too bewildered to say anything.

"Fairy powers." Finn flexed his fingers, his face serious. The knife wound in his palm was gone. He placed his hands over the teeth marks on Monte's arm. Almost instantly, the lacerations were healed.

"Very good, Finn." Mrs. Darrow's voice was thankful. "Now help Mr. Shaw and the others. We need to move him and everyone else away from here." She weaved back to where Mr. Darrow knelt on the ice. "Esca, we have to leave," she urged. "Who knows what other dangers loiter here."

Mr. Darrow stared at his hands, his lips pale.

"Esca, the kids . . ." Mrs. Darrow said.

Monte stepped backward, his legs suddenly wobbly. "But we can't go. Uncle Jarus . . ." He swallowed the massive lump in his throat. "He's not gone for good. He's not."

"Monte, he's not coming back," Garrick said, his voice dense.

"How can you say that?" Monte spun to face Garrick. "After he sacrificed himself for you." He stared at his mother, pleading. "There has to be a way. You could conjure him back."

Mrs. Darrow bowed her head. "I wish I could, son, but . . ."

"Your mother's right," Mr. Darrow rumbled, defeated, as he gradually rocked to his feet. "Jarus is gone. We must go."

"I can't . . . I won't." Monte's chest constricted.

Suddenly, he was running, his legs like great tree stumps. He clambered across the ice, through the rubble, and into the gaping rift in the cave wall. Mrs. Darrow's protests pelted after him, but he didn't stop, following the shallow tunnel to the outdoors. Brian Shaw. Moira. Uncle Jarus. The names tore through him, unrelenting and torturesome, the last puncturing his heart. He inhaled deeply, heaving and choking as he tried to balance his breathing. A thin band of light at the bottom of the horizon indicated approaching dawn. The heavy patches of cloud from the night before had cleared, leaving behind feathery remnants that wisped across the pale sky. In front of him, stretching up the mountain, was a steep, muddy path. The trail climbed for many yards, finally ending in a wide platform that extended into a broad ledge.

A shuffling noise announced that Monte was not alone. Cameron traipsed from the mouth of the cave. She stopped at his side and gazed toward the ledge where, just hours previously, they had summoned the Unicorn Witch.

"Your parents are preparing Mr. Shaw and the Norms for transport," she said, tenderly. "Finn and Garrick are helping."

He nodded, his voice lost to the abyss of shock swirling inside of him.

"Still the purest spot on this mountain." Cameron pointed to the ledge. Her arm brushed against Monte's, her touch soothing. "Look," she whispered as the sun peeked over the horizon, splashing across the rolling stone peaks before them.

A beam of light streamed from the ledge, the brightness giving way to a queenly creature. Farwen. She pranced across the platform, her white coat glowing in the receding darkness, her mane like strands of sunshine. She reared back and pawed her front legs in the air as the marriage of sunlight and unicorn radiance forged an outstanding palette of hues.

The colors rushed over Monte. He reached for Cameron's hand as the rainbow slowly vanished, his shock lessening, his grief awakening. He blinked, fighting back the residual tears. And in that instant, Farwen, Queen of the Unicorns, disappeared.

CHAPTER 24

The Grand President of the IMB

"Master Darrow, I understand that you're tired, but I really require your full attention." The Grand President's voice penetrated Monte's sleepy thoughts. Finn stretched his arms and yawned at Monte's side, while Cameron, normally poised and rigid, looked as though she could collapse at any minute. Were it not for the gentle tick of the mantel clock on the Grand President's desk, the office could've passed as some sort of outdoor sanctuary. The cozy room had a serene quality, lined with mahogany paneling and tartan wallpaper the color of forest-y greens. Even the carpet, like spongy moss beneath Monte's feet, felt good enough to lie on.

Monte snapped back to attention, the chair's cushion comforting against his aching neck. The smell of mint, mingled with fresh bark, hung in the air, a soothing aroma that added to his growing fatigue. He lifted his head, grabbing behind his neck. "Sorry, your Honor." His voice felt thick in his throat.

"We're almost finished," the Grand President reassured. She patted at her nose with an ancient-looking handkerchief. Her pointy ears poked through abundant locks of silvery hair as she leaned forward, her dusty violet eyes searching. "As I was asking," she began. "You expect me to believe that Farwen, Queen of all Unicorns, one of Britain's most ancient and legendary creatures, appeared to you and assisted in the defeat of Moira Bryce?"

"Aye." Finn wiggled impatiently in his chair.

The Grand President nodded, a hint of astonishment sparking over her face. "Remarkable." She offered a feeble smile, her eyes gentle. "I will release you to your families soon. But first, there is a matter of great importance that I must address." She raised her hand and conjured something in the air in front of her. Moira's glass basin, tarnished yet stunning, appeared with a tiny pop. It bobbed through the air, forcing Monte to duck as it scooted through the office, toppling books from the shelves as though possessed.

"Oh, come now." The Grand President snapped her fingers together. Instantly, the bowl froze. "That's better." She signaled it forward with her hand. "Do any of you three know what this is?"

"You mean do we know what it *was*?" Finn corrected. "Before Farwen destroyed it?"

Cameron shot him a look of caution.

Monte craned his neck up. The basin hovered above the desk, its symbols no longer vibrant, its once crystalline surface marred with black streaks. "That's Moira's glass bowl thing-y," he finally said.

"'Tis true," the Grand President said, her voice hushed. "But do any of you know its proper name?"

Monte exchanged quizzical glances with Finn and Cameron.

"This, my young friends, is called a cairn basin," the Grand President said.

"Like a primeval summoning bowl?" Cameron sat forward. She placed her fingers on the edge of the desk as the basin lowered.

"That's correct." The Grand President pulled a slender wand with a silver coating from her desk. "Cairn basins are constructed of lava glass, along with the most precious of all metals. They are very rare relics. Some even date back to the Viking Period." She spun the bowl through the air with her wand, clearly not wishing to touch it with her bare hands. "I'm sure the story of how Ms. Bryce procured it is a frightful one."

"How's that?" Monte asked, suddenly curious.

"Because, Master Darrow," the Grand President began, "cairn basins, though beautiful, have become blemished over time. They are extremely uncommon." She rested her wand on the desk. "But know with certainty that if you do happen across one, it has been obtained by impure means." Her voice was melancholy. "Today, these artifacts are only used for the darkest of enchantments, I'm afraid. And sadly, once a basin is used for dark magic, it is forever dangerous. This one very well could've been the gateway to the Nuckelavee's return."

"So, you believe us, then?" Monte asked. "About the Nuckelavee? And the wolves and the cat siths?"

The Grand President flicked her hand at the basin, which slowly fell to a padded cushion at the side of her desk. "It takes a very strong and ethereal magic to destroy a cairn basin," she said, her voice reflective. "And that is no ordinary puncture." She tapped her wand over the hole Farwen's horn had created.

"Too right, it's not," Finn said, his eyes like emeralds.

"Which is why we owe you three, and Farwen, many thanks," the Grand President said.

A knock rapped on the door behind them. The Grand President stood, a jeweled pocket watch dangling from her waistcoat. "Mr. Calder," she said as Kiernan crept into the room.

"Your Honor." Kiernan's lanky limbs folded into a grand bow.

*Pleb*, Monte thought. *What's he doing here?*

"You have good news for me, I hope?" The Grand President flapped her hand at Kiernan, who was still bent in half. "Enough now."

Kiernan snapped back to attention. "It is pure, Grand President," he said. "Our inspectors ran it through every test imaginable and found no power. Nothing untainted. And nothing corrupt."

"In fact, we found no traces of magical activity at all." Comerford thumped into the office, pulling a small silky pouch from his pocket.

The Grand President's shoulders stiffened as the leprechaun presented her with the pouch. "Thank you, Comerford." She slowly lowered herself to her seat, stroking her fingers over the pouch. "That will be all," she whispered. Comerford nodded and quietly backed out of the room, the door shutting with a gentle click behind him.

"Have a seat if you must, Mr. Calder," the Grand President said to Kiernan, who lingered at the side of the desk like a spoiled dog awaiting praise.

Kiernan retreated to the corner window, his beady eyes triumphant beneath his thick eyebrows.

"So, this," the Grand President whispered as she peeled the pouch open, "is what started everything in the first place." She pinched the Firepearl from the silk case, its metallic sheen gleaming despite the dimness of the office.

Monte's heart began to thump against his chest. He leaned forward.

"So small, but so desired." The Grand President's voice was thoughtful as she rolled the Firepearl between her thumb and index finger. "And now, so devoid of power."

Monte gripped the arms of his chair, his hands clammy. Farwen had warned him about keeping the Firepearl safe. But here it was, vulnerable, cold, and trapped within the Grand President's nimble fingers. The precious stone had been stripped from him shortly upon arriving to IMB headquarters earlier that morning. He had received little choice in the matter. But now, his senses were returning. He needed that pearl back, for more reasons than one. He swallowed his dismay, wishing that Cameron could use her Influencer powers on the Grand President. Yet that was probably beyond even her capabilities. Instead, he cleared his throat. "So, can I get the pearl back? Now that it's been examined?"

The Grand President looked up, her eyes hazy. "As much as I'd like to grant you that request, Master Darrow, I'm afraid I cannot hand the Firepearl over to you. Not yet."

A flame erupted in Monte's chest.

"But it's Monte's," Finn demanded.

"It *was* Monte's," the Grand President corrected.

"What?" Monte protested, struggling to maintain his decorum.

The Grand President sighed. "Brave laddie. This is the Firepearl; one of the most sought-after gemstones of all time. I cannot risk it falling into the wrong hands again."

*But I'm supposed to look after it*, Monte thought. *What will happen if I don't have it?*

"Although it appears to be in a state of harmless dormancy, the Firepearl is still a potential weapon." The Grand President's voice was dry and wispy. "And it is my responsibility, as president of the IMB, to oversee the safety of the Mystic public." She cinched the Firepearl back inside the tiny satchel and stowed it in her vest pocket.

"But it's not harmful," Monte demanded, suddenly feeling betrayed. "It's saved many lives—mine, Garrick's, Mr. Shaw's."

"You are a very valiant lad, Monte." The Grand President extracted a fancy slip of parchment from her desk. "And I'd like to extend a tremendous thanks to you, your family, and your friends for the astounding services you've rendered to our Mystic community here in Britain."

"So that's it?" Monte asked. "You're just going to take the Firepearl away? After all that's happened?"

"The matter is no longer up for discussion." The Grand President signed the parchment and rose from the desk, her face solemn. Kiernan, who had obediently remained in the corner, scurried forward, with his eyes eager.

"I can report to you with great satisfaction that this document will dismiss your brother, Garrick, from all grievances involving his terrible transfiguration misfortunes. It likewise contains the official alleviation of the accusations rendered toward your parents."

Kiernan's mustache seemed to droop in defeat.

The Grand President pointed her wand at the folded parchment. A drop of black wax dribbled from the tip, sizzling against the paper's folds. She unscrewed the silvery handle from her wand and pressed the knob, which bore the IMB's crest, into the wax. "All is well here, and I give the mightiest of thanks to you three." The Grand President swept her eyes across the trio as she pulled the knob away. "Because of you, Ms. Moira Bryce is no more."

Monte shot to his feet, his frustration mounting. "So, you expect us to just go home and forget any of this ever happened? To forget about the cavern? The Firepearl? To forget about all that Moira did?" A hollow, dead space filled his chest. "My uncle died at the hands of that terrible lady!" There. He finally said it. Died.

The Grand President stared at Monte. "Your uncle was an honorable Mystic," she finally said, quietly. "Believe me when I say that you have my most sincere sentiments of sorrow for your loss." She strode to the office door, her jeweled pocket watch swinging against her hip. "Now, go home and get some rest. We'll be sure to contact you with any further updates." She towered over the threesome, like an ancient, majestic tree. "Kiernan will escort you to your families."

"So, I'll never get it back?" Monte asked as Kiernan crept toward them. "The Firepearl?"

"As I said, it could be dangerous." The Grand President patted her pocket.

"The Firepearl is legendary, Master Darrow," Kiernan's oily voice slid through the air. "The Grand President is only taking the necessary precautions. It is safest here, at the IMB headquarters."

"As if you would know," Monte nearly shouted.

"Master Darrow." The Grand President pushed the office door open. "Please, go home and get some rest. Perhaps we can readdress this another time."

Monte's feet remained glued to the floor, his legs unflinching. "I'm not leaving without the Firepearl."

"Monte, let's go, mate. You're knackered," Finn urged. His eyes darted from the Grand President to his friend.

"Young Finn is right," Kiernan said. He wrapped his spindly fingers over Monte's shoulder.

"Get your hands away from me!" Monte shook off Kiernan's grasp. Disappointment and anger flooded over him. "I'm not going anywhere."

The Grand President sighed. "Fetch the lad's parents," she said to Kiernan.

"My parents won't help you any," Monte said. "They saw what happened in the cave. They know that the Firepearl is harmless." He staggered backward, his throat thick.

"Monte," Cameron said.

Monte turned to face her, the room tilting around him.

"It's going to be okay," Cameron said softly.

Farwen's words spun through Monte's head as Cameron's soft eyes settled upon his. *In time you will learn how to best defend the Firepearl. Trust your instincts and learn to control the fire within.*

Monte took a deep breath.

"The fire within, Monte." Cameron brushed her fingers over his chest. "In time you will learn," she repeated Farwen's counsel in a whisper.

"What's going on here?" Kiernan re-entered the room. He stared at Cameron. "What's she doing? She's making that weird face again."

"Monte." Mrs. Darrow darted into the office. Concern framed her face as she passed her hand over her son's clammy forehead. "Dear me, you've worked yourself into quite a state." She looked from Cameron to Finn, who both appeared as exhausted and as deflated as Monte felt. Her eyes flashed protectively. "Grand President, these children have been through quite the ordeal. I insist on them getting some rest now."

"Yes, Mrs. Darrow. I agree," the Grand President said. "Although they're hardly children." The corners of her eyes creased in thought. "No. These three have acted most admirably indeed, like the refined Mystics that they are." Her gaze fell upon Cameron. "Miss Basu, though you are more than capable of handling yourself, I think it's high time we made some special arrangements for you."

"Special arrangements?" Mrs. Darrow asked.

"Aye," the Grand President answered. "Cameron deserves a roof over her head. A permanent residence. A home." Her eyes twinkled. "I will have something organized for you straight away."

Cameron smiled, her face weary.

"Now, off with you all." The Grand President nudged her head toward the open door.

Monte hesitated, his head cloudy, his joints aching. He could feel Cameron looking at him. Her stare, for once, was settling. *And always remember that sometimes our most valuable possessions exist right before our eyes, even if we can't see them.* Farwen's wisdom trickled through his head.

"Let's go," Mrs. Darrow urged, gently.

Monte exchanged a special look with Cameron as they shuffled from the room, Finn already in front of them. He didn't know how, but something told him that he'd see the Firepearl again.

CHAPTER 25
From Bodmin to Brian Shaw

The next few days drifted by in a blur and then it was back to business as usual. Or as usual as could be expected for someone who had saved the country from impending doom. After sleeping for nearly an entire week, Monte found himself struggling to re-adjust to the rigors of standard life. He stared out the taxi window, the sights of Edinburgh blurring past him, adding to the fog in his mind. He sighed and attempted to clear his head as they pulled to a stop somewhere on Princes Street.

"Here yeh are, as requested," the Norm driver said as Monte, Garrick, and their parents slid from the taxi. "The Princes Gardens are just there." He pointed across the street to a lush, grassy piece of land lined with walkways and clusters of trees.

"Aye." Mr. Darrow nodded, handing over the fare. "Cheers."

The driver quickly counted the money and then sped off, his taxi filtering into the congested line of public transport buses.

"We're taking a portal next time," Mrs. Darrow said out of the corner of her mouth as the family weaved across the street amongst double decker buses and blaring horns.

"Ah, come now," Mr. Darrow said, shivering as a cold mist began to spray from the sky. "I thought you might appreciate the scenery." He led them to a striking statue of a military-clad Norm, stalwart and rigid atop an equally as striking horse. The entire structure stood on a moss-coated stone platform that overlooked the gardens—the grassy, gentle slopes building into the historic, rocky plug that hosted the Edinburgh Castle.

Monte traced his fingers around a large iron plaque on the stone platform's front. "In memory of the Royal Scots Greys," he read out loud.

"Aye." Mr. Darrow craned his neck up at the statue. "Impressive monument, this." He pulled a silver coin imprinted with a rearing unicorn head, just like the one from the portals in Salem, from his pocket. "Now, if I can just find the emblem." He scanned over the plaque, turning the coin over in his hands before stopping in the lower left corner. "Aha. Here it is." He pressed the coin into a matching indentation in the plaque and a tall stone castle materialized before them.

"Whoa, what just happened?" Monte looked around, concerned for the wellbeing of any Norm onlookers. The sudden appearance of a castle was enough to give anyone a heart attack.

"Is that the hospital?" Garrick stared up at the mighty establishment, the Edinburgh Castle now completely blocked by the Mystic building.

"Aye," Mr. Darrow said. "The Edinburgh Hospital for Severe Mystic Cases. It's one of the oldest—not to mention one of the best—Mystic specialty hospitals around."

"And the Norms can't see it?" Monte stared at the castle's great towers in wonder.

"It's protected and masked with powerful shield charms," Mrs. Darrow explained.

"So, we're invisible to the Norms right now?" Monte asked as the family ascended the staircase to the grand entrance.

"Correct," Mrs. Darrow said.

"Bizarre," Monte said as something flashed at the top of the hospital's highest spire. "What was that?" He squinted at the tower.

"What's that, son?" Mr. Darrow halted.

"A purple flash." Monte pointed to where he had seen the light. "There." Another fleck of violet streaked across the spire.

"I don't see anything," Garrick said.

Mr. Darrow looked up, shielding his eyes from the spittering rain. "Oh, there's a portal system up there," he said. "It allows the medics to transport the more critical patients faster."

They continued up the stone steps, the sounds of busy living and the smell of city grime completely fading as they left the Norm realm behind. "Do you think Bodmin, I mean, Mr. Shaw, will remember everything that happened?" Monte asked as they pushed through the lofty brass-plated doors. A smooth slate sign with gold lettering read "Mystic General Entrance."

"Don't know," Garrick muttered, his lips suddenly pale.

"Well, it hasn't been that long since . . ." Monte paused to look at his brother. "Since everything happened in the cave," he said quietly. He thought of Uncle Jarus, wondering if the pain of loss would ever diminish. Even Maren seemed to be handling her grief better than he was.

"Yeah." Garrick's hands trembled.

A nurse cloaked in plaid escorted the family to an elevator. Garrick looked as though he might keel over. *This must be hard for him*, Monte thought, coming to a sudden realization. To visit another survivor of Moira's cat sith potion. Monte's own nerves started to tighten as the elevator continued to climb. *What if Mr. Shaw is mad about what I did to him?* he wondered. *Or even worse—what if he's crazy?* Suddenly, he wasn't so sure he wanted to see Brian Shaw. Yet, the Mystic himself had requested they visit. *It's cool. Everything's cool*, Monte reassured himself as the elevator doors slid open. *It'll be all right.*

The nurse led them down a shadowy hallway dotted with flickering lanterns. Large, flat stones lined the floor and walls—cold, clean, and barren.

"The patient has this entire floor to himself," the nurse whispered as they trekked down the narrow hallway. "That way he can roam the corridors whenever he pleases, away from our other patrons."

"It's cold up here," Monte said with a shiver.

"The patient prefers it that way," the nurse said as they huddled to a stop near an open door.

Monte held his breath, trying not to be the first one through the doorway as the nurse herded Mr. and Mrs. Darrow into the quiet room. Monte tussled with Garrick, who looked just as hesitant to enter, finally yielding as his brother shoved him over the threshold.

A four-poster bed with burgundy drapes sat regally in the corner of the spacious room, the bedding smooth and free of creases. A rickety wooden chair, draped with a woolen blanket, was perched near the only window, the chair's shabby skeleton contrasting with the jewel-studded sill. Paintings of vast Scottish landscapes decorated the walls, companions to muted lanterns like the ones in the corridor. A portrait of a Highland cow, framed in intricately carved ash wood, hung near the bed. Monte smiled as the cow stared at him through its shaggy ginger coat, its expression almost playful.

The nurse placed her hand on the back of the rickety chair. "You have some visitors," she said in a hushed voice.

The chair's joints creaked, the blanket ruffling as though alive. A man's head popped from the wooly folds, his hair tangled with static.

"Mr. Shaw." The nurse helped the man to his feet. She handed him a thick, knobby cane. "This is the Darrow family."

Brian Shaw's face, now free of dirt and whiskers, brightened. "Aye," he said, a look of recognition glinting in his pale eyes as he shuffled toward them.

"Oh no, don't stand on account of us, please," Mrs. Darrow said.

"Nonsense." Mr. Shaw waved his hand at her. "I owe meh rescuers a proper greeting. Besides, it's about time I stirred meh bones." His voice was raspy and rich with Scottish intonation.

"I'll leave you to it, then." The nurse grabbed a silver tray full of finger sandwiches, fruit, and fine cheeses. Like the bed, the food appeared undisturbed. "Call if you need anything," she said, bustling from the room.

Mr. Shaw grunted and brushed a calloused hand through his hair. Though the same age as Mr. Darrow, he appeared twice as old, the wrinkles around his mouth harsh from months of mountainous exposure. "I'm very pleased te make yer formal acquaintance," he said, shaking everyone's hand. He paused when he got to Monte, his eyes deep and far-reaching.

"How're you feeling, Brian?" Mrs. Darrow asked.

"Better than yeh'd expect." Mr. Shaw limped back to his seat. "Meh mind was getting quite confused—even dark—as a large cat, so it's nice te see things as a Mystic again."

Garrick shifted beside Monte, his feet twitching like he wanted to bolt from the room.

"Although," Mr. Shaw continued. "I do wish they'd feed me more meat. A steak on the rare side, perhaps. Or some undercooked sausage rolls. Rabbit or deer would be bangin' as well."

Monte looked down, tugging on a ringlet. *Well, he's definitely not angry*, he thought. *Just mad.*

Mr. Darrow exchanged an uncomfortable glance with Mrs. Darrow. "You've experienced a most grave transfiguration indeed, Brian. I'm sure the adjustment has been difficult."

Mr. Shaw gazed through the window, brooding. "Beautiful place, this Edinburgh." He rested his chin on the cane's contoured handle. His spine poked from beneath his hospital gown. "I only came te the city once or twice as a lad, te walk the Royal Mile and see all the sites. I grew up in the Scottish Hebrides, yeh see, as a member of Clan McKnight."

"The unicorn clan?" Monte asked.

"Aye, Clan McKnight protects and raises unicorns."

Monte nodded. "My gran has talked about you guys before."

"Aye. Meriweather Darrow is a close comrade te the McKnight clan," Mr. Shaw said. "As was her husband, Lawrence Darrow."

"You knew Granddad?" Garrick asked, suddenly focused.

"Indeed, I did." Mr. Shaw nodded. "And what a fine man he was. He would've frowned upon meh associations with Moira Bryce, though." He smashed his knuckles into his forehead, shaking his head. "I should've never taken that potion. I am changed forever, a mere wisp of the Mystic I used te be." Misery lined his face.

"Not true," Garrick said, almost whispering.

"You'll come back around, I'm sure," Mrs. Darrow added, her expression soft.

Mr. Shaw chewed his fingernails, leaning back against the chair. His fine hair danced over his head with the static in the woolly blanket.

There was a knock on the door. "All right, Brian." The nurse shuffled back into the room. "It's time to re-dress your wounds." A tray lined with vials, sponges, and bandages floated in the air beside her.

"Mm-hm." Mr. Shaw frowned. "More medicine. Another wound te dress. Always something." He opened his mouth like a helpless baby bird as the nurse shoved a thermometer under his tongue. "Always poking and prodding," he slurred, the thermometer falling from his mouth.

The nurse snatched the thermometer as it rolled down his chest.

"Hey. Watch where yeh put yer hands, will yeh?" he complained.

"Sorry, Mr. Shaw." The nurse tucked the thermometer away, clearly accustomed to his crotchety remarks.

"Right. Well, we won't keep you," Mr. Darrow said, his cheeks flushing. "Thank you for letting us drop in, Brian. We're so glad to see you pulling through."

Mr. Shaw wobbled to his feet as the nurse prepared the bandages. "No, thank you for coming. It wouldn't have felt right, not seeing yeh all again, especially after everything yeh did for me and those Norm lads. And after what happened to Jarus . . ." He bowed his head, the room growing even quieter than before.

Monte looked at his feet, an unwelcome gloomy feeling pooling in his chest.

Finally, Mr. Shaw looked up, turning his head at Garrick. "You, lad. It's Garrick, isn't it?"

"Yes, sir?" Garrick said with a look of discomfort.

"Feel free te reach out te me whenever yeh need, aye?" Mr. Shaw frowned as the nurse sat him back down. "We're sith siblings now, practically brothers."

"Yes, of course. Thank you, Mr. Shaw." Garrick backed away, scuffing into the hallway.

"Poor Garrick." Mrs. Darrow looked from the doorway to Mr. Shaw. "You two have been through so much."

A noise like a purr rumbled from Mr. Shaw's throat as the nurse began to sponge his face.

Mr. Darrow rubbed the back of his neck, the redness in his cheeks spreading to his ears. He glanced at Mrs. Darrow who stared at the floor as if just discovering her toes for the first time. "We'd best be off," he said, pinching Mrs. Darrow's elbow.

The purring halted as Mr. Shaw's attention shifted from the nurse's sponge to Monte.

"Please, sir," the nurse said. "I'm nearly finished."

Mr. Shaw batted his hand at the nurse, his gaze never leaving Monte. "Might I have a word with young Master Darrow before yeh leave?"

"Oh," Mrs. Darrow said, hesitation in her voice.

"Perhaps another time, Brian." Mr. Darrow reached for Monte. "We've taken enough of your time as it is."

"Oh, nonsense." Mr. Shaw tried to escape the nurse's grasp.

"Just a moment." The nurse wrestled a bandage around Mr. Shaw's arm. "Hold still. Nearly there."

"Fine." Mr. Shaw slumped back into the chair with a grunt. His eyes bored into Monte. "I'll only be a moment with the lad," he insisted.

"Vanessa?" Mr. Darrow glanced at Mrs. Darrow.

"It's okay, Dad." Monte focused on Mr. Shaw's desperate eyes. *He has something to say*, he thought. *Something he doesn't want the others to hear.*

Mrs. Darrow bit her lip. "Sure. What harm could it do?"

"Two minutes," Mr. Darrow said, his voice stern as he led Mrs. Darrow from the room.

"There you are." The nurse looked relieved as she tied off the bandage. "All finished. Mind you don't tear this dressing off like you did the last," she warned as she bustled from the room.

"Psh!" Mr. Shaw picked at the bandage. "She wound it too tight the last time. Had te bite it off with meh teeth."

Monte hid a smile as Mr. Shaw limped toward him.

"So sorry te trouble yeh, Master Darrow." Mr. Shaw stopped in front of Monte, his breath damp and wreaking of dead things. "It's only that . . . well, yer different, laddie."

"Different?" Monte wanted to hold his nose.

"Unique." Mr. Shaw looked Monte up and down. "Yeh see, I spent much time with Moira. She's a very powerful Mystic. Not many can match her talent and skill. Yet . . ." He dug inside his ear. "I can sense something special in yeh. An energy that I was particularly sensitive te when I was an animal."

"Oh, I dunno. I—"

"Listen." Mr. Shaw held his palms up. "I don't claim te know much, but I do know that a Mystic such as Moira should've been able te easily influence that pearl of yers."

Monte cringed at the mention of the Firepearl.

"Moira could not command the Firepearl." Mr. Shaw licked his chapped lips, excited. "But you, Master Darrow, could."

"At first I thought I was mistaken, that I had only imagined the power I sensed in yeh," he continued. "After all, being caught in a great feline's body presented a constant battle of logic over primal instinct." He leaned forward, his icy eyes cutting deep into Monte. "Part of the reason I invited yeh here was te decipher whether or not I was correct. There's no doubt in meh mind that yer different than most Mystics, Monte." Mr. Shaw peered into Monte's face. "I'd wager yeh possess rare, magical capabilities."

"I'm nothing special, Mr. Shaw," Monte mumbled.

"But yeh are, laddie," Mr. Shaw implored. "Like yer Grandfather Darrow, in fact."

"Like Granddad?" Monte looked up.

"Aye." A smile stretched across Mr. Shaw's gaunt face. "Blimey, I wish he were still here. He'd know what te do."

"To do?" Monte asked. "About what?"

"About everything," Mr. Shaw replied. "About you, yer Firepearl . . . about Jarus."

"What about my uncle?"

"Monte," Mr. Darrow appeared in the doorway. "We're needed in the east tower. We've gotten permission to take the hospital's portal back to Fort William."

Monte gaped at Mr. Shaw. *What does he mean?* he wondered, desperate for an answer.

Mr. Shaw stared back at Monte, a look of promise in his eyes. "Come up te the islands and visit me, will yeh?" He slapped his hand over Monte's shoulder. "They'll be moving me back te meh clan soon."

Monte opened his mouth to protest, to ask more about Uncle Jarus, but Mr. Shaw's face suggested caution.

"And mind yeh keep a watch on that brother of yers for me," Mr. Shaw continued.

"Okay," Monte said as he backed away, reluctant to leave.

"That's a good lad." Mr. Shaw clunked back toward his chair. He tossed the woolen blanket onto the floor and fluffed it with his cane, forming a nest. With a great yawn he sunk to his knees, burrowing into the blanket like a beast preparing for hibernation.

"Monte," Mr. Darrow urged, pulling his son into the hallway.

Monte dragged his feet, curiosity flickering through him as the door creaked shut.

"What'd Mr. Shaw want?" Mrs. Darrow asked as the family walked down the hallway.

Monte glanced at Garrick, who looked more at ease now that they were leaving the hospital. "Granddad," Monte replied. "He said I reminded him of Granddad."

# CHAPTER 26
## Possessions Returned

The cracked window of Strathmartine Academy's science lab welcomed a warm, lazy breeze as the sky, like a bright blue current, hosted tufts of cottony clouds. A clock chimed from the tower outside, the bells echoing across the vibrant green hills of Fort William. The sun—a rare sight—splashed into the room, urging the students to come and play.

*Only a half hour more*, Monte told himself. He stared at the back of Mr. McCormack's head. The teacher's hairpiece, still obvious, wiggled at the base of his gangly neck as he scrawled his final notes across the blackboard. Monte recalled the time he had cast a hovering spell on the ratty clump of hair. *I can't believe I did that*, he thought. *Eejit*. His neck prickled with embarrassment, yet at the same time he couldn't help but wonder how he'd done it. It had been so long ago. He was starting to question how he had done many things—the floating toupee, the flying chalk, the Norm kids at the park in Salem. Weeks had passed since the incident on Ben Nevis, since the Grand President had confiscated the Firepearl. Since Uncle Jarus and Moira had vanished.

"Ahem, excuse me," a female voice whinnied from the door.

*No*, Monte whined inwardly as Babs Campbell entered the classroom.

"Mrs. Campbell," Mr. McCormack said. The toupee shifted against the back of his head as he turned from the blackboard. "I mean, Headmistress," he apologized. "What can I help you with?"

"Oh, I'm just here for a student," Babs warbled, scanning the desks.

Monte slumped lower into his chair. He was still getting used to the idea of Babs as the new headmistress of Strathmartine Academy. He hated to imagine what she'd done with Uncle Jarus's office.

"Ah, Master Darrow." Babs's great, bulbous eyes fell on him. "May I see you for a moment, please?"

Monte heaved himself from his chair. *Of course she wants to see me*, he grumbled to himself. At least this time it wouldn't involve rotten eggs . . . or a flying toupee.

"Thank you, Mr. McCormack. You may proceed with your lesson," Babs said with an air of importance as she escorted Monte out the door.

Finn waited for them in the hall. "Hiya, Monte," he said, twirling his lunchbox from one hand to the next.

"'Sup, Finn." Monte grinned. "You in trouble as well?"

"Who me?" Finn asked, his face softening in mock innocence. "Never." He tossed his lunchbox at Monte, who barely had time to lift his hands before it whizzed into his chest.

"Ooft!" Monte choked, still not accustomed to his friend's super fairy strength.

"Oops, sorry mate," Finn apologized as Babs closed Mr. McCormack's door behind her.

"You lads ready for the summer holidays?" Babs asked, oblivious to the Mystic exchange. A large chunk of kale waggled between her teeth.

"Excuse me?" Monte asked, trying not to gape at the soggy piece of vegetable as he slung the lunchbox back to Finn, much more gently.

"Your summer holidays. They're nearly here." The kale slid across Babs's front tooth. "I expect you're looking forward to your time off?"

"Um, yeah," Monte replied. "Sure am." Was she trying to be friendly?

"Very good." Babs tapped her stubby feet over the shiny wooden floor. She bounced on her toes, her brown bangs as fluffy as a sheep's winter coat.

"Sorry, but did you need something?" Monte asked, feeling uneasy. What ridiculous thing was she going to surprise him with this time?

"Oh," Babs said, the kale finally slipping into her mouth. "Yes. I have something for you." She fidgeted inside her jacket pocket, pulling out a small copper coin encased in a silver pendant. She held it out for Monte to see, her bright red nails glinting against the dullness of the metal.

Monte cocked his head to the side, puzzled. "Is it an award or something?"

"Yes," Finn piped in, a playful smirk pasted across his face. "You finally passed grade one. Congratulations, mate."

"Master Smith, please." Babs eyed Finn weightily before turning back to Monte. "This was your Uncle Jarus's. He always kept it in his desk. I found it there when . . ." She paused, her eyes even more watery than before. "Well," she sniffled. "I found it in his desk, and I thought you might like to have it."

"Thanks," Monte said, practically whispering. He took the pendant, his eyes stinging for the first time in a while. He rubbed his fingers over the coin's face which was completely blank except for a plain dark crow imprinted in its center. "Thank you very much, Babs. I mean, Mrs. Campbell."

"Please, Master Darrow. We're almost on holiday." Babs wiped at her eyes. "You can call me Babs in eleven minutes, as soon as the bell rings."

"Oh. Right," Monte stammered. He tucked the coin inside his trouser pocket, smiling weakly.

Babs returned the smile, her eyes sympathetic. "Well." She cleared her throat, turning to Finn. "Come, Master Smith. The bell's about to ring and I promised your nanny I'd keep you clear from the halls."

Amusement flitted across Finn's face. He nodded and squared his shoulders, hardly in need of adult supervision. He could probably take on any one of the bigger students now. But everyone had agreed it'd be better to maintain consistency. Things were finally settling down and the last thing they needed was for Norm suspicions to flare again.

"Tell your parents I'll drop by Downfield Place soon for a visit," Babs said over her shoulder as she escorted Finn down the hallway.

"She'd better not show up with friendship bracelets," Monte muttered as the pair disappeared around the corner. Then again, maybe Babs wasn't so bad after all.

A classroom door burst open behind him. "It's a braw day, the day," Garrick's voice, threaded with Scottish intonations, hopped down the hall.

"Indeed. It *is* a fine day." Monte grinned at his brother. "You're a regular Scotsman now."

Garrick shrugged. "What can I say? The place has grown on me." He ran his hand along the wall of lockers, stopping at a compartment labeled 2522. "You ready to scram?" he asked as he cranked the locker open. A messy pile of books stared back at them.

"You've no idea." Monte peered down the hall as the bell clanged overhead. "Hurry up and clean that thing out, will ya?" The hall swarmed with students. "I wanna get to the beach before the sun disappears."

"Okay, okay." Garrick scooped the untidy pile from the locker and dumped it into his backpack. He snatched up a stray ruler and then slammed the locker shut. "Let's go."

Monte trotted down the hall after his brother, the thrill of summer at his heels. The sun, sand, and ocean were calling.

Monte kicked through the sand, the fine granules clouding around his bare ankles in silvery puffs as he plodded toward the shoreline. Although he missed his beach in Salem, with the huge sea stacks and the Pickering Lighthouse, the beaches of Scotland were just as charming. This one, small and quaint, offered the calmest ocean and the softest sand he had ever seen. With its black boulders and surrounding bunches of trees, it was an ideal spot for a Mystic picnic, especially on days like today, when the sun decided to make an appearance. Grandmother Meriweather's dogs tore past him, announcing their arrival with joyful bellows. Brotus paraded into the water, Saladin splashing after him.

"Mind those dogs don't get too sandy!" Grandmother Meriweather yelled from a small cluster of boulders. She grabbed a platter from Maren, who was unpacking a large wicker basket full of picnic supplies.

"Yeah, Monte," Garrick shouted, spreading a large towel across the sand. "Get right on that!"

"Har-har!" Monte shouted back.

The Widow Smith staggered through the sand above Garrick, searching for a suitable place to settle herself. "Keep up, Finn Cornelius. I can feel the sun on meh back." Finn rushed forward with an umbrella. It swayed above him as he struggled to keep it over her head.

"Monte!" Cameron darted from the picnic area. "Wait up!"

"Hey, Cameron." Monte swept his friend into a hug, enjoying her warm, earthy smell. "How're things at Grandmother Meriweather's? She have you plan any Fairy parties yet?"

Cameron giggled as she pulled away. Monte couldn't recall the last time he'd heard her laugh, but he hoped to experience much more of it, especially now that she had a permanent place to stay. The Grand President's decision to place Cameron in the home of Grandmother Meriweather Darrow had been a wise one. Monte's once timid friend had blossomed into quite a vibrant comrade.

"Your gran has me work in the garden a lot." Cameron held her hands up. Calluses dotted her fingers.

"Better watch out," Monte said. "Soon you'll develop a green thumb, literally." He snuck in a wink.

Cameron smiled and folded a loose strand of hair behind her ear. Monte looked away, noting how pretty she was. Her hair—black, thick, and long—trailed down her back, almost to her elbows. Around her wrist she wore her dainty golden bracelet with the tiny gem. It sparkled perfectly against her russet skin, as if the ornament had been designed specifically for her.

"Cameron . . ." Monte asked as they reached the shoreline. He skimmed his toes through the glassy waves.

"Hmm?" Cameron responded, the sound whimsical.

"Are you happy?"

Cameron looked up. She stared at Monte with searching eyes. He wondered if she could sense his thoughts. "Yeah." Cameron's voice was soft. "Of course I am."

"Even . . ." Monte hesitated. "Even without Baap?"

Cameron's delicate lips straightened. "Yes," she finally said, her voice tender.

"Sorry," Monte mumbled, feeling foolish. "It's just something I think about from time to time. Especially with Uncle Jarus being gone, too."

"It's okay." Cameron touched Monte's arm. "I miss my father a lot. But it helps to know that . . . well . . ." She stared down at the sand.

"That he's not suffering?" Monte offered, gently.

Cameron nodded.

"When I learned what happened to Baap . . . When my dad told me what Moira did to him. When I heard that she had ended Baap's life . . ." Monte struggled to find the right words. "It hurt me greatly, Cameron," he said. "I'm sorry for everything that Moira put you through. Please know that. It wasn't right at all, what she did."

"Thanks," Cameron said. "It's hard to know that Baap's gone for good. But it's like the Grand President said—my father would want me to be happy. To enjoy life. To cherish everything Baap taught me."

Monte nodded, impressed by Cameron's maturity. He wanted to hug her again. To tell her that she'd always have a home with his family. But he felt shy suddenly. Her hand swept against his as they continued to walk. Butterflies whirled in his stomach. Whether her touch was by accident or on purpose, he didn't care.

"Oi, you guys!" Finn's voice sung from behind. "I hope you're not scared of kelpie nets," he yelled as he darted for Cameron, a long strand of seaweed dangling from his hands.

"Ew!" Cameron shrieked as he flung the slimy rope at her. "Get back here, you imp!" She snatched the seaweed and darted after Finn.

"All right, yeh crazies!" Grandmother Meriweather beckoned, interrupting the pursuit. "Come and get something te eat. I have sandwiches and sausage rolls." She waved her hand over a card table spread with baked savories and other picnic confectionaries.

"Brilliant." Monte licked his lips as Brotus and Saladin barreled past him. He stumbled after them, Finn's laughter and Cameron's squeals circling around him.

"But certainly, so much fresh air can'nae be good for a young lass like yerself?" the Widow Smith said to Maren. The pair sat perched on a fallen tree trunk near the small table, Maren's countenance as bright as the Widow's was drab.

"Oh no, Mrs. Smith. Quite the opposite," Maren explained. "A weekend away in the outdoors does wonders for the body. Plus, I think some time spent hiking the trails around Loch Ness will do me good."

"Psh, that old loch." The Widow shifted her squashy backside along the old stump. "Too many tourists up that way, if yeh ask me. It's a shame the officials don't ban all of the visitors."

"It's where my dad liked to go." Maren sounded wistful. "Loch Ness. It always reminded him of my mother. They shared many memories there."

The Widow's face softened. She patted Maren's shoulder.

Maren offered a smile, her eyes sad but appreciative. Admiration streaked through Monte. He knew the regrets his cousin harbored, the remorse she felt for not following her dad to Ben Nevis despite his orders for her to stay put. There was no question that Uncle Jarus's disappearance had been hardest on the daughter he'd left behind, yet Maren wore the loss courageously, each day mustering the pluck to carry on with life in her father's absence.

"Finn Cornelius!" The Widow Smith's skin folds flapped over the sun bonnet tied at her chin. "Finn Cornelius, yeh get over here this minute. Yer complexion is not suitable for this weather. The sun will burn yeh all crispy-like."

"Nanny, I'm fine." Finn plunked into the sand beside her. "Really!"

"Look at yeh," the Widow squawked as she plastered sunblock all over his face. "As pink as a lobster."

Monte chuckled, enjoying the show as he loaded Grandmother Meriweather's goodies onto a napkin.

"That greasy concoction will be about as useful as a chocolate teapot." Grandmother Meriweather jabbed her thumb at the Widow Smith's tub of lotion. "It's gotta be over twenty years old."

Monte grinned as Maren stepped in to help the Widow smooth the clumpy lotion over Finn's white skin.

"All right, all right." Finn squirmed and slipped away from their grasp, a glob of lotion sliding from his nose. "I'm not a wee bairn anymore."

"Finn Cornelius," the Widow bellowed. "I've not finished yer neck!"

"But I'm starving, Nanny." Finn dashed to the small table, leaping nimbly over Garrick, who lay outstretched on his beach towel.

The Widow Smith snorted. "Well mind yeh don't eat too much. Who kens what's in those pastries. Yeh'll get terrible indigestion."

"Ah, come off it, Doris." Grandmother Meriweather rolled her eyes. "I brought nothing but the finest treats for meh friends . . . no matter how daft they are," she added out of the corner of her mouth.

"Hiya, everyone!" Mr. Darrow appeared from a woody cluster of trees above them. "Sorry we're late," he said as he escorted Mrs. Darrow down the gentle slope. He lugged a long, slender bag over his shoulder. "We got held up with business but were thankfully able to use a portal not too far from here." He kicked off his shoes and socks.

"Welcome, son," Grandmother Meriweather greeted him, her eyes softening. "You and Vanessa come get some savories." She put her arm around Mr. Darrow. "I prepared loads."

"Thanks, Meri." Mrs. Darrow's smile was weary. "I'm quite famished, actually. The Bureau has us running around like mad, tying up loose ends before the close of the big case in a few days."

"Aye, no doubt." Grandmother Meriweather's eyes turned the color of a stormy sea.

"Kids." Mr. Darrow nudged his head at Finn and Monte. "I've got something for you." He hefted the awkwardly shaped bag from his shoulder.

"Where's Cameron? I have something for her too." He sank into the sand, signaling for everyone to gather around. He scanned the shoreline to ensure they were alone and then unzipped the large bag. "This was recovered from Moira's cavern." He pulled out a long, polished stick with bristles.

"Cousin B's broom," Finn said in disbelief.

"It sustained considerable damage from the icicles in the cave," Mr. Darrow explained. "And it took ages for the Bureau to examine and repair it. But it's finally yours again." He handed the broom to Finn. "Might I suggest that you boys leave the flying to Cousin B, though?" His face was stern as he looked from Monte to Finn.

"Aye." Finn propped the broom at his side.

"Good lad," Mr. Darrow said. "And now for Cameron . . . I believe these are yours, pal." He pulled a long strand of gems from the bag. They clinked together, radiant in the sunlight.

Cameron's face was solemn as she took the rainbow lights from Mr. Darrow. "Thank you," she whispered, cradling the crystals in her fingers. A tear rolled down her cheek. "These used to be Baap's. I thought they were gone forever."

Grandmother Meriweather squeezed Cameron's shoulders from behind, her eyes glistening.

"You're quite welcome," Mr. Darrow said. The sound of the ocean waves rolled gently around them. "You'll find that the necklace is complete once more. It's a privilege to be able to return it to you."

Cameron strung the rainbow lights around her neck with a grateful nod.

"Monte." Mr. Darrow tilted his head toward the shoreline. "Let's have a quick wander."

Monte followed, the sand squeaking beneath his bare feet as they left the rest of the party behind.

"I met with the Norm police today," Mr. Darrow said as they lazed toward the shallows. "The three lads from Hibernian Field are finally back to normal, thanks to the IMB's Human Restoration and Trauma Initiative."

"That's good, then," Monte said, staring into the distance. Then a thought occurred to him. "What about their parents?" he asked. "They're not suspicious of magic or anything?"

Mr. Darrow shook his head. "The IMB did an excellent job of mending things, though it has been a lengthy and demanding process."

"And Officer McTavish?" Monte pressed. "I'm sure she's had lots to say about all of this."

An amused smile spread over Mr. Darrow's face. "I tried to stave off McTavish for a while, but she's a stubborn old hen. Clever, too. She's suspected us since she was a wee lass, that one."

"So, she knows? About magic? About Mystics?"

"She knows," Mr. Darrow sighed. "But she's sworn to secrecy. She's been onto us ever since that night at Hibernian Field. A flying broomstick is a hard thing to forget, and the IMB frowns upon complete memory wiping."

Guilt tingled up Monte's neck.

"Mind you, she's been a massive help to those goons and their families," Mr. Darrow continued. "It'll serve the IMB to have her as an ally."

Monte frowned. He wasn't buying it. The Bureau had such high standards of secrecy. It wasn't like his father to bend the rules. That had always been Uncle Jarus's job.

"And . . ." Mr. Darrow lowered his voice. "There's also the issue of the Munro Majesties."

"Aren't they gone?" An image of Connery and the coppery wolf roaming Ben Nevis came to Monte's mind.

"Well, they seem to have vanished . . ." Mr. Darrow paused, reflective. "Your mother and our entire team spent endless hours sweeping the Munro mountain range. No signs of those wolves remain."

"What's the big deal, then?" Monte asked.

"We've never seen this sort of thing before, Monte. The type of magic Moira employed on those wolves . . . once Mystics. It's different. It's dark and unfamiliar. It will be good to have a Norm like McTavish on the inside. Someone who has access to all of the Norm files in case . . ." He sighed. "Well, there are some things not even magic can handle."

Monte rubbed at his arm, the scars from the Firepearl bumpy against his fingertips.

"But not to worry, son." Mr. Darrow stopped at the edge of the water, his eyes meeting Monte's. "We'll be ready if those wolves ever do show up again." The delicate waves lapped around his ankles as he slid a cherry-stained wand from his pocket. "I can't quite believe I'm returning this to you, again."

"Granddad's wand," Monte said in disbelief.

"It was found in the ice cavern," Mr. Darrow said. "Before the IMB obliterated everything."

Monte wiped the wand with his t-shirt and sighed. He thought of Uncle Jarus's coin, now stowed safely in his room at Downfield Place.

"I miss Jarus too, son." Mr. Darrow read Monte's thoughts. "There's not a day that I don't long to have him back." They made their way back up to the others. "It's a terrible thing, losing a brother. Jarus was my closest mate."

Monte stared at his own brother as they approached the picnic nook. Garrick lay on his beach towel, his chest rising and falling in calm waves as the sun bathed his face. He couldn't imagine losing his brother. It made him feel cold and empty inside just thinking about it.

"I know it doesn't feel like it right now, Monte, but with time, the pain will continue to lift," Mr. Darrow said as a cloud drifted over the sun, smearing a shadow over Garrick's face.

Monte exhaled, his chest loosening as he stared across the dancing shoreline. Farwen's words soared into his mind, not for the first time; *And always remember that sometimes our most valuable possessions exist right before our eyes, even if we can't see them.* He smiled to himself as Cameron's laugh sailed across the waves, accompanied by Finn's musical chuckles. Just then, something flinted through his peripheries, breaking the reverie—a lone figure running along the beach. Her bushy red bangs bobbed against her forehead as she raced toward the picnic party, her speed impressive despite her heavy police attire. "No way . . ." Monte said, alarmed.

"McTavish?" Mr. Darrow exclaimed as the Norm officer approached. A long, narrow ribbon of parchment fluttered in her hand. "Now what could she want? Surely not a message from the IMB." He fumbled inside his jacket, pulling out his telestone.

Something twinged against Monte's thigh. "Ouch! What the blaze?" he muttered, his heart thudding uncomfortably as he reached into his pocket. His fingers closed around something smooth, dense, and round. Carefully, he pulled the object from his trousers and looked down at his palm, baffled.

It was the Firepearl. And it was warm.

# ACKNOWLEDGEMENTS

Mystic Invisible went through many hands, sets of eyes, and seasons (including a pandemic) to get where it is today. It's been quite the journey and I sincerely couldn't have done it without my army of supporters. You all kept the fire burning and were kindling in my hardest hours.

To my little girls: Skye, Islay, and Falyn. Thank you for your patience and resilience while I learned to balance writing with home life. May you someday grow up to love this story just as much as I do.

To my husband, Liam. Thank you for being my rock in life; for your grounding support and for your quiet confidence in me.

To Angie Fenimore, the Calliope Writing Coach. "Thank you" will never be sufficient for what you have given me. But I will shower you with thank yous nonetheless: Thank you for being the first to sense my potential, for pulling me out of the dust, for showing me that I'm worth it and that I can do this. Thank you for all the writing tools; for coaching me through the many, many hurdles as I navigated the road to publication. For teaching me how to effectively land a pitch and how to score a great literary agent. Thank you for being my first alpha reader and editor. Thank you for the belly-rolling laughter (poor Cameron, the little waterfowl) and for all the em dashes! Thank you for letting me lie on the floor in unflattering positions during our Zoom calls when my morning-sickness took over. Thank you for staying with me through all the grappling, all the writing insanity, and all the late nights and early mornings.

A huge acknowledgement to my agent, Stephanie Hansen of Metamorphosis Literary Agency. Thank you for fighting past the many rejections, never stopping until Mystic Invisible had a home. I look forward to many more years in the Metamorphosis family.

Thank you to my parents. You both launched me into this journey in very different ways and I will be forever grateful.

Thank you to my in-laws, the inspiration, and the direct vein to Scotland—my cheerleaders across the pond.

Thank you to my dogs, my furry writing buddies. You were with me for every minute of this, literally by my side. Thanks for your snuggles and your snoring while I wrote and revised (and maybe sometimes cried) late into the night.

Thank you to my inspiring peeps at Calliope Writing Coach, especially those of the pilot Inner Circle course. You will forever be my writing family. Keep writing, never stop.

Thank you to my beta readers: Bethany, Michael, Victoria, and the Metamorphosis team. And to the Fast Track group at Calliope that helped me nail down that difficult first chapter. Your feedback, input, and encouragement greatly elevated Mystic Invisible, from the first page, to the very last.

Thank you to all the babysitters who watched my kids for countless collective hours while I accomplished this dream. Namely, Crystal and Makenna Higbee, Noelle Maes, Elizabeth and Eliza Leavitt, Nicole Zobrist, and Andrea Whittle. And to my siblings and sisters-in-law: Bethany, Lindsay, Gentry, Kelsey, Spencer, Andrew, Collin and Katy (virtual help from miles away), Whitney, Kimberlea, and Victoria. You often found yourselves tending to my girls during weekends or during your time off and it didn't go unnoticed! It really does take a village to write a book.

To Jill, my soul-sister and fellow Harry Potter fanatic, and to my brother, Spencer. Both of you were there at the very beginning, before I even knew this book was going to happen.

Thank you to Milissa Lauren for all of your help with the website and to my brother-in-law, Jason, for pushing me forward even when things felt bleak.

To all my friends: old and new, young and young-at-heart. Thank you for your encouragement and excitement and for your genuine interest in my book.

To the amazing writing communities on Facebook, Instagram, and Twitter. Thank you for your constant support and enthusiasm.

And a very large thank you to the team at Winter Goose for your impeccable work in getting Mystic Invisible out into the world—amidst the COVID-19 pandemic at that—and into the hands of readers. My readers are the reason I write, and Winter Goose turned that reason into a reality.

## ABOUT THE AUTHOR

Ryder Hunte Clancy has lived most of her life in the desert, but her heart belongs to the sea; her happy place, where brine and mist abound and allusive waves caress expansive stretches of compacted sand. A tried-and-true stay-at-home mom, she is often found scribbling notes between diaper changes or connecting plot points while everyone else sleeps. She survives off of toddler snacks like apple slices and cheese and has just as much trouble keeping up with her fictional, teenage characters as she does her three small children. Mystic Invisible is her debut novel, the inspiration of which was gleaned from her husband's homeland of Scotland, where fantasy, mystery, and folklore are rich, and hits of adventure linger around every corner.

CPSIA information can be obtained
at www.ICGtesting.com
Printed in the USA
LVHW111406190321
681922LV00035B/1622

9 781952 909054